"Very well, I agree." Celina brushed at her eyes with an angry gesture and lifted her chin before swinging around to face him.

"You agree to…?"

"Your proposition. My honour for yours, just payment for compromising your status and your principles. I ask only that you make the blooding of my brother as painless and without permanent damage as you may arrange. That was the bargain, I believe."

It was the last thing Rio expected. Tears, pleading, more recriminations perhaps, but not capitulation. It left him stunned.

He closed the distance between them with a slow stride. He pulled her to him, the crush of her skirts against his thighs an incitement beyond belief. He bent to taste her lips, absorbing the feel of their soft, tender curves, drinking in their luscious innocence like a man dying of thirst.

But he wanted more. He wanted grasping, desperate response. He wanted her to want him, and he would have that. In no other way could he be satisfied. To take the lady being courted by his enemy, to send her tainted to his bed – what could be more fitting? All he had to do, Rio saw clearly, was abandon honour.

He could not do it.

Could he?

Jennifer Blake ". . . evokes everything alluring about New Orleans. She brings the bayous and the mansions, the foggy mornings and heated evenings to life." —*Romantic Times*

Jennifer Blake is a *New York Times* bestselling author who writes contemporary as well as historical novels. She draws upon her experience of the American Deep South where she was born and raised. Jennifer Blake and her husband live in Louisiana in a house styled after an old Southern planter's cottage.

Jennifer Blake is also the author of

GARDEN OF SCANDAL

The Louisiana Gentlemen series

KANE
LUKE
ROAN
CLAY
WADE

Watch for the next book in her new
***Master of Arms** series*
Coming 2006

CHALLENGE TO HONOUR

Jennifer Blake

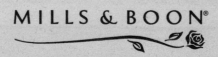

*MILLS & BOON and MILLS & BOON with the Rose Device
are registered trademarks of the publisher.*

*First published in Great Britain 2005
by Harlequin Mills & Boon Limited,
Eton House, 18-24 Paradise Road, Richmond, Surrey TW9 1SR*

© Patricia Maxwell 2005

ISBN 0 263 84519 2

153-0805

*Printed and bound in Spain
by Litografia Rosés S.A., Barcelona*

ACKNOWLEDGEMENTS

I am indebted to the staff of The Historic New Orleans Collection, Chartres Street, New Orleans, for their aid in locating obscure tomes and fascinating facts concerning the city's Golden Age, 1830-1850. Without the many details unearthed in their painstakingly preserved manuscripts, photos and microfilm, this story would not be the same.

For my loyal readers who have asked
so many times, "When are you going to
write another historical romance?"
with many thanks for their patience.

1

New Orleans, Louisiana
February, 1840

"A lady to see you, Monsieur Rio."

Rio de Silva, lounging in a wing chair with one booted foot thrust toward the low-burning coal fire and a brandy snifter in his hand, did not move or open his eyes. When he spoke, it was with deliberation that told its own story for those with the wit to hear it. "Inform her that I am not at home."

"I did so, of course," Olivier, his majordomo, answered softly. "It did not suffice."

Rio opened his eyes then, and something in his expression made the majordomo step backward so quickly that the flame of the candle he held wavered in the draft. "The devil you say."

"She is most determined."

There was a warning in the sensitive lines of Olivier's cinnamon face, Rio thought. The problem was that he was in no temper or condition to heed it.

Women did not come to him as a rule. Rather, he went to them, climbing walls, swarming up posts and downspouts to reach balconies, ghosting through the pedestrian gates of porte cocheres that had been left unlocked for his convenience. The widows and neglected wives of New Orleans who participated so eagerly with him in the diversions of the bedchamber were grateful for his discretion, and why not? To be seen in his company in the light of day would cause a whirlwind of speculation; to visit his rooms at this hour of the night was to court certain scandal. Added to that, the throughway known to the French as the Passage de la Bourse and the Americans as Exchange Alley was forbidden to respectable women. This pedestrian mall, with its brokers' and lawyers' offices, tailors' shops, barrooms, gaming rooms and many fencing salons was the exclusive province of men. Some few females might tarry under its shadowed arcades after dark, but they could not be called ladies.

Moreover, Rio did not encourage encroachment. A fastidious disinclination to exploit those forced to hire out their bodies made him steer clear of street women, and there was no place in his life for the *jeunes filles* or comely widows of a lower class who might have been available to him. No, he preferred his accustomed liaisons. Intense but straightforward, they seldom lasted past a few meetings. His paramours were women of experience who preferred to satisfy their desires without risk to their social positions or their emotions, and certainly without attracting attention. They were much too discreet to appear on his doorstep.

Through his teeth Rio said, "Get rid of her."

A rustling of skirts came from somewhere behind him. "He has found that impossible, *monsieur*. Perhaps you would care to make the attempt."

Those words, spoken in clear, bell-like tones, cut

through the brandy fumes in Rio's head like the slash of a rapier. Cultured, a little scathing, they were the hallmark of New Orleans French Creole aristocracy. They were also unfamiliar; he would stake his life on it. And he might well be forced to do just that if she were discovered here alone with him.

He drained the snifter and placed it on the table beside him, then rose to his feet. Turning with an exaggeration of his usual lithe control, he faced his visitor where she stood just inside the open doorway.

She glowed there in the dim room—there was no other word for it. Her pale skin was luminous with health and vitality. A cascade of golden-brown ringlets spilled in lustrous splendor from the crown of curls on top of her head, draping over one shoulder to lie on her breast. The gown she wore was of white silk shot with gold that caught the candlelight in a dazzling shimmer, especially at the bodice, which rose and fell with her quick breathing. Her cloak of heavy bronze satin was thrown back to reveal its lining of iridescent rose and coral, which reflected the firelight's warm glow.

Olivier twitched into movement toward the lady, almost as if he meant to protect her. "*Mademoiselle*, I regret—"

"Stay." Rio accompanied the command with an uplifted hand followed by a swift gesture of dismissal. Both were made without removing his gaze from the woman in front of him.

Olivier, his expression veiled, bowed himself from the room. He did not close the door, however, an omission Rio noted without surprise. Ladies of quality impressed his slender dandy of a majordomo, and he harbored tender, exalted impulses toward them. Rio was not so susceptible.

"Now, *mademoiselle*," he said in trenchant softness, "to what do I owe this honor?"

"Concern, apparently an excess of it," the lady answered with precision. "If this is the way the great Silver Shadow prepares for a dawn meeting, it appears I trouble myself for nothing over your appointment with my brother."

Comprehension and anger came at the same time. Rio paced forward, a slow and predatory advance. "Mademoiselle Vallier, I presume, if Denys Vallier is your relative?"

"As you say, Celina Vallier."

Rio saw her eyes widened slightly as she watched his approach, but she did not retreat. That might have been in her favor if it were not the opposite of what he had intended. "Denys sent you to plead for him?"

"Never!"

Rio stopped, but not before he was within easy arm's reach. "Then it was your decision to intervene."

"Mine alone."

He studied her lifted chin and straight gaze while recognizing the shift inside him of warring inclinations. She was no chocolate-box beauty in the current fashion, all rounded curves, pouting lips and rosy cheeks. Her features were too well defined; she lacked the requisite dimpled softness. Regardless, it was almost impossible to look away from the shading of her dark, wide-spaced eyes, like the tawny gold wine of Jerez, the sculpting of her high cheekbones and perfect lines of her mouth. She had a powerful allure that came from inside, one made all the more potent for being unintended. She was, no doubt, as innocent as the white gown she had worn on this opera evening for receiving eligible suitors in her family box in the city's time-honored mode of presenting nubile young women to society. Added to that, she was entirely too valiant for his purpose. He hardly knew whether to curse her daring or salute it.

In a deep voice layered with suggestion, he asked, "Your decision, made without regard for the consequences?"

"Consequences?" Confusion clouded her eyes. "I wanted only to speak to you a small moment, to ask if it is really necessary to inflict injury on one who is far less skilled. I thought to discover if there is any circumstance that might persuade you to call off the meeting."

He studied her, allowing his attention to move from the oval of her face down the slender column of her throat to the white expanse of her shoulders above a low décolletage. The curves there were tender, enticing in their smooth, blue-veined firmness. Lifting his gaze once more, he saw that hot color flared in her face and her eyes smoldered with resentment for his appraisal. That was good. "Am I to understand that your brother wishes to apologize?"

"Certainly not. You are well aware that he could not do so without being accused of cowardice. Anyway, he doesn't, that is…"

"He has no idea that you are here. Nor, I would venture, does anyone else."

She swallowed, a delicate movement of her throat that made him think, suddenly, of pressing his lips to the fine-grained skin. It was a moment before he could attend to her reply.

"As you say."

He eased closer. "And your mother, your chaperone, your maid—whichever of these guards your chastity—where have you deposited them?"

"My maid is outside," she said with a trace of uneasiness burning its way into her eyes. "Though I fail to see what difference it makes."

His lips curved in a mirthless smile. "I would not want her to become too uncomfortable while waiting on my convenience."

"I will not be here that long."

"Won't you?" The words were suggestive.

"No, indeed. It should take no time at all to…"

"To ask clemency for Denys, or else request that I avoid the dawn meeting altogether?"

"If…if you please."

"Either course must compromise my position. You'll have to agree that it's only fair to expect some recompense?"

She moistened her lips, a gesture that he followed with more attention than was comfortable. When she spoke, her voice wobbled a little.

"If you speak of monetary compensation, my access to any sum that might be useful to you is limited. However, I have a few pieces of good jewelry."

"I have no use for your baubles." Rio did his best to prevent his distaste for the idea that he might be bought off from sounding in his voice, but he was not sure he succeeded.

"My mare. She is a fine, blooded animal, well suited as a mount for a gentleman, as well as a lady."

"No."

"Then I'm truly sorry, but I have nothing else to offer!" She compressed her lips, her expression defiant.

"Nothing?" He lifted a brow and waited.

She was innocent but not stupid; she saw what he insinuated. But she either could not believe such a thing in connection with her person or else doubted he had the audacity to carry it out. In the last, she was much mistaken.

Looking at a spot somewhere in the vicinity of his open shirtfront, she said, "I am at something of a standstill, unable to imagine what might attract you."

"You could." He reached to touch the petal softness of her cheek with his callused, swordsman's fingers, then brushed the pad of his thumb across the fullness of her bottom lip. "I might well court disgrace for the sake of a night in your arms."

He expected her to recoil in horror, swoon, possibly strike out at him. She did none of those things, though he felt the sharp intake of her breath feather across his lifted hand, saw the blood recede from her features. A tremor ran over her slender form, and then she was still.

"Impossible."

Rio had expected no less, still his stomach muscles clinched as he heard the finality of her refusal. He skimmed his hand over the clear line of her jaw, slid a finger into the soft spiral of the curl that lay on her shoulder. With lethal softness he asked, "Now, why?"

She met his gaze, but made no attempt to avoid his touch. "It's dastardly. No gentleman would require it."

"Oh, agreed. But as you are no doubt aware, I am not a gentleman."

"That is not what people say of you," she countered with desperation shading her tone.

He could almost be persuaded to retreat for the sake of that sentiment, and might have if he had drunk less deep. But there was a devil riding him that would not dismount, one that mocked old habits, old manners, old dreams. "We speak of your brother's life, after all. What prevents you from exchanging a few hours of your time for the sake of such a boon?"

"My honor."

"Which is greater than mine, of course. This is understood." His smile was crooked and not without pain. "But mine, you see, is all I have."

Silence descended, endless vibrating minutes of it while she appraised him, examining his features one by one, pausing on the scar that marked his jaw, braving his steady regard as if she meant to plumb his soul. Then a lump of coal shifted in the grate and the flames leaped, casting wavering orange-tinted shadows on the walls. The reflections shone in her eyes, illuminating their darkness.

"I see," she said abruptly. "You never intended intimacy between us, but only sought to prove a point. Yes, and perhaps extend a warning."

"I salute your understanding."

"It's doubtful, I would imagine, that you would accept the sacrifice if I were to fling myself into your arms."

The flush of heat and pressure that raged through him at that image was amazing. He forced it down, though something of it lingered in his tone as he said, "I don't advise putting that to the test."

"No. But don't you see that it is precisely because of your repute as a man of honor that I venture to interfere? What can it avail you to meet my brother? You are a *maître d'armes,* a master swordsman who teaches other men the art of fighting with a blade. You have engaged in dozens of passages at arms and never lost. You have skills, tricks and strengths that none can match, and have proved it in public exhibition against the best teachers of swordplay in New Orleans. If you neglect to appear on the field, who would dare accuse you of cowardice? Where is the dishonor if you avoid the assassination of one who has no hope of besting you?"

The heat behind her words was impressive, but Rio could not allow it to weigh with him. "You realize that it would finish your brother just as effectively if I refused to appear? Death by ridicule is no easier to bear than a thrust to the heart."

"Then meet him, but don't…"

"Don't touch him?" he suggested, cutting across her words. "Don't put him to the trouble of defending himself? You feel, perhaps, that I should allow myself to be slashed once or twice just to set him up in consequence."

"I didn't say that!"

"You didn't, no, but tell me it wasn't in your mind?"

She was wise enough, apparently, to try no such thing. Instead, she said, "My older brother, Theodore, fell on the field of honor three years ago. My mother and younger sister died of yellow fever the next summer while my father took the waters at White Sulphur Springs for his chest pain. Denys and I escaped only because we traveled with him. Now Denys is the last of the Valliers. If he should...should fall in the morning, it will kill my father as surely as if you had thrust him also through the heart."

"Melodramatic," Rio said. "He would still have you."

"A daughter?" Her lips twisted as she smiled. "It's not the same."

Rio knew very well what she meant. Among the French in New Orleans, a daughter would be loved, might be petted and enjoyed as one takes pleasure in the antics of a kitten. Still, she was a threat to family honor until a marriage could be arranged that would cement financial, social or political advantage. Failing such an alliance, or lacking funds for the dowry and trousseau that would secure her future, she would waste away her life caring for elderly parents or as an unpaid housekeeper and nursemaid in the household of her brother or some other relative, or else be encouraged to embrace the convent. A son, on the other hand, was the proud bearer of a man's name and hope of immortality. He embodied a father's honor, relieved some portion of his family and social obligations and, of course, inherited the major portion of his estate. Simply put, a daughter grew up as a liability while a son was ever an asset.

Rio knew these things well because it had been much the same among the grandees of Spain. Such conventions had once seemed natural to him, though he had been embarrassed as a boy when his father displayed partiality in front of his sisters. That self-same standard had caused him to become a target after his father and the rest of his family had died in the fire that destroyed their summer home in the mountains of Catalonia.

"Perhaps it was your father who sent you, then?" Rio tilted his head as he made the suggestion. "If he values you so little, allowing you to plead for his only son could seem reasonable."

"You do not know him if you think so. He has far too much pride and no reliance whatever on feminine appeal."

It was an intriguing admission, one Rio might have delved into at greater length had circumstances allowed. They did not, and so he contented himself with a single comment. "He is a fool."

"Hardly."

"No? Then a man, rather, who sees his daughter merely as an ornament. I wonder," Rio said meditatively, "what he would do if he learned you had risked your good name by coming here."

"He won't learn of it." She pressed her lips together so tightly that the blood left them.

"What of your maid?"

"Her loyalty is to me."

"I congratulate you. Still, it's surprising that you chance so much."

"It was necessary given that I seem to be, however inadvertently, the cause of this meeting."

So she knew. He had wondered. "Your brother told you, I suppose. That was ill-advised of him."

"Denys and I were always close in childhood, and

have become more so these last three years. There is little concerning him that I fail to learn eventually."

"A gentleman does not worry the ladies of his family with such matters."

"Oh, please," she said with scathing irony in her voice. "The canons of the Code Duello may be sacred to men, but they seem ridiculous to a mere female. What I don't understand is why you felt it necessary to speak of me in a public gaming establishment. You can know nothing of my character, for good or ill. To my knowledge, we have never met, never so much as exchanged a word before this night."

It was true enough. Her father, brother, distant male cousins and acquaintances might rub elbows with a man such as himself, a mere *maître d'armes*. They would acknowledge him in bars, restaurants, gaming hells and at races, cockfights, bullbaitings, and even at the public subscription balls. They might frequent his fencing atelier, might imitate his style of swordplay, the cut of his waistcoat, or the grace of his bow. But he was never invited into their homes or to the private balls where their daughters, sisters and female cousins danced under the watchful eyes of chaperones, never formally presented to such protected flowers.

These things had once been open to him as a young man of land, fortune and infinite future, but not now. Not now.

"No," he said quietly, "we have never met."

"Our paths have never crossed?"

"Not in the sense you mean."

"I have never harmed someone near and dear to you?"

"No."

"Then I fail to see how you could possibly find anything to say to my discredit. I am forced to assume that the innuendo used to force this duel was feigned."

"An unwarranted conclusion."

Her eyes sparkled with her anger. "Indeed? Then tell me why I was brought into this affair."

"You might call it an accident. I did not know your name at the time but spoke of the prospective bride only in general terms." Rio did not account for his actions as a rule. Yet he thought on reflection that she deserved to know that much.

"You wanted this duel."

"No."

"But why else...?"

"The purpose was my own and not one I care to discuss. I will tender you an apology in form, however, if it will soothe your wounded consequence and persuade you to take your leave."

"My consequence has nothing to do with it! I refuse to allow a few words uttered for no apparent reason to be the death of my brother. If you spoke wrongfully then you must, in all honor, retract the slur."

"That I cannot."

"Then I was right. You forced this duel on Denys."

"It was never my intention to meet your brother. He overheard a comment meant for another and was quicker to resent it."

"Meant for...?" She paused and then said faintly, "Oh."

He inclined his head as he watched appalled comprehension rise into the sherry-gold of her eyes. "Once his challenge was issued, there was no turning back."

"Explaining being out of the question, of course, just as it is now."

"Precisely." His agreement was short, since he'd presented her with far more detail than he'd intended or knew to be wise.

"It's madness! The games gentlemen play are beyond belief, slashing at each other with swords and shooting off pistols over trifles. To risk death for a mere nothing has little to do with honor and everything with stupidity."

"More is at stake than you realize."

"Tell me what it is, and perhaps I may agree with you. In the meantime, I believe your notions of honor require adjustment. There is none to be had in skewering a young man with scant knowledge of swordplay and because of a slur spoken for unnamed reasons."

She was correct and Rio knew it. That fact was largely responsible for the half-empty brandy decanter that sat on the table beside his chair. Denys Vallier was not the man he had expected to face at daybreak. Rio did not want to meet him, had no desire to injure him, much less be responsible for his death.

The object of a duel was not to end a man's life, of course. Honor could be, and usually was, satisfied at first blood. Yet all too often a slip of the wrist, weakened parry, or lunge with more anger than finesse behind it bought another cemetery plaque reading, *Mort sur le champ d'honneur.* Dead on the field of honor.

"My skill with a sword is my livelihood," he said, driven to defense against his will. "Compromise it, and I am done. The men who frequent my salon will find other masters to teach them the art of staying alive. More than that, I will become a target if I allow an untried youth to best me. I shrink from no man's challenge, but neither do I court frivolous meetings."

"Only this one in which my brother intervened. I understand." She turned abruptly in a silken swirl of skirts, moving away a few steps where she stood staring at the bust of Napoleon on a bronze pedestal that occupied a corner of the room. Then she brushed at her eyes with an angry gesture and lifted her chin before swinging around again. "Very well, I agree."

"You agree to…?"

"Your proposition. My honor for yours, just payment for compromising your status and your principles. That was the bargain, I believe."

It was the last thing Rio expected. Tears, pleading, more recrimination perhaps, but not capitulation. It left him stunned.

"Well? What are you waiting for?"

"You can't realize what you're saying."

"You have made it very clear to me," she said crisply. "But I will not hold you to the letter of it. I ask only that you make the blooding of my brother as painless and without permanent damage as you may arrange. Then you may ask of me what you will."

Brandy and overheated blood did not mix well. Rio could feel his heartbeat pulsing in his brain, surging along his veins with alcohol-generated impulses that gathered, throbbing, below the fastening of his pantaloons. He should refuse this sacrifice at once, he knew, should do it with such brutal finality that Celina Vallier fled from him in horror. It would be a kindness to her and much less dangerous for him than any pact.

The words would not come. Instead, there seeped into his mind a vision of perfect vengeance. Far better than a simple sword thrust to the heart, it was more calculated and ultimately more devastating. To take the lady being courted by his enemy, to send her tainted to his bed, perhaps even impregnated with a child who would become the man's rightful heir? What could be more fitting? All he had to do, Rio saw clearly, was abandon honor.

He could not do it.

Could he?

As in a dream, he saw himself close the distance between himself and Celina Vallier with a slow stride. He took her hand and carried it to his lips, touching the smooth skin across her knuckles with the heat of his mouth. Then he placed her lax fingers on his shoulder and reached to encircle her narrow waist, drawing her against him. The feel of her whalebone stays, the crush of her skirts against his thighs were an incitement beyond belief. Her scent, like warm, powdered rose petals, mounted to his head. The liquid sheen of her eyes was a reproach that he blotted out by lowering his lashes, glancing at the moist, trembling curves of her lips. Then he bent to taste them, absorbing the feel of their soft, tender curves, drinking their luscious innocence like a man dying of thirst.

She didn't resist. A small shiver moved over her,

then she was still, absolutely quiescent in his arms. There was no passion, no answering desire, but only mute and passive surrender.

He wanted more. He wanted grasping, desperate response, a seductive madness of need. He wanted her to want him, and he would have that. If he must give up his soul for this revenge, then he wanted the same in return. In no other way could he be satisfied. He would give to his enemy a wife who yearned for another and might never find pleasure or surcease in the arms of her aging husband. It would be the final irony.

He released her mouth with lingering gentleness and stepped back. His voice a hoarse rasp in his throat, he said, "Later. When the meeting is over."

"Then?"

"Then I will come to you, when you have seen that I keep my promises." He would, God forgive him. And what he would do then the devil alone knew, for he certainly did not.

She lifted a hand to her lips, touching them with only her fingertips. Her eyes were huge in her pale face as she searched his features. "Please, I…"

"Have no fear," he said quietly. "No one will know, your good name will be safe. This I also pledge."

"Yes." It was little more than a whisper.

He took her arm and turned her toward the door, seeing her into the entrance hall and out to the maid who waited with Olivier in an anteroom. As the two women moved toward the stairs to the lower level, he noticed with approval the veil the maid draped over her mistress and the way she closed the edges of her cloak over the revealing whiteness of her gown. He stared after them for long seconds, listening to their footsteps and the soft brush of their skirts on the stair treads.

He might have offered his escort if being seen with him were not so damning. As it was, he spoke quietly to Olivier. Seconds later, Rio donned the coat, hat and gloves brought by the majordomo. Then taking his sword cane from the marble-topped stand beside the door, Rio went out into the night.

He trailed Celina Vallier and her maid along the pedestrian passage, then down the side street that intersected with the rue Royale. Staying well back, he kept the women in sight as they passed under the gaslights that illuminated street corners, crossed the stone paving of the section of rue Royale, and moved alongside courtyard walls with the perfume of sweet olive and jasmine spilling over them along with the sound of hidden fountains. A block or two more, and he watched them enter the Vallier town house that was located above a millinery shop in the style of the city where living quarters at street level were considered both dirty and dangerous. The pedestrian gate, set into the wrought-iron barrier to the porte cochere, clanged shut behind them. Minutes later, the glow of candlelight appeared behind the shutters of a corner room, beyond the traditional blue-green painted iron railing of the upper balcony.

Rio noted the location with care, since discovering it had been as much his purpose in following the pair as making certain they arrived home safely. Still, ~~didn't move away but stood with his attention fas~~ ~~n the shifting shadows behind the heavy louvered shutters. Satisfaction and doubt warred inside him, along with a strong current of feeling made up of protective instinct and possessiveness, anticipation and disquiet.

Celina Vallier was his for the taking. She had placed in his hands the final and perfect touch to complete his long quest. Concern for how it might affect her need not trouble him, since she would be ten times more blessed to have her first taste of intimacy at the hands of a man, any man, other than her prospective husband. Regardless, the contact between them must be a brief and singular event. When it was done, he would never speak to her again; never meet her face-to-face. Whatever secrets she carried to her marriage bed and beyond into widowhood would remain between the two of them.

That was understood, the inevitable way of their world. No reason whatever existed then, for the inconvenient remorse that attacked him, no purpose for the regret that settled, aching, in his heart.

Still, beneath that remorse was a burgeoning suspicion that held him rooted to the spot. Celina Vallier was a lady of spirit and courage, innocence and honesty. The likelihood that she would conspire against the groom chosen by her father was so farfetched that Rio thought he must have been drunker than he knew to entertain it for even a second was desperate to save her brother, but th could betray her future groom then k him on her wedding night and ever impossible.

And yet Celina Vallier had il's bargain. She had paid li

but finally turned to him in all her shining, virginal finery and given her solemn word.

He swore in a virulent whisper and slashed the air at his feet with his sword cane. Dear God, but he was a fool. She must have a reason, some plan or purpose that had slipped past him in his concentration on the novelty of her plea and his flagrant reaction to it. Surely she did, but what was it?

Why in the name of all that was holy had she agreed?

2

What had she done?

That question tolled like a church bell in Celina's mind as she stood in the center of her bedchamber while Suzette worked at the back buttons of her evening gown. It was incredible to her that she had found courage for the agreement with Rio de Silva, much less words to seal it. She had gone to him from concern for Denys's life and had come away with the means to reclaim her own. But first, she must submit to the will of the Silver Shadow.

Suzette drew off the silken folds of her gown over her head with a practiced movement. Stepping to the rosewood Mallard armoire to put it away, she spoke over her shoulder. "Well?"

"Well, what?"

"Are you going to tell me what passed between you and this so infamous *maître d'armes*, or must I guess?"

"I thought surely you overheard." Celina avoided her maid's gaze, bending instead to tug at her petticoat tapes. "Or were you too well entertained by his majordomo to notice?"

"We spoke, yes," Suzette answered with a shrug.

"He is very handsome, is he not?"

"Olivier, you mean? Or Monsieur de Silva?"

For the briefest of seconds, Celina could see in her mind's eye the master swordsman as he had been earlier. The strong yet severe cut of his features and the silver lightninglike facets in his storm-gray eyes were indelibly imprinted on her memory. An old scar had angled from just under the lower lashes of his left eye to his jawline, a thin, pale streak in the bronze-tinted skin of his face. He was taller than most men of her acquaintance, with wider, more muscular shoulders caused by the constant wielding of foil, épée and rapier. His physical condition was superb as disclosed by the lithe control and silence of his movements, as well as the well-defined thigh muscles under the close fit of his pantaloons. Self-assurance just short of arrogance had been in the set of his head, the lift of his dark, peaked brows, the indented corners of his mouth. And every second she had been with him, he had studied her with predatory interest.

Her voice sharp, she said, "You know very well I spoke of this Olivier."

"Ah, yes," Suzette agreed, her glance sly. "Most agreeable, I thought. He is not a slave, you know."

"No?"

"He and Monsieur de Silva met in Havana, or so he told me. Olivier was a free man of color. His grandmother had been a slave, but was freed by her white master when she had his child who was Olivier's mother. It was a love match, so Olivier claims, and his grandmother and his mother lived in his white grandfather's household. His mother was even educated by the nuns. Afterward, she married a Boston shipping merchant, though the man neglected to tell her that he'd left a family behind when he came to Havana. The merchant went back to Boston before Olivier was born and was never heard from again. Olivier was sent to Spain, to be educated at the university in Toledo."

"I thought there was something cultured about him," Celina said with interest. It had been there, hidden behind his quietly deferential attitude.

Suzette gave a nod. "But now the story is not so nice. On his return from Spain, Olivier was given the position of factor for the family sugar plantation. He worked in it until the death of his grandfather. An inheritance was to have been his, but one of the legitimate heirs, a gentleman of wealth and power, hired thugs to set upon Olivier as he left the office a few nights after the burial. They came very near to killing him, and would have except for Monsieur de Silva. He happened upon the attack and drove off the thugs with his sword cane. Afterward they came to New Orleans together, Monsieur de Silva because he had business here, Olivier because to stay in Havana would be to risk death. Olivier owes his life to this *maître d'armes*, therefore will serve him all his days."

"A romantic tale," Celina said. "Do you suppose it's truc?"

"But yes, I think so. Olivier said as well that Monsieur de Silva does not believe in slavery because once, when he was only a youth, he was a slave himself. This seems strange to me, but Olivier swore to it."

It seemed unlikely to Celina as well, though she did not say so. "You and Olivier found quite a bit to talk about."

"Indeed. To listen was no hardship since he speaks so well. Even so, he is not as handsome, I think, as the Silver Shadow." The maid's quick glance over her shoulder was more than a little arch.

Celina feigned a shrug. "You think so? I was sure that none could surpass Croquère in your eyes."

Bastile Croquère, a mulatto sword master who kept a well-patronized atelier a few doors down from that of Rio de Silva, was considered to be the most handsome man in all New Orleans. Well-known for his elegant taste, he was equally famous for his collection of cameo rings and stickpins.

Suzette gave her an amused smile. "You've heard the latest about him, yes?"

Celina shook her head.

"It's said that he wore a cameo bracelet to the opera last Tuesday evening, fine cameos carved from shells. A man had the audacity to snicker over his choice of adornment. Croquère challenged him for it of course, but was denied the privilege of a meeting."

"A pity." Men frequented Croquère's fencing salon for the sake of his skill and finesse, Celina knew, crossing swords with him there in scant regard for the black blood that ran equally in his veins with white. Still, being a mulatto made him ineligible for the dueling field. What man could be expected to defend his honor against one not considered his peer?

"No matter. Monsieur Pasquale took it on himself to resent the slur on Monsieur Croquère's behalf. The laughing one will learn to keep his opinion to himself next time."

"Pasquale, the Italian sword master?"

"Just so, the one they call La Roche." The maid came close again, offering Celina a steadying hand as she stepped out of the ruffled heap of her petticoats.

"Do you suppose either name is his own?" It was common knowledge that many of the more than fifty sword masters with salons on the Passage de la Bourse operated under a nom de guerre. Pasquale in Italian meant Easter, she thought, an unlikely birth name.

"Who can say? But I am not to be distracted with talk of these handsome men, *ma chère*. What did Monsieur de Silva do to make you run away as if the hounds of hell were after you?"

"I didn't run."

"It was no pleasant stroll, our return here. Did he offer you insult?"

"No. At least…" Celina paused for a distracted instant as she recalled the touch of his mouth on hers, the unyielding feel of his arms around her. There had been something about him, a dangerous sense that he was capable of compelling her surrender if he wished it, and had the power to persuade her to wish it, as well.

"I knew it! Did I not tell you it was a great mistake to go there? Did I not warn you such a man could not be as noble as he is painted? You were lucky to escape unmolested."

"He would not have gone that far, not while knowing you were just outside."

"Much he would have cared, I'm sure. He cannot be allowed to get away with this."

"Shall I inform Denys so he may challenge him yet again? Or do you think my father would like the pleasure of facing him with sword in hand?"

"*Mon Dieu!* What has this man done?"

"Nothing so very terrible," Celina said as she turned to allow Suzette access to her corset strings. "At least, nothing that didn't suit me."

"Worse and worse. Tell me at once what passed between you before I imagine complete disaster."

To withhold the conditions of her bargain with Rio de Silva would be useless. Suzette had been the keeper of Celina's secrets for years, since she'd been presented as a gift from her grandfather to her mother on the day she was born. Zuzu, Celina had called her when she was learning to talk, and still gave her that *petit nom* at times. Though the maid was older by two years, the two of them had grown up together. They had slept in the same room, shared pranks and scrapes and childhood illnesses, and studied the same lessons until Celina was sent to the Ursuline nuns for training in music, domestic arts and fine embroidery. For weeks, they both cried every morning when the time came for Celina to leave for her classes with the nuns. Sisters could not be closer.

More than that, Suzette might no longer sleep in a trundle pulled from under Celina's tall, canopied bed, but she still had the intimate care of her bed-chamber, her clothing and her person. It would be impossible to keep any clandestine visit from her. The only way the appointment with Rio de Silva could be kept was with her maid's aid and cooperation.

The café au lait color of Suzette's face turned dusky red as she listened. As Celina fell silent, she set her hands on her hips. "He is Satan himself, that one!"

"Perhaps." Celina frowned. "Though I think…"

"What?"

"That what he proposes isn't mere deviltry." She allowed Suzette to slide the loosened corset off over her head.

"What can you mean?"

"That he may be more interested in injuring the count than in invading the fastness of my bedchamber."

Suzette moved to put the corset away, returning with a nightgown of embroidered lawn that she held while Celina located the openings of the long sleeves. "And that matters to you?"

"It isn't particularly flattering." Celina gave the maid a wan smile as her head emerged from the soft folds of cloth.

"You are lucky he didn't have his way with you there in his rooms. I told you it was folly to go. But when did you ever listen to anything I have to say?"

"Often, and you know it. Still, I swear there was no question of anything really improper."

"You needn't sound disappointed."

"I was terrified, if you must know. It's plain that Monsieur de Silva is everything they say of him, a gentleman and ultimate master of the sword, yes, but also a coldhearted duelist who plans carefully before he strikes and cares nothing for the pain and heartbreak of man or woman."

Suzette breathed an imprecation even as she straightened the folds of the nightgown, and then moved to stand near the dressing table where she waited for Celina to be seated. "This is the man who will claim his reward for sparing Denys, and you expect me to look the other way?"

"It won't be like that."

"No, no, certainly not. I'm sure he promised a sweet courting with love notes and trinkets and compliments whispered in your ear. You can't be so foolish as to believe it?"

"When have I ever had hope of such things, much less depended on them?" Celina gave her maid a brief glance in the mirror above the dressing table as she seated herself before it. "Only witness the courtship of the count."

Suzette studied her with a troubled expression. They were both aware that Celina's formal appearance at the opera house and balls and parties of the *saison de visites*, the winter social season, had been delayed by three long years of mourning, first for her older brother, then for her mother and younger sister. Celina had been dangerously close to the age when an unmarried woman was advised to throw her corset on top of the armoire and resign herself to spinsterhood by the time they were over. To everyone's amazement, she had immediately attracted the attention of the social lion of the moment, the Spanish count who was sojourning in the city.

Romantic sensibility had played scant part in his pursuit, however. The two of them had exchanged fewer than a dozen words, and those in public, before the count approached her father. The only compliment he had paid her was to observe that she appeared healthy and quite capable of producing the heir denied him by his two deceased wives. The nuptial arrangements were initiated over a glass of brandy, and would have been completed then and there except for a small difficulty with the settlements. Her father insisted that a large portion of her dowry should be kept in her name, a stipulation not at all to the liking of the count. The issue was still being negotiated.

"It is the way of such things," the maid said with a shake of her head. "Men respect their wives and dote on their mistresses, while women respect their husbands and love their children."

"Yes, and it is the way of things for young men to die beneath Allard's infamous oaks, but Denys will not be among their number if I can help it."

"To fight death is senseless, Mam'zelle. You cannot stop it, no matter how hard you try." Suzette wet a cloth in the basin on the nearby washstand and handed it to Celina for removal of the rice powder and carmine oil that were her only cosmetics.

Celina accepted the cloth but refused to meet Suzette's eyes again, knowing the sympathy and understanding for past sorrow, past regret, that she would find there. "I have given my word. It's too late to draw back now."

"I wonder," Suzette began.

A light tapping on the door interrupted her. Almost immediately, it opened and an elderly woman wearing a frilled nightcap from which fine curls sprang like silver wires put her head inside. Small-boned and gently rounded in shape, she had smiling eyes and a voice like the happy yet grating chirp of a cricket.

"Oh, good, *chère*. I thought I heard voices. Praise the saints that you've returned. I was beginning to worry."

"I'm sorry, Tante Marie Rose, though I did tell you that I would not be long behind you."

"I'm still persuaded your father would think it remiss of me to not to have gone with you to inquire after Félicité Parmentier's bout with *la grippe*. My duty was to attend you." The elderly woman moved into the room with her hands clasped together in her agitation.

"And contract her virulent cough? You know how easily you become ill. It doesn't bear thinking of, particularly when I've returned without incident. You may rest easy, my dear aunt."

"And how is poor Félicité?"

"Much better," Celina answered firmly. The errand she had used to escape being chaperoned after leaving the Theatre d'Orleans, known to all as the opera house, was no fabrication. She had spoken briefly with her friend's mother. Still, deceiving her aunt left a bitter taste in her mouth.

"Denys did not return with you, I see. I peeped into his room just now and his bed was empty."

Her brother was sleeping elsewhere to prevent concern over his dawn appointment with Rio de Silva, though he had given her instructions in what to say if he was missed. She was heartily glad of it now, since it also served to make it appear she had enjoyed his escort after leaving Tante Marie Rose. "He met Hippolyte Ducolet outside the opera house and was invited to join his party in an outing to a cockfight or some such thing after seeing me home. No doubt he will be offered a spare bed in the Ducolet *garçonnière*."

"Such a nice young man, Hippolyte. What a comfort he is to his mother."

Hippolyte was in fact a hellion who seldom went to bed before dawn, which was doubtless why her brother had chosen him for his second. Being a notorious sleepyhead himself, Denys had need of someone who would rouse him in time to see that he was punctual for his appointment under the oaks.

"You are a dear to worry about us," Celina said. "But shouldn't you be in bed? Remember that tomorrow is your day to sew for the orphans at St. Joseph's."

"But of course, though I feel so unwell that I may send my regrets. My liver, you know. I should never have had the pear tart at dinner. Pear tart always makes me bilious."

It did indeed, but she always ate it and always complained. "Perhaps a tisane might give you relief."

"I was just on my way down to make one when I stopped in here."

"Really, Tante Marie Rose, you should have rung your bell."

"So you and your father always tell me, but I so dislike causing a fuss at this hour."

Her aunt hated imposing at any time. A sister to Celina's mother, she had come to visit for a week or two following the death of her husband and remained for these twenty years. Self-effacing to a fault, she was a pleasant guest and convenient chaperone, though a martyr to illness in its infinite and fascinating variety. "Perhaps you would like Suzette to prepare it? You know she has a way with herbs."

"I would be most happy," the maid said at once, though there was irony in the glance she sent Celina, as if she knew the errand was an excuse to be rid of both maid and aunt.

"No, really," Tante Marie Rose said in agitation. "I could not ask, that is, I don't expect...truly prefer..."

"You know just how you like it," Celina supplied in soothing tones.

"Precisely," her aunt agreed with a relieved sigh. "I shall just toddle along down to the kitchen, but you may be very sure I will leave all in order. I know how much your dear father dislikes it when Cook gets into a temper over misplaced cups and cutlery."

"He is at home?"

"No, no, still out with Count de Lérida, I believe. Isn't it providential that they have so much in common? Well, good night, *chère*. Sleep well."

"And you," Celina said, then sighed as she listened to her aunt's footsteps pattering away toward the back stairs that led to the outdoor kitchen.

"We really should get you into bed without delay," Suzette said, turning down the bedcovers. "Tomorrow could bring anything."

"Meaning they may bring Denys home on a window shutter in the morning, or that my husband-to-be will introduce my father into some gaming house where he may lose everything, including my dowry."

"He isn't your husband-to-be until the marriage contracts are signed, and your father has more sense than to plunge too deep at the tables."

"He is impressed with the noble Spaniard, and anxious to have him as a member of the family."

"You know he wants only what is best for you."

"He wishes to prove that he is ready to provide for me, in spite of it being my fault that—"

"No, *chère*," Suzette said in sharp interruption. "He cares for your happiness."

"Cares so much that he is ready to marry me to a man older by decades who wears a corset stronger than mine and is addicted to *écarté* and high-stakes poker."

"None of which you have any business knowing, and would not except for Denys."

"Ignorance of it would not make me resigned to this match."

Suzette did not look at her mistress as she reached to remove the white camellia Celina wore tucked into her high-piled curls, then pull free the combs and pins that held her hair. "Women have always given way to such arrangements."

"Because they have no wit or backbone."

"Because it's the way of the world. They may cry and plead, but they obey in the end for how are they to live otherwise? Often they grow to love their husbands and are happy in their new homes."

"And sometimes they are so miserable that they can exist only if their senses are dulled by orange flower water laced with laudanum," Celina said in fierce tones. "They dance and wager at cards as if their lives depend on it, let illness or the rigors of

childbirth take them, or even do outrageous things
so they may live separate from their husbands."

"Outrageous, *chère*?"

Celina refused to be drawn. "It's stupid, and I will
not follow in their footsteps if it may be prevented."

"Yes, but can it?"

Celina made no answer. Sitting there in only her
thin nightgown, she felt suddenly chilled. She
couldn't get the image of Rio de Silva out of her mind,
his stalking advance, the silvery sheen of his eyes
and intense concentration on his features as he
reached out to touch her. Her cheek felt branded
where his fingers had brushed it. And in spite of the
protests she'd made, she was perfectly aware that he
need not have stopped there, that only his will and
consideration had kept him from further encroach-
ments.

"Mam'zelle, you're shivering. Come, let's finish
this, then perhaps I should make a nice tisane for
you to calm your nerves."

"I'm fine."

"Of course you are," Suzette scolded as she put the
camellia and hairpins to one side, then picked up a
hairbrush with coarse boar bristles and began to pull
it through Celina's tresses.

Celina closed her eyes momentarily, relaxing a little with the pleasure of the brush moving over her
scalp, which was sore from the pins holding the
weight of her hair. Nothing could distract her for
long however. "What if Monsieur de Silva fails to
keep his word? What if Denys is killed?"

"What if he lives!" Suzette said, her face grim.
"You have made an appalling bargain, Mam'zelle,

and I don't see how you can keep it without being ruined."

"I shall never marry, so it will hardly be of consequence."

"And what will you tell your papa? Or Denys for that matter? This is madness. I should never have gone with you tonight."

"You are not to blame. I suppose it was foolish to interfere, but I thought…"

"You thought to save Denys yet again. When will you learn?"

"He is my brother, all the family I have left."

"There is your father."

"Yes." Celina let that one bleak word stand without embellishment.

Suzette gave a quick shake of her head. "What is done cannot be mended. Now, into bed with you. The morning will come soon enough."

"I'll never be able to sleep."

"Thinking about what may or may not happen is of no use." Suzette held back the gauzelike netting of the mosquito *baire* while Celina mounted the bedsteps and lay on the high mattress. "Put it from your mind."

"Easily said, but not so easily done," Celina told her, and closed her eyes with a sigh. Even as she lay there, she could see in her mind's eye two men facing each other with drawn swords in the early light of dawn. After a moment, she lifted her lashes again. "Suzette?"

"Mam'zelle?" The maid turned from where she was tidying the dressing table.

"Do you suppose we could…?"

"No!"

"But you don't know what I was going to say," she protested.

"I know you, and I've been waiting for you to decide that the best way to look after Denys still further would be to be an observer at this duel. It isn't done. Besides, your papa would be furious."

"He wouldn't have to know."

"You think you could send to have the carriage brought out at dawn without his hearing of it? The coachmen would not dare obey without checking first."

"You could go and fetch a hack, and I could slip out to meet you at some corner away from here."

"And what am I to use for money? Neither of us has more than a few piastres to our names."

That much was true, Celina thought with a frown. Though her father was a man of wealth and she was free to spend a reasonable amount on her wardrobe and feminine furbelows such as gloves, fans and parasols, her purchases were put on account and the bills sent to the town house. Even when she went to the French market, it was either Suzette or the butler Mortimer who haggled with the vendors on her behalf and handed over the money, just as it was they who carried the market basket. It was assumed she had little need for funds other than to buy a praline or rice cake from a street vendor or put a donation in the box when she lit a candle at the cathedral.

"There must be a way," she said, almost to herself.

"Don't think of it, I beg you," Suzette said. "Only consider how the tongues would wag if you were discovered. Consider your poor aunt, who would be consumed with guilt that she did not stop you. Consider

Denys and how mortified he would be to realize you do not trust him to conduct this affair like a man."

Celina cared very little for the wagging tongues and though she had every sympathy for her aunt's position, was well aware that she would be little blamed. What Denys might feel was a different matter. She would not like to embarrass him before his friends. Still less did she like the idea that she might distract him at a crucial moment.

"How I wish I were a man!" she said passionately. "It would be perfectly natural that I go about the streets on my own or wish to be present at this duel."

"But you are not, and so you must wait."

"Yes." Celina closed her eyes again. "I do pray that Monsieur de Silva will keep his word."

"And I fear that he may," Suzette replied in grim tones. "I do greatly fear it."

3

Olivier knocked softly on Rio's door at a little before five. Rio was awake, standing at the long open window of his room, watching the last of the darkness give way to a pink glow in the sky beyond the great curve of the Mississippi River. He had dressed with care in knit pantaloons that gave easily with his every movement. With them he wore a fresh linen shirt fastened with onyx studs, cravat of white silk tied in a loose knot that would release at the first tug, waistcoat with gray shadow-stripes and a black frock coat. Though he didn't care for the current fashion of heavily pomaded hair, he had used a little to prevent the morning breeze from blowing strands into his face. His beaver hat lay ready beside the case that held the rapier he preferred for these affairs, as well as two others of slightly varying sizes in case of need.

"*Alà vous café*, Monsieur Rio."

He turned to take the cup from the tray Olivier held, sipping from it before he said a brief word of thanks.

"A fine morning for the business."

Rio lifted a shoulder in a moody shrug. It appeared to be, since it was fair with only a trace of fog.

"You should have waited on the cravat," Olivier said, eyeing the three wrinkled and discarded silk cloths that lay on the bed. "I could have saved you a great deal of trouble."

"I woke early."

Olivier gave a judicious nod, as if he had guessed as much.

"There was no need for both of us to lose sleep."

"You are concerned?"

Rio gave him a sardonic glance. "This meeting should not be taking place."

"It will soon be over."

"Yes." Rio tossed back the demitasse of hot, strong brew and set the cup back on the tray.

"The visit last evening of Mademoiselle Vallier—"

"Don't!" Rio said sharply.

Olivier veiled his gaze and was silent.

Rio hated that servile attitude. Its purpose, he thought, was to goad him into the explanation he was reluctant to give. As a prelude to the inevitable, he said, "Thinking about women before a meeting is as stupid as spending the night with some cocotte."

"Just so," Olivier murmured.

"Not that Mademoiselle Vallier's interference is of any moment. I simply prefer not to be reminded."

"You had no intention of killing her brother even before she arrived."

"I'm not a murderer," Rio said shortly.

"No. The question then is why you did not tell the lady and be done with it."

"What, and pass up a perfect opportunity to have her in my debt?"

"As if that matters."

"She thinks me honorable." The words were dry.

"And is she wrong?"

A knock at the entrance door on the ground floor made it unnecessary to answer that question. It would be Caid Roe O'Neill and Gilbert Rosière, his good friends and fellow *maîtres d'armes* acting as his seconds today, come to escort him to The Oaks. They were on time. It was a good omen.

Caid, his chief second and an Irishman only recently arrived in the city and Passage de la Bourse, had hired a barouche. It waited for them on the rue Saint-Pierre. Gilbert took charge of the sword case, and the three of them walked along the Passage and turned onto the side street where the vehicle stood with its top down on this mild winter morning and the driver perched in front. They rode the short distance to the home of Dr. Kiefer, who had been engaged for the event. A genial man and imminent physician from Vienna with much experience in these matters, he came out of his house at once with his black surgeon's bag in his hand. Bows were exchanged along with a few genial comments as they started off again.

The wheels of the barouche bounced over the uneven paving stones of the rue Saint-Anne and through the offal of the muddy street that skirted Congo Square. It picked up speed as it rattled from the confines of the Vieux Carré, or Old Square, the grid of streets laid out by French engineers more than a hundred years before with surrounding walls and protective forts. In the outlying area beyond the Faubourg Marigny, the upstanding skeleton-like studs and braces of houses under construction gave indication of the spreading growth of the city.

They traveled in the direction of Bayou St. Jean, eventually reaching the outer limits of the Allard plantation. Rio stared out at the palmettos, cattails, purple asters and tall grasses that filled the ditches, waving in the breeze of their passing. Beyond that weedy tangle lay a solid green wall of sugar cane. It would soon be harvested, cut down by the sharp knives of the field hands at the height of its vigor and sweetness. He turned away with his face set in grim lines.

After another mile or so, they came in view of the live oak grove that had become the chosen spot for affairs of honor. The leaves of the trees had a mirror-like sheen in the early morning light, while the gray moss that hung from their branches looked like rags of silver lace. The shade was dense underneath, and the lush grass that grew there showed only a little yellow among the green blades. At the edge of the grove was a pair of oaks known as The Twin Sisters that provided the perfect combination of protection from slanting rays of the rising sun, which could blind a duelist, and flat turf for nimble maneuvering. The barouche pulled up a short distance away from that spot and they got down.

There was no sign of Vallier. Gilbert looked at Rio and raised a brow. "It appears we may breakfast alone, *mon ami,* and without a bloodletting to spoil our appetites."

"Give it time, Titi," Caid told him with a smile, using the nickname that was in the alliterative fashion of the French Creoles, and the other sword mas-

ter's cross to bear. "We're a little early since there
was no need to roust our good friend here from his
bed."

"Just so. He's disgustingly alert, don't you think?"

Rio spared a cynical look for his friends, knowing
that they would have been no less prepared in his
place. They were both exceptionally fit, as required
of those at the top of their chosen profession. Gilbert,
though Italian by birth, looked the complete French-
man, the effect no doubt of patronizing French tailors, French cobblers and French tonsure parlors.
Expansive and ebullient of personality, he was one
of the few sword masters who was married and kept
his family above his salon.

Caid was taller and more heavily muscled than
Gilbert, nearer to Rio in size, and lacked any hint of
Gallic style. Though he hailed from Erie, he was
Black Irish in appearance, as if one or two female an-
cestors might have met a Spanish raider on the beach.
His hair was dark and curling, his eyes the blue of the
deep North Sea, and his manner alternately charm-
ing and blunt to a fault. Both men had great dexterity with a blade and a higher degree of skill than the
average *maître d'armes*. On the few occasions when
the three of them had paired off in any combination
on the fencing strip, they had either fought to a draw
or else the outcome was dictated by purest chance.

Just then, the sounds of wheels came from down
the road. A hired hack bowled around the bend, racing toward them with a foam-flecked horse in the traces and a comet of dust trailing behind. It pulled up,
and the Vallier party jumped down. The two groups
saluted each other, and Denys Vallier came forward.

"My apologies for keeping you waiting, *messieurs*. The hack arrived late."

It was impossible to dislike the young man's frankness and courtesy, Rio thought. It was also impossible to miss his resemblance to his sister, though the aristocratic refinement of his sister's features took on a masculine cast in young Vallier's case, one emphasized by a light beard and side whiskers in the style of the Romantics. Rio could feel the knot just under his breastbone coil tighter. Soon he must make the decision that had eluded him during the night.

"Not at all," he replied in curt tones. "We were early."

Denys Vallier inclined his upper body in acknowledgment, and the two parties separated to a distance of some twenty feet. Dr. Kiefer and the surgeon attending on Vallier, Dr. Buchanan, withdrew to the side, where they laid out their instruments on cloths of white linen. The two chief seconds met at the halfway point to execute their remaining responsibilities. An offer to inspect the weapons was made and refused after it was established that standard *colichemardes,* a type of triangular-shaped rapier, would be used, with matching thirty-six-inch blades, eight-inch handles and the usual bell guards. The field, it was agreed, would be restricted to the standard fifteen paces, and this area was marked off with chalk to indicate the area within which the contestants would confine themselves. A Mexican silver dollar was produced and tossed high several times, with the calls deciding which duelist would face the sun or the wind and who would give the signals. Caid won, and all was in readiness.

During these preliminaries, Rio removed his coat
and waistcoat and folded the sleeves of his shirt to
his elbows. As he pinned the folded cloth into place,
he noted the arrival of more carriages bringing
spectators. They were an integral part of the proceedings, and their rumble of comment and shouted
wagers could not be allowed to impinge on his
concentration.

Many of the *maîtres d'armes* relished the presence
of an audience, seeing any duel fought as a form of
exhibition from which they might gain new clients.
They welcomed, even sought, the challenges that
would allow them to display their skill. Rio had only
contempt for such tactics. To his mind, the grounds
surrounding The Twin Sisters resembled the Circus
Maximus of ancient Rome where men fought to the
death for the entertainment of the crowd. He took no
pride or pleasure in being one of those whom the
gathering men had come to see engage in combat and
perhaps leak away his life from his wounds.

Caid moved to Rio's sword case, which lay open
on the ground, and tested the blades. After a small
grunt of satisfaction, he glanced up. "Your prefer-
ence?"

Rio indicated the plainest and sturdiest of the set and
accepted it as it was extended, handle first, over Caid's
arm. Allowing the tip to trail to the ground, he rolled
his shoulders to relax them and then stood waiting.

The morning was advancing, the first rays of sunlight striking through the trees, turning the leaves to
small, glittering mirrors and swaying the hanging
moss. A breeze laden with the smells of dust and
trampled grass made a quiet rustling overhead. A

squirrel chattered some distance away, and cardinals flashed among the trees like streaks of blood. Somewhere a crow called three times, then fell silent.

Rio and his two seconds advanced to the center of the field, where they were joined at once by Vallier and his friends. He and Denys executed their formal salutes with flashing, whistling blades. Their attendants stepped back out of the way, standing a little to the right on each side.

Caid glanced at Rio. Their eyes held for a long second of silent communication. Then Rio gave a short nod.

"On guard," Caid called.

Rio brought up his blade. It slapped the end of his opponent's sword with a bell-like clang. As the two of them fell into position, he looked beyond the crossed blades. Denys Vallier's face was flushed and his eyes burning but free of active hostility. He held himself well, and there was only a faint tremor in his extended arm.

"Begin!"

At Caid's command, Rio felt the familiar alertness and mental dexterity settle upon him like a mantle. His concentration narrowed to the point of his sword while he accepted the handle, guard and blade as if they were parts of his body. With a movement of satinlike smoothness and perfect coordination, he launched into an attack.

Seconds later, he knew that he could kill Celina's brother at will. It was not surprising, still Rio had thought he might have more of a fight in front of him, given that Vallier was entered as a pupil at Croquère's salon.

The voices of the spectators grew quieter, then faded away. Most had some skill with a blade, no doubt, so knew of a certainty that the best of amateurs had little chance against a master. It had to be glaringly obvious that Vallier, for all his courage, was something less than the best.

A brief flare of anger moved over Rio for whatever suicidal impulse of pride or folly had caused this young gallant to challenge him. Honor had been the driving force, of course; Denys Vallier could not let the remarks made about his sister pass. Not for the first time, Rio cursed both his ill luck in having a witness to that oblique reference to Celina Vallier and his own stupidity in using it. Still, he wondered if there had been something more to the challenge for Vallier, perhaps the notoriety of meeting a premier sword master. There were those who hoped to gain a measure of fame by besting one of his repute. It would not be the first time he had been forced to risk his life for such small cause.

The young man had agility and a quickness of eye that together allowed him a show of defense. Regardless, his moves were without finesse. There was little control in his thrusts, and his wrist was far too rigid. He lunged so recklessly, parried so widely that it was difficult not to impale him by accident. Reading his play, Rio drew him out with care while searching for some way to end the passage at arms without making a mockery of the whole affair.

Vallier's face was white now, and his lips blue-tinged as he breathed between set teeth. His eyes, so like his sister's, were shaded dark brown with desperation. He must be aware that he could not meet a professional standard, had to expect to feel cold steel pierce his chest at any moment. It was cruel to keep him suspended there, hopelessly striving to hold his fate at bay.

Rio had killed his man on more than one occasion, though always because his adversary would accept no other form of defeat. In common with most of French New Orleans, he followed the European dueling form wherein honor was satisfied at first blood rather than the Americanized version that expected every contest to result in death. A final end always seemed barbaric, smacking of revenge instead of the defense of honor. It appeared even more so now.

No decision was required, after all. The only course he could take in good conscience was the same one that would place Denys Vallier's sister in his hands.

It was a reasonably easy matter to target an antagonist's right forearm. A turn of the wrist and it was done, though an experienced swordsman could readily parry the attempt at injury. Before the thought had fully formed in Rio's mind, he swirled into the designated attack. He executed the move and felt the tip of his blade slice skin and muscle.

Vallier gave a stifled cry and dropped his sword. Rio stepped back, even as the seconds called out the order to halt and ran forward. Both he and Vallier turned on their heel and walked a few paces in opposite directions. A murmur ran through the crowd, though it was impossible to say whether it was one of sympathy or disappointment.

Vallier's surgeon hurried forward to inspect the wound and swab it with a handful of cotton soaked in pungent alcohol. He pressed his thumb into the flesh of the young man's wrist, holding tightly. Vallier's seconds huddled around them. A brief conference was held, after which the chief second stepped forward.

"Dr. Buchanan gives it as his opinion that our man has been injured in such a manner as to put him in danger of bleeding to death if he continues. The duel must not go on."

He had touched an artery then, Rio thought. That had been his intention, though a chancy venture. He prayed he had not severed tendons that would leave Vallier with a useless arm.

Handing his sword to Caid, he turned to Gilbert. "Ask if I may approach, Titi. I would like a word with my worthy opponent."

Gilbert Rosière went off on the errand and soon returned with the requisite permission. By that time Rio had rolled down his sleeves and donned his frock coat. He strode across the grass to where Mademoiselle Vallier's brother stood, coming to a stop with a brief bow.

Vallier was pale, but the previous feverish anxiety had drained from his face. His expression was calm and a little shy as he met Rio's. "You wished to speak to me, Monsieur?"

"Indeed," Rio said, his voice grim. "Is there anything I or my surgeon may do to help here?"

"Nothing," Vallier's doctor replied. "I have the bleeding in hand. It will stop in a short while if there is no further strain on the arm."

"Excellent." Rio turned back to Vallier. "Permit me to say, then, that I regret your injury as much as my remark that brought about this meeting. I ask that you forget both, if you please."

His adversary might have pressed the point, could have demanded to know if this was an apology in form. He did not avail himself of that privilege. Putting out his good left hand, he said, "Done, and gladly."

That magnanimity lifted Rio's impression of the boy another notch. Accepting his hand, he said, "When your injury allows, I would consider it a great pleasure to cross swords with you again under more pleasant circumstances. Perhaps you will visit my salon in good time?"

"Monsieur, I…you do me too much honor," Vallier stammered.

That might prove to be true, but Rio had no regrets. Having pledged his word to Celina Vallier, he might as well observe it to the limit. "Then I shall see you there."

"You may count on it."

Rio inclined his head then turned away to rejoin his friends. Moments later, they were bowling away back toward New Orleans.

"Handsomely done, that apology," Titi said. "I never knew you had it in you."

"I was wrong and said so. That's all." Rio knew his words were curt, but there was little he could do about it.

Caid gave him a droll look. "You know that you'll have every young sprig in town stepping on your toes and elbowing you in the ribs."

"Nonsense."

"Just wait. They will decide you have gone too soft

to be dangerous, or else hope to become an object of pity and private lessons."

"I took no pity on Vallier."

"You let him live for the sake of his *beaux yeux*, I suppose. Or possibly for his sister's?"

Rio turned on his friend. "What do you know of it?"

"Nothing, nothing, except that you retracted your remark, which must mean you no longer think it true that she's desperate for a husband after delaying her debut for three years of mourning. And what could change your mind except the fair lady herself?"

"I merely had second thoughts."

"I hope so, *mon ami*."

"Meaning?"

"You know very well. You and I may gain entrance to the home of a daring widow such as Maurelle Herriot, recently returned from Paris where Romantics, Bohemians and other outré types are accepted in fashionable circles. With a female of marriageable age in New Orleans, it's a different thing altogether. Step too far over the line and your clients will melt away faster than ice on a steamboat churning downriver."

"I'm in no danger of forgetting that point," Rio said, his voice grim.

"What about ignoring it? No, forget I said that. You couldn't be so foolish."

Rio gave Caid a hard look, but Titi broke in before he could speak. "A drink, as usual, to celebrate the favorable outcome of this business? I, for one, am more than ready for it. "

"And breakfast," Caid agreed. "Where shall we go?"

That was of course a serious question, food and drink being subjects of primary importance to those who called the Vieux Carré home. A number of possibilities were discussed, but the final choice was the restaurant at the St. Louis Merchant's Exchange and Hotel. Not only was the chef at Alvarez's superb, but the place fronted on rue Saint-Louis, opposite the entrance to the Passage de la Bourse, so was only a stroll away from their salons that would soon be thronged with students.

The Exchange was a hive of activity. Open less than four years under the management of James Hewlett, it had taken over the custom of the old Maspero's Exchange on rue Chartres, becoming the place to be seen and do business in the city. It was a magnificent structure with the bar and restaurant on the lower floor, and upstairs the Exchange itself plus guest rooms for two hundred and a pair of grand ballrooms. Surmounting the open center of the second floor was a great, echoing dome designed by architect Charles Bingley Dakin in imitation of a Greek temple in Athens by Lysicrates. It carried the same Lantern of Diogenes theme, so set a high tone for the commerce that took place beneath it. Under that echoing vastness were held the frenetic auctions of steamboats, city property, plantations and farm animals during the week, with slave auctions on Saturday.

The combined smell of strong coffee and sugar-drenched beignets was like a thick fog they had to wade through to reach their favorite corner table. Within minutes, they were sipping the roasted brew of the bean laced with hot milk and brandy while sharing a large platter of fried pastries.

From time to time, they greeted men who had visited their various salons, or were members in good standing or private pupils. They also nodded at other sword masters who were making their rounds, among them the latest arrival in the Passage, Nicholas Pasquale, who had been promptly dubbed La Roche, The Rock, by the fencing brethren for his immovable fighting stance. At one point they watched with some irony as José Llulla, known as Pépé, entered, followed by a group of young men who wore thin mustaches that drooped past the corners of their mouths in imitation of the style of this quiet but deadly sword master. No one knew how many men Llulla had slain on the field, but a macabre joke ran that said he needed a private cemetery to hold them all. It was Pépé who had proposed that they hold a tournament matching all the *maîtres d'armes* of the Passage against one another. This exhibition was to take the place of the separate bouts usually mounted as a means of attracting men to their salons. The idea was still being discussed among them, with a few stiff-rumped masters calling for a certificate issued by a well-known training academy as a condition for entry. Some claimed this was a flagrant attempt to exclude Pépé and other masters like him who had no such certification. What would come of it was anyone's guess.

Pépé Llulla had not yet spotted them or he would surely have joined them, Rio thought. Since the thin, saturnine master hailed from the Balearic Islands, they were countrymen of sorts and had struck up as close a friendship as was possible between competitors. As they watched, he veered from his path at a hail from the back reaches of the room. A dandy with a Don Quixote beard and an exquisitely embroidered waistcoat rose to perform a punctilious bow then sweep his hand toward a vacant chair in an obvious invitation to join him and his companions. Llulla hesitated, or so it seemed, before he accepted.

"Who might that be?" Caid asked with a nod toward the young Don Quixote. "I don't believe I've seen him around."

"An envoy from Mexico, or so I'm told." Gilbert paused to allow the waiter to refill his coffee cup. "He's supposed to be en route to Washington where he hopes to block the acceptance of Texas into the Union."

"Not a popular stance here." Rio had no particular interest in the former Spanish colony or in Mexico, but most New Orleanians, he knew, held a different view. Ties between Texas and Louisiana had been strong since the days of the Spanish dons, when the king of Spain had held power in the area and the El Camino Real, or the King's Road, had run from Natchez in what was now Mississippi to Natchitoches, then across to San Antonio in Texas and on down to Mexico City. New Orleans had been in ferment over the struggle for Texas independence four or five years back, and would not look kindly on any attempt by Mexico to annex the young republic now.

"Most of the states favor admitting Texas," Caid agreed. "Mexico already controls a major portion of the western plains and desert countries, not to mention the area called California. If they reclaim Texas—which they may well do if statehood is denied—then the frontier will become the boundary set by the Louisiana Purchase. Westward expansion will cease. New Orleans will forever be the jumping-off place for the border between this country and Mexico."

"It could happen," Gilbert said. "Antislavery factions in the northeast seem adamant in their objection to having Texas entering the Union as a slave state."

"No doubt, but the politicians can hardly risk losing such a vast stretch of new territory."

"War will come if Mexico invades," Gilbert said with finality.

"There may also be war if Texas gains statehood," Rio pointed out. "The authorities in Mexico City will consider it a land grab by the States."

"Which it will be, of course," Gilbert agreed with a wry grin. "And when this fight starts, New Orleans will be in the thick of it."

Caid leaned back in his chair. "More business for us then, my friends. The army of Mexico is made up of swordsmen. A saber is part of the uniform. Men heading for Texas to face naked blades will require extra instruction in the art of defending their hides."

Rio nodded mechanically but had ceased to listen. The table favored by journalists from the nearby offices of the daily news sheet *L'Abeille*, or The Bee, was emptying. The removal allowed him a clear field of vision for the gentleman seated with the envoy and Pépé Llulla.

The man's face was florid and his jowls purple where they rolled into a pair of double chins above his gold silk cravat. The clothing he wore was impeccably tailored, yet fit him like the skin of a sausage. The pomade on his hair contained dye to darken the sparse locks and was so heavy that it glistened in the morning light through the windows. The nosegay in his lapel was far too large, and the fobs that hung from his watch chain were so heavily ornate that they clanked on the tabletop as he bent forward to push a pastry into his mouth. Rio cataloged the details of the man's appearance, and the enmity in his heart was so cold that he shuddered, abruptly, from its chill.

"Mon vieux," Titi said as he reached to touch his arm. "What ails you? Did someone tread on your grave?"

Rio managed a thin smile. "You might say so."

"That's the Spanish count," Caid said, craning his neck to follow the path of Rio's gaze. "Our noble visitor, come to invest in cotton and sugar and, so they say, possibly increase his fortunes by taking a rich planter's daughter as a bride."

"Don Damian Francisco Adriano de Vega y Ruiz, Conde de Lérida in the Spanish style," Titi supplied. "As pompous as he is stout, though there are those who forgive him anything for the sake of his title. He buried two wives back in Spain, one of them in unhallowed ground as a suicide, or so it's said. He's thought to be dangling after the Vallier girl." He stopped abruptly, a considering expression in his dark eyes.

"What else do you know of him?" Rio asked, his voice soft.

Titi exchanged a quick glance with Caid who shrugged, then, clearing his throat, he continued. "The count arrived in the city from Havana a few weeks ago. He has set up a pretty quadroon in a house on Rampart and visits her as regularly as some men take a physic. They say also that he's seen frequently at the gaming houses where he plays for high stakes but is a poor loser."

"Go on," Rio said as the other sword master paused.

"He has run up tremendous bills of account with the tradesmen along Royale and Chartres. Also with Hewlett here at the hotel, where he has one of the best suites of rooms. The count is dedicated to his morning chocolate, drinks at least three cups before getting out of bed. Hemorrhoids are his particular cross to bear—well, along with weak knees. They say he requires at least two stout menservants to remove him from the chamber pot if he ever gets down on it." He grinned. "Is that enough?"

Rio gave him a jaundiced look. "Where did you come by these details?"

"Slave gossip, the heart's blood of New Orleans. Never think that those who serve you don't know every detail of your existence. What else would you care to hear?"

"The count's chances of persuading Monsieur Vallier to accept him as a husband for his daughter."

"Good to excellent. Monsieur Vallier, after a protracted period of mourning during which he was seldom seen about town, formed an alliance recently with a pretty young woman named Clementine whom he met at a quadroon ball in the count's company. He has also taken to appearing nightly at Davis's gaming houses in tandem with his new *compadre*. Odds are two to one here at Alvarez's bar that the contract will be signed momentarily and the wedding celebrated before Lent."

"And how does Mademoiselle Vallier view this prospect?"

Titi shrugged. "No one has asked her."

It was a lack that should be remedied, Rio thought. And it would be, soon.

4

"Denys!"

Celina, standing at the top of the stairs that descended from the upper gallery into the courtyard, called out her brother's name as she saw him emerge from the porte cochere. Tears of joy and relief sprang to her eyes, blinding her so she nearly tripped as she ran down to meet him. "You're safe!" she cried, flinging herself against him. "I can't believe it. You're safe!"

"Well, of course I'm safe, *stupide*," he told her, his voice husky as he held her close. "Did you think a little thing like a duel with a sword master would be the end of me?"

"One such as de Silva? Why would I not?" She smiled a quick welcome for his friends, Hippolyte Ducolet and Armand Lollain, who followed him out of the shadows of the tunnel-like carriageway, before turning back to Denys. "How did you escape? You must tell me. Tell me all!"

"It was fantastic beyond anything," her brother said. "Monsieur de Silva looked quite deadly, I promise you."

"Denys faced him as coolly as if he fought a duel

every morning before breakfast," Hippolyte interjected. "We were truly amazed."

"Thank you," Denys said in dry reproof for the implied insult. "But Monsieur de Silva was most generous, Lina, so generous that you will hardly believe it."

"Was he, indeed?" Her voice was not quite steady as she turned, moving up the stairs with one arm around her brother while the other two young men trailed behind them.

"I swear he could have slain me ten times over if he had wished it. Yet he held back for reasons I can only begin to guess. He allowed me the privilege of sparring with him for nearly five minutes by the clock, then ended it with such aplomb that..."

"What do you mean, you can guess?"

"He made me an apology, Lina, and handsome it was. But that was afterward. Before then I quite expected the slight nature of the injury he'd inflicted would require the duel to proceed. It was not to be. The doctor declared me unfit, and de Silva accepted it without a whisper of protest."

"You were injured? Where? Let me see?" She dragged him to a halt at the top of the stairs, running her gaze over his slender form. Dark spots sprinkled his boots and right leg of his pantaloons, and she followed their path upward until she saw the bandage that peeped from his coat sleeve.

"It's nothing," he said, pulling away from her grasp. "A scratch only."

"You would say so. But if the doctor stopped the duel, then it must serious."

"An artery was damaged," Armand said. "He was bleeding like a stuck pig."

"It appeared worse than it was," Denys insisted. "It's my opinion that Monsieur de Silva knew exactly what he was about. The expression in his eyes, *chère.* You should have seen it, such intensity, such purpose, such deadly concentration. I thought...I thought by now you would be stopping the clocks, turning mirrors to the walls and searching for your discarded crepe."

"Don't!" she commanded, suppressing a shiver.

Denys paid no heed to her squeamishness. "And there is more, Lina. You will never guess. The maestro suggested that I cross swords with him in private at his salon, a privilege reserved only for the best and most promising."

"It's unheard of from de Silva," Hippolyte said as they all reached the upper gallery and took chairs at a table that was laid for breakfast. "I was grass-green with envy."

"And I," Armand declared. "Emerald-green!"

"Banana-leaf green." This from Hippolyte with a broad gesture at the plants growing in the courtyard below, surrounding the edges of that stone-paved space and hanging over the wrought-iron fountain that bubbled quietly in a corner.

"Oak-leaf green!" Armand said with a glance at the old live oak beyond the fountain before he gave Hippolyte a quick shove. "And nothing can possibly be greener."

"It's a great honor, I take it?" Celina asked in an attempt to divert their escalating high spirits brought on by near-giddy relief. It was understandable, to be sure, but could lead to horseplay that might be dangerous to the furniture, as well as to Denys's injured wrist.

"An incredible one," her brother replied. "I am humbled beyond words by the invitation. Beyond words, I promise you."

He and his friends had a great deal more to say about Rio de Silva, regardless. His skill, physical condition, marvelous restraint and, most of all, condescension in making any kind of apology were described in detail. A part of their high spirits, she realized after a few moments, was due to the strong drink they had all apparently stopped to imbibe on the way home. She really didn't mind, since it seemed her brother deserved the release it provided after his ordeal. She didn't mind anything so long as he was alive.

The three young men were still fighting the duel, giving her a move-by-move description complete with sound effects, when a door opened farther along the gallery. Their father stepped out, wearing an ankle-length brocaded robe in the Persian style and with his tasseled nightcap still on his head.

"Papa!" Denys said, starting up from his chair. "Did we wake you? I would not have done so for the world if I'd known you were still abed."

"Nonsense." Their father's voice was gruff. Coming to the table, he caught his son in a quick embrace. "Why in the name of *le bon Dieu* must I learn from strangers that my son is to meet an assassin on the field of honor? I returned home the instant I heard but you were not here."

"I would have told you, Papa, if I had known where to find you."

A small silence fell. The slight flush that appeared on their father's face made his bloodshot eyes seem redder and the broken veins in his nose more prom-

inent. "Yes, well. But you survived, for which I thank
the Holy Mother and entire pantheon of saints. Truly,
you were blessed, or so it seems from what I hear of
this de Silva." The older man released him and
waved him and the other two young men, who had
stood as a mark of respect, back into their seats. Taking the chair at the head of the table, he went on. "Tell
me at once of your escape. I perceive that you have
an injury, but how does it happen that it isn't fatal?"

Celina had heard all that she could bear. Rising
with the murmured excuse of seeing to breakfast,
she went down to the kitchen located beneath the
garçonnière, which sat at a right angle to the house.
Telling the cook to send up coffee, rolls and cheese
omelets for what had become a male party, she re-
traced her steps back along the stone-floored lower
gallery that connected the kitchen wing to the main
house and, like the gallery above, acted as a passage
from one room to another. She could hear the low
rumble of voices overhead. In no hurry to return to
the masculine company, she paused for a moment to
lean against a brick pillar plastered with ochre stucco.
It was only as she felt its firm, sun-warmed support
against her back that she recognized the weakness in
her knees.

She breathed deep, trying to calm her unsettled
nerves while staring at the sunlit courtyard. It was an
oasis, pleasant, fecund and orderly. The great live
oak cast lacy, moving shadows on the stones beneath
it as a light wind shifted heavy limbs lined with dark
green parasitic fern. Winter violets played hide-and-
seek among hardy ferns in the side beds, and a mock-
ingbird drank from the basin of the fountain that was

overhung by tall bananas and palms that had not felt the touch of frost so far in this protected space. It should have been a peaceful scene, yet there was little calm in it for Celina.

Rio de Silva had kept his word. He had allowed her brother to escape with the least possible injury. More than that, he had arranged that Denys was neither snubbed nor humiliated, but set up in his own regard and that of his friends.

She should feel grateful. Some part of her did, in all truth. But deep inside was a strident voice that questioned the ease of her victory and asked, fearfully, what the sword master meant to demand from her in return for such magnanimity.

There was no answer, nor did she come closer to one as the day wore on. Her brother's friends took their leave, and Denys retired to his room to change his clothes, rest and perhaps study his Blackstone a little, since he was reading law with prominent attorney Judah P. Benjamin and meant to become a lawyer. Celina spoke to her father about her evening plans. Given that Denys was somewhat indisposed, he reluctantly agreed to escort her and her aunt to the soiree being given by her mother's cousin, Madame Sonia Plauchet. They discussed the dinner menu as well, and afterward he dressed and went to the market below the rue de la Levée with Mortimer, his butler and body servant. Her father returned after an hour with Mortimer carrying the shopping basket. In it reposed a wet grass sack of fresh shrimp, a fat hen, four or five yellow apples, salad greens, and a small clay pot of sassafras filé from the Choctaw Indians. Celina's father spent some few minutes instructing the cook in the preparation of these items for dinner, and then left the house again without saying where he was going.

Tante Marie Rose returned from her sewing meeting in midafternoon. Fatigued from her labors and the joy of hours of gossip with her friends, she lay down to rest. Celina worked at her embroidery frame for some time, and found a certain peace in setting stitches and blending the rich colors of the silks. Toward dusk, she bathed and changed for the evening. Since the soiree was little more than a family party, she wore a simple gown of sea-blue silk with a triple-flounced skirt and white kid slippers. Suzette put up her hair in a coronet of braids, fastened around her neck a plain gold locket suspended on a black silk ribbon, then handed her a gold velvet cape.

The soiree was pleasant. Monsieur Sloman, a tenor of some note who had recently given a benefit at the St. Charles Theatre, sang a number of comic songs. Afterward, there was dancing, since no evening would have been complete without it. The cream pastries served during the supper were particularly fine and occasioned much comment. The count, favored guest of the season, did not appear as promised, which mortified the hostess but did not trouble Celina at all. It rained off and on during the evening, commonplace in what was proving to be a wet season, but stopped long enough for Suzette and Celina and her father to walk back to the town house rather than sending for their carriage. After seeing her home, her father went out again.

In its details, then, it was a day much like any other. But at no time during all its long passing did

Celina forget what she had promised or to whom she had given her word. Hardly a moment went by that she did not ask herself if Rio de Silva would come to her that evening.

She had watched for him on the streets as they walked the few blocks to her cousin Plauchet's house and back again. He was not among the strolling *beaux*, nuns in their habits and vendors of flowers and pralines that they passed on the banquettes, as the walkways beside the streets were called for their resemblance to small bridges above gutters filled with muddy water and other refuse. By the time they reached home again and Suzette undressed her for bed, Celina had almost convinced herself that she was worrying for nothing. Probably the sword master had never meant to come, threatening it only to make her see how wrong it was of her to interfere in his affairs.

Suzette wished her pleasant dreams and went away to her own bed, which was located on the upper floor of the kitchen wing. Celina tried to read from a volume of the macabre poet, Poe, but could not force her mind to appreciate the verses. Finally she put out the bed candle and lay staring into the darkness relieved only by the dim bars of light falling through the shutters from the whale-oil streetlamp on the corner.

It was raining again with a faint drumming and splatter. The music of a guitar drifted to her, a melody in a minor key played by some street musician perhaps taking refuge in a nearby doorway. A carriage rattled past accompanied by an echoing clip-clop of hooves. Dogs barked several streets away, as if they chased some unfortunate cat or a pig rooting in the gutters. Celina sighed and let her eyelids fall, holding them closed with determination.

"Good evening, *mademoiselle*. I trust that I haven't kept you waiting long?"

She sat bolt upright with a sharp gasp. Her gaze searched the room, fastening on the French door that opened onto the balcony overlooking the street. A man's tall form was silhouetted against the street-lamp's glow before he closed the outer shutter and pushed the door shut. Though indistinct beyond the gauze of the mosquito netting, she would have known his tall, graceful form anywhere.

Rio de Silva.

"How…how did you get up here?" she asked.

"Nothing easier, my sweet." He flourished some-thing in her direction that might have been a coiled whip or a circle of rope. "So easy, in fact, that I've never understood why those who live above the street feel so secure they seldom lock their balcony doors."

"But someone might have seen you!"

"I made certain they did not, though I am honored by your concern." He tossed the coil to one side and followed it with his hat.

Her heart jolted in her chest. She could not think straight, could hardly breathe. "I'm not concerned," she said with a wary eye on his approach. "At least only for…"

"For your good name? That is in my keeping, I think, and safely so."

What answer could she make to that? In any case, there were more important things between them. "I must thank you for the consideration you displayed toward Denys. It was well done and…and I truly am grateful."

"I gave my word," he answered, moving toward the bed. "As you gave yours."

"But still…"

"In any case, I would have thought your concern would be for other things."

"Meaning?"

"The consideration I might show toward you."

It was on the tip of her tongue to ask him what he meant, indeed, what he meant to do to her, but she bit it back. She would not give him that satisfaction. More than that, she was not at all sure she wanted to know in advance. "I rely on your promise that I will come to no harm," she answered with only a small quaver in her voice.

He was silent for long seconds. Then he stepped forward to lift the mosquito baire, draping it behind the bedpost. Mounting the lower tread of the bed step, he seated himself on the side of the mattress. She felt it give under his weight, and clenched her hands on the sheet and coverlet over her to control the instinct to fling herself off the other side.

"Harm," he mused. "I would say that might depend on your point of view. Or possibly that of the man you are to marry."

"I don't see—" she began, then stopped abruptly. "Oh."

"Oh, indeed."

The grave amusement in his comment grated on her nerves. She had always hated having anyone laugh at her. The irritation it brought was a welcome antidote for her fear. "I suspect he will overlook any small...damage for the sake of my dowry."

"Will he indeed? It hardly sounds like a love match."

"Certainly not," she said with a snap in her voice. "It is an alliance."

"A different thing altogether, I perceive." He tilted his head. "I recognize what the groom will receive, a lovely young bride with a fortune attached. But just what is the attraction for you?"

His face was in shadow, which made it difficult to know what he meant by asking such a thing. With little to guide her, she was left with only the truth as an answer. "Nothing attracts me."

"Not the prestige of attracting the count's notice?"

"Nothing."

"You have no wish to be the Condesa de Lérida and make your curtsy before Queen Isabel in Madrid? To be mistress of a house like a castle and an estate that stretches for miles?"

"Never. I don't want to leave New Orleans at all. Everything I know and love is here, my family, my friends, everything."

"Then why did you accept the match?"

"I didn't."

"Surely the man spoke to you, made some attempt to learn if you were willing?"

She thought the sword master frowned as he spoke, but could not be sure of it. "I saw him twice, once in the family box at the opera house, another time at a ball. We exchanged fewer words than you and I have spoken together, and never alone. He called on my father a week after our first meeting. A half hour into the visit, my father sent for the Napoleon brandy."

"It was arranged so quickly?"

"The settlements are still being negotiated. Apparently the count requires either complete control of my dowry or else the payment of a considerable sum before he will condescend to marry me." It felt remarkably liberating to be able to speak her mind. The man who sat so close was one of the few people to whom she could express her disdain without fear of censure.

"Then there is still hope," he said with the sound of meditation in his voice.

"You may see it. I cannot." She stared at him a moment there in the dark while curiosity rose inside her. "But what is it to you?"

"Nothing except interest in the happiness of a valiant lady."

It was an evasion, she was sure of it. "Do you know the count?"

"Let us say we have met."

"And you don't care for him."

"Why would you think that?"

"You suggested, I think, that you wished him to resent your comments instead of Denys."

"Did I?"

He was giving nothing away. It might be that he thought he had said too much earlier or else that she had no right to probe. It was he who had brought her into his too-masculine sphere by his disparaging comments, however, so had no one to blame for her curiosity except himself.

The darkness and rain beyond the window created an intimacy that seemed almost familiar. The longer Rio de Silva sat unmoving on the side of her bed, the more natural it felt. She wondered if he realized it, perhaps even counted on it as a man with experience at calming the fears of women. She also wondered if he recognized her nervous questions as a means of keeping him at a safe distance.

"Who are you, really?" she asked as she adjusted her pillow for support, then drew her hair, woven into a single long braid for sleeping, forward over her breast.

"No one, just a fencing master."

"You haven't been in New Orleans long, I think."

"Not long, no."

His voice was stiff, as if he didn't care to talk about himself. That was intriguing. "Why did you come? Do you perhaps have family here?"

"I am alone in the world."

"No family at all?" She could hardly conceive of that, of being the last of one's bloodline. Though her close family was small since the deaths of her mother and two of her siblings, she still had Denys, her father, Tante Marie Rose and any number of other aunts, uncles and cousins in the city. "What of your mother and father?"

"Dead in a fire, along with my sisters."

"How horrible. This was in Spain?"

"As you say, and many years ago." Pain edged his voice.

"You escaped in some manner. That was fortunate."

"Accidental, rather."

She tilted her head. "Meaning?"

"I was not there."

The words were short, dismissive, yet she thought she heard in them an echo of anguish. "We seem to have something in common then. My mother and my younger sister died while I was elsewhere. I've always thought…"

"Yes?"

She shook her head. "Nothing."

"Please. What was it?"

"That I might have done something to keep them alive if I had been there," she said with a small, help-less gesture. "Nursed them more faithfully, perhaps, held on more tightly."

He neither spoke nor moved for long seconds. Then he said quietly, "You felt it was unfair that you had escaped when they did not."

"As you say. My little sister cried out for me again and again, or so I was told. My aunt meant well, let-ting me know. She only wanted me to realize how much little Marie Therese loved me and longed for the comfort I could give her. Still I am haunted by the thought of it."

"I've wondered if my mother and my sisters cried out, if there was something I might have done to pro-tect them and my father if I had been—" He stopped abruptly.

"How did it happen that you were not in the house?"

It was so long before he answered that she thought he did not mean to speak. When he finally did, his voice was rough. "I had just reached an age, barely, when I had left my tutor and was ready for the uni-versity. I had a short time before study began, so was out doing all the things available to a young man of fortune and interesting prospects."

"The priest says it's vanity to blame ourselves for illnesses and accidents, that we are not powerful or important enough to be responsible for these things."

"It was no accident that they died."

She stared at him a long moment there in the semi-darkness. "You are saying that…that someone killed your family?"

"They meant to kill me, as well. They tried again when it was discovered that I had not died in the fire. Only the would-be assassins decided to collect twice, once for my supposed death and again for selling me to the captain of a ship bound for Morocco with a cargo for the dey of Algiers."

"So you really were a slave. Suzette had this from Olivier, but I could hardly credit it."

"He talks too much," Rio said in grim tones.

"Suzette has that effect." She smiled a little, though she wasn't sure he could see. "Tell me how it is that you survived. Also how you gained your freedom."

"Purest chance. The French captured Algiers less than two weeks after I was brought there. All the slaves were set free."

She thought from the grim note in his voice that he was being less than forthright. He was not the man to bend easily to the yoke of slavery, she thought, or to stand idly by while others fought for their freedom. The exact chain of events was probably something she would never discover, but he had clarified at least one thing for her.

"I knew you had not always been a teacher of swordplay," she said with satisfaction.

"No."

"You learned the trade in Spain perhaps?"

"A little. The most useful skills were picked up in France where I was taken after I was freed."

"That explains your command of the language. And did you ever return to Spain?"

"Once. Nothing remained for me there."

Did he mean literally nothing, or simply no familial ties? She would have liked to ask, but feared that would be probing too deep. "So you came here instead. Why is that?" She gave him a quick glance through her lashes. "I mean, you appear and establish yourself on the Passage de la Bourse but have no connections in the city that you've yet mentioned, no reason for choosing it over any other place."

"It's a city of immense wealth where the Code Duello is still observed in all its niceties. Men have need of the skills I can supply."

Another evasion, she thought. "So the money is all you're after?"

"I make my way as best I can. Unlike some."

"Meaning that I am rich, so have no understanding?" she asked with precision. "My father is wealthy, not I. His wealth was gained because he had the courage to mortgage everything he owned in order to buy land and plant sugarcane. He took the gamble when other men were unwilling to accept the risk."

He eased closer on the mattress, close enough to reach out and pick up the thick rope of her hair where it shone against the white of her gown. "You are an able champion for his cause, especially considering that he means to marry you off to a man more than twice your age."

She had been lulled by their conversation into thinking that his presence held no threat. It appeared she was wrong. He had merely sought to soothe her fears so she would not scream when he pounced. Not that she had any intention of such a display. She had invited his touch, after all. Avoiding it now would be foolish.

Yet it was difficult to sit still while he drew her hair into his hard swordsman's fingers. It seemed that every strand communicated his touch, tingling along her nerve endings to spread throughout her body. She tried to ignore the sensation, though her breathing quickened and her heart throbbed so hard against the wall of her chest that it visibly shook the fine lawn of her nightgown.

"What, no answer?" he asked, the words quietly mocking.

"I…didn't realize it was a question."

"You don't resent having your future decided by someone other than yourself?"

"My father feels it's his duty to provide the best possible husband for me, one of equal or superior social position who will honor and keep me with the least change in circumstances."

"Change in wealth, you mean."

She shook her head with a movement that pulled against his hold. "Not exactly."

"In caste, then, and class."

"You make it sound so cold!"

His attention was on his hands where he had begun to loosen the braid he held, spreading the entwined swaths of hair so they caught the dim light with golden gleams. "Isn't it? Not on your part, of course—the decision has been made for you. But do you have no opinion? Have you been so trained to obedience that you can bring yourself to care for whomever is presented to you, or does it make no difference who occupies your bed as long as he is suitable?"

"I…I must respect my father's decision. He knows much more about men than I do."

"Since you have met so few outside your family and been closeted alone with fewer still? As we are alone now?"

She couldn't quite meet his gaze, even in the semidarkness. "Yes."

"Still, suppose your father is no judge of character or easily led to believe things that are untrue?"

"How can you…?" she began.

"What of love?" he asked, cutting across her question.

"What of it?"

"Aren't you curious? Don't you wonder about it, since you are curious about so many other things?"

Naturally she wished to know about love, how it felt, what difference it might make between a man and woman, what effect it could have on a marriage. Admitting it seemed fruitless, however. At something of a loss, she stared at him a second, until she recalled what Suzette had said the night before. "Women respect their husbands and love their children."

"And men?"

"That is a different matter."

"Yes," he agreed, as he spread out the hair he had loosened so it covered her chest like a gilded breastplate. "But should it be that way? Should there not be love, as well as passion in the marriage bed?"

"I'm told I will grow to love the husband provided for me," she said a shade desperately.

"Now there's a gamble." He smiled with his focus still on her hair. "Are you sure you want to make it?"

Moistening her lips, she said, "You are suggesting that I refuse to marry the count?"

"It seems a sensible thing to do."

"And what then? Women who balk at the alliances made for them have been locked in their rooms, even beaten. At the very least they are made to feel that they have failed their families. If no other match appears, they must embrace the church or resign themselves to a life of dependence."

"No one said it would not take courage."

She sat watching his shadowed features, trying to penetrate the mask he presented, to see into the deep wells of his eyes to the man inside. It was not possible. The room was too dim. More than that, he was much too contained, too armored within himself.

"It's the count, isn't it?" she asked finally. "You care nothing for what happens to me as long as you disrupt his plans."

"You give yourself too little credit," he said, the deep timbre of his voice like a caress. "You are a beautiful woman who deserves more than to be bartered off to a man who may lust after you but expects to be paid for having you."

His plain speaking brought heat to her face. "Monsieur de Silva, this is too…"

"Rio," he said. "Considering how familiar we shall become, formal address between us seem overdone."

"It's the custom even between husband and wife." The awkwardness of the moment made the words sound absurdly stilted.

"Perhaps." He took her hand and lifted it to his lips while his gaze remained on her face. "But I am not your husband. Nor am I the kind of man who wants to hear the woman in his arms cry out some formal salute in the throes of passion."

"Monsieur de Silva—Rio, please."

"Please what? Please don't touch you? Don't take you? Maybe this isn't what you expected. You thought I would spare you when the time came for you to make good on your word?"

"No, but it seems that talking of it is so..." She stopped, uncertain of what she meant.

"You prefer not to speak of it, is that it? You want it quickly over and done? That's hardly flattering."

"I mean that it seems so callous, a mere business transaction."

"Passionless, yes—rather like marriage, after all."

"Yes. I...is that the point you intended to make?"

"Perhaps," he said, his voice dropping lower. "But if so, it's no longer of importance."

He reached to encircle her waist, drawing her across the mattress with unhurried ease until she lay in his arms. His mouth, warm and possessive, came down on hers. The smooth surfaces of his lips matched hers with exactitude, rousing in them such instant sensitivity that they felt on fire. She could feel his heart, a fast, steady beat beneath her fingers that were trapped between them, sense the faint prickle of the smooth-shaven skin near his lip line, taste the sweet flavor of him. The onslaught of sensations was so stunning that she slid her hand higher to clutch at his shirt collar, though she wasn't sure whether she meant to push him away or pull him closer.

There was more, much more. He traced the line of her lips with the moist abrasion of his tongue, an exploration so exquisite that she trembled with it. To draw swift breath through parted lips was natural, but allowed his entry. The invasion was so unexpected that she was still, lost in the spiraling emotions it produced, an odd assault of enticement mixed with disbelief, marveling coupled with an insidious languor.

The kiss was a trial. This she knew in some distant corner of her mind, as if he wanted to discover her every secret, to know her in ways no one else ever had or could again. He meant to take her in the most intimate meaning of the word, to make her a part of him even as he made himself a part of her.

He touched her breast. She felt the warmth of his hand as he cupped the soft yet resilient fullness, slowly encompassing the rounded shape until it fit his hand as if molded for it and no other. He brushed the nipple with his thumb and desire erupted inside her, spreading like a contagion. He caught his breath and gathered her closer, the hot thrust of his tongue driving deeper. She met it and was caught in the flare of unimagined need.

Abruptly, he released her mouth and lifted his head, though he did not remove his hand from her breast. His voice not quite even, he said, "Yes, well. I think we've established my point. Now let us see if we can discover just what, besides your brother's life, you expect to gain from this sweet sacrifice."

"What?" she asked, too dazed to be more co-herent.

"Something tells me you have your own purpose in agreeing to our bargain. Would you care to convince me that I'm wrong?"

She attempted to remove herself from his grasp, but he would not allow it. Forced to resort to words, she exclaimed, "You must be mad!"

"Oversensitive, perhaps. Still, it occurs to me that you are not quite outraged enough at this turn of events. In fact, you came close to inviting them."

"I only agreed to your proposition!"

"After you understood why it was made and that I had no expectation whatever of an acceptance. It occurred to me to expect an ambush here, only what would be the point? Unless you were more enamored of your noble suitor than seems possible."

"I would not do such a thing!"

"Apparently not, which leaves the mystery still unsolved. Why would you risk having me come to you? You don't seem the kind of female who is anxious to experiment or excited by risk. What does that leave, then?"

"Since you seem to have given it so much thought, perhaps you have a conclusion." She had meant to answer with pride and dignity, but the words came out sounding waspish instead.

"I can venture one. You are, I think, something less than the dutiful daughter you pretend, meekly resigned to the marriage arranged for you. I wonder if you aren't seeking a way out of this alliance. If perhaps, you saw an avenue of escape in my ill-considered suggestion and grasped at it with both hands."

She did not care for that description of herself but was in no position to refute it. Voice stiff, she said, "I fail to see how one thing is supposed to affect the other."

"Allow me to make it clearer. What would be the effect, do you think, if you claimed to have been seduced by a man whom your chosen groom is unwilling to face with sword in hand?"

Celina felt the rise of sick dismay. He was not supposed to be so penetrating. "How very calculating you would make me. But what you fail to address is that my father or Denys would be more likely to demand satisfaction."

"True." He paused. "That must mean that you intend to sacrifice yourself."

"Oh, please."

"That's it, isn't it? You will refuse to name your seducer so there will be no one to challenge. It won't matter if your groom declines to defend your damaged honor. It will be enough to claim the violation and provide the required evidence."

She said nothing for long seconds, only staring at his shadowed face above her. "If I entertained such a plan," she asked finally, "would it be so terrible?"

"Not of itself," he answered in dry tones. "Still, I prefer to be consulted before being embroiled in a situation with such potentially damaging consequences."

"And if your motives for being here are not readily obvious, I'm sure you will explain them just as exactly."

A short laugh left him. "As bright as you are beautiful. Remind me to be more careful with my accusations. The lamentable truth is that I'm not sure why I came. I only know that it was impossible to stay away."

"We have scarcely been acquainted long enough for you to say such a thing," she said in tart denial.

"Sometimes it takes only a moment."

That was mere flirtation she was sure and therefore easy to brush aside. She allowed a moment to pass, one in which her thoughts moved rapidly toward a conclusion.

"Well, *mademoiselle*, what is your answer?"

She glanced at him, then away again. "Are there circumstances, ever, where it's permissible to do a dishonorable thing for the sake of a greater good?"

"Now you are a philosopher?" The question was tentative, as if he required time to think.

"I thought you might be familiar with the temptation. I mean, it would so easy for you to use your skill to right the wrongs you see around you or remove anyone who stands in your way. What prevents you?"

"Many things," he answered. "Foremost among them is self-preservation. I also have a strong disinclination to be hanged for murder in the prison yard on some fine Friday morning."

She lifted a brow. "I'm not sure I believe that."

He made no answer but sat with his head tipped in a listening pose. After a second, he released her and rose from the bed with an effortless flexing of muscles. "Too bad, but we must continue this fascinating discussion another time. Someone just entered the house at the porte cochere and is coming up the stairs."

"You're leaving?" Amazement sounded in her voice in spite of all she could do.

"You would rather I stayed?"

"I didn't say that!"

He laughed and reached for her hand, carrying it to his lips. She felt their warm, tingling brush against her knuckles before he released her. "I can always pretend."

She had no answer for that, even if there had been time for one. Footsteps were heard on the stairs, followed by a low murmur of voices as Mortimer let someone into the house. Mere seconds later, a knock fell on her door.

5

"Lina? Are you still awake?"

It was Denys. She swung her head toward Rio. He was on the far side of the room, retreating toward the French door so silently that she had not heard him move. With his coiled whip and hat in his hand, he drifted through the opening like the Silver Shadow he was called. Then he was gone, closing the door and shutter behind him with a faint double click.

"You're home early, *cher*," Celina called out to her brother. "Is your arm paining you?"

The door opened, letting the light from the bed candle her brother held in his good left hand spill into the room. "Not enough to speak of. I didn't wake you, did I?" he added as he glanced around the dark room. "Old Mortimer said he thought he heard your voice not long ago."

"I must have been saying my prayers," she answered with a silent plea for forgiveness for the lie. "Not that it matters since I'm not really sleepy."

"Good." Leaving the door open behind him, he stepped into the room and set his candle in its silver holder on her bedside table. Then he moved to lean one shoulder against the tall rosewood post of her bed.

It wasn't unusual for Denys to visit with her for a short time after he arrived home in the evening. She had become his confidante since their older brother was killed. He liked to tell her where he'd been, who he'd seen and what he'd heard around town as a way of unwinding enough to sleep. He was a gifted mimic and had a droll sense of humor, so usually left her laughing at some ridiculous thing he had seen or heard. Tonight, however, his mood seemed more somber.

Before she could launch into questions about his evening, he leaned to scoop something from the foot of the bed. "What's this? Your headpiece for the evening?"

He was holding the stem of a rosebud tied with trailing ribbons. Flushed with pink that deepened to the rosy blush of sunset in the center, the rose was perfectly shaped and included three glossy leaves on its stem. Still fresh in spite of the late hour, it was certainly nothing that she had worn that evening. In fact, it had not been on her mattress or anywhere else in her room before the arrival of Rio de Silva.

He had left her a freshly plucked token, but of what? A rose in the popular language of the flowers meant love. That was clearly ridiculous, of course, unless it referred to mere physical union.

"A token from an admirer this evening," she said, trying for a careless shrug even as she thought that she would have much to remember at her next confession. Her fingers trembled a little as she held out her hand for the stem.

Her brother passed it over without comment. That was disturbing as well, since he liked to tease and she had half expected that he would make her beg for the prize.

"Is something wrong?" she asked, searching his face as she sank back on her pillow and lifted the rose to inhale its fragrance. "Mortimer said Hippolyte and Armand came by earlier. I thought perhaps you had gone out with them for a while."

"We strolled over to Canal Street for dinner then back to a gaming house on Chartres. I wish I had remained at home, or else gone to Cousin Plauchet's soiree with you and Tante Marie Rose."

"To such a dull family party?" she inquired with lifted brows. "You alarm me! Are you sure you aren't getting a fever from your wound?"

"No, I mean it," he insisted. "Everything is different since the duel, and with this." He waved the black silk sling that confined his right arm.

"What do you mean?"

"It's the most stupid thing. I hardly know how to tell it."

"Denys," she said in a warning tone.

His smile was brief before he looked down again, pretending to examine the bandaging. "All that was talked about tonight was the meeting with Monsieur de Silva. Every man we met seemed to know of it."

"That cannot have been a surprise."

"No, but not one of them seemed to think it was anything to my credit that I survived. Speculation is that de Silva has lost his fighting spirit. If it were otherwise, I'd not have escaped so lightly."

"Oh, Din-Din." The childhood name sprang automatically to her lips as she envisioned the slights he must have endured as this conclusion was brought home to him.

"I don't mind for my sake, you know. I thought at the time that he must have felt sorry for me."

"How can you say such a thing? I'm sure you fought as well as you were able." She was also sure that she was the cause, at least indirectly, for Denys's low feelings just now. It did not make her think better of herself.

"That's just it, Lina. Men of experience with a blade have only to watch a match for a few minutes to judge the play and know at once who the better swordsman may be."

"Then why would they doubt Monsieur de Silva's competence?"

"You don't understand. What they doubt is his will to dominate an opponent on the field, or perhaps to cause permanent injury."

"So you came off with a minor wound not because of your brilliant swordplay but due to his dullness?"

He gave a short laugh. "Something like that. It makes me feel sick after he was so lenient toward me."

"It isn't something you can help."

"No, but it's unfair that he must suffer for it."

"Suffer?" She sat us straighter.

"It's like the mastiffs at a bullbaiting. The instant they get the scent of blood, they start to close in for the kill."

The image was more than a little disturbing. "What are you saying?" she asked sharply. "Did someone force a challenge on Monsieur de Silva? Is that it?"

"Four." Denys held up his good hand, curling his fingers as he counted them off. "One this morning, two this afternoon and one earlier this evening. Four fools determined to have the glory of defeating him."

"You can't mean it!"

"It's true, I assure you. Any number of people made certain that I had the news."

"Whatever possessed him to accept so many?"

"There was no way he could avoid them and retain his repute as a *maître d'armes*. He will meet all four men at dawn tomorrow."

Four duels. Four meetings on the field of honor that Rio must face because he had shown mercy toward Denys as she had asked.

Four duels, and he had said not a word to her of them.

When dawn rose over the city and Allard's oaks, Rio would meet these ambitious opponents one after the other. One or two might be foolish amateurs but the others could be men of expertise, even other fencing masters. And whatever happened, for good or ill, would be her fault.

After her brother had gone, Celina got out of bed and removed the ribbon from the rosebud Rio had left behind before clipping the stem and putting it in water. Staring down at it, she touched the petals with a gentle fingertip. How very strange that he had brought a flower, leaving it behind him without a word.

Or perhaps not, who could tell? He was a stranger, this man she had given the right to enter and leave her bedchamber at will.

That she might be the cause of his injury or death

was insupportable. The challengers were accountable for their own actions, yet it was her deed that
had led them to meet the Silver Shadow. Rio had
tried to tell her how it would be. In her concern for
Denys, she had refused to listen.

Disturbed beyond imagining, she paced the floor
with the fullness of her lawn nightgown swirling
around her ankles and her loose hair swinging
around her like a shining cloak. She would stop the
round of duels if she could. Yet try as she might, she
could conceive of no way to intervene. It was a thing
of male pride, male honor.

The Silver Shadow must and would prevail. She
refused to consider any other outcome.

What then?

Would he come to her again?

Denys's return had prevented the consummation
of her agreement with the sword master. Her brother
would not always be so conveniently at hand, however. Celina was almost sorry that the encounter between her and Rio de Silva had been interrupted.
The intimacy to which she had agreed would be over
and done by now, a thing of the past. Dread would
no longer be necessary, nor would she have to face
Rio de Silva's anger over the dawn exercise he was
forced to undertake because of her.

There had been little sign of that fury while he
was with her. He had not indicated by word or deed
what the morning held for him. That was true
sangfroid, cold blood indeed, or else an extreme form
of male courtesy. Of the two possibilities, she could
hardly decide which disturbed her more.

He had come to her, just as he said he would. The

risk he had run by climbing to her bedchamber was incalculable. Her father or brother would have had every right to annihilate him on the spot. Had the night watch discovered him, the result might have been prison. If a neighbor had caught sight of him entering, then she would have been ruined. She shuddered to think of him coming to her again but did not doubt that he was capable of it.

Returning to her bed, she lay staring at the shuttered French door that opened onto the balcony. That Rio might step through it again at any moment, that he could do so when he chose, gave her an odd sensation in the pit of her stomach. It wasn't fear exactly, though that was a part of it.

The Silver Shadow was so very male, with an aura of danger that both attracted and repelled her. He made her long for things she had thought never to know, imagine things best ignored. His touch had sent a frisson along her nerve endings, and his kiss had been a revelation. She had expected to pay the debt she owed him with dutiful compliance and her eyes closed tightly. She had never dreamed there might be excitement in it.

She could not, did not, sleep.

Dawn glimmered behind the shutters at last. The rain had slowed and finally stopped. Rio would be arriving at the dueling ground about now, and the other men, as well. All would be rigidly correct as they paced off the field and took out the swords. The grass would be wet, so the danger was increased tenfold.

Yesterday at this time she had been consumed with fear for Denys as he faced Rio. Today it was otherwise.

Abruptly Celina flung back the covers and slid out of bed. Moving to the prie-dieu that sat at the foot, she knelt on the narrow bench covered with burgundy velvet, took the pearl rosary that lay in the tray above the wrist rest and then bowed her head. Rio might have no need of her prayers, but it helped her feelings to make them.

The morning proceeded much as normal. The rain had brought a weather change, and she pulled on a burgundy velvet robe *à la française* against the increased coolness before joining her aunt in the breakfast room. They sat down alone to the repast of warm brioche and café au lait. Her father was still abed, and Denys had left the house early, undoubtedly to be a spectator at the duel.

Tante Marie Rose was oblivious to the events taking place around her. The season, now at its height, occupied her thoughts, therefore her conversation.

"The Rochebriants have finally arrived, did you notice?" she asked while applying peach preserves to her brioche with a liberal hand. "Their windows and doors were open yesterday, and smoke was rising from the kitchen chimney. I am surprised they came at all since her father-in-law expired only a few days before Christmas. I suppose she has come to replenish her wardrobe. We must leave cards immediately, though they are sure to be very quiet. I am told her sister, Madame Decou, will be late this year as well, perhaps even after Mardi Gras. Her second-to-eldest son broke his leg while hunting snipe and cannot travel just yet. Such a pity, for he is a dear boy. Oh, and I saw Hélène Payne yesterday as she came down the street in a pony cart. What a figure of fun!

Why her husband doesn't provide her with a decent carriage is a great mystery, for he could easily afford it. Her mother-in-law was with her, of course. Such a disagreeable woman, always looking as if she has bitten into a green persimmon."

"And Madeleine?"

"The oldest daughter? No, though I saw her the other day, sitting on the balcony. You were at convent school with her, were you not?"

"For a year only, since she was younger."

"Now she will be coming out. What would you think of her as a wife for Denys?"

"More than acceptable," Celina replied. "Though I rather thought that Madame Payne was a fairly close family connection."

"No, no. Her grandfather was the youngest of thirteen, a brother to your great-grandfather rather than your grandfather. That would make Madeleine, let me see, a fourth cousin to Denys? Except that the grandmother was a second cousin, wasn't she? Isn't that right? *Mais non!* The grandfather was the child of a second wife, while your great-grandfather was the child of the first who was the cousin, so they are barely related at all."

Celina did not even try to follow that web of relationships. Families were large and intermarriage common among the French Creoles of New Orleans. Once, the cause had been isolation as a colony of first France and then Spain, but now was in reaction to the invasion of the Americans with their sharp business and political dealings and hurried manners—or lack of manners at all. Only older women with sharp memories could unravel these knotted skeins of kin-

ship. Such exercises were a chief occupation of the
morning calls of the *saison de visites*, the social season
that ran from the first of November, when the summer fever season was presumed to be over, until the
first of May, when heat and mosquitoes made evening entertainments unbearable.

"My approval hardly matters in any case," she
said in dry tones. "Denys may wish to choose a bride
for himself."

"So he may." Tante Marie Rose reached for another slice of brioche. "Still, a little guidance in these
matters can do no harm."

Was that how her aunt looked on her proposed betrothal to the count, a matter of benign guidance? Or
was her relative being willfully optimistic about her
future happiness?

"Your own marriage was arranged, I think," Celina said with a glance at her aunt from under her
lashes. "Did you not mind?"

"That is past history, *chère,* long past." Her aunt
popped the piece of brioche into her mouth and
reached for her coffee cup.

"Yes, but what did you think of it? Did you come
to love Uncle Alphonse? Were you compatible? Had
you no regrets?"

Tante Rose Marie swallowed, drank from her cup,
then set it back carefully in its saucer. "We
were...suited. It was not unbearable."

"But not particularly happy, either, I think."

"There was his gambling that made us paupers."

"Is that all?"

"Surely it is enough! I thought many and many a
time that we would have to go to debtor's prison. It

was still possible in those days, though it hardly happens now and the lawmakers threaten to abolish it. Then he died and your mother was sweet and generous enough to take me in, or I don't know what I would have done."

"We have been most fortunate to have you with us. Still, I am curious. Did Uncle Alphonse have a mistress at the time of your marriage, and did he keep her? If he did so, did you mind?"

"Truly, Celina, you must not ask me these things!"

"Who else am I to ask when my mother is gone?" she replied with conscious reason. "You must tell me what I am to expect."

A troubled frown knit Tante Marie Rose's soft white brow, which seldom reflected anything other than pleasant thoughts. Pushing her plate of brioche aside, she used her napkin with care. "I do see what you are saying, though I'm sure your dear papa would not like it."

"This is my life, my future. Why should I not go into it armed with the truth?"

"You have much right in that." Her aunt sighed and put down the napkin. Folding her small plump hands, she leaned closer and lowered her voice. "I must have your promise that you will never repeat what I say, never mention it to anyone."

"You have it, I swear." As she said those words, Celina was seized with a sudden need to call them back. What if the things her aunt said were too awful to hear?

"Marriage is not an easy thing for a woman. She must give up her freedom, her will, her body to become one with her husband. She trades the tyranny of a father for that of a strange man who may have little care for her comfort or well-being. Children are said to be a woman's solace and reward, yet to produce a baby every year or two is a painful and wearisome thing."

Celina had observed these things for herself so could find little new in them. "Still we are told that we will come to love the man chosen for us."

"Some find true companionship, true meeting of the minds. Others go through the motions while keeping their thoughts and feelings buried deep inside. Women find consolation in their homes and society, men in the company of their male friends and all the amusements open to them. And here is where the real secret resides, my dear Celina. If a man philanders, his wife will often turn a blind eye, not because she is ignorant but because it suits her purpose. She is content for her husband to have other women, since it frees her of an onerous duty that could lead to unwanted childbirth."

Celina drew back a little in her chair. "But surely if a husband had any consideration…"

"So few do, my love. They are told that it is right and natural for women to have children, that God has ordained that they bring them into the world in pain and sorrow, and it is a husband's privilege and pleasure to get them on us. Why should a man deprive himself or exercise unusual control when nothing compels it?"

"Oh, Tante Marie Rose."

"I've shocked you, I can see it. Oh, I knew I should have kept quiet!"

"No, please, I wish to understand how it is between a man and woman. I need to understand. If there is pleasure for a man in the marriage bed, is it not the same for a woman?"

Her aunt flushed but met Celina's eyes with determination. "Sometimes, though often of a mild sort and short in duration. There are men who have the skill and consideration to make it more, but I fear most lack the will or self-control. Well, or else they are so flustered and embarrassed by the…the high passion they feel that they treat it as an itch to be scratched as quickly as possible."

"Tante Marie Rose!" Celina's amazement was for hearing such things on her staid aunt's lips rather than for the idea itself.

"Oh dear, oh dear. I do apologize, but you would have the truth."

"Yes, and I am grateful for it," she said, reaching out to touch her aunt's hands, which were clasped so tightly in front of her that the knuckles were white. "Still, I am puzzled that knowing these things, you can still recommend marriage to the count."

"It is a woman's lot to marry, love. But if you must suffer the indignities, then you may as well do it in comfort with a man of wealth and position."

Tante Marie Rose spoke from her own disappointment and experience of poverty, Celina thought. All alliances were not quite so dismal; of this she was fairly certain. Several of the young women with whom she had attended convent school were married with a baby or two, and seemed happy enough with the bridegrooms provided for them. The husbands were, in the main, near their age and of their close circle, the sons of friends and acquaintances of their parents. Often, the two young people had played together as children, attended church together or noticed each other while walking on the levee in the evening or attending the theater. A distant cousin from France or some upriver plantation had been chosen for one or two, but even then the couples had enough in common to cement the union between them.

"If I must wed, I would prefer someone not quite so aged," she said judiciously. "Yes, and a little more attractive."

"What he looks like will make little difference in the dark, *chère,* and an older husband may make you a widow sooner rather than later. Then there is the count's acquisition of a house on the rue des Rampart. You must not mind if he fails to put aside the little quadroon *placée* that he keeps there, for you can see that the arrangement has its advantages."

Mortimer entered just then, bearing a card on a silver tray. It was the first of the morning, but had to be added to the dozens piled on the marble-topped console in the salon, just inside the main entrance. The stack of white pasteboards imposed a duty to make return calls, and Tante Marie Rose turned with every sign of relief to planning the best order for them.

A short time later, they were dressed and ready for the outing of three morning calls followed by a stop at the book dealer. Celina would have preferred to remain behind, but it was impossible. The visits were primarily for her sake, a means of introducing her to the older women who kept the fabric of society in good repair while also preparing her to take her place among them after she was safely wed. She cared not at all what she wore, but donned what

Suzette had laid out. Today it was a silk redingote of the ash-gray known as *couleur cendre,* one with lapels like a gentleman's waistcoat that opened over a pleated cambric *chemisette,* sleeves full at the shoulders and tight to the wrists, and *rouleaux* decoration down the open front edges of the skirt. Over her center-parted hair she placed a bonnet of rice straw that was sunburst-lined with gray silk and enhanced by ribbon and silk pansies in lavender and yellow. Pulling yellow kid gloves onto her hands, she followed her aunt down the stairs of the town house and into the carriage.

Three excruciating hours later, after endless glasses of orange flower water concoctions served with candied violets, petits fours, and cakes flavored with molasses and orange peel, they arrived back home again. Celina, her nerves stretched to the breaking point by inane chatter and the recitation of the ailments meant to be interesting in the current Gothic fashion that glorified ill health, snatched off her bonnet and flung it onto the bureau along with her beaded card case. She was just reaching for the bell pull when the door opened to admit Suzette.

"Tell me at once," she said, swinging to face the maid. "Is there news?"

An odd smile came and went on Suzette's face. "There is, if you are able to read the signs."

"Meaning?"

"This was delivered for you, along with instructions to present it only when you are alone."

The maid removed her right hand from among the fullness of her skirts, bringing out a spiral of white paper tied with twine.

Celina took the paper in her hands and lightly unrolled it. A handful of looped ribbon was revealed, to which was attached a rosebud that was a twin to the one Rio had brought her the night before. She closed her eyes, whispering, "Thank God."

"Mam'zelle?"

At the questioning sound of Suzette's voice, Celina looked up. "I'm relieved, as who would not be? To have the death of the sword master or that of any man on my conscience would have been distressful." She paused. "Were injuries mentioned?"

"Not for Monsieur de Silva. For the others, the first man received a cut similar to that of Monsieur Denys, the second was pierced through the shoulder, the third had a slash to the face, though it missed anything vital and the fourth suffered a punctured lung. The doctor is in attendance on the fourth man, but he is expected to recover, the saints willing. The entire series of affairs lasted less than an hour."

Celina, carefully untangling the ribbon from the rosebud, did not look up. "If only that's the end of them."

"Olivier seems to have little hope of it."

"It has to stop. It must!"

"There is no need for agitation," Suzette said with the lift of one shoulder. "Olivier assures me that the Silver Shadow can take care of himself. It is his profession, after all."

"His profession is teaching men to defend themselves with sword in hand, not facing death every morning."

"Take care, Mam'zelle. You almost sound as if you have a personal interest."

"My interest is the same as for any man in the same position," Celina answered with asperity. "I caused these meetings, after all."

"That may trouble you, but Monsieur de Silva and his friends disport themselves as usual. Olivier paused here on his way to purchase tickets for the masked ball to be held tomorrow evening at the Marine Ballroom."

"Sword masters put in an appearance at such subscription balls to attract clients, or so I've heard. I expect Monsieur de Silva wishes to prove that he doesn't shrink from public entertainment that might spawn further meetings."

"My point exactly," Suzette murmured.

If Rio showed himself, Celina saw, then he might invite more passages at arms. The thought did nothing to allay her worry. Still, there was little she could do about it.

Or was there? A possible solution came to her in midafternoon. She could not manage it without Denys's cooperation, however, and he was still not home. Patience was not her greatest virtue, and the little she had was exhausted by the time she was finally able to speak to him just before dinner.

"No." Her brother's refusal was instant, coming even before he heard her out completely. "No, *chère*, no indeed."

"But why? It's such a small favor."

"You would not care for it and Papa would be furious."

"He need not learn of it," she said, stepping close to finger the silver bull's head fob that dangled at the end of his watch chain. "How should he, when he takes so little interest these days in what we do? Soon I'll be married and must sail away to Spain where everything is incredibly dull and formal. Why should I not have this small adventure?"

"What of Tante Marie Rose? You know she will not condone it."

"I only dared mentioned it because this is her card night, and she will be with her friends at the Thierry town house. We are certain to be back before she returns." Just as her aunt had her set day to sew for the orphans, this evening was her night for cards with her old friends. Tante Marie Rose clung to her habits in the main, though was ready enough to change them if needed as a chaperone.

"This ball is to be a masked affair, a *bal de guisé*. It could become more exciting than you might like."

She drew back a little. "Surely it won't actually be rowdy?"

"Perhaps not, but neither will it be as sedate as the private affairs you normally attend, or even the balls held at the St. Louis Hotel. Americans from uptown will be there, Lina, along with whoever can manage to persuade the sponsors to sell them a ticket. Many may be quite respectable, but hardly the crème de la crème. Others may be downright rogues."

"It sounds fascinating, much more amusing than attending the same balls where the same people appear night after night. Please, Denys. I'm so fatigued with always being proper and doing what is expected. If all Spanish nobility are as stuffy as the count, I may never have such a chance again."

"Poor Lina," he said, brushing a forefinger under

her chin as he smiled down at her. "Do you dislike so much the idea of becoming a countess?"

"How can you even ask?"

His eyes darkened a fraction. "Is that all, *chère?* I mean, has the count given you cause to take him in dislike, or perhaps something more?"

"More?"

"I don't know. Mistrust, perhaps?"

"Do you mistrust him?" She watched her brother, trying to guess at what was in his mind. It was difficult, since he would not meet her gaze.

"I can't forget how he stood aside and allowed me to face de Silva when it was plain the quarrel belonged to him. Still, Papa must know what he is about with this betrothal."

"I wish I could think so." She hesitated and then went on in a rush. "The influence of the count has been great in these weeks since the season began."

"I had noticed. The gaming is particularly troublesome." Her brother's boyish face had turned grim.

"Then there is this second household."

"I wasn't sure you knew of that."

"One hears these things."

"He appears to be quite infatuated."

The discomfort in Denys's face suggested he thought it indelicate to mention their father's paramour. Celina had no such reserve since it seemed vitally connected with her future. It was not as if she were discussing the amorous activities of her future husband. Those were not yet her concern, something for which she was devoutly thankful.

"Is she very beautiful?" Celina asked.

"Indeed, one of loveliest quadroons of the season. Her personality is amiable, even sweet."

"You've met her?"

"Briefly," Denys said with a twist of his lips.

He must have seen her at one of the quadroon balls where such young women in search of protectors were presented. It was possible he had desired her. It would have been much more normal and appropriate for a father to guide his son in such an arrangement rather than taking a *placée* for himself. The liaisons, not unlike the maintenance of the little lights o' love known as *Les Lorettes*, kept by Parisians in apartments near Notre-Dame de Lorette, provided an outlet for young male energy and deflected any tampering with young ladies of their circle. For the quadroons, the unions represented security in the form of settlements that included title to a house, an allowance and funds to educate any children. Such arrangements usually ended when the young man married, though not always. However, to seek such a mistress in later years was considered undignified.

"I'm glad Papa is happy," she said. "But it is strange. His family had seemed everything to him since the fever took Maman."

"The time of mourning ended, and I think…"

"What?"

"That he sees himself growing older, fears the pains he's been having around his heart, and maybe hears the footsteps of death behind him so he runs from it. Taking a mistress allows him to pretend that he's young again."

"Poor Papa." They had each been damaged by the deaths in the family, even Denys who was trying so desperately to be the older son and family protector now, as witness his challenge of Monsieur de Silva.

"Yes. It will pass, I think. In the meantime, little can be done about it."

"I suppose." She gave her brother a quick look from under her lashes. "But as I was saying, his pre-occupation makes it unlikely that he will notice what we may do."

Denys shook his head. "Lina, Lina, you have always been able to talk me into whatever you wanted, haven't you?"

She gave him a small smile. "To my sorrow."

He gave her a hug. "We are alive and well because of it. There can be no fault in that."

"If I had not insisted that Papa take the waters at White Sulphur Springs…"

"Maman was worried about his heart, as well. We all were. And you know how she hated traveling."

Celina's smile was crooked. "The journey might as well have been to the moon as far she was concerned."

"And she knew Papa would be lonely without some of his family with him. She had the company of both Tante Marie Rose and little Marie Therese, and preferred seclusion following Theo's death. I'm sure she was glad we were not here to be taken by the fever."

Celina caught her brother's hand and held it against her face, unable to speak for long moments as memory of that terrible summer came back in a flood. No fever had been reported in the city before they boarded the steamboat that would take them to Kentucky where they would hire a carriage for the remainder of the way. A week after their departure, a ship arrived from Havana. Another week, and both yellow fever and cholera raged in the city. Hundreds of people became ill in the following month, their mother and younger sister among them. Tante Marie Rose had nursed them unceasingly since she had survived the Yellow Jack, as she called the fever, when a child and could not contract it again. It had not been enough to save them.

Celina's younger sister had been eight, a sunny sprite with fine, silky curls who idolized her older sister. Celina had treated her like a doll, brushing her hair, playing with her, enjoying her chatter. Marie Therese had cried for her constantly as she lay ill, begging that Celina come home, or so Tante Marie Rose had told her. Somehow it seemed that if she, Denys and her father had not left the city, if she had not conceived the idea of going away, then her mother and her sister might still be alive. She had changed all their lives without meaning to, and none of them would ever be the same.

"Perhaps you're right," she said with a sigh. "It might be better not to tempt fate by attending this ball."

"No," Denys said abruptly. "If you really want this, we will go."

"Truly?" She searched his face with mingled hope and fear rising in her chest.

"I can't bear to think of you languishing in some place far away, dreaming of lost opportunities."

"I'll never ask anything of you ever again, I swear it."

"Of course you won't! Not ever!" He gave her another quick squeeze as he laughed down at her.

"Oh, Denys."

"I'm only teasing, *ma chou*," he said, using the cabbage-head endearment that had been a favorite between them since childhood. "Make your disguise. We go to the masquerade."

6

Rio stood with Caid near the back wall of the Marine Ballroom. The two of them had mingled with the crowd, trading bows and pleasantries, before the dancing began. Now they watched from a safe distance while waiting for a decent interval to elapse before making their departures.

"This is my least favorite part of our calling," Caid said. "I'd like to wring the neck of the idiot who started the practice of strutting around like a damn peacock to attract clientele."

Rio gave him a jaundiced glance. "You have better things to do?"

"Anything would be better. Don't tell me you aren't bored to distraction, because I won't believe it. You're half-asleep on your feet."

"It's crossed my mind that hiring a man to bang a drum and shout my accomplishments through the streets might be just as effective."

"Show me a man who hasn't heard of your exploit this morning, and I'll show you a dedicated recluse or a blockhead."

"Notoriety wasn't what I had in mind," Rio answered in grim tones.

That he and Caid were of a mind about affairs such as this was a given. Acquainted only a few weeks, they had found a common bond in the fact that they were both recently arrived in New Orleans, both new to the fencing salons of the Passage de la Bourse. Caid was an uncomplicated man, with no hint of professional jealousy about him. Upright and honorable in his dealings, he scorned the flamboyant tricks other sword masters used to gain clients as well as the deceits with which they stole them. He had his secrets, Rio was sure, as did they all, but kept them decently to himself. An agreeable companion, he was often an amusing one, too.

"Notoriety is yours whether you want it or not," he returned now with scant sympathy. "Only think— with any luck at all, you may come across a good half-dozen more dueling partners before morning. That's if any man here is foolish enough to ignore the warning you've provided thus far."

"I'd as soon not repeat this morning's performance, thank you. Lying in bed past dawn tomorrow has definite appeal."

"I can see that you're worn to a frazzle by all your efforts."

Rio barely acknowledged the cheerful scorn in Caid's rejoinder. His attention was on the ballroom doorway. A man and woman had just entered. Both were masked, though they had avoided the kind of elaborate costumes worn by many of the guests. The man was slender and held his arm in a black silk sling, proof enough of his identity as Denys Vallier if any were needed. It was not. Rio would have known him instantly by the woman at his side.

Celina Vallier, gowned in straw-colored silk with a draped corsage *à la grecque* and wearing a gold velvet mask across the upper portion of her face, had a regal grace that set her apart from every other female in the room. Her hair was arranged in a crown of curls that caught soft gleams from the candles in the massive chandelier overhead. The sheen of her skin and fascinating curves of her mouth were too-familiar torments. Still it was not these things that brought recognition but rather the sudden, tingling alertness he felt inside, like a hunter sighting his prey.

At that instant, she turned her head and caught his gaze. Her eyes were darkly mysterious behind her mask. For the space of a heartbeat, it seemed a message hovered there for him alone, a silent command that he come to her now, at once. She reached up with one gloved hand to touch the pair of roses that nestled in her hair, their ribbons twining with the curls that cascaded down one side of her neck.

His roses. She had worn them.

She did not look away or move from where she stood. She did nothing at all, yet abruptly his heart surged against the wall of his chest and the back of his neck felt fever-hot. A wild urge beat up inside him to march across the room and take her away to some private place where he could carefully demolish her exquisite perfection and see to it that she grew as hot and fervid with longing as he felt at that moment.

He took a quick step in her direction before the idiocy of what he was doing froze him in place. He wanted her. God help him, yes, he wanted her. Still, it was more than that. In some strange way he could not quite fathom, she had come to represent all that he had lost. She was innocence and hope, freedom and joy, favor and respectability and all the other half-forgotten rights and privileges he had once enjoyed. And he, jaded, bloodstained and irretrievably déclassé as he was, could never have her, just as he could never reclaim his vanished heritage.

Oh, he could take her; Rio knew that now. He could enter her virgin bedchamber, possess her in sweet consummation and blind disregard for the consequences. She was his by right and her sworn oath, and she would not gainsay him if he chose this very evening to strip her naked and join his body to hers. He could have her, yes, but only once and without honor. And that meant that he could never have her at all.

"On second thought, it might be better if no one crosses you tonight," Caid said, lifting a brow as he watched his face. "The poor devil could find himself spitted and roasted for your breakfast."

"It's a possibility." Rio's reply had a savage edge as he watched a gallant dressed as Cardinal Richelieu approach Celina Vallier and make his bow.

Caid followed his gaze, then pursed his lips in a silent whistle. "Isn't that…?"

"Yes."

"Why is she here?"

"I have no idea."

"But you would like to know, I think. Shall I find out for you?"

"Not," Rio said distinctly, "if you value our acquaintance."

A startled look crossed Caid's face. "Now this is interesting. I thought you were only concerned with the fiancé."

"Matters have changed."

"I can see that. What I would like to know is how, also why?"

"That's something between me and the lady."

"I wonder if the count is aware," Caid said in narrow-eyed consideration.

"He isn't, and won't be if I can help it."

"Stop staring, then, or everyone in New Orleans will know it."

It was good advice. Rio was just not certain he could heed it.

Protected mademoiselles such as Celina Vallier seldom appeared at these things. That she was here on the arm of her brother meant something. The problem was discovering what that might be while still keeping his distance. The last thing he wanted was to compromise her at this point, accomplishing in a public forum the very thing he could not do in private.

The evening advanced. Rio and Caid were joined by Titi Rosière and Bastile Croquère. A round of the gaming houses was suggested. Caid agreed, but Rio declined, though he could give no good reason for remaining. The best he could explain it to himself was a strong sensation of being unable to leave a guard post.

The crowd grew thicker. Rio had no objection; the greater the throng, the better able he was to blend in with it. To aid in that regard, he slipped on a half mask taken from his tailcoat pocket. He had little expectation of passing unnoticed behind the concealment, but it allowed others the option of failing to recognize him if they so desired.

The air reeked of candle smoke, perfume and the camphor used to prevent the depredations of moths and insects that destroyed silk and wool overnight in the near tropical climate. The wine and punch served in an adjoining room were barely passable. Still the polkas, waltzes and quadrilles were excellently played by an orchestra made up of *gens de couleur libre*, or free men of color as those not enslaved were known. Dancing was sprightly but still decorous. The company included several notables, among them the mayor and several of the more prominent businessmen from the big houses above Canal Street, in the American section known as Faubourg Ste. Marie.

There were plenty who were not of this caliber, however, and their numbers increased as the evening deepened. They formed noisy enclaves with others of their kind, including one or two women whose behavior behind their masks left their virtue open to question. Their movements in the dance were a little too wide, a little too showy. They drank too much, talked and laughed too loudly. Several altercations created by them were settled only by intervention of the gentlemen who served as hosts for the occasion.

The company began to thin as the more respectable element took their leave. Rio expected that Vallier would lead his sister away soon after. It didn't happen, though he saw the two of them whispering heatedly once or twice as if in argument. He thought of approaching to suggest it but restrained himself. Denys Vallier might be gratified at receiving an invitation to face him on a fencing strip, but that did not mean he would appreciate interference in the escort of his sister.

Circling the room, stopping now and then to talk to a client or another *maître d'armes*, Rio managed to keep Celina in view. As his vigil stretched into its third hour, he realized that she was being selective in her dancing partners. She turned away most invitations with a smile, and avoided others by strolling around the perimeter of the floor on her brother's good arm. When she did award a dance, it was to Denys or young men who were apparently his friends. He saluted that proof of discretion even as he wished her gone from the ballroom.

She enjoyed being on the floor, that much was plain. Moving with smooth grace, she seemed to float in precise rhythm to the music. Her body yielded bonelessly to the movements of her partner, and her eyes glinted with pleasure behind her mask. Observing from where he leaned on a fluted pillar, Rio had a brief but gut-wrenching vision of what it might be like to have her move in just that way against him, meeting and matching the pace he set, following his lead while held close in his arms. He was forced to take a cooling stroll on the nearest balcony long before the music ended.

It was a little after eleven when he noticed the count. That portly gentleman was handing his great-coat, hat and cane to an attendant. He made a party with two gentlemen Rio could not identify behind their masks. With them as well, was Aristide Broyard, a *maître d'armes* of unsavory reputation who had his atelier across the Passage from Rio's.

Broyard was one of the flashier sword masters, a

man who lost few opportunities to force a challenge and was quick to speak of his kills on the dueling field. His temper was surly, and his anger always near the surface. Thin of build and only average in height, he had unusually long legs that gave him a gangling but distinctive appearance. As if to distract from this deficiency, he affected complicated cravats and gold-embroidered waistcoats, wore his dark hair long and combed straight back with pomade and his beard in a point below his chin. Though his salon was popular, his teaching methods relied on a mixed bag of sly tricks rather than the hard practice that built muscle, instinct and skill. He cultivated no friend-ships among the other sword masters, considering them as competitors who had to be beaten. Rumored to be a rapacious Casanova, it was also whispered that blackmail sometimes figured in his conquests. One young woman of good family had taken poison and died after an affair with him. Broyard swore she had been unstable, a hysteric distraught over his end-ing the arrangement. Others claimed that she took her life from shame, because she had given herself to him to save her young husband from a challenge.

What purpose could the Count de Lérida have in encouraging such a man? Rio frowned as he consid-ered the possibilities. At the same time, he wondered what the count's presence meant for Celina. Was this a rendezvous between them, one held under her brother's watchful eye to further their acquaintance before the final step toward marriage? Or would Ce-lina prefer to avoid being seen by the nobleman? If the last, would the count recognize her behind her mask? Rio had certainly done so, but then he was accustomed to looking beneath the surface, to searching for subtle clues, the hint of purpose that could mean life or death.

The count was very Spanish this evening, dressed in the flamboyant costume of Andalusia. Since it was designed to flatter a horseman's narrow-hipped physique instead of the rotund shape of a self-indulgent gourmand, the choice was unfortunate. The glittering beads that decorated the short jacket reflected the gaslight in bright spots on his quivering jowls, and the clubbed hairstyle emphasized his thinning hairline.

Rio realized abruptly that the nobleman was aging, and none too well. It was a revelation.

A short time later, Rio saw Aristide Broyard making his way across the room toward where Celina stood. She had her back to the sword master while she chatted with a shepherdess in a gown with so many white flounces that she looked much like one of the sheep she was supposed to be guarding. Broyard came to a halt and made his bow, and Celina turned toward him with her lips parted in surprise. He made a sweeping gesture in the direction of the polished dance floor, but she shook her head, murmuring something that was doubtless a cordial refusal.

Broyard's sharp features turned ugly. He spoke with the sound of insistence in his voice. As Celina stepped away from him, he actually put a hand on her bare arm above her glove. She answered him again in clearly negative tones, though the words were indistinct. At the same time, she tried to draw her arm away. Broyard did not release her, but pulled her closer with his mouth set in a thin line.

Denys, engaged with a friend a short distance away, turned at the sound of his sister's voice. Count de Lérida, separated by no great distance from Denys, appeared to notice the young man's alertness and followed the direction of his gaze. Both men were too far away to offer protection to Celina or prevent her from being dragged onto the dance floor.

Rio did not hesitate. Shouldering through the dancers awaiting the start of a waltz, he strode to where Celina stood. With a smooth bow, he said, "I beg your pardon, *mademoiselle* of the golden mask. I am inexcusably tardy, but I believe this is our waltz?"

"Yes, of course." Relief was strong in her voice as she held out her free hand. "I had almost given you up."

Rio took her gloved fingers and placed them on his arm. For an instant, he thought Broyard would not release his grip. Then the rival sword master stepped back a pace. Malevolence glittered in his eyes as he spoke. "An untimely intervention, Monsieur de Silva."

"Is it?" Rio's gaze was narrow and unsmiling.

"Most untimely, since it prevents my design. I would dislike discovering that it was a sham."

"But you feel it might be?" Rio paused as he awaited an answer. His gaze encompassed Denys and the count, who had just arrived on the scene, halting a few steps away. The look in Denys's brown eyes, so like his sister's, was troubled. The count watched the proceedings with his moist lips pursed and his features unreadable.

"*Messieurs*, please," Celina began with distress clouding her face.

Broyard ignored her, his focus on Rio. "It would not be the first time you have interfered where the lady is concerned, or so I hear. One wonders at it."

"My actions, like my motives, are none of your affair." Rio could feel the rush of the blood in his veins, keeping pace with the rise of his anger. It crossed his mind to wonder if Broyard had approached Celina solely to create this situation. That would mean he understood the connection between them, which was highly unlikely. Another possibility teased at his mind, but he had no time to grasp its outline, much less unravel it.

"It is my affair if they affect my pleasure."

"Your pleasure?" Rio repeated with deadly softness.

Broyard gave him a smile with a sneer in it. "I was before you with *mademoiselle*, I think."

"An injudicious turn of phrase. It indicates the need for instruction in how to speak of a lady, as well as in gentlemanly conduct."

"And you will supply this lesson?" Broyard laughed with a barking sound. "Excellent. My seconds will call on yours."

Rio turned toward Denys. "Monsieur Vallier?"

Celina's brother blinked then flushed scarlet. "You wish me to…but of course." He bowed. "I would be honored to serve as your second in this matter."

"Thank you."

Rio inclined his head and then turned once more to lead Celina onto the dance floor and away from the altercation. She moved beside him willingly enough, but as he faced her and placed his gloved hand at her waist, her body was rigid.

"Is this what you have been doing all evening?" she demanded. "Seeking out quarrels?"

"You object to the defense of your honor?" He drew back a little, in part to see her face. It was also necessary to avoid the stiff bell of her skirt that felt too much like being pressed against her very bones.

"I object to being made a part of that charade just now. And I despise being the cause of another duel."

"Perhaps you feel I should have allowed your brother the honor of chastising Broyard."

"There was no need for anyone to fight him."

"He was being entirely too forward with you. He also had the effrontery to accuse you of lying to avoid him."

"Which I did, of course."

Her brown eyes flashed golden fire as she glared at him. It was insane that he should enjoy her anger, yet he did. It spoke of a passion she normally repressed, passion waiting to be released by a man who could equal it in heat and strength.

"That may be," he said as evenly as he was able. "But it has no bearing whatever on how a gentleman is permitted to address you. You may not object to his behaving as if you were a trollop, but I do."

"By what right?"

"The right of any man to uphold the standards of respect and common decency."

"Even without personal involvement?"

"We are involved, my sweet, whether we like it or not," he said through his teeth. "You saw to that."

"To my great regret!"

"And mine!" He swung her into a turn that sent her silken skirts swirling out behind her and effectively prevented a reply. A moment later, he slowed again, saying abruptly, "Forgive me. That was as ill-mannered as anything Aristide Broyard may have done."

She looked away with a hectic flush across her cheekbones. "I was equally rude."

"But with more cause," he replied with a twist of his lips.

"The truth is that I was dismayed to find I had embroiled you in yet another meeting. That was not my intention when I came here."

"And what was your intention?"

"To see you, speak to you. I thought to discover if there is some way I may undo what I seem to have set in motion by visiting your rooms the other night."

"You wish to be released from our agreement?" he asked with a squeezing sensation in his chest.

She swung her head to stare at him. "That isn't what I meant. What I want is to prevent more ridiculous swordplay. I can't stand it that you've had to defend yourself against four men because of your leniency with Denys. I hate it that you must meet another in the morning. I never intended to put you in danger."

Her honesty made him want to comfort her, to tell her she could be as rude to him as she liked if she would also let him hold her. He had known that dancing with her was a mistake. God, but he wanted her, needed her with an ache so fierce that moving to the music with her in his arms was an exercise in self-torture.

"Your concern does you credit," he said, "but any

blame for the current state of affairs rests on my shoulders. I did agree to your request, after all."

"Yes, but…"

"And I'm not sorry for it."

He was sorry for nothing, and that was the biggest mistake of all. His one prayer was that the error would not be fatal.

She stumbled a little, and he was forced to step closer, supporting her with an arm about her waist until she regained her balance. He stepped away the instant she was steady again, resuming the rigorously correct distance. Her clasp was still tight on his hand, however, when she spoke in low desperation. "I can't stand this, I really can't."

"Because of your older brother who died in a duel, I do understand. Was his opponent by chance a sword master?"

"It was a match with pistols," she answered with a quick shake of her head. "Just a stupid quarrel over a game of cards."

It was a relief to hear that, though he did not bother to ask himself why. "Sometimes the senseless deaths are hardest to bear."

"Yes." Her grip tightened on his hand. "Is there nothing you can do to stop these endless duels, nothing at all?"

"I could always kill a few challengers, but that seems an extreme deterrent."

"You wouldn't! I mean, not just to relieve my mind?"

His smile was forced. "Not deliberately, though it could happen. And I might make an exception in Broyard's case."

"Please don't make a jest of it." The golden-brown depths of her eyes were shadowed as she gazed up at him.

"No," he said soberly. "It's really nothing to jest about, nothing at all."

7

Celina was at Bourry d'Ivernois, the dry goods emporium on the rue de Chartres, when the carriage bearing one of the *maîtres d'armes*, apparently injured, came slowly down the street. Young boys racing alongside it, shouting up at the coachman while dodging among strollers on the banquette, helped to identify it. Other emporium patrons hurried to the front door to watch it pass. Celina joined them, though a single glimpse of the vehicle was enough to relieve her mind. She drew a deep breath, her first of the morning, and then let it out again.

It was not the Vallier carriage that Denys had taken out that morning to transport Rio, his other second and the surgeon to The Oaks. The wounded duelist had to be Aristide Broyard. Rio had been victorious once again.

Celina listened shamelessly to the comments exchanged around her. One gentleman was sure the match had been a vicious one, given that the opponents were so skilled and evenly matched. Broyard was not a man to stick at seizing any advantage that was offered. If de Silva had won, then he had proved himself not only superior with a sword but sharp at guarding against unscrupulous tricks. Another man agreed, adding piously that the saints sometimes fought on the side of right.

As the carriage came opposite, an elderly gentleman called out to the driver, asking if the occupant was dead. The reply was that Broyard still lived but was grievously injured. The surgeon was riding with him to his rooms where the repairs begun on the dueling field would be completed. No, the coachman didn't know how the other gentleman fared. He thought he was injured, also.

"Suzette?" Celina glanced around with a frown.

The maid stepped from the place she had taken near a window. "Yes, Mam'zelle?"

"We should return home. Denys may have sent word." She met the eyes of her maid for a second of silent communication.

"Indeed, Mam'zelle. If not, then there are other ways of learning news."

Celina gave a quick nod. A clerk was wrapping her purchase, a bolt of Italian embroidered muslin for new summer curtains to go under the draperies in her bedchamber. Bourry d'Ivernois had advertised a shipment from Le Havre of spring goods of all kinds, from tartans and cashmere shawls to Swiss goods, and she had come at once to look at the merchandise before it was gone. The shopping expedition served mainly as an excuse, however, for she had known she would have news of the meeting much more quickly on the street than sitting in her salon.

With Suzette carrying the basket, they made their way back toward the town house. The sun was bright, and they kept to the shady side of the street where overhanging second-floor balconies protected them from its poisonous rays. Ordinarily Celina walked sedately, exchanging greetings and enjoying the lacy shadow patterns cast on the banquette by wrought-iron railings of the upper balconies that had been hammered out in the workshops of Seville. She was in far too great a hurry for such things this morning. She brushed past the apothecary shop and the bakery without noticing their distinctive aromas, spared not so much as a glance at the collection of tortoiseshell hair combs, shaving brushes, razors and knives that were laid out in a haberdashery window. Her greeting for Madame Freret, glimpsed through her courtyard gate where she watered her geraniums, was perfunctory in the extreme, and she pretended not to hear the invitation to step inside for cakes and *eau sucrée*. She spoke to a pair of nuns in black habits and white wimples met in passing, and curtsied in response to the bow of one of her father's friends. Regardless, the steady click of her heeled slippers on the paving stones never slowed until they reached the Vallier town house.

Denys was not at home.

"*Tiens!*" she exclaimed impatiently as she snatched off her bonnet without fully untying the strings. "I suppose he could not resist having a drink to celebrate the success of his principal."

"It would be strange if he did not, Mam'zelle."

"When he knows I am here waiting? How could he?"

Suzette reached to take Celina's bonnet, which was in danger of being crushed as she slapped it against her skirt. "Calm yourself, *chère*. He has no inkling that his news is of anything more than passing interest."

"Nor is it," Celina said instantly. "It only upsets me to think Monsieur de Silva may have been injured for my sake." Suzette had naturally been at the Marine Ballroom the evening before, in case repairs were required for a disintegrating hairstyle or torn petticoat. What she had not heard about the challenge as soon as it was issued, she had gotten from Celina afterward.

"But, yes, of a certainty." Suzette turned to put the bonnet beside the basket she had deposited on the salon table, a furniture piece that served as a general catchall, as well as a repository of visiting cards.

Celina narrowed her eyes. "Surely you can see that."

"Naturally. Would you care for café au lait after all? You had no breakfast and Cook could make you a nice omelet to go with it."

"I'm not hungry. Are you saying I should not be upset?"

"No, no. It's only that I wonder…"

"What do you wonder?" Celina began to remove her gloves, dragging them from her fingertips with quick, jerky movements.

"If you are the cause of this meeting, after all." Suzette glanced at her then went on in a rush. "I mean, think, *chère*. Twice in one week you have been at the center of an affair of honor, and neither time through any blame of your own. Something else may be at stake here."

Celina felt as if a band constricting her chest had begun to ease. Suzette had just put into words a feeling that had haunted her from the beginning without her being able to put a finger on it. "But what can it be?"

"Monsieur de Silva was present on both occasions."

"And the count."

"Monsieur Denys, as well, though as your escort that is natural enough."

Celina agreed. "What of Broyard last evening? His presence was such a random thing."

"So it seems, but was it indeed? What if someone asked him to accost you?"

"Really, Suzette!"

"It could happen."

"But why?"

"Perhaps to put you under obligation for the rescue?"

"You are accusing Monsieur de Silva then."

Suzette made a brief, negative gesture. "He intervened, but was not close by when this Broyard first approached."

Celina was not so sure. He had never been far away during the evening, though her plan for a meeting had very nearly come to nothing. But if Suzette was not thinking of Rio, that only left one person. "The count has no reason to wish me to feel obligated."

"Unless he suspects you dislike the match and fears your father will listen to your objections."

Celina considered that a mere second. "I saw no sign that he meant to play the gallant."

"It is difficult to imagine, yes," Suzette agreed, then gave a light shrug. "Perhaps my instinct is wrong. Monsieur Broyard is, or was, a *maître d'armes* with a sizable following and the ambition to make it larger. That's reason enough for him to force a challenge."

"But not for him to think he could reach the Silver Shadow through me."

Suzette gave her a glance from under her lashes. "So?"

"So how could he know? The agreement between Monsieur de Silva and myself was private. He has been most discreet."

"Sweeping you onto the dance floor at a subscription ball shows discretion? Then I dread to think what he may do next. Or what will happen when your father hears of that waltz."

A flush heated Celina's face. "We were both masked if you'll remember, and the dance was well meant. Anyway, the challenge had already been issued."

"True." Suzette picked up the discarded bonnet again and turned in the direction of the bedchamber, no doubt to put it away. "Then I can only suppose that Monsieur Broyard accosted you for the usual reasons."

Celina was forced to agree though it still seemed too easy.

Suzette paused in the doorway. "You understand that the situation has changed since this last challenge? The duel, along with the sensational string of them that went before it, will be rehashed over every luncheon table in the Vieux Carré."

"Yes," Celina said in grim recognition as she stared at the sunlit courtyard that lay beyond the French doors. People would talk, and she might well be at the center of these conversations if even one person had identified her. Then she glanced at her maid. "You mentioned an errand before?"

"I'm going, I'm going," Suzette said. "Though let us pray that everyone thinks I traipse up and down the Passage de la Bourse because of my interest in Monsieur de Silva's manservant instead of yours in the *maître*."

It was some time before the maid returned. She was a trifle disheveled, her lips swollen and her news scant. Rio had been pierced in the shoulder by Broyard's sword. The surgeon had attended him on the field, but he had not yet returned home. That was all that Olivier knew, or at least all that he would say.

Celina fumed, muttering under her breath about the discourtesy of males such as Rio and Denys who could not tear themselves away from their amusements long enough to relieve concern over them. It was most unfair that she was not only prohibited from viewing the contest but denied direct news of it. Then less than a half hour later, a delivery arrived. Brought by a young boy, the son of one of the Italians who sold flowers and vegetables at the Levee Market, was a red rose sprigged around with rosemary and tied up with blue ribbon.

Celina's anger died away. Turning the rose in her hand, she stared down at it. Rosemary for remembrance. He had not forgotten that she would be waiting to hear, after all. But to give a single red rose meant to give one's heart. What did the flower signify then? What were any of these meant to convey? Or did they mean anything at all beyond mere flirtation from a man with the reputation as a lover of women, a Silver Shadow whose movements in swordplay were so swift they could not be seen, and who ghosted in and out of beds other than his own but never lingered?

As the morning passed, Celina sent for a seamstress, a free woman of color who measured the bedchamber windows with a length of string before entering into a long discussion about rod pockets and hem depths. Visitors interrupted the consultation, and Celina joined her aunt in the salon, leaving Suzette to give the seamstress refreshment before sending her off with the muslin.

It was not their normal day to be at home for callers. Left to herself, Celina would have had Mortimer deny them most politely and take the visitors' cards. Her aunt delighted in having the company of old friends such as these, however, and would be far too curious over why they had come to renounce the pleasure of the visit.

Celina could guess what had brought the two elderly ladies. She should have told Tante Marie Rose of the previous evening's events early that morning instead of rushing out of the house before her aunt left her bed. She had delayed too long, and now had to bear the consequences.

The eyes of the visitors were bright and devouring as Celina joined them in the salon. Still they spoke only of the usual things over the cordials and savories: a carriage accident on the river road, a lady or two who were enceinte with a third or fourth child, and friends who had come down with putrid sore throats or *la grippe*. Her aunt chatted with élan, but her puzzlement grew increasingly evident as the normal half hour granted for such a call passed with no real explanation for it or sign of departure.

Celina realized finally that it was her presence that deterred the older women. Since they were her aunt's friends and she had paid her due respects, she was not compelled to stay. Bowing to the inevitable, she made her excuses and left them.

The instant the pedestrian gate closed behind the callers, Tante Marie Rose sought out Celina where she had taken refuge in the deepest corner of the front gallery. "What impudence!" she exclaimed, coming toward her with high color staining her cheeks. "Those two viragoes actually thought that I would tattle about you behind your back, filling their ears with your affairs. I've never been so incensed in my life!"

"Tattle." Celina felt a sinking sensation in her stomach.

"Another duel fought by this so terrible Silver Shadow person, and you are said to be at the center of it. Ridiculous! You may be assured that I told them so, and much more besides."

"Oh, Tante Marie Rose. I am so sorry."

The color fled from the older woman's face. She took two faltering steps and dropped into the rattan chair opposite where Celina sat. Above the chair's protesting creaks, she cried, "Never tell me that it's true!"

"I fear it may be," Celina answered, reaching to take one of her aunt's hands. "But first you must tell me exactly what is being said."

"That you were seen last night at a subscription

ball, a vulgar affair where you became embroiled in another quarrel between Monsieur de Silva and one Broyard. Oh, *chère*, please tell me you were not there."

"I cannot do that, but I was masked and at no time removed the disguise."

"Useless, completely useless. You are too distinctive, my dear heart. Besides, Denys was nearby, and the count as well, which would naturally lead people to assume…"

"Yes, I see."

"But that is not all. The count has been most vocal over the affair, declaring that this business of dueling in New Orleans is barbaric, a travesty of manners that casts a bad light on the fair lady whom he expects to make his wife. The upshot of the matter is that everyone now knows that you were involved."

"What idiocy," Celina said in annoyance.

"Very true, but only think. He may be so disgusted that he will break off all discussion of the betrothal!"

Celina lifted her chin. "I'm sure I shall live over it."

"But everyone expects an interesting announcement any day, even any hour. If he is seen to have taken you in disfavor, then no other man will have you this year or possibly ever." Her aunt's face crumpled and her faded eyes filled with tears. "I have failed you, *chère*, I who should have protected you from such a pitfall."

"You could hardly protect me from something you knew nothing about," Celina said, sliding from her chair to kneel at her aunt's feet. "Don't upset yourself, it will be all right. I'm only sorry that you had to learn of it from someone other than myself. But the whole thing seemed so minor, the merest triviality. I went to the ball only to see Monsieur de Silva and discover if…"

"No! Tell me you were not so indiscreet?"

"I had to see him. It's my fault that he has been forced to meet so many on the field of honor."

Her aunt moaned and fell back in her chair. "Your father will turn me into the street, I know he will. He is certain to think this tragedy my fault entirely."

"No, no, he is too aware of my nature for that. Please, don't cry," she said, taking the elderly woman's hands in her own. "Please."

"But what a scandal! It's too awful. How are we to face people?"

"I did nothing, I promise."

"That matters not at all," her aunt said on a low moan. "You were there, and that is enough to sink you forever. Oh, dear. That it should come to this when everything was so bright just a few days ago."

Celina was still trying to comfort her aunt and explain the sequence of events that had transpired when her father returned to the town house. The two of them fell silent on hearing his voice. Celina thought that he was speaking to Mortimer, instructing the butler to bring refreshment while divesting himself of hat, cane and gloves. Then they heard another man accept an offer of sherry. His voice held such grave pomposity that it could belong to only one person.

"The count," Tante Marie Rose said with a catch in her voice. "He has come to disavow the betrothal."

"May the Holy Mother hear you," Celina murmured.

"*Chère!* Bite your tongue. I tell you, if he deserts you now, you are ruined."

"But free, which doesn't seem so great a disaster."

"It would be in all ways terrible," Tante Marie Rose said earnestly. "Everyone will assume the worst. No one will know you. Your friends will not be allowed to call, and no invitations will be sent. You may as well be dead."

Her aunt was right, Celina knew. She was aware that she would despise being the subject of speculation, hate being cut off from everyone. Still, she could not prevent the rise of hope.

A bare ten minutes after a tray bearing glasses of wine had been delivered to the study, Mortimer came to say that her presence was required there. Celina had half expected the summons, so made herself ready, running a damp cloth over her face to cool her hectic flush and smoothing her hair. Changing her gown crossed her mind, only to be dismissed. She had no particular desire to please the count.

She entered the study at her father's reply to her knock. Her father stood, indicating a chair placed before his desk and next to that of the count. The count began to struggle from his seat, but she forestalled him with a lifted hand.

"Thank you for joining us, Celina," her father said as he resumed his place. "I thought it right that you should be here, since the count has laid a disturbing charge before me."

It was as her aunt had suggested. The betrothal might be at an end. She schooled her features to conceal her elation. "Yes, Papa?"

"I understand you attended a ball last evening,

one which you knew neither I nor your aunt would approve. Can this be possible?"

"It was only an impulse, Papa, to see how such affairs were conducted. I promise there was no harm in it."

"If you had thought it would be allowed, you would not have waited until your aunt was otherwise engaged."

She lowered her gaze. "Yes, forgive me."

"I am disappointed in you, and doubly so that you embroiled Denys in the business. Do not trouble to deny it, for I know he would never have escorted you without strong persuasion. In any case, what may be acceptable for him as a young man about town has no bearing on what a sheltered female may do without consequences."

Celina clenched her teeth against the urge to speak. It would do no good, and might make matters worse. To be reprimanded in front of the count was painful, however, especially as the look on his face seemed to suggest that he approved. Nevertheless, it would soon be over, and the result would be worth the embarrassment.

When she made no reply, her father turned to his guest. "You were telling me of the events that resulted in my daughter being dragged into a vicious quarrel, Monsieur le Comte," he said, using the French form of address for his title. "Perhaps you will be so good as to continue?"

"Certainly, though I take no pleasure in being the one to make the matter known to you." The count took a handkerchief from his sleeve, releasing a wave of heavy musklike scent before using it to blot the moisture from his upper lip. "Mademoiselle Vallier was in conversation with a young man whom I believed to be a friend of her brother when she was approached by the fencing master, this Rio de Silva. He solicited a waltz and she refused him, much to her credit. He pressed her to alter her decision, even daring to place his hand on her arm. Her protest attracted the attention of another fencing master of note, Monsieur Aristide Broyard. An altercation then arose when Broyard remonstrated with de Silva over his lack of manners."

"No, it wasn't like that at all," Celina began.

Her father gave her a quelling look. "Allow the count to speak, if you please."

"But Papa..."

"You surely would not insult an honored guest by implying that he lies? Pray allow him to continue."

"My gratitude," the count said, lowering his eyelids as he tipped his head. "As I was saying, Monsieur Broyard objected to being pushed about, not unnaturally, and felt the conduct of this de Silva required mending. The result was a challenge. Then Mademoiselle Vallier was carried out onto the dance floor by the man who had accosted her."

"That is completely untrue. It was Monsieur Broyard who would not accept my refusal. Monsieur de Silva rescued me from his unwanted attentions."

The man to whom she was almost betrothed only shook his head with a condescending smile. "The sensibilities of a lady such as your daughter are beyond delicate, are they not, monsieur? I fear she was so disturbed by the confrontation that she has become confused."

"Apparently," he father said in grim tones.

"I assure you that I am not, Papa," she insisted, speaking through her father since her suitor seemed determined not to address her directly. "If the matter had proceeded as the count indicates, surely he would have felt moved to rescue me himself?"

Her father lifted a brow, and for an instant she thought she might have made an impression.

Then the count gave a rumbling laugh. "Broyard had the situation well in hand. Moreover, I was not certain that *mademoiselle* disliked having two men fighting over her. She has great spirit. It also seemed to me that she was more pleased than not at what must surely have been flattering attention from a man of de Silva's amorous reputation."

Celina caught her breath at this outrageous accusation. To her father, she said, "So I was abandoned to de Silva by the count while he allowed another to defend my honor? There is scant surprise there, sir. It was much the same before, in the situation that resulted in Denys and Monsieur de Silva crossing swords."

"Celina! You will apologize at once for this insult to an honored guest."

She closed her lips tightly as she sat straight and proud in her chair. She would never apologize for speaking the truth.

"I take no offense," the count said with a wave of his handkerchief, though his face was the color of a ripe plum. "I would only point out that *mademoiselle's* own words prove this de Silva to have been at fault in the first instance, which suggests similar blame in this one. But we will not quarrel, my bride-to-be and I over the events. With all due respect, I insist that I am not here to take such a lovely creature to task but to prevent the further besmirching of her fair name."

"Take me to task?" she repeated, swinging on him. "That is not your right even if it were necessary, which it is not!"

"You are mistaken, I believe." His smile held the glimmer of triumph. "I have just this minute signed the marriage contract. We are bound as man and wife by law, if not yet in the eyes of the church. This gives me the right."

Celina felt her heart leap like a trapped thing in her chest. Turning back to her father, she demanded, "Is this true?"

"Indeed, *chère*, or will be when you have signed."

"Then I shall not."

The count snorted, answering before her father could speak. "You must, *mademoiselle*. The scandal caused by your willful disregard for convention makes it imperative."

"Papa!"

"The count is correct," her father said with a sigh. "The matter has been settled between us. You should be thankful that he still wishes to escort you to the altar."

"I am more inclined than ever," the count said smoothly. "In fact, I can hardly wait to claim a bride so attractive that men fight at sword point for her favor. Rather than risk further scandal, however, I suggest the nuptials be celebrated at once. Say next Friday, Monsieur Vallier?"

"No!"

Her father looked judicious. "The proposal has merit."

"But Friday is hangman's day!" Celina exclaimed, seizing the first excuse that sprang to mind.

"Pardon?"

Her father made a fatalistic gesture. "Forgive me, Monsieur le Comtè, but it is customary here to abstain from being wed on Friday. Executions were once carried out at the Place d'Armes in front of the cathedral on this day. That the first thing seen by a bride as she emerged from the church should be a hanged felon was not considered a good omen for marriage. The superstition attached to the day remains."

"Saturday then," the count said with ill-disguised impatience. "Let it be Saturday morning, early."

Celina could hardly believe her future was being decided in this precipitous manner. She sat forward in her chair. "I can never be ready in so short a time. More than that, such haste will only make everyone think we have something of which to be ashamed. Please, Papa, I would like to speak to you alone."

"For what purpose?" he asked. "Everything has been arranged."

"But I have no wish to be married."

"You must marry sometime and the count offers you—"

"I don't want to be a countess!" That was as plain as she could speak without so angering her father that he might order her immediate obedience.

"You aspire to be the wife of a fencing master, I suppose," Count de Lérida said with a sneer.

"Not at all." The attention she turned on him carried hot contempt. "Monsieur de Silva has too much sensibility to ever expect it."

The count glanced at her father. "This fencing master's sensibility now exceeds mine, you see? Next, she will be running away with him. Let her be married to me on Saturday and I guarantee that such foolishness will be at an end."

"No!"

"Celina Celeste Amalie Vallier!"

The use of her full name was a warning, but one she could not heed. "This is against my will, Papa. To sign the contract is to sign away my life."

"Mere dramatics, *chère*," he said, his lips tight. "A woman requires a husband."

"Not this man and not like this," she said stubbornly.

"You are too young to judge. Allow me to know what is best for you."

"I know you have my best interests at heart, but I tell you that this is wrong."

The count cleared his throat by way of interruption. "If I may, *monsieur*?"

"Please."

"Permit me to plead my case, I beg. Now that the betrothal is official, there should be no obstacle to a few minutes alone with my future bride?"

Her father considered the request only a moment before rising to his feet. "I see none for a man such as yourself."

Alarm threatened to choke Celina. Before she could find suitable words for further protest, her father moved to the door. It closed behind him, sealing her in with the count.

Oppressive quiet descended on the room. In it, Celina could hear voices in another part of the house, the rustle of a light wind in the live oak outside, the rattle of a wagon over the stones of the street and cooing of the birds in the pigeon cote at the end of the carriage house. A fire had been set ablaze in the fireplace on the count's arrival, but it had not had time to take the dampness from the air. She felt chilled as she clasped her hands in her lap, staring down at them while she tried to think of some way to escape both the study and this marriage. There was only one that she could see.

The count levered himself out of his chair and moved to the window overlooking the courtyard. He stood staring out, or perhaps watching her father's retreat along the upper gallery, before turning to face her.

"I am not a fool," he said, drawing himself up to a stiff posture. "I realize that young women dream of a handsome man who will court them with flowery speeches and promises of undying devotion. But such things fade away after a few years of marriage, and what is left? Respect and comfortable circumstances, even high position, if one is fortunate. These are the things I can give you."

"I am aware…" she began.

"Allow me to finish, if you please. I was not born the Conde de Lérida, you know. Noble, yes, but not the firstborn son destined to inherit my father's title and estates. That was the right of my older brother under our ancient *mayorazgo* system, which decrees an estate must be handed down *in toto*, without division among a nobleman's children. My brother was trained for the title, brought up a grand *hidalgo,* keeper of the *estancia,* master of all that lay before him. I was instructed in the duties of his steward. I served him and his family most humbly because I was the second son."

For the first time since they had met, she saw a shadow of dignity in his bearing, recognized sincerity in his face. He had suffered under his brother's dominion, she thought. Perhaps not physically, but in the thousand and one small slights and humiliations those in a position of power inevitably inflict on those beneath them. It was an uncomfortable insight, since she had no wish to feel sympathy. "I'm sorry," she said, "but I fail to see how this affects me."

"I am speaking of my circumstances and how completely they changed. For you must know that an accident overtook my brother and his family. Suddenly, the honor and wealth that had been his were mine. I was unprepared, scarcely able to recognize my new position for grief, reluctant to step into my brother's shoes. Still, it was required that I accept the challenge. I know what it means, then, to go from a simple life to an exalted one. I understand your fear. But I will be at your side, supporting you as you come to enjoy your elevation, this noble status that awaits you. You will find it worth the lack of youth and a handsome face across the breakfast table, I promise you. And permit me to relieve your mind on this important score. You will have a virile husband in your bed."

She would have liked him better if he had left the last unspoken. Not that anything could, or would, persuade her to accept his suit. "I have no need for honors, *monsieur*. Nor is a handsome face of extreme importance to me. But I do require to feel something more for the man I marry than mere tolerance."

He took a step toward her, his expression intent. "This is something that will come in due time."

"It…seems most unlikely."

"You require proof? That can be arranged."

The flare of heat in his eyes sent alarm skittering along her veins. Springing from her chair, she put it between them. "All I require," she said a shade breathlessly, "is time."

"Nonsense." He stepped closer. Putting out a hand, he closed his fingers on her wrist that rested on the chair back. "The passion of the marriage bed forges a bond between husband and wife. It is a thing of great power, an almost overwhelming force. I think a demonstration may be worthwhile."

"Not at all, I promise you! Why you would wish to claim a reluctant bride is beyond my understanding. Almost as much a mystery is why you seek an alliance here in New Orleans when you must know more eligible females in Spain. There is much I don't know about you, *monsieur*." She tugged at her wrist, trying to break his hold, but he clamped down so tightly that her fingers began to feel numb.

"I sought only investments until I saw you," he said, licking his plump lips so they shone moist and red. "Your beauty enthralled me. I was reminded of my duty to my name, which includes the responsibility to produce an heir."

"You must seek one elsewhere." She jerked against his steady pull on her arm while shoving against the

chair between them so it pushed against his belly.
"Let me go, sir, or I will call out."

"Do you think anyone will come? Can you actually believe that your father failed to understand my
intention when I spoke of pleading my case? Have
done with this foolish resistance. Come to me."

"You forget yourself, *monsieur!* My aunt will be
sent to join us. You will be discovered." She hoped
devoutly that it was true, prayed that even if her father had left her to the count's attentions, it would
not be for long.

Her struggles seemed to excite the count. His eyes
glittered and his grasp tightened. Abruptly he thrust
the chair out of the way and dragged her against
him. His body odor, mixed with the smells of warm
wool and sour wine, assailed her senses. She could
feel the rotund shape of his belly pumping obscenely
at the lower part of her body. His massive weight and
strong, heavy arms suffocated her while he fumbled
at the back of her head, trying to force her face up to
meet his wet mouth. Blinded, unable to breathe, she
twisted in his grasp while disgust rose with the taste
of bile in her throat. The sound of a seam ripping
loose at the fitted shoulder of her day gown touched
off a small explosion of panic.

He released her wrist, which was caught between
them, trying for a better hold. As her hand was freed,
she struck out with curled fingers, reaching for his
eyes. Her nails raked down his face. He gave a hoarse
yell and staggered back.

Celina jerked clear of him and whirled away to a
safe distance. For an instant, they stared at each other.
He raised a hand to his face, touched the livid

scratches, then looked at the traces of blood that came away on his fingertips. Rage burned its way into his eyes. He seemed to swell like a bull about to charge as he started toward her.

"Celina!" Tante Marie Rose cried in breathless tones from the doorway. "I am here, *ma chère*." She came forward with jerky movements. "Count de Lérida, as duenna in this house, I am appalled. Such familiarity as I have just witnessed is not allowed. Celina's father may have been lax enough to permit encroachment, but not I!"

"My dear lady," he began.

"No, *monsieur*, I will hear no excuses. You are not yet my niece's husband. If you cannot restrain yourself, then you must take your leave."

Anger still mottled the count's face, but he apparently recognized defeat when he saw it. "Forgive me, *madame, mademoiselle*," he said through set teeth. "I forgot myself for a moment."

Her aunt turned to her. "Celina?"

"Yes, certainly," she said, holding a hand to her abdomen where nerves still fluttered. "I do think it will be best if the count should leave us now."

Her aunt turned on the nobleman, whose heavy breathing could still be plainly heard. "I regret the necessity, *monsieur*, but we must bid you good day. In your absence I shall endeavor to discover if there is any hope for you and your suit."

"For that, I will be grateful," he said in tones only a hair away from sarcasm. "Your servant, *madame*."

He turned to Celina, inclining his upper body in stiff obeisance. "And yours, *mademoiselle*."

Celina and her aunt stood in silence while he

turned with ponderous dignity and took himself from the room. His treads sounded along the gallery, then could be heard descending to the courtyard. Before they passed out of hearing, Tante Marie Rose turned to her and opened her arms.

"Thank heaven you arrived when you did," Celina said with feeling as she relaxed against her aunt.

"Whatever made the man believe such conduct would be permitted?"

"Ego, I should think. He makes much of being a count. But no matter. You were formidable just now, *ma chère tante*. I am amazed at the way you stood up to him."

"Indeed, I amaze myself, but I could not fail you again." Her aunt gave a shaky sigh. "You are my chick, Celina, and no man shall take advantage of you while I breathe, no, not even if he is your betrothed and ever so noble. I shudder to think of you enduring such insult."

For an instant the memory of a different embrace hovered in Celina's mind. Those few minutes in Rio de Silva's arms, the touch of his mouth, had not been at all frightful. In spite of what her aunt had said before, it seemed all men's embraces were not the same, whether in dark or daylight. A small shiver feathered down her spine.

"There, I knew you must be more upset than you appeared," her aunt said, giving her another fierce hug.

The stir of hope was a warm, yeastlike rising inside her. "Perhaps now you begin to see my objection to the count."

"I have always understood, truly I have. The difference in your ages, your unequal stations and the severance from your family that marriage will bring—all these are difficult considerations. And yet it would be foolish to allow what has just taken place to weigh too much with you. Men are impetuous creatures and frequently at the mercy of their desires."

"You cannot say you still think I should accept him!"

"He may improve on acquaintance," her aunt said, though the sentiment was more optimistic than her expression. "I cannot but wonder that your father did not choose someone more suited, however, a pleasant young man who will adore you and be proud to have you at his side."

Celina hesitated and then said quickly, "I have wondered if he troubled himself to look into the credentials of the count."

"Persons such as the Count de Lérida seldom present credentials, love. It's hardly necessary. A great number of people in New Orleans have Spanish connections from the old days, if you'll remember. Many know of him, of his estates and position at court. A lady of my acquaintance spoke of it just a few days ago, at the sewing circle for the orphans."

"Perhaps, but is there no way to be sure?"

Pity clouded her aunt's face. "I fear that you are grasping at straws."

"But what harm can it do?"

"None, I suppose, if it will resign you to this betrothal."

"You will look into it? Oh, Tante Marie Rose!"

"I can promise nothing."

Her aunt's words were a strong indication of how little she expected to find to discredit the count. "Any scrap of knowledge would be welcome, even confirmation that he is just as he represents."

"Very well," her aunt said unhappily. "Allow me to think on it a little and we shall see."

Her aunt's promise of aid in the face of her father's will was courageous, and Celina honored her for it. Still, she could not trust her future to so frail a possibility.

Something more would have to be done. The arrangements were in place, had been since her visit to Rio de Silva's atelier. All that was necessary was to proceed.

She had little time, only a week, if she must be wed next Saturday. Whatever she was going to do, it would have to be soon.

8

"I must get back."

Rio set his glass on the table and rose to his feet. He had been saying that he needed to leave for the past hour. This time he was really going.

They had stopped at the roadhouse near the Allard Oaks for a celebratory drink, breakfast and a quiet place where the surgeon could stitch up the flesh wound in his left shoulder. The food had been slow in coming, the drinks had multiplied and there had seemed little reason for leaving. Now glasses and plates covered the table, and he'd had enough. If Caid wanted to go with him and Vallier wanted to transport him in his family carriage, well and good. If not, he would find his own way back to town.

"I'm done," Caid said, draining his glass then pushing back his chair.

"And I." Denys Vallier looked around for his hat and cane, which he'd discarded on entering.

The young man's movements were deliberate, but Rio didn't believe he was seriously befuddled. One of the spectators who had joined them was not quite so hard of head. He lifted his glass, regarding them with bleary-eyed bonhomie. "A last toast to your so-great victory over Broyard."

"Another time, my friend," Rio answered, his tone more brusque than he'd intended. "I have affairs awaiting me in town."

"I'll wager you do." The other man gave a hiccuping laugh.

Rio sketched the briefest possible bow and turned away without a reply. It was better than his first impulse, which was to knock the man's teeth down his throat.

He needed fops and dandies such as this man, those who thought they cut a large swath because they attended his salon. Their money helped pay his bills, and their swaggering added to his repute as a sword master. Enduring their company tried his patience, however, particularly in his present temper.

His muscles were stiff, his shoulder ached with a vicious and steady throb, and he was aware of the accumulated fatigue brought on by several mornings of dawn meetings. More than these, however, was the black disdain that often gripped him after a duel. He had not been brought up to earn his daily bread by hacking and slicing at his fellow men. Never was he more aware of that fact than after he had bloodied his sword yet again.

The match had been hard fought, and the end uncertain until the last. Rio had felt the wings of the angel of death beating around his head more than once. Broyard had been thrusting for his heart when he'd deflected the lunge so it sliced into his shoulder. If the rival swordsman had been a shade faster, or his own reaction a fraction slower, he could have died.

A contest between masters was always more difficult. Only when it was enjoined was it possible to tell who had the most skill, greater stamina, or deeper bag of tricks. Even then, a thousand small details could tip the balance—the angle of the sun, the dampness of the grass, how much or how little an opponent had eaten, drunk or slept the night before; what was on his mind. Broyard had been good. He had fallen victim, finally, to his need to grandstand for the audience. His play had included an extra edge of flamboyance that wasted strength and effort. His concentration had been divided for that split second that allowed his guard to be breached.

His own blade had touched the man's lung, Rio thought. Even if Broyard recovered from the injury, it was unlikely he would take the dueling field again. The thin sword master had brought it on himself, but Rio was not proud of the outcome.

He wondered how Celina Vallier felt about it.

The need to know, to find out if he would see approbation or repugnance in her face when they met again, was so strong that much of the drive into town was spent searching for an excuse to accompany Vallier to his home. That was far too rash a course. He had to rein in his inclinations, bide his time.

The meeting with Celina would come. He would see to it.

It was the second night after the duel before he could make the opportunity. Suzette had informed Olivier that her mistress would be spending a rare night at home. Olivier had arranged to meet his new inamorata, since it was a Sunday and she would be off duty. The small pedestrian gate that was inset in the larger wrought-iron barrier of the porte cochere would be left open for the majordomo's entrance, and Olivier would not secure it behind him.

Rio could have climbed to Celina's bedchamber again, but was wary of using that route too often. It was too easy for him to be seen from the street, or perhaps from one of the windows of the houses opposite. Besides, the possibility of being overheard or interrupted, as they had been before, was great. He cared not at all for himself, but he'd come as close to compromising Celina as he cared to on the night of the subscription ball.

It was near midnight when Rio strolled past the town house. He glanced through the gate into the inner court. It lay quiet and peaceful under the glimmering light of the moon; nothing moved in its open area or the deep shadows cast by the big oak at the rear.

The street was empty also, and the windows of the facing houses were blank and dark. Lamplight shone from behind the draperies of the Vallier town house, including those of Celina's bedchamber. He opened the pedestrian gate with care, but it still let out a protesting squeak. He spared a quick thought, as he stepped into the porte cochere, for the need to instruct Suzette to rub the hinges with soap. Moving quietly down its length, he paused to review his options where the stairs rose to the upper floor.

He could look for Suzette and Olivier in order to send the maid to fetch her mistress, or mount the stairs and search out Celina in hope that she would be alone, or even tap on her French door to attract her attention. The first choice was the safe one, but he was growing tired of caution.

Footsteps sounded on the gallery above him. Someone was coming toward the stairs. He stepped back and flattened his spine against the wall.

A skirt hem appeared first at the top of the stair steps, flaring out to expose a froth of lace-edged petticoats and quick-moving, slippered feet. He had a glimpse of white silk stockings outlining trim ankles, and then Celina came into view. Her head was down as she watched where she was going, and she was in a hurry.

He took a long step forward as she reached the ground. Sweeping an arm around her waist, he lifted her off her feet and swung her into the shadows under the staircase.

Most women would have cried out or fought him. She only gave a convulsive shiver and clutched at the lapels of his coat as he slowly allowed her to slide down the length of his body until her feet were on the ground again. That was fortunate, since the strain on his shoulder would have made the outcome of a struggle doubtful. He released her with reluctance, placing a hand to his bandaging as he breathed deep against the tearing ache.

"Are you all right?" she asked. Her features were pale and serious in the light falling from the room set back behind the gallery railing above them.

"Well enough, or I will be in a second." Or perhaps not. Her nearness made the blood throb in his veins. Every breath filled his lungs with her essence, mind-swimming drafts of clean, fragrant female warmth.

"I know you were injured. Is there anything I can do to help?"

"Nothing. I just...forgot." It was a stupid thing to say but the exact truth. He had been far more intent on snatching her into hiding with him, far too aware of her softness within his arms, her narrow waist and the resilience of her breasts against him, and her acquiescence.

"A sword wound being so common an event that it slipped your mind."

He dipped his head toward her a fraction as he heard the coolness in her voice. "Did I hurt you?"

"No."

"Frighten you then?"

"Not at all. I knew you would be here, for Olivier told Suzette. I thought I heard the gate."

It was a moment before he could accept the meaning of the words. "You came downstairs to meet me?"

"It seemed preferable to having you come to me."

Her concern was for her reputation and the secrecy of their meeting. He'd thought for an instant that it might be something different. More fool he for entertaining such a notion.

He reached for her hand then, carrying it to his lips while noting its faint tremor, which told him she was not quite as calm as she appeared. "If I had known you would be so cooperative, I might have come sooner."

"Unnecessary, I promise you. I am aware that you have duties and appointments that are more important than relieving my mind."

"Were you concerned?" He had to ask it, though he had little hope of an honest answer.

"Why would I not be, when I am the cause of your injury?"

The low music of her voice with its trace of disturbance made his chest feel tight, while the touch of her ungloved fingers under his stirred him profoundly. Her skin was smooth and firm, and he could not prevent his imagination from leaping to thoughts of similar satin firmness under her layers of clothing, and the hot and tender treasure that might be found by delving beneath petticoats and lace, knotted tapes and ribbons. The knowledge that only his own code prevented him from discovering the reality of his imaginings was like a live coal burning red-hot in his brain.

"If you are the cause, it's only indirectly," he said with emphasis. "The real culprit was Broyard with his lack of manners. His injuries are far worse, you know. I'm sorry that the business had so drastic an outcome, but it couldn't be helped."

"I'm sure it could not. I…I haven't thanked you for defending my good name. Please accept my gratitude."

"It was only the due of a lady."

She withdrew her hand with a small tug and reached to adjust her India shawl, which had slipped halfway down her back as he caught hold of her. "Yet it seems odd that you risked so much when just a few days ago you were defending yourself against Denys for a similar reason."

"Not at all similar," he answered in stiff tones.

"Still."

He hesitated a moment. "Does it upset you to be the cause of such meetings?"

"Of course it upsets me! I have no wish to be blamed for any man's death."

"No one should fault you. If blame there must be, let it to be laid to the Code of Honor."

"That is mere hairsplitting and of no comfort whatever, nor would it be any solace if you had died—or Broyard, if it comes to that."

"At least I now seem to be among those for whom you worry." He kept the words light, as if they were no more than the usual gallantry exchanged between men and women in her circle.

"I had hoped you would come," she said, pulling her shawl closer around her as if chilled. "The matter of my betrothal has reached an impasse. Try as I may, I see no way out of it without your aid."

"Command me." He knew instantly that his willingness had as much to do with removing the troubled look from her face as with his own plans. When had that come about?

The tale Celina unfolded was brief and not too surprising. Rio heard her out in thoughtful silence. When she came to the end, he said, "Your father seems to be much under the count's influence."

"They have become great friends, always in each other's pockets. But if you believe my father would rather please the count than his daughter, you would be wrong. He loves me, but truly feels this marriage is to my advantage."

"Not simply a matter of pride in achieving the family connection?" The question had to be asked, regardless of his admiration for her defense of her parent.

"There is that, of course," she said with a slight

hunch of her shoulders. "The ties to Spain are many here, since we were a part of that country until a few decades ago. A Spanish title has a certain cachet."

"But not for you?"

"Not if the count comes with it."

He could not help smiling a little at her vehemence. "Surely your father will relent if you can make him realize your distaste?"

"You don't know him. He is a lenient man, but that very fact makes him obstinate in the extreme about those few things that he does command."

"You actually fear he will force you?"

She moved away from him with quick footsteps, following the arcade formed by the posts that supported the upper gallery, moving deeper into the courtyard. "I don't know," she said over her shoulder. "I really don't know."

"No priest will perform a marriage ceremony over an unwilling bride," he argued as he followed after her, unwilling to allow distance between them.

"As we have discussed before, ways exist to insure willingness," she said darkly.

Accepting a coerced woman as a wife was beyond comprehension to Rio, but there were many men less fastidious, particularly when a fortune was at stake. Keeping his mind on such matters wasn't easy, however, not while watching the enticing sway of her hips that made her skirts swing gently around her. "What will you do if he resorts to these measures?"

"I had hoped that our agreement might provide suitable reason for calling off the match."

"You mean..." Rio stopped, unable in that instant to find words innocuous enough to express what he thought she meant. His heart beat against his chest like a gong, filling his mind with such a clamor that he could not think.

"Surely the count would refuse to accept a bride who was not, that is, one who was less than…"

"Less than what?" he asked as she paused and turned to face him.

"Pure. Less than pure."

The implication behind her words was stunning. Desire sliced into him like an unexpected sword slash, taking his breath, leaving him momentarily off guard. Between one instant and the next, he was hot, thickly heavy, and more than ready to fulfill any need she might be bold enough to express. His voice vibrating deep in his chest, he said finally, "You mentioned before, I believe, that purity or lack of it would matter little as long as the dowry was paid."

"That was mere cynicism. Besides, I thought it was what you wished to hear, that it might remove any impediment to…to intimacy between us."

"Therefore preventing this marriage regardless of whether I wished to be part of the scheme. But what of other suitors? You will surely wish to marry at some time."

"I shall take the veil as a nun."

"Impossible." His reaction was as swift as it was instinctive.

She gave him a scathing look before turning away again and stepping off the end of the arcade, moving into the deeper shade of the big live oak near the end of the carriage house. "If you think so, then you don't know me at all."

"I know it would be a terrible waste. Besides, you haven't the temperament."

"Self-denial and passionate devotion are not necessary," she said evenly. "Much preferred is a strong stomach and a cheerful disposition."

He moved after her again with deliberate, predatory steps. "You realize that you may be called on to supply proof of this impure state?"

"Papa will take my word for it."

"The count is unlikely to be so accommodating." He damned the man in virulent enmity as he thought of what she would have to endure at some doctor's hands to establish that she had been deflowered. It was one thing for him to contemplate that deep probing of her tender body, but something else to picture another man, even a medical man, taking such liberties. Rio didn't like it. He didn't like it at all.

She stopped and faced him once more, her lips pressed together in a mutinous frown. Then she looked away with a sigh. "I suppose."

"My point," he said softly, "is that it isn't something you can merely pretend."

"It will not be a pretense, not if you will be so accommodating as to execute our bargain."

At that moment, Rio caught a flicker of movement near the ground-floor kitchen from the corner of his eye. He caught Celina's arm, drawing her with him as he stepped back against the carriage-house wall. As he halted, she stumbled. He caught her with one arm, sweeping her close so she was pressed to his long length from breasts to knees. They stood still, locked together in the sudden embrace.

He could feel the warmth of her skin under her

whalebone stays, the full curves of her breasts, the firmness of thighs padded by petticoats, catch the faint rose-petal perfume of her hair. Her lips were parted, her eyes like deep pools of ancient allure, ancient knowledge. He felt his mind drifting on a tide of sensual awareness, recognized the powerful interior struggle between inclination and will, hunger and principle.

"Cat," she whispered, her breath fanning his mouth.

"What?"

"Over there."

It was a gray tabby, weaving in and out among the gallery columns before stalking into the open space of the court. It paused to watch a lizard scurry to a hiding place under one of the breast-high clay ollas, water jars that lined the inside wall. After a moment, it moved again, coming toward where they stood. Sitting down no great distance away, it licked a front paw, then began to groom its head and ears.

"Of course. A cat." His voice sounded strangled in his throat. He shifted to allow space between them again, marginally grateful for the animal's appearance, which gave him a chance to gather his scattered thoughts. "As to the point you were making…"

"Yes?"

"The accommodation you require is to be relieved of unwanted purity?"

Her lashes flickered but she did not look away. "If you please."

Oh, he pleased. The urge to take her there in the dark was so strong that his body felt fevered and aching with it. The problem was that he was certain she would regret the act with every fiber of her being the instant it was done.

"Why me?" he asked to gain time and breathing room.

"You suggested it."

"To prove a point."

"But you did, nonetheless, and I agreed. The arrangement seemed destined because I would never have dared make such a request of a man otherwise."

"I should think not." The very idea made the hair rise on the back of his neck.

"Then you are perfect for the purpose, or so it seems, a man of experience with women instead of a mere youth, one feared by other men and therefore unlikely to be troubled by repercussions. Though known for your conquests, you avoid young women of good family so would be unlikely to continue beyond the initial contact, and being outside customary society, you would be ineligible as a husband."

"Ineligible."

"At least in the eyes of my father," she said in haste.

He smiled with a sardonic twist to his lips. "So he would prefer sending you to the convent rather than inviting me into the family."

"Are you insulted? I meant only that—"

"I know what you meant," he said shortly. He had swallowed greater slights before and doubtless would again. Why this one galled him so he wasn't sure, but thought it stemmed from her calm assumption that he would never have any claim on her.

"This is why you agreed to what I asked, because it suited your purpose?" Instinct had told him there was something behind her sudden change of heart. He should have listened.

"Is that so terrible?"

"Not at all. But it might have been more polite to let me know from the start."

"You had other things on your mind, I think, intentions of your own."

That much was certainly true, though he could not allow it to weigh with him now. "What if, when your virtue has been sacrificed, you discover that you are unfit for the convent after all?"

"Unfit?"

"By nature," he answered with precision. "To be a nun may require no passionate devotion to the church, but it must certainly be helpful if your desires are not aroused in other directions."

"I don't believe…" she began.

"Don't you?"

The words were a challenge couched in a whisper. Even as they were spoken, he reached to pull her into his arms. Then he set his mouth to hers.

She was a sweet intoxication, a fever in the blood. The tender surfaces of her lips enticed him, enthralled him. He tasted them, tracing their smooth and gentle outlines with his tongue while inhaling the scented essence of her. His brain felt on fire. His body strained against self-imposed restrictions. He wanted to drink her like a heady draft of priceless wine, to take her into himself and make her a part of him. He wanted to strip away the clothing that made a barrier between them, holding her in naked splendor.

Lost, he was lost in the spiraling sensations she

created inside him by lying quiescent in his arms, allowing him access, denying him nothing. Nothing except herself, nothing except mutual response, that clarion call of passion to passion.

It was not what he wanted or needed, not what he had intended at all. He drew back a little in the first move of a careful release that would allow them both the time to regain balance and reason.

Abruptly, as if on some decision made and accepted, she closed her hands on the lapels of his coat and caught him closer. With a sigh that feathered across the plane of his cheek, she angled her lips against his, letting him feel their heat.

His muscles clenched with the staggering onslaught of white-hot need. He gathered her more tightly against him. With one hand, he smoothed along the narrow span of her backbone to the tender nape of her neck. Tangling his fingers in the massed curls at the back of her head, he deepened the kiss, taking everything she offered and more, much more.

She tempted him, beckoned with her sweet, virginal desire. She was sensual magic, a pure element so necessary to life that his need was like that of a man dying of thirst. He swept into her mouth, absorbing the delicate textures while his mind spun into a vortex of pleasure. Her skin was so smooth under his fingers, the bones finely turned under her skin. The gentle curve of her breast swelled to his touch, pressed into his palm as if it belonged there. He brushed his fingers along the small frill that edged her bodice, and heard her swift-drawn breath, felt with rich, burgeoning joy the tight budding of her nipple.

Dear Lord, but he wanted her, wanted her innocent surrender as an antidote to past pain and a promise of future glory. He needed her belief, her trust and the benediction of her smile to make him feel whole. And he could have her. He could take her there in the surging ardor of the moment, while her will and newborn determination ran swift and hot, and she had no real idea of what she was doing or doing to him. He could take her against the carriage house wall in a froth of petticoats and a rich plundering of the flesh and the senses, and she would abet him.

She deserved better. She deserved vows and candlelight, music and a slow and gentle introduction to bliss in a soft bed if not a wedding bower. And he deserved a more fitting memory, if that was all he was to be allowed.

He was a fool. He had meant to prove she was unsuited for a convent by showing her the enticements of the flesh. He had not intended to hand her a weapon that might bring him to his knees, begging to be allowed to compromise her.

With a swift, wrenching movement, he let her go. Then he caught her hands, which had somehow crept around his neck, and brought them to his hot mouth. Her fingers closed on his. He pressed his lips to her taut knuckles again, and then set her from him. Turning away, he put one hand on the carriage-house wall, pressing hard enough to feel the grain of the wood and the ache in his shoulder while he fought for reason and control over the hot beat of his heart.

"Why? Why did you stop?"

Her voice blended with the whisper of the leaves in the oak above him, affecting him like a caress. His voice was harsh in response to the exquisite pain of it as he answered. "Because I can't."

"I offended you, displeased you in some way?"

"Dear God, no. It's just…a matter of principle."

"Principle." Her voice was flat.

If he looked at her, he might well weaken. He stared blindly at his hand on the wall. "To cause that kind of harm, to change your life, your future, would be worse than unscrupulous. It would be criminal."

"Even if I wish it?"

"Even so."

She was quiet for long seconds while the breeze rustled around them, sounding like quiet laughter among the banana plants near the fountain. "Permit me to understand you," she said, moving a step closer in a silken slither of skirts. "If I had not told you of my intentions, if I had simply kept to our bargain while leaving you to believe that I would go from your arms to those of the count, then you could have compromised me without a qualm?"

"Something like that."

"But would you have done it?"

It was an excellent question. He wished he knew the answer. "Possibly."

"What is the difference, then? No, don't tell me. Honor, it's always a question of honor."

He turned finally to look at her as the angry despair in her voice reached him. "Is that so difficult to accept?"

"It's the perfect excuse, isn't it? The unanswerable reply to anything and everything that you don't wish to explain. But tell me this, if you were uncertain that you meant to hold me to our bargain, why then did you spare Denys? Why did you come to my bed-chamber that first night at all?"

"Why not? You are a lovely woman."

"Meaning that you were toying with me out of boredom? Maybe you thought I longed for the excite-ment of a lover rumored to be the most dangerous man in New Orleans? Or perhaps you were simply curious to see if such an innocent would shrink from the final surrender?"

"None of those things." She had effectively killed his ardor. The problem now was repressing his grow-ing annoyance.

"No, it wouldn't be, would it? Shall I tell you what I believe? I think you had no intention of harming Denys beyond a superficial wound because he was never your target. You hold the count in disfavor and would like to face him sword in hand, but he refuses to condescend so far. My part in this affair is minor, and only because of the count's request for my hand. If you had any designs at all on me, it was merely for—"

"For what?" he asked, pushing away from the tree and moving toward her with menace in every slow stride. "You think I don't want you? You think I would risk so much for any trembling virgin that caught that petty nobleman's eye? Can you actually have so little conceit that you think only revenge brought me to your bedchamber?"

Her eyes widened a fraction and she took a step backward. "*Monsieur*, wait. Rio…"

"God in heaven," he breathed, matching the

words to his slow stalking. "I would like to take you away somewhere, now, this minute, where we could close out the world and be alone. I'd love to take the pins from your hair, unfasten the buttons of your gown one by one, and take away your petticoats and chemise like stripping the petals from the heart of a rose. I would hold you, taste every inch of your skin, feel your heart beat only for me as I teach you about love and desire, freedom and possession. And I would do all these things with the utmost pleasure and regardless of the consequences, except for…"

"Honor." That completing word was breathless as she came up against the wall of the house.

"Yes, eternally damned and inescapable honor." He placed his left hand against the wall beside her head as he leaned over her, inhaling her sweet scent, speaking the hot words that boiled up from inside him against the cool, smooth skin of her cheek. At the same time, he pressed a knee between her thighs, opening them even as he spread his right hand over her rib cage and smoothed his palm upward until her breast and her heart beneath it were trapped under the heat of his hand.

He took her mouth then, thrusting inside in a single hot glide, giving her a taste of his power and surging desire, a minute sample of the tumult that he could make for them both. It was a tempered assault based on virulent need, frustration and sympathy, one a part of him watched in bleak condemnation. But it was not without purpose or recognition of its dangers. Nor was it without self-hatred.

Wrenching free once more, he stepped back, well away from temptation, before sketching a stiff bow.

"Yes," he said, "for honor. And you are fortunate at this moment that I have a little, a very little, of that commodity left to me."

Turning, he walked away with swift purpose. He crossed the courtyard with no attempt whatever at concealment, no thought of anything until he was outside in the street once more. Only sheer, blind luck prevented his discovery.

Turning homeward, he swore at himself and his lack of control, cursed the count and Monsieur Vallier and all the Fates and furies that had dogged his steps since the night he met Mademoiselle Celina Vallier. She was acute, far too much so for his comfort. She saw what no one else had noticed, suspected the vengeance that drove him. He had tried to stop that accusation, to obliterate the line of reasoning that had led to it. How successful he might have been, he could not tell, and he could not afford to stay to discover it.

All his plotting and cunning, and it had come to this, an absurd conundrum that defied solution. If he completed his bargain with Celina Vallier, taking her maidenhead and revealing possibilities for bliss that she was unlikely to find in the count's bed, then she would refuse to marry. If he failed to take her, then she would marry but there would be no personal revenge for him against the count. And between the two choices lay a growing conviction that he could not win, either way.

No matter what he did or did not do, she would remain forever beyond his reach.

9

"Are you mad?"

That question was hurled at Rio from out of the dark. He whirled, dropping into an instinctive swordsman's crouch. His hands were empty. He had left his sword cane behind as an impediment to stealth when he set out for the Vallier town house.

An instant later, he relaxed and straightened to his full height as Caid emerged from the shadows of a tall doorway. His friend and colleague stepped into the dim and flickering light from the corner street-lamp and sauntered toward him.

"I could ask the same of you," Rio said. "You might be a dead man if I'd been armed."

"I'd have been more careful if I had not noticed that you were weaponless. And it's a toss-up which is more downright stupid, walking the streets that way or paying midnight visits to a belle of the *haut ton*."

"Your concern touches me deeply."

"Don't let it go to your head," Caid recommended without noticeable humor. "It's not your welfare I'm worried about. Keep up this game, or whatever it may be with the Vallier girl, and you're going to give *maîtres d'armes* a bad name that we can ill afford."

"It's fear of losing salon members that troubles you. I should have known."

"That, and having the place next door to me come up for lease before time."

"Meaning?"

"That you are going to get yourself killed over this affair, and then I'll have to put up with some ass like Broyard poaching my clients and leaving his sour wine barrels stacked outside my door."

"You can handle it."

"I'd rather the devil I know. Speaking of which, just what the hell were you about here?"

Rio gave him a straight look. "Minding my business?"

"Just so, as is your right," Caid said stiffly. "But don't say I didn't warn you."

"No, you've done that twice now, if memory serves. My question," Rio added in tones freighted with irritation in spite of being both quiet and softly pleasant, "is what you were doing loitering outside this particular town house?"

"Waiting for you, since I saw Olivier when he emerged just now and he said you were still inside."

Rio sighed. "I suppose you had a reason?"

"You can be sure of it. I have better ways to spend my time than kicking my heels while you play Don Juan."

"Tell me about it over an absinthe," Rio said abruptly. "I think I need it."

The nerve-tingling anise smell of the popular drink permeated Absinthe House, greeting them at the bar's tall door and dragging them inside by the nose. Only a few candles stuck in old wine bottles lit the place. Custom was slim. One or two men stood at the long polished bar and an elderly gentleman near the door peered blearily at a book through a pince-nez. Rio and Caid headed for a back table. Moments later, they were seated with glasses of the cloudy, greenish liquid for which the bar was named sitting in front of them.

The first sip was always a test of resolve as it grabbed the back of the throat and threatened to dissolve a man's stomach. Past that point, it went down dangerously easy. More than a few men in the Vieux Carré were drooling slaves to its flavor and effect.

"So?" Rio asked as he set his glass back on the table.

Caid leaned back in his chair while studying the swirling liquid he still held. "Rumor is that our friend the count has been making discreet inquiries among the brethren of the sword."

"Indeed?"

"He'd like someone to slit your gullet."

"Bloodthirsty of him."

"For a price, of course."

"A high one, let us hope. Has anyone in particular expressed interest in this work?"

"Broyard may have been the first, at a guess. Then the Italian La Roche, this Nicholas Pasquale, was seen in conversation with him. There could be others."

Rio gave a short nod. It made sense, more than he liked to think. A lethal duel was an excellent way to dispose of an enemy, particularly if the opponent was a man of Pasquale's mercurial temperament and consummate skill. That the count would descend to it was not surprising.

"I frighten him, you think?"

"I think," Caid said in laconic agreement. "Though Broyard's annoying Mademoiselle Vallier in order to provoke you has certain implications."

"Meaning he is aware of my interest in that quarter?"

"You have an interest? I mean beyond the obvious."

Rio made no answer, but only returned his friend's gaze with unsmiling intentness.

Caid looked away first. "Yes, well." He took a pensive sip of his drink. "But how was he to know?"

It was a good question, Rio thought. His acquaintance with the lady was slight, at least to public knowledge and up until the subscription ball of the night before. "He couldn't unless he, or more likely the count, has set someone to watch my movements."

"Damn cheek. But for what reason?"

"Count de Lérida may look like a buffoon, but it would be a mistake to take him for one. No doubt he was suspicious of my interest in his marriage plans."

"For which he can hardly be blamed, though his methods of looking into it may leave something to be desired."

Caid's voice held a shadow of inquiry as he spoke. Still, holding his own counsel was a habit Rio was reluctant to break. "You wonder about my meddling in the affair? Let us say the happiness of the count, conjugal or otherwise, is not an object with me. In fact, I pity any female unlucky enough to attract his notice."

"Because of his bad luck with wives?"

"Among other things."

"You knew one of them, perhaps?"

"As it happens." The interest had been mild and not especially pertinent, but the lady had not deserved the unending abuse that had caused her to take her life.

Caid watched him from across the table, his eyes measuring. "But that isn't all."

It was a monumental understatement, Rio thought, though he kept his voice even as he replied, "Let us say there is enmity between us and leave it at that."

"As you prefer. I only wanted to drop a word in your ear. It seems that if you are the count's enemy, he returns the favor in kind."

"A thousand thanks for the warning," Rio said. "I'll remember it."

Caid regarded him for long moments without speaking. Then he pushed his half-empty glass to one side. "I don't know what you're doing, my friend, but I have a suggestion."

"And that would be?"

"Watch your back."

They spoke of other things, the progress of President Harrison who had been chosen as the Whig party presidential candidate, also the British campaign in China and its effect on the opium trade. However, their most intense discussion was reserved for conditions in France where the worst flood in 250 years had inundated 20,000 acres, and the body of Napoleon had been returned at last from St. Helena for reburial under the chapel dome of the Hôtel des

Invalides. This last inevitably segued into the attempted military coup of Prince Louis Napoleon earlier in the year. The great Napoleon's nephew had hoped to use the current nostalgia for the glories of Bonapartist imperialism to make a bid for the throne. Why he had failed and whether he could ever succeed, even if he could escape his present prison in the fortress at Ham, occupied them until their glasses were empty.

Still, even as they talked and later strolled homeward toward the Passage, Rio could not stop turning over in his mind the problem of Celina and her betrothal to the count. What was he going to do? Should he try again to force the count to the field of honor, or bow out, leaving New Orleans before he caused more damage than he had already? Did the fire of his revenge still burn hot, or could he be content to allow the mills of the gods to grind away, hoping the count's mistakes would catch up with him? Yes, and was it concern for Celina's welfare that moved him, or only a growing reluctance to risk his life for an oath sworn so long ago that he had lost all resemblance to the boy who had whispered it into the noisome darkness of a ship's hold?

The answers eluded him. And when morning sunlight woke him to a new day in which he could go from his bed to the fencing strip without a detour to The Oaks, he thought he had to have been either drunk or blue-deviled to even consider the questions.

The salon was packed by midmorning. So many men crowded into it that the French doors were flung open for air and so they could spill out onto the bal-

cony. Rio was kept busy welcoming new arrivals and
seeing that they had their choice of wine or *bière* Creole, also in pointing out errors of form and technique
to those shuffling back and forth on the strips, or
taking up a foil or épée to illustrate a point or give
private instruction. He was allowed ample space as
he moved from room to room, and none showed the
slightest inclination to resent anything he said or did.
The most frequent comment he heard was congratu-
lations for his prodigious feat of defeating six opponents in four days. Rio passed these off but was
pleased enough to hear them for what they represented. It seemed the original incident was behind
him, and if no one quite understood his leniency toward Denys Vallier, they at least had no doubt of his
willingness to impale any number of other men on
his steel.

Celina's brother arrived at midmorning. Rio heard
the sudden quiet followed by a ripple of too loud
talk. He turned in time to see the young man pause
in the doorway with hot color rising to his hairline.
Uttering a polite request to be excused to the client
with whom he'd been talking, he moved to intercept
Vallier.

Olivier was before him, offering the young man a
claret cup. Denys declined with a shake of his head.
"Monsieur de Silva," he said, his expression earnest
as he made his bow. "If I might have a moment?"

"Certainly," Rio answered. "Remove your coat
and make ready, and I will be with you shortly."

"I don't want…that is, I didn't come for a fencing
lesson. I would like a word in private, if you can
please."

Rio didn't care for the seriousness in the young man's face. It seemed he might have congratulated himself too soon. "Privacy is in short supply here," he said with a twist of his lips. "Still. If you will follow me?"

He led the way downstairs and out the back where a small green area lay between the rear of the salon and the back wall of a house that faced on the rue Chartres. It was nothing like the spacious courtyard of the Vallier town house, but had a wrought-iron chair under the thinning shade of a chinaberry tree that scattered narrow yellow leaves over the rank green grass.

Rio indicated the chair with a wave of his hand, while he put his back to the chinaberry and crossed his feet at the ankles. "How may I be of service? Is anything wrong at home?"

"Nothing of moment. That is, not with me. I come to you about another person, another matter."

"And that is?"

"My sister, Celina."

Rio felt his chest tighten. That his visit of the night before had been discovered seemed a distinct possibility. "She is unwell? Something has happened with her?"

"No, no. It's only that I am concerned for her future."

"The sentiment does you credit, I'm sure," Rio said, studying Vallier's flushed features, which were set in such resolute lines that his lips had a blue tinge. "But how does it touch on me?"

"It's your part in what has befallen her that troubles me."

"I am at a loss," he began.

"Please, *monsieur*, let us have done with pretense. You have twice made her an object of your attention, thereby bringing her to public notice. That is not our way. The name of a gently bred female should be on people's lips only twice in her life, when she is wed and again when she leaves this world. Nothing else is acceptable. I must ask, then, what you intend toward her?"

"Intend?" Rio asked with irony. "I am well aware that furthering the acquaintance is out of the question."

"If you go on in the way you have been, if you continue to embroil her in your quarrels, you will surely damage her good name."

"You were glad enough to allow me to rescue her from Broyard."

"True," Denys said with his chin at a defiant angle. "I should have insisted on doing more than acting as your second. But that was before I realized how it could be construed, how it might be twisted to suggest…"

"To suggest what?" Rio pressed.

"Some clandestine connection between you and Celina. It is being used as a weapon by the man who wishes to marry her, used to put forward the wedding to a date less than a week away."

Rio crossed his arms over his chest. Denys must be allowed to bring out Celina's reluctance to accept the match. Rio could admit no prior knowledge of it. "She should be safe enough from scandal then. Please present my felicitations."

"I'm not so sure felicitations are in order."

"Meaning?"

"I dined with my father last night. He and my sister's betrothed have been together much of late. Over the pears and Camembert he spoke of a proposition broached by the count, one touching on an agreement with the envoy from Mexico. Since then, I've heard more of it."

Rio's attention sharpened. "What sort of an agreement?"

"The count feels that my father, by virtue of long residence and widespread family ties, should have access to the minds and inclinations of men of influence in the city. The count may move in these same circles but does not, let us say, have a cordial personality. My father is… is quite the opposite when matters proceed according to his desires."

It was plain that Denys had difficulty overcoming family loyalty enough to talk about his father. It was an excellent quality in a son, but not what Rio required at the moment. "The count was interested in these opinions of your father's friends?"

"Very much so," Denys said with a grateful smile. "He offered to divide with my father the money that he would be paid for gathering them."

The count was being paid to persuade others to look favorably on Mexican interests. Now that was interesting information. "Particularly as this influence pertains to the vast territory west of the Sabine River?"

"The sums mentioned were not small."

They wouldn't be if they were designed to entice the count. Rio summoned a careless air. "Reprehensible, I agree, but not criminal."

"Perhaps not, though it's hardly in the interest of the United States. Nor can it be good for Louisiana if Mexico overruns the new Texas Republic and we wind up with its army camped on our border."

"General Santa Ana would hardly dare invade U.S. territory."

"Which is why Texas must become a state."

"And the slavery issue?"

"An emotional question that keeps running into the fair and practical need to reimburse those who have all they have amassed in a lifetime of effort tied up in this human commodity. Certainly it's not something politicians thousands of miles away should be allowed to decide for the citizens of a sovereign country such as Texas. There is little to be gained by the debate then, and much to be lost."

"Your father agrees with this stand?"

"He has in the past, but I fear he may take a different view now. Favoring Mexican pretensions could recoup the large sums lost while gambling in the count's company."

"I see the problem," Rio said. "But it doesn't tell me where I come into it."

"That is because I don't know. It's what I came here to find out."

"Forgive me, but…"

"I beg you will credit me with a little sense. Your actions in recent days suggest one of two things—you either have a grudge against the count or you are enamored of my sister. My care is not for your feelings—these are your affair. What I would like to know is if you have plans to end my sister's betrothal?"

Rio felt as if he had been punched in the stomach. Denys, being one of only three people who had heard the slighting remark spoken about Celina, was in a unique position to guess at his aims; still it was disturbing to have them spoken aloud. On the other hand, it was possible that Denys had not come solely because of his misgivings.

"You are reluctant to welcome the count into your family?"

"Celina is equally opposed."

"I can take it, however, that you are not her emissary?"

"*Mon Dieu*, no!" Denys frowned and then gave a quick shake of his head. "She would never essay such a thing."

The brother refused to expose his sister's foibles to a stranger, Rio thought with approval, though he might suspect her of more daring than he admitted. "Even when it bears greatly on her future?"

"Even so. She may protest, in fact has done so, but will comply with my father's wishes in the end."

"She has made her opposition clear to her father, then, as well as to you?"

"And to the count. He was not discouraged. In fact…"

"Yes?" Rio's voice held a clipped demand as Denys came to a halt with a troubled look on his face.

"He insisted on speaking to her alone. She did not care for his method of persuasion."

"He laid hands on her?"

"With little concern for her resistance, apparently."

Celina had not mentioned that portion of the interview. Rio felt a leaden sensation invade his chest as he realized that he had used much the same tactics as the count. "It's safe to say, then, that she won't be shattered if the count should withdraw his offer?"

"Withdraw?" Denys looked at him as if he had grown horns. "That must make it appear that he has discovered some fault that would render her unsuitable as a wife. He must not be able to say he is withdrawing."

Rio lifted an ironic brow. "In other words, he should be unable to speak? In fact, you want him dead?"

"No such thing! I am not asking you to become an assassin."

"You relieve my mind. But let's have it in plain language. What is it you're asking?"

Denys turned away, taking a few hasty steps before he turned back again. "I wish him to cease pressing to marry Celina. He must accept her refusal and go away, preferably back to Spain. Surely there is some pressure that can be brought to bear, some threat that will make this nobleman see reason?"

"You want me to challenge him, then, or at least make him think he may be required to meet me."

"Something of the sort." Denys looked away an instant while he drew a deep breath, then let it out in a rush. "I apologize. I had not thought how it must sound when put into plain words, had not considered the risk to you."

"I have not refused," Rio said softly.

"No, but I can see that I was wrong to come to you. This is not your affair. I can't imagine why I felt so strongly that you could best—" he stopped himself.

"But don't consider it another moment. Forget it completely, if you please."

Denys Vallier turned toward the salon's rear entrance, his slim back stiff under his dark frock coat with its narrow waist and fashionably full length. Rio allowed him to take two long steps before he spoke. "What are you going to do?"

"Please don't concern yourself. This is a family matter. I must settle it without outside aid."

Rio was ready to grant him that concession but didn't care for the necessity. Celina's brother was levelheaded, intelligent, and felt exactly as he should on the things that mattered, but was still young. That meant he was proud, high-tempered and far too ready to pick up the gauntlet in defense of his honor. More than that, Celina loved him. If he were to die while trying to make the world right for her, she might never recover.

"Should you come upon a situation you can't handle, feel free to call on me," he said to the young man's back.

Denys Vallier made no reply, nor did he stop walking.

Rio did not move, but stood in frowning consideration for long moments. He tore a twig from the chinaberry and stood stripping off the leaves, dropping them on the toes of his soft leather boots. He felt as if he had failed Denys, yet what could he have done differently? To give up his own plans and purpose was more than anyone should ask.

Wasn't it?

Olivier was in the storeroom of the lower floor that served as a raised basement when Rio finally ran him to ground. He heard the manservant humming to himself and followed the sound into the area kept as a wine cellar. Wearing a leather apron over his white shirt and dark trousers, Olivier was decanting wine from a keg resting on wooden supports into a thick glass bottle. Two corked bottles sat on the table beside him while nine others waited to be filled.

"You sound exceptionally happy," Rio said as he stepped inside.

Olivier turned his head, surprise on his cinnamon features. "*Monsieur?* You had need of me?"

"In a manner of speaking. The Valliers' maid—this affair between the two of you still progresses?"

Olivier smiled a little before turning back to his task. "With Suzette, yes. You don't object, *monsieur?*"

"Not at all, if she is the reason that you sing." He paused, aware suddenly of the rich, grape-flower scent of the claret as it rose around them, blending with the smells of dust and mice. "But I wonder…does she ever speak of her mistress?"

"At times."

"Would one of those times be recent, and concerned with her betrothal?"

Olivier glanced up at him, then back down at what he was doing as he opened the keg's spigot wider so the wine gurgled into the bottle of thick green glass. "As it happens. You wish to know about it?"

"I do if it touches on the count's conduct toward her and how she felt about it."

"She was upset, as any lady would be, or so Suzette said. I gathered that he laid hands on her, attempted a kiss and other intimacies. There were bruises and one of her sleeves was torn."

Rage swept over Rio like a hot wind. It took his breath with its fury, and turned his expression into such a black scowl that he was glad of the relative darkness of the storeroom, illuminated only by a high window and light from the open doorway. His voice sliced like a rapier when he could speak.

"Attempted?"

"She was like a wild cat, I understand. The count will regret his impetuosity every time his valet is forced to shave around the scratches. Her aunt, who serves as her duenna, completed the rescue."

"Where in hell was the duenna before then?"

"Occupied elsewhere while *mademoiselle* was closeted with her father and her future fiancé. Monsieur Vallier left her alone with the count for a few minutes, since he had signed the nuptial agreement just moments before. It was a mistake."

"Apparently." Rio had seen Celina afterward. He knew she was all right. Still, the need to see her again, now, this instant, was so strong that it was all he could do not to pick up his sword and storm the Vallier town house. "Mademoiselle Vallier will be away from home this evening, I suppose?"

"So I believe," Olivier said in carefully neutral tones. "I could discover where she goes if you wish it."

"I wish it," Rio answered. As Olivier topped off the bottle he was filling, corked it and reached for another, Rio repeated, "I wish it now."

Olivier lifted a brow. Then his mouth tilted in a grin and he began to remove his apron.

Rio watched the other man for brief seconds while his thoughts revolved in a steady circle, then stopped at the inevitable conclusion. "And while you are out," he said deliberately, "there are other things that require to be done."

10

It had not been the most enjoyable evening of the season for Celina. She had spent much of it sitting alone. Her aunt excused herself soon after they arrived, going to speak to an elderly friend. That lady was a relative of the Baroness de Pontalba, a New Orleans woman, heiress to the wealthy old Spaniard Don Almonester y Roxas, who had been wed at fifteen to the son of the Baron de Pontalba. She had sailed away to France and a miserable married life filled with disputes with her in-laws over her dowry. Just five years before, she had been shot and wounded by her father-in-law who then turned the weapon on himself. More recently, she had gained the legal separation of her assets from those of her husband, and it was said that she was returning to New Orleans to begin improvements to inherited property that included run-down rental houses on either side of the Place d'Armes. Naturally, Tante Marie Rose wished to learn more.

She had left Celina sitting next to Marthe Desiard whom she had known all her life, supposing that she would be well occupied for at least a quarter of an hour. The two of them were somewhat isolated since the other young women who had been sitting nearby had drifted away one by one.

Marthe seemed ill at ease in her presence, sending curious glances her way when she thought Celina wasn't looking. They had talked a bit about the promised entertainment, a program of prestidigitation by the great magus, Monsieur Adriant, who was currently appearing at Bank's Arcade. He was to saw a woman in two, or so their hostess had said. Celina was less than enthralled since she was certain there was a trick to it, but the other girl shivered in delicious horror at the idea. Afterward, there would be billiards and cards, also dancing for the younger set to an ensemble of French horn, violin and pianoforte, with supper to follow.

Finally Marthe leaned closer, touching Celina's arm as she whispered at her ear. "I am dying of curiosity, *ma chère*, so you must tell me. Is it true that the infamous Silver Shadow has fought a dozen duels in your honor?"

"Certainly not!"

"A half dozen, then? I'm sure it must be a prodigious number, for Maman says it is scandalous and that you have surely done something most outrageous to attract his notice."

"I assure you—"

"Please don't say there is nothing to it, for I think it the most romantic thing in the world! Just imagine, a man willing to face death for you, not once or twice but several times over. What passion, what fire! What is he like, this so formidable *maître d'armes?* Is he as handsome when near as he is at a distance? Come, *chère*, tell all!"

Celina could feel the heat in her face. Added to the embarrassment, however, was a definite reluctance to speak of Rio, as if that might be to share the man himself. "There is nothing to tell, I promise you. It was all a mistake."

"Yes, of course, and I suppose there's no truth to the rumor that the Spanish count has a *tendre* for you and has spoken to your papa? What excitement, and yet you keep it all to yourself. I think it is mean of you. Or else you know you are soon to be a *condesa* and so exalted that you will no longer acknowledge your old friends."

"No, truly," Celina protested. "I don't want to marry the count. I don't want to marry anyone."

"Because you are in love with the *maître d'armes* and know it can never be? Oh, *chère*, I see now the tragedy. He fights from despair, hoping to be killed and therefore stop the pain of knowing that you must marry another man, even the so-old count."

"That isn't it at all!"

"Then tell me what transpires between you."

"Nothing! Nothing transpires."

"But Denys fought him, then was his second and has since become his most valued client. Today they spoke alone for some time on a subject most serious."

"How do you know?"

The other girl shrugged. "My brother was at de Silva's salon and chanced to glance out the window to where the two stood in the garden. He said the Silver Shadow appeared very angry. It made my brother shudder in his boots."

"Angry with Denys?"

"So it appeared. You must ask him. Or perhaps you have no need since you should know what might be a sore subject between them, yes?"

"No." Frowning preoccupation made her answer short, though she saw an instant later that this had been mistaken for rudeness.

"Very well, keep your secrets then, Celina Vallier, for what comfort they may be to you."

Marthe rose and left her with a miffed tilt to her nose. Only a few steps away, she met another friend and the two of them put their heads together, talking rapidly behind their hands.

No one else approached her, and during the dancing after the great magus performed, it was some time before Celina took the floor. Then it was only with Hippolyte Ducolet, the special friend of her brother.

"Have you seen Denys?" she asked her partner. "Is he at the card tables, perhaps, or smoking in the courtyard?"

"I couldn't say, Mademoiselle Celina. Is he even here?"

"He was supposed to be, but went out earlier in the day and had not returned when my aunt and I left the house this evening. My father saw us here, but had another engagement. I thought Denys might arrive in time to escort us home again."

"He will show up, I have no doubt. If not, I volunteer most gladly to do the honors." Hippolyte stumbled a little as he almost trod on her toe. He was an uninspired dancer and talking interfered with his mental counting for the waltz. Added to that, he was not a natural gallant.

"That's very kind, but I'm sure it won't be necessary. Denys will not fail, I know. If you should come upon him, please tell him I'm ready to go home now. I have the headache."

"But of course, *mademoiselle*. Perhaps your bad head is because of the weather. It's turning colder, don't you think?"

"Perhaps." It was an attempt to redirect the conversation, she knew, though servants were busy at the windows, closing out the too-cool breath of a sweeping north wind. After a moment, she said, "Monsieur Hippolyte?"

He lifted a brow inquiringly as he smiled at her, his eyes almost on the level of her own.

For an instant, Celina allowed herself to be annoyed at the formality that existed between men and women. She had known Hippolyte for years. They had played together as children, yet to use their given names was not done. The purpose of such a custom was to maintain distance, preventing the familiarity that might interfere with the plans of their parents. Still, it made great difficulty out of asking a simple question. "Tell me, if you please," she said finally. "Are people talking about me?"

"Of a certainty. You have snared the catch of the season. Why would they not?"

"Is that all?"

"Isn't it enough?"

He was being polite, she thought. "Some seem to think that I have an involvement with Monsieur de Silva."

He followed her gaze to where Marthe danced with a young man in the garb of a Romantic whom they both knew to be her cousin. "That one? Pay no attention. She's only jealous because her future is so dull, you know."

Celina did know, though she'd almost forgotten. Marthe had been betrothed in her cradle to the son of a friend of her father's, a country gentleman with a plantation on the Red River. Not precisely a great beau, he was said to greatly prefer hunting snipe and deer and running his fox hounds to journeying to New Orleans during the *saison de visites*. The wedding was planned for late spring, after Easter that was in mid-April this year.

Celina suspected Hippolyte of merely being polite. It seemed best to allow it. She spoke of other things, keeping up a light flow of conversation until the music ended and she was returned to her aunt.

Afterward she was left again to make tapestry, as the saying went, remaining in her chair among the chaperones. When Denys did not appear in a reasonable time, she suggested to her aunt that they go home early. She and Tante Marie Rose walked the short distance to the town house while bundled up against the increasing north wind and under Hippolyte's nonchalant protection. That gentleman bowed and wished them good-night at the foot of the entrance stairs before returning to the soiree. He also promised to inform Denys, if he saw him, that his escort was no longer required.

Suzette had not been needed for such a quiet evening so had stayed at home. She appeared to have fallen asleep while waiting for Celina to return. She looked so peaceful that Celina was loath to wake her, but the maid roused anyway as the bedchamber door clicked shut.

"Did you have a nice time?" she asked, stretching and giving herself a small shake before coming fully alert.

"In truth, it was rather dull," Celina answered as she tossed her shawl aside and began to remove her gloves.

"Was no one special there?"

"No one." The words were clipped.

Suzette pursed her lips. Moving forward, she turned Celina and began working on the buttons that fastened up the back of her peach silk gown. "Something has upset you. Tell me what it might be."

Celina complied. It was a relief to speak of it to someone who understood and could also be trusted not to spread the story.

"Pay no attention to such gossip, Mam'zelle," Suzette said when she had finished. "It will mean less than nothing when you are wed and far away from here."

"I would prefer to remain in New Orleans and be at least somewhat respectable."

"Something you should have considered before involving Monsieur de Silva."

"I know very well that I have only myself to blame that it turned out badly."

"Monsieur Denys is alive because of it, even so."

"Is he? I think perhaps he would have been anyway."

"You cannot know that." Suzette lifted the gown off over her mistress's head and put it away in the armoire, then took Celina's nightgown and wrapper from their hook and slung them over her shoulder. Returning, she began to work on the tapes of Celina's petticoats and her corset strings.

"Perhaps not," she said, and then went on to tell her of Denys's failure to appear that evening. "It isn't like him," she said as she came to an end. "Something is wrong."

"Don't fret over it, Mam'zelle, or you will really give yourself a headache." Suzette took away her petticoats and helped her don the nightgown. "That is, unless your bad head was not an excuse. Does it hurt? Shall I rub your temples with cologne or make you a tisane?"

"No, no. I'm fine. I'll just take down my hair and brush it myself."

"I could…"

"I'll take care of it, really. You've done enough. To bed with you, I mean it."

It was a relief when the door closed behind the maid. As much as she appreciated everything Suzette did, knew how lucky she was to have her, there were times when she wanted nothing more than to be alone. This was one of those occasions. She needed to think, even if her mind traveled the same well-worn pathways.

With the soft lawn of her nightgown and wrapper swirling around her feet, she moved to her dressing table. Removing the pins from her hair, she pulled the long swath over her shoulder, then she picked up her hairbrush. She ran the brush over the length of her tresses, smoothing tangles while she turned to the French door. Suzette had not closed the shutters. Beyond the glass, the gaslight of the corner street-lamp wavered as its heavy square globe was infil-trated by the north wind. A roll of hay, dropped from some wagon or feed bag, tumbled down the street along with a man's dusty top hat. A low moaning sounded around the eaves, disturbing a roosting pigeon so it let out a sleepy protest. Shivering a little, Celina opened the door, then reached for the shutter to close out the noise and chill draft.

"Permit me."

She gasped and whirled even as Rio reached above her head and closed the heavy shutters and the door. "How did you... I mean, when..." she stammered.

"The usual way," he answered with a crooked smile. "Suzette was asleep when I slipped in, and I saw no reason to wake her, or alarm her if it came to it. I waited there."

She glanced in the direction of his nod, toward the Watteau screen that marked off the corner opposite her dressing table. It concealed the usual chamber pot and the hat-shaped tub she had used earlier for bathing. "Alarming me being a matter of no concern?"

"It was, yes, but seemed unavoidable."

The amusement that layered his deep voice did odd things to her heartbeat. Or perhaps it was his powerful masculine presence, his height and breadth so close beside her and the fresh outdoor scent that clung to the cloak that hung from his shoulders. He really was as beautiful to look at close up as from a distance, just as Marthe had suggested. His hair grew in shining black waves over his head, his brows were thick and slightly arching, and his eyes held such pure silver glints that they seemed like polished mirrors in which she should be able to see herself, or see into his soul. Even the thin line of the scar down his face did not detract, but only added to his dangerous air.

The silence between them was lengthening. This would not do. Grasping at her scattered thoughts and the echoes of the words he'd spoken, she inquired, "I assume you put yourself to the trouble of coming here for a reason?"

"Probably, though I seem to have forgotten what it might be." He took the hairbrush from her lax grasp, then lifted a silken tress and began to brush it. His touch was gentle, his focus on his task, where the tendency of the shining filaments to twine around his hand seemed to fascinate him.

"We have established that our bargain is impossible to keep," she said, her voice not quite steady. "What else is there?"

"A question, now that you put me in mind of it." His expression did not change, nor did his voice as he continued. "Why is it that you failed to tell me the count had put hands on you?"

She jerked away a little so that her hair stretched taut between them. He did not seem to notice, nor did he release her. After a moment, she said, "When last we met, you were at pains to impress upon me all the reasons why there should be no contact between us. How was I to know you would be interested?"

"In such a telling threat? I'd have expected you to use it for your own sake."

"As an illustration of my fate should you fail me, I suppose. But that was always obvious, with or without the church's blessing."

"You accept it, then?"

"I abhor it," she said distinctly. "For what good it may do me."

"But you don't want me to rid you of the threat in the most final way possible."

"By killing the count? I've told you what I think of that solution." She waited, hardly daring to believe that his purpose in coming to her again now might now march with her need.

He spread the hair he held over her breast, following along its length with the glide of the hairbrush. "So the count resorted to a violent wooing. I should not have expected it of him, but I suppose your reluctance piqued his vanity."

"His consequence, rather. I was to be stunned into compliance by my good fortune in having such an exalted personage make advances. That I resisted amazed him as much as it annoyed him."

"And yet," he said with his gaze on the shimmering, gold-colored filaments of hair that sprang from under the brush, "you did not resist me."

"That was different."

"My methods were much the same. For that, I owe you an apology."

A frown drew her brows together. "They were not at all the same."

"Not in intent, perhaps, but in execution." Reaching for her wrist, he pushed back the sleeve of her wrapper, exposing the purple splotches of bruising. He smoothed over them with a gentle thumb, then bent his head and pressed his lips to the discolored skin.

Her pulse leaped into a frantic beat. She wondered if he could feel it against his mouth. The night was cool and she had no fire in the grate beneath its mantel, but she was suddenly warm from her head to her toes. She swallowed with difficulty as she sought words.

"You made your point, nonetheless."

"Meaning?" He lifted his head to meet her eyes, though he did not release her arm.

"The purpose, if I remember correctly, was to illustrate my unsuitability for a nun's existence. The demonstration was convincing."

His silver-gray eyes held a tarnishlike darkness, hiding mysterious currents of thought. "You are now resigned to marriage?"

"I didn't say that. I merely accept that the convent holds no refuge for me."

"Then you choose to be a spinster."

She gave him a strained smile. "I have no vocation for that position, either, it seems. In fact, if my response to your lesson is any indication, I should become a courtesan."

"A courtesan." His face and voice were both devoid of expression.

"Not in New Orleans, of course. I'd thought of Paris. There are men of wealth there who can afford to keep me. If I must be separated from my family and friends while going to some man's bed, then I should at least be free to choose the man."

"Is that a threat?" he asked in deadly softness.

"Now why would you think so? My life is my own and nothing to do with you since you repudiated our bargain."

"I agreed to nothing," he said in hard tones. "There was no bargain."

She was unperturbed, at least on the outside. "It was implied. Nevertheless, I have accepted your decision and must adjust my plans accordingly. That is the end of it."

"And when do you leave for Paris?"

"Soon, I think, before my freedom can be curtailed as a persuasion to accept the count."

"It will take money, both to travel and to live until you find a protector."

"Yes," she said pensively. "Then there is the matter of insuring that no one comes after me to drag me back. I have to wonder if there may not be merit in my first solution, that of first giving myself to a successful *maître d'armes*. I should not like to live as a creature of depravity among those I know, but beginning that way seems expedient."

"By creating a scandal, you mean." His voice was a low rasp in his throat, and his eyes suddenly carried molten heat.

"That seems near to accomplishment, though it was not my intention. Since it has, then..."

"Then you may as well continue."

"As you say."

"Blackmail."

The look she gave him was clear yet a little surprised. "There are other *maîtres d'armes* in the Passage de la Bourse."

A sound left him like the stifled grunt upon receiving a blow. He released her wrist, turned from her and moved away a few paces. Frowning at the white-plastered wall with its carved wood crucifix, he asked, "You've made your choice, then?"

"A second choice, you mean? Not as yet."

He was silent for long seconds. Then he turned to face her. "You don't know what you are suggesting. The life you speak of in such easy terms is brutish and unsafe. Marriage to the count, as bad as it might be, would be infinitely better."

"You fear I shall become a woman of the street? It's unlikely, you know. My mother was an heiress, the only child of a doting father who was quite elderly when she was born. He taught her to manage his affairs before he died, a task she did not relinquish when she married. My father was content to have it so as he has no head for business, and I have handled the details of property purchases and sales, rentals and leases, suits for debts, and so on since she left us. In truth, much of it is my inheritance. I may have need of a protector for a short while, you see, but not for always."

"Your father may object to releasing what's yours."

"Then I shall find redress in the courts as the Baroness de Pontalba has done."

"You are adamant, then? Nothing will induce you to accept this Spanish marriage?"

"I would rather die."

Celina meant every syllable. She had been too nearly independent for too long to easily accept the physical servitude and loss of free will. More than that, she had caught a glimpse of something more, a hint of mental and physical closeness that had nothing to do with conjugal rights and demands, crass domination by sheer bulk and weight or embarrassing fumbling and pain in the dark. She wanted that with the heartfelt yearning of overextended hope. She would settle for nothing less.

"And what if, when you have prevailed upon one of my kind to serve you as you wish, the gentleman decides that he prefers to marry you himself?"

"You mean…" she began, then stopped. Of course he did not refer to himself; it wasn't possible.

"Heiresses have been forced into marriage before, compliant or not, on being discovered in bed with a man," he said when she failed to complete the thought. "Or they have been carried off and kept under lock and key until they are ready to speak their vows."

"What an opinion you have of your fellow swordsmen."

"Of my fellow men, rather, where money and a beautiful woman are concerned. You would be wise to trust none of them, not even me if by chance I should agree to this mad scheme of yours."

She blinked a little and moistened her lips with her tongue before she spoke. "Am I to assume that you might, after all?"

Outside the wind moaned and a street sign creaked in steady rhythm as it swung on its chains while a loose shutter banged in the distance. The bed candle burning on a side table fluttered in a stray draft so the flame popped on its wick.

"If I did, then what?" Rio asked finally as he crossed his arms over his chest. "Would you remain here under your father's roof, assuming he was able to send the count packing, or would you still sail for France? Would you opt for the position of maiden aunt or leave everything and everyone behind?"

"If my father could be brought to break off nego-tiations quietly and keep the details secret so Denys would not feel compelled to challenge you, then I would gladly remain here. To live as a spinster until I find someone with whom I can live otherwise is all I've ever asked."

"You would trust me in your bed and out of it? You will wager your future that I won't demand to share it and whatever wealth you may possess?"

"If you were not trustworthy," she said carefully, "then this conversation would not be taking place. If you meant to tie me to you by nefarious means, then it would have been done days ago and without advance warning."

"Logical," he said as he took a swift step toward her, then bent to thrust one arm behind her knees and the other across her back, sweeping her up into his arms. "But that doesn't make it correct."

"Monsieur!" The move was so unexpected, so dizzying, that she almost forgot to keep her voice down.

He paid no attention, but moved quickly to the bed and mounted the first tread of the steps, where he elbowed the mosquito baire aside. Placing a knee on the mattress, he lowered her to the padded surface. Then he followed her down, imprisoning her with a steel-hard arm as he stretched out alongside her body. Hovering above her with his weight on one elbow, he stared into her wide eyes for a long instant, his own dark and challenging. "Rio, call me Rio," he whispered. "And never say you were not warned."

For a single, blind moment, Celina knew the instinctive terror of a leap into the unknown, a paralyzing fear that what she was doing was wrong. Then his mouth touched hers in the candlelit dimness. She felt his heat and his power, tasted the sweetness that had become achingly familiar to her. Doubt faded, and terror was no more.

His body was warm against hers yet hard in its planes and angles. His strength surrounded her, supported her as she lay in his grasp. She could feel the throb of his heartbeat, the lift of his chest with his every breath.

A shiver moved over her, catching her by surprise, and a small sound of distress caught in her throat.

"Are you cold?" he asked, clasping her closer against him.

"No, I just…"

"I know. Overstrained sensibilities. It will pass."

His voice was soft and deep, with a hypnotic timbre that seemed to touch a chord somewhere deep inside her. He had been in this position many times before, she thought, so probably understood her misgivings as well as she did, if not better.

"Have you known as many women as they say?" She had clutched the facing of his frock coat as he lifted her. Now she uncurled her fingers and smoothed the fine broadcloth with her fingertips.

"Far fewer. The gossips love to exaggerate."

"Even so, they will have been more experienced than I. Do you mind?"

"I think," he said, brushing her forehead with the smooth surfaces of his lips, "that I can manage to overlook it."

"You're laughing at me."

"No, no, only teasing a little. Few men truly object to being the first."

His warm breath feathered her temple and he followed it with his lips, stringing small kisses down her hairline and across the ridge of her cheekbone, then over the fine-grained curve of her cheek. At the same time, he stroked her back, smoothing in slow circles that seemed to unravel the knots inside her, bringing a melting sensation.

"You must tell me what to do," she began as she felt his lips against her eyelids where he tasted her lashes with the moist edge of his tongue.

"The first thing is to stop thinking," he whispered. "Feel instead. Only feel."

He knew what he was doing; she could trust in that much. He would not hurt her, or at least no more than was necessary. How strange that she knew that about him when she had no such confidence in any other man she could name. It required trust, this surrender to the caresses of someone who was, in spite of everything, a stranger. How did women dare it with men who had been selected for them, sometimes without their knowledge or will, and knowing that it was irrevocable, a nightly surrender for the rest of their lives? It was barbaric to expect such mindless compliance, and yet women did it every day.

"Don't think," he said again, as the heat of his lips touched the tip of her nose, then pressed the corner of her mouth. "Only feel."

"How…" she began, but the words were smothered as his mouth covered hers.

The searing adhesion of his lips, the exotic taste of him, was oddly gratifying. They assuaged some deep hunger that she had not realized she had, fed a rising curiosity to discover what more he would do. Not that she was completely ignorant of the process. She wasn't, couldn't be, as a plantation-bred female where animals disported themselves in plain sight and men discussed their breeding as a matter of economic interest. More than that, Suzette had answered her more curious inquiries long ago, drawing on knowledge gained in the slave quarters where the only thing more precious than privacy was modesty. No, she knew the bare facts and had no special fear of the process. What she had not expected was the rise of anticipation, the sensual hunger that rippled through her like the river swelling toward flood stage.

Blindly she accepted the careful invasion of his tongue, taking pleasure in the sinuous and thorough exploration of her tender tissues and the porcelain edges of her teeth. In unfurling boldness, she followed his retreat to taste the smooth inner flesh of his lips, abrading the slick surface of his tongue with her own, then invited his further incursion. If accepting him into her body elsewhere was like this, then it should not be so difficult.

Spurred by the need to touch him, she slid her hand along the strong column of his neck, trailed her fingers over the square turn of his jaw and then the faintly stubbled plane of his cheek. Her fingertips found the old scar that slashed downward there, soothed it and passed on to the chiseled firmness of his mouth where it held her own. To trace the joining of their lips was such an exquisite sensation that she made a small, involuntary sound of pleasure deep in her throat.

He caught her closer, plunged deeper. She held her

breath, engulfed in mounting excitement, needing to lose herself in this wondrous blossoming of the senses. The muscles of her abdomen fluttered and she eased nearer, pressing against him in aching need of firmer, more vital contact.

He kneaded the narrow turn of her waist, clasped her hip to hold her against the radiating heat and rigidity of his lower body for an instant, then smoothed over her hip to her thigh. She shivered as he skimmed down to caress the sensitive inner surfaces through layers of fabric, gasped as he cupped the softness at the apex of her thighs. Then he gathered the fullness of her nightgown and wrapper, easing them upward. Releasing her mouth, he kissed the point of her chin, touched his eyelids and then his mouth to the slender curve of her neck, then tested with lips and tongue the pulse that beat frantically at the base of her throat.

The blood poured through her veins like heated wine so her skin seemed fevered, glowing from the inside with heightened sensitivity. Intoxicated by his caresses, she reeled under their onslaught to the point of near abandon. Yet some small, barely acknowledged voice inside her whispered of caution.

"The door," she said in low entreaty. "We should lock it. And the candle…"

"Leave them," he commanded.

"But what if…"

"How can it matter?"

He was right, or would be if she didn't care that he might be embroiled in her disgrace. But she did care. "Please. I could not bear, now, to be interrupted."

His muscles went taut, that stone-hard muscula-ture of a sword master who worked on the fencing strip most days of his life. Then he released her, turned with lithe power and slid from the bed. The key grated in the lock as he turned it. Then he swung and started back toward her. He made no attempt to douse the candle, however, and he shed clothing as he walked, stripping off his coat, wrenching free the buttons of his waistcoat, slipping the knot of his cra-vat and flinging it from him. His movements were economic and purposeful, every one an unconscious demonstration of male power.

Then, jerking the studs from his shirtfront one by one, he shoved them into the pocket of his pan-taloons and stripped off his shirt.

Celina's breath was trapped in her throat. His chest, in the gilding light of the candle, had the per-fection of a classical statue by some master sculptor. The hard planes and shadows, the ideally propor-tioned triangle of curling hair that dipped to his waist and under the band of his pantaloons, were sheer en-ticement. She was mesmerized by his male grace and primal strength, enthralled by the hunger and prom-ise she saw in his eyes. The urge to feel his naked skin against her made her breasts tingle as the nipples tightened to stinging buds.

Then she saw the white bandaging that marked the site of his injury high on his shoulder. A flush of chagrin suffused her.

"You were wounded, I had forgotten. I'm so sorry. If it will interfere, that is… I would not cause you pain."

"Nothing will interfere, I promise you."

"You're certain?"

"You have my word," he said, and smiled into her eyes, his own as silvery as a polished blade.

Placing one hand on the mattress then, he kicked out of his boots and sprang up to join her once more in a movement so quick and sure that the bed hardly bounced. As he reached for her, she came to him in boneless, fervid surrender.

"Now you," he said, and proceeded to strip away the yards of embroidered lawn and heavy velvet that she wore, taking them from her without ceremony until she lay covered only in candlelight before him.

"Dear God, you are so lovely, a woman to be adored. And will be if you allow it."

"I could not bear, now, to be denied," she whispered, the tight ache inside her adding a tremor to her voice.

They came together like the clash of steel against steel in the first attack of a duel of hearts. His touch was tempered, controlled, sure, a testing of strength and nerves. She responded, advanced with her own explorations of purpose and intent, each caress both an attack and its defense, each sigh an acknowledgment of the ultimate touché. She shivered, melting under his touch, drowning in the sweet intensity of the enticement he offered and the pleasure.

She had known he was skilled, but not that he was patient beyond accounting, tender beyond imagination. That he might take pleasure in the rapture he gave while still holding to his restraint was astounding, that he could share the unselfish joy was a revelation. The knowledge sent desire through her like a storm of the senses, racking her with sensual tension so she strained against his caressing hands and mouth. She was consumed, wanting nothing, needing nothing except the sweet magic he offered. Yet in some distant corner of her mind was a tremulous fear that it was too fervid, too exalted, that it might prove a snare more binding than any contract of betrothal.

Still she sought the hot caress of his mouth on the tight nipples of her naked breast, yielded, shivering, to the inexorable slide of his lips down her abdomen and along the flat surface of her belly. She arched toward him, writhing under his hands. Her quick-drawn breath seared her lungs while her body clung to the ceaseless incursion of his long, aristocratic fingers. Her heartbeat grew frantic, jarring in her chest. Shuddering pleasure spread through her in overwhelming waves. Her lower body was suffused and heavy, aching for a deeper pressure, a more fervid touch.

The pyrotechnic explosion of sensation that burst over her caught her unaware. Its sweet ravishment swept in on her so suddenly that she stiffened, twisting against Rio with a low cry in her throat and her hand gripping his good shoulder. It was endless, a panting eternity of pulsing beguilement. Still Celina thought, as she clung to him, half-stunned with pleasure, that there should be more. A fretful distress gripped her, an urgent need that hovered, waiting.

Rio shifted, cupping her face, tasting her mouth once more. Then with a few swift moves, he skimmed from his pantaloons and eased between her thighs. She urged him nearer, and he fitted their bodies together, entering her like a sword into its carefully prepared sheath.

The sting was sharp and burning. She felt stretched, unbearably full. Then came an easing, a slow slide into beatitude that beckoned, promising certain glory.

He moved above her then, supporting his weight yet letting her feel his strength, soothing that deep internal throb while gathering speed and power in a race toward distant surcease. She met his cautious movements, matched them in passionate gratitude for his care and concern, clenched her body around him with trembling muscles and pounding heart.

They strained together in the escalating tumult, blind with fretted pleasure and a restrained fury of effort. The candlelight glowed in the moisture that dewed their bodies, shone behind their tightly closed eyelids. They were matched, mated, loving opponents who strove to win, to live with honor and no thought of defeat.

It came to them, that bright moment of victory. Bursting over them with scalding heat, it was an internal, pulsing cataclysm of bliss. It took them, transfigured them with such ineffable grandeur that they clung together with the feverish joy of survivors, forgetting to weigh the consequences, never thinking to ask the price of the rescue.

11

Celina awoke with a start. One moment she was drifting in a languorous half dream, half memory, and the next she was staring wide-eyed at the tester above her head with its enclosing fall of mosquito netting.

She was alone in the bed. Quite alone.

The house was quiet, but from the street came the call of a coffee vendor touting her wares, followed by the musical cry of the hot rice-cake woman, *"Calas! Tout chaud calas!"* A pig squealed where it rutted in the gutters, and a cock crowed several streets away. Above it all floated the musical clanging of the cathedral bells.

The noises were ordinary, heard every morning. It was the sudden knowledge of change that had awakened her. She had won. Her bargain with Rio de Silva was done.

She felt little different physically. Beyond a small amount of soreness here and there, she seemed much as usual. Was this all there was to it? Should not something so significant be more obvious? Her sense of well being was almost enough to make her question the entire principle of purity. If her virgin state could be so easily forfeited, then how could its lack be so vital?

For her, it meant that she would be free.

She had to see her father at once and make the change in her situation known to him. How he would take it, she had no idea. Once she might have guessed, would have said that his attitude would be one of disappointment followed by resignation. He had been so different since coming under the count's influence. His autocratic pronouncements during the interview in his study were disturbing. He might be angry, even violent.

She could endure anything if it meant the end of her betrothal. The sooner it was done, then, the better. Afterward, the pleasure of knowing she was free would make whatever happened worthwhile.

She would not betray Rio. Her father and the count might guess he had been her lover, but they could not be certain. It was unlikely that either of them would act without proof, and she would not give it to them. Rio deserved that much, deserved her silence and her loyalty.

For an instant, she could almost feel his touch on her skin, the hard strength of his arms, the purpose and intensity of his attention. Desire, so easily aroused in the night, threatened to engulf her again merely from these fleeting images. In some deep recess of her mind, it seemed wrong that he had to leave her, wrong that a man like the count had the right to court her when Rio was forbidden the opportunity.

Not that the Silver Shadow would avail himself of a change in circumstances if such a thing were available. Permanency, it seemed, did not figure large in his life.

She turned her head toward the window where she had last seen him as he left her. A tall figure in the dark, he had turned back to look at her one last instant, as if half inclined to return to her bed. Then he had sketched a bow and swung with a swirl of his cloak to disappear into the night.

She had known he must go, expected nothing else. Yet she had felt incredibly alone afterward, bereft by the sudden knowledge that the bargain was sealed, the interlude with him over.

Remembering, she stared with unseeing eyes at the bars of morning light, behind the draperies, falling through the outside shutters. She was still lying there minutes later when the bedchamber door opened.

"Good morning, Mam'zelle," Suzette said as she stepped briskly inside the room, bringing with her the scents of coffee and scalded milk from the silver tray she carried. She moved to the bedside table to deposit her burden, and then whisked around to pull back the draperies and new muslin under curtains and throw open the French doors to push the shutters out against the walls. Drawing the doors closed again to keep out the coolness, she glanced around the room as if checking for other tasks.

Celina sat up in bed to fill her coffee cup and add hot milk, then thrust her pillow behind her back and leaned against the headboard. Suzette came forward and picked up the other pillow from where it had landed on the floor. Celina, leaning forward a little to allow it to be tucked behind her, glanced at her maid's set features.

"What is wrong?" she asked abruptly. "Have you been crying?"

"It's nothing." Suzette averted her face.

"Something has upset you. You haven't cried since we were children. You must tell me at once."

"You will think it foolish."

"Suzette," Celina said in warning tones.

"And you may not like some parts of it." She swung away, moving to the foot of the bed. Taking up the hairbrush that Rio had left lying there, she began to pull the trapped hair from the bristles with jerky, almost uncoordinated movements.

Celina swallowed a sip of coffee while frowning a little as she watched her maid. "Why is that?"

"Because…"

"Yes?"

"Olivier was with me last night."

Celina could feel her face burn as she wondered if Olivier's visit had been anything at all like that of his employer to her room. Suzette appeared normal other than the teary redness of her eyes but, as she had discovered, that meant little. "What is wrong with that?"

"Nothing, really. Being a free man instead of a slave, he had no need of a pass."

"So?" Celina wondered at the bitterness in Suzette's voice. To require a pass was commonplace enough, for otherwise there would be no way to distinguish between runaway slaves and those on errands for their masters.

"We talked for a long time, very long. He…he kissed me."

"Is that all? He didn't hurt you, did he?"

"Never! He is the soul of gentleness. To be in his arms is...is beyond heaven." Suzette looked up, her eyes drowning in tears. "I would have denied him nothing."

Celina set her coffee cup aside and sat forward. "Then what is the matter?"

"He didn't want me!" The words were a wail as Suzette turned her back to conceal her face.

"That can't be true," Celina objected. "He came here to see you, after all. There must be something else."

"No, Mam'zelle, he said it plainly. I am forbidden to him. He will not chance bringing a child into the world who must become the property of another man. No child of his will ever be born a slave."

Pain rose unbidden in Celina's chest as she saw the full nature of the problem. A baby born from the union of a slave mother and free man always followed the condition of the mother. It was the law, and had been for more than a hundred years, since the Black Code was promulgated soon after Louisiana became a French colony. Or perhaps it was older even than that, stretching into Greek and Roman antiquity. "Oh, Suzette. I'm so sorry."

"So am I. So is Olivier. So are we all, for what good it may do."

"You don't think he can be persuaded?"

Suzette gave a decided shake of her head. "He is a man of...of much control."

Celina had some inkling of what was meant, since she had known firsthand Rio's ability to hold his more passionate impulses in check. "But that doesn't mean Olivier doesn't want you."

"It only makes it worse, don't you see? But for a piece of paper, we would be free to love. But for freedom we could marry and have a family. Without these things, we must remain forever apart from each other."

"Perhaps if I spoke to my father," Celina began.

"You think we haven't thought of that? Monsieur Vallier would expect to be paid for my loss, and why not since money was paid to purchase my mother years ago? Sometimes, I know, free men and women of color purchase slaves, but Olivier has not the money. He thinks Monsieur Rio would perhaps lend it to him if he had it. He doesn't, for everything *monsieur* makes is spent on his salon or else saved for his so great quest."

"His quest? What is that?"

"Olivier would not say. It seems something Monsieur Rio has worked long and hard to gain. To accomplish it, he started from nothing and worked like a demon to build his skill and reputation with a blade. It is almost within his grasp, or so it appears. Olivier feels that to take anything from him now would be unfair since it could mean the difference between success and failure."

"How mysterious."

Suzette's smile was wan. "Deliberately so. Olivier says little for fear of giving away something that may harm the man who has his loyalty unto death. I had to read between the lines for the little I've just told you."

"Monsieur Rio must be an exceptional man to warrant such loyalty." To speak so of him gave her an odd pleasure, though she knew she should resist the impulse.

"According to Olivier, his maître saved his life when he could as easily have thrown it away, then refused to enslave him when it would have been to his advantage. His gratitude approaches worship. I could be jealous, if I had the right."

"It seems to me that Olivier is protecting you, as well as any future child. It would be difficult for you if you *were* to conceive."

"Yes, but I would prefer that he did not think so much. I would like him to love me wildly, as I love him."

"To give in to natural instinct is easy. It's controlling it that is rare and difficult in a man." She spoke from experience, Celina thought, though she tried not to let it leak into her voice.

"Yes," Suzette said with tears again welling into her eyes. "But it hurts all the same."

Celina could think of nothing to say that would not make matters worse. Reaching for her coffee cup again, she took refuge in sipping the hot liquid. She would still speak to her father about Suzette's freedom, but she must choose her time. She could hardly expect him to give consideration to such a matter after she presented him with her own news. It was entirely possible that he would not even be speaking to her.

After a moment, she said, "I also had a visitor last night."

"I know," Suzette replied quietly, looking away as she wiped her eyes, then moved to the folding screen in the corner. Pulling it aside, she dragged the hot tub further into the room.

"You know? But I thought…"

"I didn't see him, no. Olivier told me he was here."

"And you didn't come to me?"

The maid looked up. "Did you need me?"

"No." Celina looked away. "It was…my choice. I think…that is, if you find certain stains on the sheets, perhaps you will save questions from the laundress by removing them."

Suzette straightened to her full height. "Mam'zelle!"

"I know, I know, but it was most necessary."

"Your papa will disown you."

"I hope he may."

"Don't say that when you know you don't mean it. I couldn't bear it if you had to go away and I was forced to stay behind. Think of Denys, think of your aunts and uncles and cousins. Yes, and think of your poor papa. Even if he sends you from him, he will miss you and long for you as for his own heart."

"If he had been reasonable, I would not have been forced to it."

"Were you forced, *chère* Mam'zelle?" Suzette moved to the bellpull beside the fireplace as she asked the question, ringing it twice as a signal to bring hot water for Celina's morning bath.

"You must know I was not. The fault lies with the count, who insists on a marriage between us. He would not release me. This is the only way out."

"That isn't what I meant," Suzette said, blowing her nose on a handkerchief taken from her apron pocket as if dismissing her own problems to confront those of her mistress. "Are you certain it wasn't a choice made because you are attracted to the sword master?"

"He is handsome and dashing and dangerous. Why would I not be attracted? But you could hardly expect me to choose someone of no appeal?"

"That isn't an answer."

She was right and Celina knew it. "All right, yes, he attracts me. He is also a man who others will hesitate to accuse or insult."

"Even Denys?"

"I hope and pray that Papa will keep the matter between the two of us specifically to safeguard him. Or at least share it with Count de Lérida alone."

"He will not dare make a lot of noise, you think, for fear Denys will feel required to defend your virtue? You preserve your good repute while gaining what you want. Clever, Mam'zelle."

Celina shook her head. "It can so easily go awry."

"And may have already." A frown gathered between Suzette's brows. "According to Mortimer, Monsieur Denys has still not returned home. He said in the kitchen this morning that he lay awake for hours last evening, listening for the bell on the gate that never rang. He checked Monsieur Denys's bed earlier and it was empty and undisturbed. Something is wrong."

Denys might not have come home for any number of reasons. Balls and soirees, gaming, cockfights, dog fights, bullbaitings, impromptu race meets outside the city—any of those could have occupied him into the early-morning hours. Afterward, he might easily have accepted a bed at the home of a companion. It was nothing to wake and find that Hippolyte, Armand or any one of a half-dozen other friends of Denys's had availed themselves of Vallier hospitality. To see them wander forth from the *garçonnière* in disheveled evening clothes, searching hopefully for café au lait and a roll, could be amusing.

Still Denys had not been home in twenty-four hours. He should have at least returned for a change of linen.

"No message arrived?"

"None."

"Not even a word sent by some street boy? You're certain?"

"I asked most particularly. No one has seen anything or anyone from Monsieur Denys."

Celina gave a small nod while concern wormed its way into her mind. To fail in providing his escort, as he had the evening before, was not at all like Denys. The lack of a message was even more disturbing. He was the most amiable and conscientious of brothers, with a tender heart that would never leave them to fret over his whereabouts.

"Is Papa at home?" she asked after a moment.

"No, Mam'zelle."

Unspoken between them was the knowledge of his obvious whereabouts. Just as plain was the difficulty in contacting him at an address of which Celina was supposed to be ignorant.

"What of Tante Marie Rose? Has she left her bed?"

"I believe so. Shall I tell her what transpires?"

"I'll attend to it at breakfast." Celina threw back the covers and slid from the bed. "But you may ask one of the stable boys to make ready. I would like a note carried around to Hippolyte Ducolet immediately."

She and her aunt were still at the breakfast table when Denys's friend arrived. He was alone except for Mortimer who had admitted him. Her heart sank a little, for she had hoped that Denys might be with him. Rising, she came forward, holding out her hand with quick words of appreciation to the slim young dandy for his prompt answer to her summons. When he had bowed a greeting to her aunt and seated himself, she took her place across from him and offered café au lait and brioche. Pouring the hot milk from enough height that it foamed into the cup, she said, "I do apologize for bringing you out so early, but we are quite worried about Denys."

"It is a privilege to be of service, Mademoiselle Celina. I only wish I might relieve your mind."

"You never saw him last night?"

Hippolyte shook his head. "I've not seen him at all since we spoke a few minutes on the street. He was on his way to de Silva's salon, I think. We engaged to have an early dinner before his appointment to escort you and your aunt to last night's soiree. That he failed to appear surprised me, but was not a real worry until now."

The implications in her brother's failure to keep at least two engagements were so disturbing that Celina felt as if her corset were squeezing the breath from her. She pushed her plate aside, suddenly without appetite. "Why did you not say so last evening?"

"I was sure he was out on some lark and would appear, all excuses and apologies, this morning." Hippolyte shifted uncomfortably in his chair. "It did strike me as odd that he had not included me, but you know how it is."

She did, at least in a manner of speaking. There was a section of New Orleans known as The Swamp where few dared go in daylight, much less after dark. Located uptown near the levee, it comprised several streets of grog shops, barrelhouses and places of ill fame that catered to riverboat men and sailors off the ships tied up at the docks. Most young gentlemen seemed to find their way there at least once before they settled down, sometimes with disastrous consequences, but no gently bred female admitted to knowing of such an area.

As the conversation faltered, Tante Marie Rose stepped quickly into the breach. "How very upsetting this all is, to be sure. I feel quite ill with it. But can you really think of nowhere in particular that dear Denys may have gone, Monsieur Hippolyte, no errand that might have taken him out of town?"

"Would that I could, madame." Denys's friend spread his arms wide, endangering the coffee cup that he held. "Denys has been little inclined toward idle pastimes of late. His thoughts have been for Mademoiselle Celina and her future. Well, and this recent business with Monsieur de Silva."

"What can you mean?" the older woman asked, her voice strained. "I thought his part in the affair over and done."

"Assuredly, if you speak of the duel. However, Denys has a high regard for the Silver Shadow. The many other meetings that stemmed from his own, not to mention the affair of Broyard, made him as blue as…that is to say, they disturbed him greatly."

"I fail to see why it should. He was not at fault."

"No, *madame*, but Denys felt it all the same."

"Yes, he would." Tante Marie Rose took out a lace-edged handkerchief and dabbed at a tear. "Such a kindhearted boy, always considerate, especially of his elders, and now something terrible has happened to him, I just know it."

"Surely not," the young man said, his discomfort mirrored in his face.

"But how can we know? He may have been set upon by thieves and robbers or attacked by some of the horrible American boatmen from the river. He could be lying injured somewhere, or taken ill and unable to send word. Oh, dear, I can't bear to think of it. Something must be done. Someone must find him."

"Calm yourself, *chère* Tante Marie Rose. He will be found," Celina said, reaching to put a hand on her arm.

She turned to Hippolyte again. "Marthe Desiard's brother saw Denys at Monsieur de Silva's salon, so we may be sure that he arrived. But did he give you no indication of his purpose in going?"

"I took it that he meant merely to look in, see who was there, watch the usual demonstrations of skill or enjoy a practice bout."

"Nothing else?"

"What else could there be?"

One disturbing possibility lay at the forefront of Celina's mind. Denys could have learned of her bargain with Rio. He might have discovered that the sword master had visited the town house in the dead of night, or that she had practically begged him to make love to her. What might have passed between the two of them if Denys had confronted Rio was something she could not bear to imagine.

"I wonder if we might impose further on your good nature, monsieur," she asked after a second.

"Only command me."

"A search must be made for Denys. I dislike having to ask it of you, but my father is otherwise engaged and I fear speed may be necessary." What she did not say but was understood between them was that the task required a man, since the places Denys might be found were forbidden to her.

"Armand will wish to be a part of this search party I'm sure, as will such other friends as can be gathered on short notice. We will comb the town from the river to Lake Pontchartrain and back again, I promise you."

"I knew I might count on you, still you have my gratitude."

"And mine," Tante Marie Rose said with a helpless gesture with her handkerchief. "Though, Celina, *ma chère*, I'm not sure what your papa will think."

"What do you mean?"

"He may feel we should have waited on his counsel, you know. What if Denys is merely detained on some private errand? It will be embarrassing in the extreme if a hue and cry is raised, then the dear boy comes whistling home in the middle of it."

Her aunt was concerned that Denys might be with a woman, perhaps even a quadroon, Celina thought. The idea had occurred to her, but she was almost certain he would have sent to let them know he was detained even so.

That Hippolyte also understood the nature of her aunt's concern was plain from the careful blankness of his features. He put down his cup and rose to his feet. "You may rest assured, *madame*, that all will be handled with the utmost discretion."

Tante Marie Rose offered her gratitude, as well as a half-dozen other misgivings and admonitions. Celina, seeing that Hippolyte was anxious to depart, walked with him to the door before expressing her own appreciation once more.

"You may depend on me in this," he said, taking her hand and bowing over it. "I will not fail, not if success is possible."

"You will send word at once if he is found? Night or day?"

"*Naturellement.* Do not disturb yourself. Denys is the most sensible one of us. All will be well with him, you'll see."

She thanked him again, and then watched him reclaim his hat and cane from Mortimer before going lightly down the outside stairs. The butler followed at a more sedate pace to see him out. Moments later, the pedestrian gate clanged shut behind him. Celina stood on the back gallery, staring at nothing until, abruptly, she turned and moved back into the dining room to rejoin her aunt.

Tante Marie Rose was waiting for her, her eyes watery and red in her pale face and her handkerchief clutched to her mouth. "Oh, *chère*," she said in a voice just above a whisper. "You don't think that our Din-Din could be…that he is—"

"I don't know," Celina interrupted, unwilling to hear the thought put into words.

"Hippolyte said he was on his way to that awful fencing salon. What if he arrived but never departed?"

"I don't know."

"Swordplay is so very dangerous, even when the weapons are blunted. Is it possible that this de Silva may have…"

"I don't know!" Celina exclaimed.

"You need not shout," Tante Marie Rose said in tearful reproach. "I was only trying to think what might have happened."

"I know," Celina whispered. "I know."

No afternoon calls were made that day. Tante Marie Rose had no heart for it, and Celina was reluctant to risk missing any news sent by Hippolyte. Yet they pretended to a normal routine. Tante Marie Rose wandered into the sitting room after breakfast where she picked up the evening pocket she was making of lavender silk covered with black netting and steel bead accents. Celina consulted with the cook about meals for the day, ordered the courtyard swept free of fallen leaves and dried mud from the carriage wheels, and watched over the filling of the giant water ollas from the water wagon that passed by, also its purification with alum. Somehow, the day passed.

A missive arrived from Hippolyte in midafternoon. The news it contained was entirely negative. Denys was not in any of the hospitals in either the French or the American sections, had visited no doctor of any known address or standing. He was not in the *calabozo*, the old Spanish-era jail behind the Cabildo where the gendarmes kept those detained for drunkenness or misdemeanors, not in the new jail nor in the parish prison near Congo Square. No barroom or gaming house had enjoyed his patronage that the owners could recall. He had hired none of the

score or more hacks that plied the streets of the Vieux
Carré, bought no ticket for the train out to Pontchartrain Lake or any other, and had not visited the Métairie racetrack. Hope was not lost, however;
Hippolyte and his friends would continue to search.

As the hours passed, it began to seem as if Denys
had disappeared off the face of the earth. Celina
stared out the windows as if her watchfulness would
make him appear on the street below. She paced,
clenching her hands together with vexation at not
being able to join the search herself. The weight of responsibility for finding him weighed ever more heavily.

A thousand times, she thought of sending for her
father. Just as often, she had the almost overwhelming urge to turn to Rio. If Denys was not in any of his
usual haunts or the obvious alternatives, then he had
to have become embroiled somehow with the seamy
elements that lurked in the back streets and alley-
ways. Of all the men she knew, Rio seemed most
likely to be able to penetrate there and emerge again
unscathed.

More than that, there were things he needed to explain, such as what her brother had discussed with
him that was so important. Yes, and why Rio had not
mentioned the evening before that he had seen
Denys.

It would be easy enough to send a note; what
would be difficult was finding the nerve to suggest
a meeting. Their agreement had ended. Applying to
him now would be awkward, as if she were attempt-
ing to cling to what had passed between them. She
could not and would not do that. If she spoke with

Rio at all, it must be on some neutral ground. They would talk with reason and logic and no intrusion whatever of inconvenient desire.

Even as she assured herself of this, she was swamped by the memory of his hard strength against her, the feel of his arms around her, his hands moving over her skin. Images of the musculature of his body outlined in golden candle gleams haunted her, as did the dark, hot sheen of his eyes as he gazed down at her. And his kiss…

No, she could not afford that distraction, dared not succumb to the temptation of it, or the wonder. She had to think of her brother. That being so, she would go to Rio only as a last resort.

Her father returned home as she was on the point of penning a message to be carried to the Rampart Street address of his mistress. She met him on the stairs and drew him into the salon, closing the door behind them. Quickly she told him what had transpired while he was away, and what she had done about it.

"Celina, my dear heart, you are upsetting yourself for nothing. It was foolish to involve young Ducolet. What is the world coming to when a brother cannot pursue the normal business of a young man about town without the interference of his sister?"

"But Papa, it's been two whole days now since anyone has even glimpsed Denys's face. Surely some of his friends should know where to find him?"

"Not necessarily." He glanced at a side table where a copy of the news sheet, *L'Abeille*, lay. As he reached to pick it up, he went on. "You mean well, Celina, this I know, but you are letting your fear override your better judgment."

"Even Monsieur Ducolet felt this was unlike Denys."

"So you have sent him on a wild-goose chase. He is a most obliging young man, particularly where attractive young women are concerned, but a poor choice as emissary for one who is betrothed. Why is it that you did not turn to the wise counsel of your fiancé?"

The idea had never crossed Celina's mind, nor could she imagine it now. "Monsieur Ducolet has a friendship with Denys, something that is naturally absent in the count."

"Even for such a cause, he may well object to these visits from another man who is not a blood relative."

"He might have that right if we were in fact betrothed. But we are not and are unlikely to be."

"Celina," her father began in stern tones.

The news of her changed circumstances that made the alliance ineligible sprang to the tip of her tongue. She bit it back with an effort. Now was not the time. She could not risk being confined to her room or any similar penalty that might prevent her from trying to find Denys. "Please, Papa," she said urgently. "I am convinced Denys is in trouble. Is there nothing you can do to help locate him?"

He seated himself and snapped open the news sheet he held. "For the last time, leave the boy alone. Go about as usual, enjoy yourself in these last days before you are betrothed. Denys will come home when he is ready."

The emphasis he placed on the words was aimed at the way she had pounced on him the instant he came in the door, Celina thought. He knew very well that she felt he had been too much away from home with his current inamorata. Neither of them would think for an instant of putting the situation into words, but it lay like a stone between them all the same.

Turning away, Celina walked to the door with her features set. She almost passed from the room, leaving him to his reading. At the last moment, she swung back to stare at the man who was her father, seeing him not as some being of supreme authority but as a man like any other, obstinate, fallible and given to snap judgments and questionable activities as an antidote to the lingering pain of loss.

"Papa?"

He did not look up. "What now?"

"Do you not care what happens to Denys or to me? Or is it just that you can't bear to think anything else may go wrong with your family?"

He raised his head from the news sheet then, but did not speak. She met his eyes, her own holding clear compassion. When he looked away again, she turned with quiet grace and went from the room.

12

It was, Rio thought, a monumentally insipid evening's entertainment, featuring a recital by the second soprano from the opera company currently at the Theatre d'Orleans. The singer, apparently a believer in the theory that embonpoint created a large voice, hurried through the first set of arias as if more concerned with getting to the food than in enticing those present to her next performance. The ensemble of pianoforte, violin, oboe and French horn that accompanied her was just as uninspiring.

Younger gentlemen were noticeably absent due to the pugilism display taking place in the arena behind the Exchange. During the intermission, elderly women gossiped with their heads together, young matrons talked with animation while one or two nursed babies and older men talked politics and planting while strolling outside to smoke. They seemed not to notice the dullness, but Rio was bored beyond endurance.

His vantage point was the garden, which may have had some bearing. Or perhaps it was just that the scene unfolding inside the house was too familiar. He could easily bring similar occasions in Barcelona to mind, even to the scent of wine and orange-flower water drinks and the sight of white camellias among high-piled dark curls. Yet for the first time in recent memory, thinking of it brought only a minor sense of exclusion.

The reason was the woman in pale aqua silk who sat with the full skirt of her gown spilling around her feet, her smooth shoulders catching the light with pearl-like gleams and ill-concealed anxiety in her eyes. She had moved from her chair only once since her arrival, and that was to exchange seats with her aunt, who wished to talk to the lady on her opposite side. Watching her through the window, noting her rigid smile and the quick, edgy way she looked around the room or snapped open her fan, Rio felt compassion shift in his chest. At the same time, impatience with her retiring pose gripped him. He had tried for the past hour to will her into rising and taking the air in the garden, but so far she'd managed to ignore his mental summons.

Other guests strolled on the back veranda or descended the wide steps to explore the white oyster-shell paths that marched through the formal garden with its hedges and secluded alcoves. Celina had, thus far, shown no inclination for such exercise. And he had thought that lying in wait for her at this expansive house on the uptown edge of the Vieux Carré would be easy.

Rio weighed the consequences of invading the house, then decided against it. Going in search of the kitchen entrance, he loitered outside it until a manservant appeared to empty a pan of scraps. A coin was passed. Then Rio scaled the garden wall again and leaped lightly down into an alcove where high shrubbery sheltered a small summerhouse from view of the main dwelling.

Celina came toward him at last like a vision from a fevered dream, all luminous and ethereal beauty, moving with such swift grace that she seemed to glide toward him. Watching her mount the wide brick step of the garden structure, with its domed roof and wrought-iron railing, he knew an aching hunger that had little to do with the heated response of his body. In some odd way that he did not fully understand, Celina Vallier had come to stand for everything he had lost and could never hope to regain, everything he could touch, barely, but never fully grasp.

The knowledge was not something he wanted to face, not yet. His only weapon against it was resentment. Driven by that near painful anger, he stepped from the concealing shadow of an iron pillar to block her path.

She drew back with a stifled gasp. He put out a hand to catch her arm. She tensed against his hold for a second, before abruptly stepping closer so her skirts caressed his booted ankles.

"At last," she said in quiet satisfaction. "I was afraid you might not have received my note."

"I had it, though I can't say I understand it," he answered. "You required a neutral meeting place, I believe. Is this neutral enough?"

"Perfectly. I apologize for taking you from your amusements of the evening, though I thank you for coming so quickly."

It was as he suspected. She wanted to speak to

him, but nothing more. This was not to be a romantic encounter. He was hardly in a position to complain, yet it annoyed him that she made her disinclination so clear. It also disturbed him to realize that he'd had no amusements for this or any other evening since they had met. Casual amours had lost their appeal. "I assumed that your need was urgent, otherwise you would not have taken the risk."

She sent him a quick glance for he saw the flash of moonlight in her eyes. "I would not have you think there might have been repercussions from our last meeting. I spoke of it to no one."

"No?" he queried softly.

"No. Other matters more important have made it quite impossible to do so."

"You relieve my mind." His words were dry. It was of course exactly what he had not wanted to hear, that the night she had spent in his arms was of minor importance in her busy life.

"You may have heard that Denys is missing?"

To focus his thoughts on her question required an effort. "I know that a nervous gentleman calling himself Armand Lollain appeared at the salon yesterday morning and inquired if I had seen him."

"And had you?"

"You think I might have?" he inquired as he heard the doubt in her voice. "You feel that if he learned of my visits to your bedchamber and chose to resent them, I could have sliced him to pretty ribbons and used them to decorate my scabbard."

"Don't! Please, just…don't." White-faced, she stood before him with her fists knotted on the India shawl she clutched around her shoulders.

"My apologies. I had the mistaken notion, you see, that since you had trusted me with your body, you must trust me in all else."

She let that pass, or perhaps failed to register it in her concern for her brother. "You seem to be the last person to see him, or so I have it from two witnesses."

"And he was hale and hearty when he said his farewells."

"Was he really?"

Had she been a man, he would have challenged those words. But then, if she had been a man they would not be having this conversation. "You require proof? Is that what this is all about?"

She swung away, taking a few steps. Over her shoulder, she said, "I suppose not. What I really require is your aid."

"In what way?" She had asked before in that desperate tone of voice for his help. He was more wary now.

"Denys is in trouble, I know it. My father is disinclined to believe it so does nothing. My brother's friends have searched all the obvious places with no success. Still, they have little real knowledge of the less desirable sections of the city, and I hesitate to ask them to brave the dangers there."

"While you have no such qualms where I'm concerned. I see."

"Are you offended? It was not my intention. I meant only that you know more of the world and are better able to protect yourself. I also thought you must have a more comprehensive idea of the ugly things that can happen to a young man, therefore should have more knowledge of where to look."

She was correct on all counts, probably more so than she realized. That did little to mollify Rio, which was a measure of his sense of betrayal. That he cared one way or the other was a chink in his armor that he did not relish having brought to his attention. "So I am to comb the dives and bordellos of New Orleans for your brother? Shall I have someone drag the river, as well?"

She made no reply, but only stared at him while her face took on the tint of white marble and her eyes became pools of pain.

"No. Forgive me," he said at once, taking a step forward. "That was inappropriate."

"It isn't that I can't envision such a thing. I've heard for years of bodies found floating near the docks or below the river bend. I simply can't think of it until other avenues have been exhausted."

"I do understand."

He understood something else as he finally bent his mind to her request. Of all those who might search for Denys Vallier, he alone knew what had been in that young man's mind and where he had intended to go when he left the fencing salon. The reflections that brought were not pleasant, nor could he mention them to Celina. She didn't need the worry, for one thing, but it would also raise questions he was in no position to answer.

"Will you help?" she asked, reaching out to touch his arm.

"Out of altruism or perhaps common decency? I can't afford the first, and you seem certain the second doesn't apply."

"I didn't say that!"

"You don't deny it, which comes to the same thing. But what does that leave by way of incentive, unless you're thinking of our past transaction. That was temporary in nature and is now concluded. Satisfactorily, of course."

She lifted her hand from his arm as if she touched fire instead of his sleeve. Her voice chill as the evening air, she asked, "What is it you want?"

He wasn't sure himself. Or no, that was wrong. What he wanted was not only obvious but carnal to the core. He wanted the unobtainable. He wanted their agreement to continue. He wanted her.

"We have had this discussion before, I think. It was established then that you have nothing that will entice me, with a single exception."

The sound of her swift-drawn breath was perfectly audible. "That is quite…"

"Vile?" he supplied as she stopped. "But I thought you saw that quality as a useful one in me."

She watched him there in the semidarkness, her eyes searching his face, probing his motives, his manners, even his very soul. To sustain that evaluation was one of the most difficult things he had ever done, far worse than facing a man over crossed blades. He wanted to take back every syllable he had spoken and kneel at her feet to ask pardon. Just as strong was the urge to hear how she would answer.

"Very well."

Caution tempered the triumph that surged through him. "Meaning?"

"As before, I agree."

The slow smile that curved one corner of his

mouth sounded in his voice, along with a warning, as he said, "This bargain has no limit."

"You...you expect it to continue after Denys is found?"

"Just so. If you aspire to the arts of a courtesan, your lessons might as well begin with me."

She moistened her lips. "But not publicly."

His smile hardened. "I am nothing if not discreet, though you will wish to throw off pretense and embrace this chosen profession at some point."

"You are enjoying this, aren't you?" she asked with a lift of her chin. "You like having me in your power."

The effort to hold the uncaring edge of his smile nearly cracked his face. "If that's the only way I can have you."

"A thorough rogue, after all."

"But at least an honest one, a consideration when engaging the services of such a blackguard. And particularly with so invaluable a payment."

"You have first to find my brother."

He reached to take her hand, turning it to release the wrist button of her elbow-length glove and expose the tender underside of her forearm. Bending his head, he pressed his lips to her pulse that fluttered there before probing that frantic beat with the hot flick of his tongue. "Given such an enticement," he drawled as he buttoned the glove again, "how can I fail?"

She drew away from him and picked up her skirts as if to return to the house. Then she stopped. "Where will you start your search?"

"What does it matter as long as Denys is found?"

"It almost seemed…that is, I thought you might have some idea of where he could be."

She really was too acute where he was concerned, a trait he did not want to encourage. "You are suggesting I might know in advance where to look?"

"I suggest nothing," she said, her regard steady. "I only thought there might be some small thing I could tell my aunt to ease her mind."

"As well as yours, I imagine. Unfortunately…"

"Oh, please. You must have a glimmering of a plan. Otherwise you would have refused me."

"Never," he said softly.

She brushed that aside with a quick gesture, though high color spread across her cheekbones. "Surely there is some place you intend to begin, somewhere you think he may be or at least could have been detained. I don't understand why you can't say so instead of being secretive. Unless you intend to exact payment for that, as well."

"An excellent idea. Why didn't I think of it?"

He advanced a step, certain she would retreat. It was a miscalculation. She dropped her skirts and stood quite still, so near that he could catch the rosewater scent of her skin, see the satin shimmer of her skin through the fine weave of her light shawl. He closed his hands into fists as he sought control against the urge to reach out, to touch, to take.

"I confess I'm at a loss to know why you didn't. It seems the natural thing."

Her words stung, as she had intended. "This garden is pleasant enough," he answered, his voice a low growl in his throat, "but lacks a certain comfort. When I make love to you, I want you naked before a warm fire and behind a door with a lock to keep out the world. I want no hurried grappling, but a long, slow stint of kisses and sweet sighs, caresses and endless joining. I want to have done with convention and pretense and all the trappings of society that make what is between a man and woman false. I want what is real and sweet and true. I want—" He came to a sudden stop, afraid he had said far too much about what he wanted when what he was allowed must be so little.

Long seconds ticked past. Then she inhaled sharply, as if she had been holding her breath. Looking away from him, she said, "Yes, well. I pray you find my brother, regardless. Should you go into places where…where danger lies, please take care. Though I have every confidence in your strength and ability, anyone can be caught unaware. Your injury is already on my conscience. I would not like to have more."

Amazement left him mute. In that stunned second, there came a call from nearby. "Celina? *Ma chère,* where are you?"

"Here, Tante Marie Rose," she said at once. With a last glance, she turned and left the small shelter, skimming down the wide step.

Rio took a hasty stride after her, one that carried him into a patch of moonlight that framed the summerhouse doorway. In that moment, her aunt came into view along the white shell path. With her was another woman, a gaunt yet elegant figure in stiff brocade and wearing an ivory mantilla draped over the tall, ornate comb in her silvery white hair.

"Mon Dieu!"

The strange lady stopped where she stood, putting a hand to her throat. The look on her face was one of aghast recognition. It did nothing for Rio's mood to realize that she was one of those females of supreme sensibility for whom a sword master such as himself was a devil incarnate. This accidental meeting would be another mark against Celina, since she was obviously just leaving a clandestine tête-à-tête with him.

"Come, Celina," her aunt said. "It's too cool to linger without your cloak."

"Yes, so it is," she answered. Without a single backward glance, she joined her relative and her elderly friend and turned toward the house.

For long moments Rio stood listening to the crunch of their footsteps on the oyster shells. When the trio was safely inside, he left the summerhouse step. Then he ran for the garden wall, scaling and flinging over it with a strong twist of his body as if there were danger behind him and the only hope of safety lay on the other side.

Olivier was not in when Rio arrived back at the salon. The majordomo was not required to be on duty, of course, but usually assigned himself the task, since he liked to make certain all was secure before he went to bed.

It was possible that he had gone to visit Suzette. Had the maid attended her mistress this evening? Rio had seen no sign of her, but she could have been in some withdrawing room. She and Olivier might also have been enjoying an assignation out of sight somewhere on the property. No one was likely to interfere with them as long as Suzette's mistress did not object.

To be on the streets at night was not without its dangers for a free man of color. He might be taken for a runaway, attacked for his purse or set upon for no reason at all. Rio hesitated a second. Then he picked up his hat, gloves and sword cane again and went back out into the night.

His majordomo was not to be found in any of the obvious places, nor was he at the musical soirée. A stroll past the Vallier town house was more productive. His informant was a young stable boy of perhaps eleven years, squatting on the banquette where he smoked a corncob pipe while watching for the return of the family carriage. But yes, Monsieur le Maître, he said, that one, Olivier, had been with Suzette earlier but had gone. His master would be home soon and he had to be there.

Rio flipped a picayune that the boy snatched from the air as if catching a fly, then he turned toward home again.

He was too restless for bed just yet. More than that, he liked walking the streets when they were lit only by gaslight or, in the poorer sections, whale-oil lanterns on wrought-iron brackets. The muffled strangeness as the mists drifting from the river wove around the glowing lights and down the narrow thoroughfares gave him a sour pleasure. He enjoyed knowing that commerce and other daily toil had ceased and everyone was either at play or asleep. Movement in the streets was slower, with less noise and confusion, less need to bow and scrape and attempt to be eternally ingratiating. Not that they were empty. Men still strolled from one barroom, cabaret or gaming house, one ball or soirée, to another. Car-

riages clip-clopped along with their side lamps giving off unearthly gleams through the fog as people
left entertainments. Soon even this small amount of
traffic would end. Though an occasional private ball
might last until dawn, most broke up near the witch-
ing hour. Later, nothing would move except stray
cats, the inebriated wending their way homeward
and those who preyed on them.

The gendarmes were abroad tonight, however. Rio
saw a pair of them in their blue dress uniforms with
bell-shaped hats set with cockades, brass-hilted
swords rattling at their sides and staffs swinging.
They crossed the street ahead of him where one of
them stopped to thud the cudgel-like symbol of his
office on the paving stones, calling out the time and
the lie that all was well.

Rio avoided the pair, cutting through the alley
alongside the cathedral and turning onto the rue de
Chartres on his way toward the Passage. As he
moved past a barroom door farther along, the smells
of liquor and stale sawdust reached out to him
through the open door. He glanced inside to see Pépé
Llulla, fellow sword master renowned for his peaceful intentions and deadly skill, at a window table.
With him was Pasquale, the man they called La
Roche.

Rio paused, then turned and entered. His temper
was still uncertain, and he remembered well what he
had been told about the *maître* with the Italian name.
If there was to be a fight, then he had no objection.
He was in that kind of mood.

"Welcome, *mon ami*," Pépé said with a beckoning
wave. He waited until Rio had bought a drink at the

bar, then moved to take a seat before he went on. "What brings you out this time of night?"

"Need you ask?" A reputation as a ladies' man had certain advantages, or so Rio had discovered, providing an excuse for many things.

"Is she lovely?"

"Aren't they all?"

Pépé regarded him with amused recognition for the evasion but did not press it. If he was aware of the talk concerning Rio's interest in Mademoiselle Vallier, he gave no sign.

"Have you by chance seen O'Neill or Croquère this evening?" Rio asked.

"Croquère was for the pugilism match, I believe. Our Irish friend may be with him since he fancies himself a master with fists, as well as with the blade."

"But of course. I should have guessed." He might have, too, if he'd paid more attention to his friends and less to the possibilities contained in Celina's note.

"The match will be ending soon. In the meantime, do you know La Roche?"

"In passing, though I don't believe we have been formally introduced," Rio answered, bowing as Pasquale rose to do the same. "My compliments, sir."

La Roche answered just as punctiliously, and the two of them took their chairs again. Conversation proceeded without undue strain, primarily at Pépé's lead. During the course of it, Rio discovered that La Roche was born in Italy of an Italian mother, but was the natural son of a young English duke who had visited his country on his grand tour. That accounted for his height and the width of his shoulders, as well as the square shape of his jaw. Pleasant spoken, with a dry sense of humor, he did not seem the kind to rent out his sword. It was unfortunate that Count de Lérida had suborned him, for otherwise Rio might have been pleased to call him a friend.

"*Eh bien, señor,*" La Roche said after a time. "You are settled here in New Orleans?"

"For a while, at least."

"No thoughts of returning to Spain?"

"There is little for me there."

"This may be so, yet the place a man calls home holds a powerful attraction."

"One that grows less with time, or so I find. You have plans to return to Italy?" Rio asked, wondering at the same time at the man's insistence.

"One day, perhaps. The summer here promises to be a trial."

"I haven't experienced one as yet."

"Nor I."

La Roche turned to Pépé. "Is it as bad as they claim?"

"The very belly of hell, my friends. I swear every year that I will not stay. Every year, I fail to leave."

"To where would you make your escape?"

"The gulf at Biloxi or one of the barrier islands, the pine barrens near the Ouachita River, the country acres of some accommodating planter—even aboard some steamboat heading to the north. The destination is really unimportant."

"Why don't you go?"

Pépé studied the wine in his glass. "It seems cowardice to run away from such puny things as heat and fever. I am not a coward."

"But if you had a family?"

"A different matter altogether, I do agree. Any precaution is acceptable in order to protect one's own. This is natural and right."

Rio turned his gaze to Pasquale. "You have no wife or children?"

The Italian shook head. "To be both a good swordsman and good husband and father is not possible, I think. Each requires a type of concentration that the other will not allow. And you?"

"The same." This was mere fencing with words, Rio thought. He decided to move to the attack. "You have been in town long enough to make the acquaintance of the Count de Lérida, I believe. Or did you know him before you came, perhaps travel out on the same ship?"

"Ah, the count, a man of parts." Pasquale's smile tightened a fraction. "But how came you to know of our meeting?"

"I don't recall." Rio leaned back in his chair. "One hears so many things."

"It's disturbing for a man to learn his personal affairs are spoken of so casually." La Roche's gaze was intent.

Pépé glanced from one to the other of them with a shadow of concern in his eyes. "Talking is the great pastime of New Orleans."

"Just so," Rio agreed. "Those troubled by it must make certain they do nothing to provide fuel for the gossips."

"Meaning?" The Italian's voice was quietly even.

"To live an exemplary life may be difficult for a sword master, but isn't impossible."

"Is there something in particular that I should avoid doing?"

Rio met the Italian's eyes, his own somber. "That is a matter for your own conscience."

The man across the table studied him for long seconds, but apparently found nothing he cared to resent in that answer. Narrowing his eyes a fraction, he said, "You are almost as new to the city as I, or so one hears. Where have you been since leaving Spain?"

"Many places, none of them that I care to call home."

"Havana, I think."

"I was there."

The other man's smile was wry. "You seem to have left several gentlemen with scars as souvenirs of your stay."

Rio felt the tingle along his veins of heightened alertness. He was not, apparently, the only person who took an interest in the movements of others. "You are well informed."

"A pleasant place, Havana, very like New Orleans. And before that you were in Rome, I'm told, and Paris."

"You were in these cities, as well?"

"It happens that we followed the same route."

"Fortuitous," Rio said, and waited to see if the Italian had more to add.

"Possibly. Shall we drink to fortune?"

La Roche was not to be so easily drawn then. It was understandable. Many of the *maîtres d'armes* of the Passage were reluctant to speak of where they had come from or how they had reached New Orleans. To ask was a blunder. Therefore La Roche must have a reason for it. Was he suggesting that he was following him? Had he, Rio wondered, injured some friend or relative of the Italian's in one of the meetings that littered his past? That might explain his gravitation toward the count. The question was whether his motives would eventually lead to a challenge.

Rio, raising his glass, spoke in tones of meditation. "To fortune, good naturally."

He left the barroom a short time later. Pépé pressed him to stay, but he declined. The disappearance of Denys Vallier raised problems that Rio was not certain he could solve. Nor was he sure how long he had for the attempt. The count was an aging wolf in the guise of a portly gentleman, hiding his teeth behind a somewhat ridiculous combination of bonhomie and hauteur, and doubly dangerous because he did it so well. He had little use for a show of strength but preferred more stealthy means of achieving his aims.

The river fog had grown thicker while he was with Llulla and La Roche. It hovered like a blanket just above street level, so thick it was near impossible to see the toes of his boots. Like the wraiths of lost souls, it curled around the corners of buildings and piled in drifting clouds in doorways. Sound was distorted, so that the squall of the cat Rio almost trod underfoot seemed far away, and the distant howl of a dog directly in front of him. Old women said it meant a death, that night howling, but that was mere superstition. People often died at night and dogs always howled.

The men appeared out of the fog like hulking ghosts, dark shapes that emerged from a recessed doorway to block his path. Three in number, they closed in fast and without a sound beyond the whip of swinging cudgels. They were brutes, dock scum intent on robbing a man they figured to be drunk and defenseless.

It was their mistake. Rio stepped back swiftly. The hiss of his sword cane as it left the sheath was a quiet and deadly warning.

The first blow came from behind him. He felt rather that saw it coming and spun away. He was not quite swift enough. It caught his injured left shoulder a glancing blow, numbing his arm to the fingertips. With a grunt of pain, he ducked and side-stepped, leaping from the banquette into the muddy street. There were five men rather than only three, and he retreated swiftly until he faced all of them.

The gang of toughs spread out with their cudgels and knives held at the ready. For a moment, it appeared that none wanted to test his steel. Then they rushed him, cursing, yelling, swiping at him with their crude weapons as if they meant to take off his head.

He slashed the first man to reach him, sending him reeling back, yelping, as he clutched the cut across his chest. The next avoided Rio's savage thrust with a quick twist, but the third caught his back-handed slice with the wood of his crude weapon. The sword bit deep and was held. The attacker tried to wrench it free, tried to jerk the blade from Rio's hand. He held on with dogged strength, though every movement sent pain lancing through his shoulder that hung useless from the blow on top of the thrust during the duel three days ago.

The sound of running footsteps impinged on his consciousness. It might be either the gendarmes or more dock trash, and he had no time to discover which. His attackers were closing in, weapons raised as they made ready to rush him.

Then he no longer faced them alone. A tall, solid presence filled the space at his left side. Steel rasped as it was drawn from its sheath. As one, he and his new friend advanced, blades flashing.

Their opponents fell back, stumbling in their desperate haste to get away from the vicious whine of the twin swords. Men cursed and yelled. Those at the fringes melted away into the fog. The few that were left turned and took to their heels.

Rio straightened and sheathed his sword, then turned to face the man who had come to his aid. It was Nicholas Pasquale who stood there, relaxed, breathing without apparent effort. A smile lifted one corner of his mobile mouth in response to the startled look Rio bent on him.

"Well, *monsieur?*"

"Well done," Rio answered, remembering his manners enough to execute a bow. "I am in your debt."

"Not at all," the Italian said politely.

"I insist."

"Now why? I'm sure you would do the same for me under like circumstances. But you are hurt, I think." He nodded toward Rio's arm, which he held against his side. "A physician is required?"

It was noteworthy that Pasquale gave him credit for knowing the extent of his own injury. The reaction was that of one no stranger to such matters. Rio flexed his fingers experimentally and lifted his elbow while clasping his shoulder. "I don't believe so."

"Permit me to see you to your rooms, then, in case our friends return."

"That is generous of you, but I doubt they will try again."

"Nevertheless." The Italian waved in the direction Rio had been headed. "To the Passage, I think? Shall we?"

To permit the escort seemed politic, if unnecessary. Rio acquiesced with a nod, then moved off beside Pasquale. They walked in silence for half a block before the other man spoke again.

"It appears you have enemies, *monsieur*."

"What makes you say so?"

"To gather so many to set upon a single man is not the way of such scum. They knew the caliber of their target, therefore the greater numbers. It suggests that someone paid to have you brought down."

The possibility had also occurred to Rio. What troubled him was the motive, though he had no intention of discussing it with a stranger who might also be an enemy. "You may be right."

"This person is known to you?"

"Perhaps."

"You prefer to keep your own counsel. Well enough, but I advise caution."

Rio gave him a hard stare. The urge to demand what he knew and the exact nature of his acquaintance with the count was strong. If Pasquale was the count's man, however, no useful answer could be expected. If he was not, then it would be imprudent to involve him in the business. "Thank you," he said, his voice grave. "I will bear it in mind."

Pasquale left him at the ground-floor entrance of the salon. Rio made his way up the stairs, but was required to unlock the door to his personal rooms himself, since Olivier was not on duty.

Rio shrugged out of his coat with some difficulty and removed the studs from his shirt using the fingers of one hand. Sliding his arm out of the sleeve, he turned his injured shoulder to the small shaving mirror that sat on his washstand. The skin was turning purple with bruising and had considerable swelling around the joint. He thought no bones were broken, but it was impossible to be certain.

"Monsieur Rio!"

He turned his head to see Olivier standing in the doorway of the bedchamber. The majordomo closed the door behind him with swift grace and came forward.

"It's about time," Rio said.

"I would have been here, but Suzette was concerned for her Mam'zelle, since she had only her aunt with her tonight. I waited to see her home."

Rio gave him a brief look as he heard the clipped tone in his voice. "You think I should have done it? I was certain any number of men would have been happy for the opportunity."

"So they were. Their host seized the honor for himself. That does not relieve the obligation."

Rio gave a grunt that was both comment and the result of Olivier's firm grasp on his shoulder.

"It's bruised only, not dislocated," the majordomo said. "Be seated and I will attend to it."

Rio swore even as he complied. "Be quick about it, and then bind it tightly."

"To be sure," Olivier said in grim tones. "It would never do for anyone to know how close you are to being hors de combat."

13

Rio slept late on the following morning, in part because of the early mornings and late nights he had been keeping, but also because of the strong tot of old cognac that Olivier had poured for him as a palliative against the pain of his shoulder. It was Caid who woke him, strolling into the room with a small tray balanced on the tips of his fingers and a crooked smile warming the rugged lines of his face.

"*Alà vous café*," he said dryly in the traditional greeting used by a servant whose job it was to wake his master in the morning. "Olivier tells me you had a bit of trouble last night."

"You could say so." Rio raised up on his elbows in bed, raked his hair from his eyes with one hand and sat up. Oliver, trailing Caid into the bedchamber, moved to place pillows against the bed's headboard, and Rio suppressed a grunt of pain as he subsided against them.

Caid grimaced in sympathy. "How's the shoulder?"

"Stiff."

"So I would imagine. And this is your day for instruction."

That was true enough. "I'll have to close, not a bad thing since other duty calls. I'll be ready again for the next round." Most sword masters gave lessons only three days per week to allow for rest between the days of exertion.

"One way or another? Take care or you'll do yourself a permanent injury. Then who will we look to for entertainment under The Oaks?"

"You can take over."

"Thank you, but I prefer less melodramatic methods of demonstration."

Others might take Caid's refusal as a sign of trepidation, but Rio knew better. Rather, it was an indication of his pacific nature. He was one of those large men who smiled, spoke softly and were slow to anger, but became quietly lethal when his temper was aroused. "Good," he said. "Then you won't mind attending me in a small task."

"Won't I?" Caid crossed to a chair near the window and sat, lifting one booted foot to his knee and grasping the ankle.

Olivier brought the extra cup from the tray and poured a stream of the hot brew into it. "Ah, Havana beans," Caid said, inhaling the aroma.

Rio glanced at Olivier with a raised brow, even as he reached for his own cup. Olivier, who made all such purchases, nodded agreement. To Caid, he said, "You've become a coffee connoisseur since being in New Orleans?"

"Hard to avoid. Besides which, I saw the notice in *L'Abeille* of the Havana shipment. The barque *Paul Emile* unloaded a big consignment of wines, too, if you need to replenish your cellar, including fifty boxes of Château Lafitte at a dozen bottles to the box."

"And you intend to supply your salon with the Lafitte?"

"Not on your life. My purse won't run to it, and the young sprouts that come to me are unlikely to appreciate it. A cask of the St. Emiline and maybe a barrel or two of the Bordeaux will do for the salon."

"Sounds as if I need the same before it disappears. Olivier?"

"I will attend to it," his majordomo said at once.

"Perhaps you could place Caid's order at the same time, since I have need of his services."

"Just so."

Caid tipped his head. "What can be so important? Come, you've tweaked my curiosity enough."

"It's young Vallier."

"What has he done now?"

"Rather, it's what he hasn't done. Unless he put in an appearance last evening, this will be the third day since he was last seen at home."

"So his fair sister has asked your assistance in locating him? Or is it that she blames you for his disappearance?"

"I blame myself," Rio said shortly, then went on to tell Caid what had taken place between him and Denys Vallier.

Caid pursed his lips, his gaze narrow with concentration. "It may be foul play, but he could just as easily be off on some lark, maybe a bullbaiting or cockfight in the country."

"Without leaving word?"

"Yes, well. Maybe he's enjoying a protracted sampling of the charms of a quadroon or one of the women who sit in second-floor windows on certain streets. It's not the sort of thing a man is likely to discuss with the females in his family."

"Someone should know of it, his friends or his father."

Olivier, moving around the room picking up articles of clothing and opening the curtains, gave Rio a narrow glance, but he was easily able to ignore it.

"True," Caid agreed.

"I don't like it, and if we wait to make certain he isn't simply amusing himself it may be too late."

"The question is where to start?"

Olivier cleared his throat. "If I might make a suggestion?"

Rio was not at all sure he wanted to hear it, but he lifted an inquiring brow.

"Inquiries could be set in motion concerning the young gentleman among those who work in these less respectable haunts, including the houses with the second-floor females."

What Olivier proposed was using the slave grapevine. It was a formidable force along which gossip, serious and salacious, risible and malicious, could travel as fast as a man could walk. If a young man of good family was currently ensconced in the arms of a blowsy female of amorous skill and scant virtue, some servant would know it.

"I leave the task, and the wine, in your capable hands," Rio said with a small salute. "In the meantime, Caid and I will scour the docks."

Caid lifted a brow. "Before or after the gaming houses?"

"Others have beaten that particular bush already, leaving us the more interesting parts of town."

"We have a lot of ground to cover then. Shall we enlist Gilbert and Bastile?"

"Excellent idea, if you think they will join with us."

"They will be annoyed if not included."

"Good. You might step down the Passage and roust them out, if you will, while I make ready."

Caid agreed at once and went off to execute his commission. Olivier lingered to help Rio into buff pantaloons, a merino waistcoat in ash-gray embroidered with black and black boots of Spanish leather. He tied his cravat in a simple knot and helped him carefully into a black frock coat with a velvet collar and gray pearl buttons, then handed him his sword cane. Turning away, he picked up Rio's beaver hat and stood brushing it a second before smoothing the nap of the fur with his sleeve.

"You will take care, yes?" he asked finally.

Rio gave him an amused glance. "You're worried, mother?"

"You are not yourself."

"I know. But the surest way to attract predators is to let them smell blood."

"So you will pretend. What if you are challenged?"

"I'll fight, of course."

Olivier shook his head. "You cannot."

"I must, or it will be all over for me here. But let us hope it doesn't come to that."

"Hope costs nothing yet can have a high price."

"I'm sure that means something," Rio said, lifting his right arm to take the beaver and set it on his head.

"A gambler may hope for luck but lose everything. A man may hope to live and find that others want him dead."

"Never fear," Rio said, reaching to clasp Olivier's shoulder. "I will recommend you to Caid if worse should come to worst. I'm sure he will give you leave to play *fainéant* at his salon if mine closes."

"I would not!"

"I know." Rio did, too, since a *fainéant* was a man who lived on the charity of his relatives or friends.

"I didn't mean…"

"I know that as well, nodcock, and thank you for it." Rio smiled as he shook his friend and majordomo a little. "Now give me no more warnings or I may take to my bed while you coddle me to death."

The program Rio had outlined was followed with all care and dispatch. Gilbert and Bastile made the rounds of the grog shops and barrelhouses in the less savory part of town. In the process, they ran across Llulla and one or two other *maîtres d'armes* who joined the hunt. Caid elected to accompany Rio to the docks, perhaps because of knowledge of the dangers there and Rio's temporary incapacitation. They spoke to stevedores rolling barrels and hogsheads up steamboat gangplanks and accountants ticking off bills of lading, walked the lines of vessels tied up at the levee and boarded a couple of barques and steamers. No one had seen a young man of Vallier's description.

Standing amid the hustle and bustle, the yells of dray drivers and calls of vendors touting their wares both liquid and edible, Rio tried to think exactly how a gentleman might be spirited away from the city and which ship was most likely to take the cargo. The problem was not that none seemed a likely candidate but that any one of them could have served the purpose.

The smells of sour molasses, spilled wine and moldy flour hung on the air along with the sweet scent of tobacco from the ship just in from Havana. Pigs rooted in the debris that littered the ground, including a trio with blue snouts that had discovered a broken keg of indigo. Just along the way, a boat was loading for the upriver run to Louisville, and passengers crowded the area where its gangplank reached across the water. Shouting farewells, calling after errant children and laggard nurses, looking around for boxes and bags and other luggage while holding on to skirts and bonnets, hats and coattails that blew in the wind, they created a scene from bedlam. It was impossible to think in the midst of such confusion, much less make any vital decision.

"He could be anywhere," Caid said, setting his hands on his hips with an expression of disgust.

"And probably is," Rio agreed.

"Such as at home with his dear sister by now, regaling her with his adventures. Have you thought of that?"

"I have."

"Then suppose we make certain we aren't wasting our time."

"I could send a note," Rio said in reluctant agreement.

"Excellent." Caid reached to settle his hat more firmly on his head. "Let us repair to the nearest barroom where you may find a pen and writing paper and I shall certainly find a drink."

They stopped in at the Café des Réfugiés on the rue de la Levée. Caid ordered wine for them both then lounged at the table, sipping from his glass, while Rio wrote and dispatched his message. It was sent to Olivier by one of the street boys who normally hung about barrooms and coffeehouses in hope of such commissions. The majordomo must once again act as intermediary.

Caid, when he was done, nodded toward a man who had entered just moments before. "Your friend the envoy from Mexico, I believe, and without the count in tow."

"So it is." Rio surveyed the dark-haired newcomer with the Don Quixote beard. "Now, I wonder…"

"What's that?"

Rio didn't reply. Drinking the last of his coffee laced with rum, he rose and went toward the Mexican. The man turned at his approach, and Rio offered a punctilious bow and the traditional, rather florid greeting of their heritage.

"You are alone, *señor*, or so it appears," he continued. "Perhaps you would care to join us?" He gestured toward Caid, who watched him in lively curiosity.

"That is most kind of you, but truly…"

"I insist," Rio said. "It will be an honor."

The Mexican envoy moved ahead of Rio to the table where he bowed to Caid as he was introduced. When greetings had been exchanged, he flipped apart the full, divided tail of his frock coat with a fastidious gesture then seated himself. "This is most kind," he said. "As a stranger here, I sometimes feel the lack of companionship. To hear the fine syllables of my own language rather than French or the barbarous English is a distinct pleasure. But you do not have the accents of Madrid, I think, Señor de Silva. Do I hear those of Barcelona?"

"You have a good ear," Rio answered with a nod of assent.

"Only because Count de Lérida, whom you know, I think, mentioned his connection to the Catalan."

"How does the count go on? I've not seen him for a day or two, perhaps more."

"He is well, you may be sure. His kind is seldom otherwise."

"His kind?" Rio's interest sharpened as he heard the sardonic inflection in the other man's voice.

"You are not a particular friend?"

"By no means."

"I would not wish to give offense. Indeed, I should not have spoken at all, and would not except for lingering annoyance. I was with him earlier in the day, you see."

"At the hotel and exchange, perhaps? I don't suppose he was accompanied by Denys Vallier?"

"The brother of the beauteous Mademoiselle Vallier whom he is pursuing? I regret, no. We were alone as the count particularly desired that I attend him in private."

Rio had expected no less. "And this discussion, I assume it was unsatisfactory?"

"I would call him out but for the reflection on my position as a representative of my country!"

"He must have vexed you more than a bit." It was

a blatant invitation to know the reason. Rio waited with strained patience to see if the envoy would accept it.

"Quite. A matter of avarice and disloyalty, though more than that I cannot say."

"I understand."

"I knew you must have every sympathy. Just as I know we must share similar ambitions."

Rio lifted a brow. "For success with a sword?"

"No, no, my friend. I speak of Mexican supremacy west of the Sabine River. As one who has the blood of glorious Spain in his veins, you must surely applaud our aspirations."

"Indeed," Rio said noncommittally. Sympathy was one thing, approval quite another.

Caid, silent until that moment, made a sound between a snort and a laugh.

"Such an upstart young country, this, don't you agree, sir?" The Mexican envoy smiled as he glanced in Caid's direction.

"Oh, aye, and brash with it. But strong."

"Due to the hopes and determination of its people, yes. One is forced to yield that argument. Still, age and experience must always prevail over youth and brawn."

The waiter arrived just then with a drink for the envoy. Caid chose that moment to rise and drop a few piastres on the table for his own libation. "Your pardon, gentlemen, but I remembered an errand that needs my attention." He took his hat from the extra chair seat and settled it on his head, tipping the brim in the Mexican's direction. "A pleasure, *señor*. Rio, I'll rejoin you in an hour or so, if I may."

If his friend had an errand, Rio didn't know it. He suspected Caid of taking himself off from either dislike for the turn of the conversation or else discretion because he had caught some slight hint that the Mexican might speak more frankly without his presence. If the latter, then he was perfectly correct. Before Caid reached the banquette, the envoy drew his chair closer and lowered his voice.

"I am happy to have this opportunity to speak more privately, Señor de Silva. It came to me a moment ago that we might discuss a matter of mutual advantage."

"Concerning?"

"Influence, in a word. The esteem in which you and other *maîtres d'armes* are held by these French Creole aristocrats, the opportunities open to you of swaying political opinion in these admirers."

"Forgive me if I err," Rio said, "but rumor indicates this function is being served for you by Count de Lérida."

"It was spoken of between us, I freely admit it." The envoy shrugged. "The possible influence of the count was slight compared to his estimate of his worth."

"He asked too much for the task?"

"His demands were exceeded only by his arrogance."

"So you could not come to terms."

"In a word, no. When told that Mexico would not beggar itself in order to gain his favor, the count suggested that he might sell his knowledge of our aims to representatives of the Republic of Texas or the U.S. government."

"Arrogance indeed."

"Such a threat is an indication of the man. I would rather my country fail in its aims than achieve them by treating with such noble scum."

"The count must be desperate for funds to attempt such extortion."

The eyes of the envoy turned as hard as obsidian. "I had heard this, which was the reason I approached him some weeks ago. He was rational enough at first, then this. Now he may die in the gutter, and I would not lift a hand to save him."

The count had made an enemy. Rio wondered if he realized it. But if he had lost this opportunity to fatten his pocketbook, he would be even more desperate for cash. To marry without delay might be imperative for him. It was not a comforting thought.

"An unpleasant business," Rio said gravely. "Also unfortunate since it puts you in a difficult position."

"One that I dare hope you may correct. It would be a signal service if you could see your way to filling the role originally designed for the count. I would go so far as to say your value in this matter may surpass his."

"You flatter me," Rio murmured, as his mind moved in swift computation.

"Not at all. Naturally, my government is prepared to be as generous as any reasonable man could expect. I feel certain we may come to an arrangement satisfactory to us both."

"The proposal has merit," Rio said, his concentration on his wineglass. "I believe it calls for serious reflection."

"As you will. I shall look forward to hearing from

you." The Mexican envoy made an expansive gesture with his glass. "Providence has arranged our meeting, I feel sure of it."

Rio was less sanguine but kept his doubts to himself.

"So," Caid said when he rejoined Rio later at his fencing salon and heard the envoy's proposal. "You aren't really going to allow yourself to be suborned?"

"When it will prevent the count from benefiting? Why should I not?"

"Loyalty to a place you may wish to call home? Dislike for smarmy intrigue? An intelligent disinclination to mix politics with your profession? Take your choice."

"It's the Republic of Texas that stands to lose. I can't imagine what loyalty I owe there."

"If Texas is lost, this young country, this land of opportunity, will be the less."

"Then its leaders, as with so many others who have much to lose, should learn the art of compromise." Rio actually had no intention of becoming involved in the envoy's plotting, but wanted to hear what his friend had to say.

"True enough, but in fact it's New Orleans that has earned my gratitude, if not yours. It's the people, the street boys who look up to us, the young men who expect us to give them skills that will keep them safe, the old men who bow in deference and extol our supposed courage, even the ladies who smile on us. They have taken us in, and for it they have my allegiance."

"You sound as if you never intend to leave, even when you are done here."

"Could be."

"What of your green island of Erie?"

"There's little enough there worth going back for to see," Caid answered, his brogue strong in the words. "I'll be content to rest here."

Rio gave him a keen look. "A man might almost believe there was a woman at the bottom of this sudden attachment to the city."

"Not for me, not yet. Oh, there's a many a darling girl over in the part of the city they call the Irish Channel, and more arriving every day. I've found none anywhere that I'd want to wed, however. Unlike some I could name."

"You're suggesting I might have intentions in that direction?"

"As to intentions, I wouldn't know. But I do think that if that lovely young female who lives on the rue Royale should only whisper the dear words, 'Come to me,' you'd be for breaking your stiff Spanish neck to get there."

Caid's comment made half in jest was easy enough for Rio to brush aside. That was until the answer to his note was delivered a short time later. The first words to leap up at him from the page were, "I must see you." He stood staring at them while white heat rose to sear his brain and desire became a need so strong it was like addiction.

He should not go. He knew that, knew it beyond doubting. "Not bad news, I hope?" Caid asked, his attention resting on Rio's face.

"Vallier is still absent. She doesn't say more than that, though it seems something may have come up. She writes that she must see me."

"And you don't think it's merely that she pines for your kisses?"

Rio gave him a hard look without speaking.

"No. My apologies. So you will go?"

Nothing could keep him away. "Perhaps."

"Suppose it's a trap?"

"Why should it be?" Impatience threaded Rio's voice for Caid's apparent disapproval.

"Why, no reason at all. Except that you are despoiling a young woman who came to you for help while risking her good name and her future, not to mention her immortal soul."

Anger moved over Rio in a wave. His voice low and hard, he began, "If you were any other man…"

"If I were any other man, you would call me out and slice me to slivers, or try it. But I have become your friend, and I tell you to your face that what you are doing is wrong."

"You know nothing of what I am doing, or my reasons."

"I know that you have become so blinded by the need for revenge that you will sacrifice anything and anyone to have it. I know that you have abandoned your principles in order to injure one who has wronged you. I know that you have endangered Denys Vallier by enmeshing him in this affair, and that you seek him now, not to save his life but in the hope that his circumstances will serve to your advantage. I know that you will go tonight to Celina Vallier, whispering of love, while the heart inside you is as cold as ice."

Rio stared at him while breathing hard and fast through his nostrils. "Are you done?"

"For the moment."

"Then let me tell you— No. Forget it. If you have no better understanding of who I am or what I must do, then my reasons can matter not at all. What I require to know at this moment is if you intend to continue the search for Vallier. Are you with me or not?"

"Oh, hell, Rio, of course I'm with you. I don't desert my friends just because they're pigheaded, stiff-rumped and have no common sense."

Rio stared at Caid in fury for long seconds. Then abruptly the humor of Caid's determined partisan-ship caught up with him, shaking a laugh free of his chest. "Good. Let us go. Now."

14

The footsteps on the stairs were slow and trudging, as if someone carried a great burden. Celina exchanged a long glance with Tante Marie Rose. The bell had not rung, and the tread was not that of Mortimer that they heard scores of times every day. It didn't belong to Denys, for he always took the steps at speed.

"Papa," she said.

"Oh, *chère*," her aunt said, fumbling in her apron pocket for her smelling salts. "I fear the worst."

Celina put down her embroidery needle with its silk floss and left her chair, moving from the salon to meet her father at the head of the stairs. He raised his head to give her a long look. His features were taut and pale, and his mouth set in a grim line. After the barest pause, he continued upward.

"You have word of Denys?" She kept her voice as even as she was able, but it wobbled a little as she spoke her brother's name.

"I've heard nothing, seen nothing."

Her father handed his hat and cane to Mortimer, who came from the darkness at the end of the gallery to receive them. Standing aside for her to precede him, he followed her into the salon. He nodded briefly to Tante Marie Rose before stepping to a side table where he poured a glass of claret from the cut-glass bottle that reposed there on a silver tray.

Celina glanced at her aunt, who sat pressing her handkerchief to her lips, her eyes huge in her face. At her almost imperceptible nod, Celina drew a deep breath and spoke with care. "The authorities must be told. Surely you agree to it now."

"In the morning," Monsieur Vallier replied. "I will call on the gendarmes then if Denys still has not appeared."

She wanted something done now. The need pushed at her like a hurricane wind. Another day had gone by without word. Hippolyte and Armand had dropped by the town house several times, but only to report their lack of progress. With every moment that passed, her feeling grew that they were losing precious time, that soon it might be too late. "What if Denys is lying ill or injured somewhere? Why not go this evening?"

"He would surely be able to give his name and habitation."

"Not if he were unconscious or out of his head with fever. Please, Papa!"

"You have already gone behind my back to have his friends make inquiries. Is that not enough for you?"

"How should it be? Denys's friends may ask about or go to his usual rendezvous, but that is all. You are his father. You are able to speak to the officials, to make them undertake a wider search, if you will give yourself the trouble. Don't you care what has become of him?"

"Of course I care," he said, turning on her. "How dare you suggest otherwise? But I also have some concern for his pride. I will not make him a laughing-stock by trailing after him like an anxious nursemaid. And I will thank you not to interfere further."

Tante Marie Rose made a bleating sound of distress, but Celina barely heard her. She faced her father squarely with her hands clenched into fists among the folds of her skirts. "You are still angry with me over the affair of the marriage contract. Please don't allow that to sway your judgment. To stand against you in either of these matters is no light undertaking. Only the most pressing conviction of disaster drives me to it."

"You view marriage to a man of noble position, impeccable lineage and fine manners as disastrous? That you can speak of it in such a way is clear indication of your poor judgment. How am I to put any credence in your fears for Denys?"

Celina allowed herself a silent and most unlady-like imprecation. It had been a mistake to bring up the betrothal. "Please, Papa," she began.

"Enough. I have said what I will do. The discussion is at an end." He emptied his glass and set it back on the tray with a musical clang. Then he strode from the room.

He was going, and she had not mentioned half of what was on her mind. With a tight set to her mouth, she whisked after him onto the gallery. "Papa, wait!"

He turned with a forbidding frown. "What is it now?"

"I thought, that is, I wondered if I might go with you when you speak to the gendarmes. To sit here doing nothing is insupportable."

"You may not. It's no proper place for a female. What good you think you might do there, I can't imagine."

"I could describe Denys, tell them what he was wearing, where he likes to go and who his friends are so they may speak with them. Oh, a hundred things that you may not have noticed in these last weeks."

"Nonsense. Denys is well-known to the watch, I assure you."

"Then allow me to accompany you for whatever else you intend doing. I will stay in the carriage, if you like, but sitting here while time passes is driving me mad!"

"Please don't make a tragedy, Celina. It is the lot of women to wait. In any case, I think you've done quite enough with your missives."

Celina stared at him a brief second. Could he be aware of the notes to Rio that Suzette had taken back and forth? Surely not, or he would be much more perturbed. He was referring to her message sent around to Hippolyte Ducolet. However, that instant of fear was a reminder of another problem.

"I suppose I must abide by your decision then," she said, lowering her head.

"There's a good girl, Celina. Now, if you will excuse me."

"Of course...except for one other thing. I don't know how to ask, hesitate to mention it at all..."

He gave a long-suffering sigh. "Yes?"

"Have you ever freed a slave, Papa? I mean, have you any strong feelings against it?"

"Do not tell me, please, that you have turned abolitionist while I wasn't looking?"

"No, no, but I…have you?"

"To free a slave is an economic decision, *chère*, not a matter of emotions. Slaves are an investment, a commodity for which money, a great deal of money, has been paid. A man cannot simply divest himself of such assets without serious consequences to his pocketbook. More than that, the owner must provide surety that the freed slave will not become a charge on the state, so that other citizens must bear the cost of his beneficence."

"Suzette was a gift from my grandfather, I think, given to my mother when I was born. She cost you nothing."

"We are speaking of Suzette, are we?"

"If you please. She is in love with Olivier, a man in the employ of one of the sword masters. He cannot, or will not, marry her because she is a slave."

"And I should dispense with her services because of this man's principles?"

"She deserves it, Papa, and I would not mind. In fact, I would be glad if it means her happiness."

"Happiness, a mere hope attached to an illusion." He shook his head. "More than likely, she would be miserable, forced to bear a child every year while living hand to mouth on the slim wages such a man might make. She will be far better off with us."

"Will she truly, while pining after all the things she cannot have, the things she cannot do, because she is our property? She loves this man, truly she does. To be with him is her only desire."

Her father stared at her for a long moment. Then he gave an abrupt nod. "Very well."

"Oh, Papa! You will release her?"

"I will give her to you as a marriage gift on the day you wed the count. If you choose to free her, it is your affair."

Celina was bereft of speech. This was coercion of a most pernicious kind. She could not believe her father would stoop to it. That he had done so was the count's influence, she knew it.

"Nothing to say, *chère?* Then Suzette's freedom must not have been so important a matter, after all." Her father turned and continued along the gallery. The door of his bedchamber closed behind him.

Celina stared after him a long instant. Then with her head held high, she returned to the salon.

"My father has turned into someone I no longer recognize."

Her aunt searched her face. "You must not judge him too harshly. I think he fears for Denys but tries valiantly to hide it. To admit the possibility of another loss would be too much."

Explaining her discussion with her father was more than Celina cared to attempt at the moment. Besides, the prospect of freedom for Suzette might change her aunt's mind about marriage to the count yet again. "I have no wish to play nursemaid to Denys, but only to make certain no harm comes to him."

"We cannot protect those we love from the world, *ma chère.* They must make their own way."

"And I must say nothing, do nothing for that reason?"

Her aunt sighed and wiped her fingertips under one eye. "You remind me so much of your mother, dear Celina. She was so serene in her outlook, yet would fight like a tiger for those she loved. Family was everything to her, as it is for your papa. He loved her desperately, you know, and depended on her counsel in all things. I think you are possibly too much like her for his comfort."

"I can't help that. Am I to sit here twiddling my thumbs because I might injure his sensibilities? Must we wait until daybreak when even now Denys may be calling out in pain, wondering why someone does not come for him? I can't bear it."

"Now, *chère*. You will make yourself ill if you don't have a care. Perhaps that nice Ducolet boy and his friend, Armand, will have better news before the evening is over."

Celina had no great hopes of it after so much time without word. Any expectation she had was invested in Rio de Silva. His note this afternoon had been comforting, a sign that he was carrying out his promise. He had knowledge and experience undreamed of by Denys's more immature friends. If he could not find her brother and bring him home to her, then no one could.

It had not been easy to pen the second request that he come to her. She had wavered over it, writing and tearing up the note a dozen times. Finally she had dashed it off and given it to Suzette for Olivier before she could change her mind. Even so, she wished it back a dozen times, wished it safely unwritten.

He would think she was infatuated with him, think she longed for more of his kisses, more of his strength surrounding her, inside her. He was possibly right; the mere thought made her feel lightheaded yet warm and heavy in her lower limbs. Yes, and to touch him, to have that right, had been incredible. The muscles that layered his body, their smooth, warm glide under the skin, had enthralled her. To have him touch her, hold her in silent possession, had been something she would never forget for as long as she breathed. Regardless, to repeat the experience might not be wise. How could anything that might pass between them possibly live up to her memory of that first time?

She had felt loved. It was very strange.

How she had managed to face Rio de Silva last evening, she had no idea. That the brides she knew had been able to laugh and talk and greet friends and relatives as if nothing had happened in the tangled sheets of the marriage bed was amazing. Such intimacy, frightening and delightful, awkward and entrancing, vulgar and soul-satisfying, changed everything. She shivered a little just thinking of it.

"Celina, my love, is something wrong?"

"No, no," she said quickly. "I was only thinking." Moving to where she had left her embroidery frame, she seated herself with the lamp's glow at her left elbow. Though she set a few stitches, she had no idea if they were long or short or even in the correct place.

Tante Marie Rose had retired for the night, but Celina was still at her frame when the caller arrived. It was late for a visit. She sat perfectly still, listening while Mortimer moved past the salon with his stately gait on his way to answer the bell.

Her first thought was naturally for news of Denys. Her second was that Monsieur de Silva had lost patience and decided to present himself formally rather than with his usual stealth. She strained to hear, but caught only the murmur of male voices. Then she heard Mortimer returning. The visitor wheezed as he climbed the stairs, and his footsteps were heavy and solidly placed.

Celina leaped up to flee through the door that connected to her aunt's bedchamber and her own beyond it. It was too late. Mortimer rapped softly, then turned the knob and stepped aside.

"Monsieur le Comte, *mademoiselle*."

She would not make the man welcome or give him her hand. Fastening her gaze at a point just past the visitor's shoulder, she said, "Inform my father, Mortimer, if you please. I am sure the count's business is with him."

The butler bowed himself from the doorway. The count sent a derisive glance after him, as if noting the door left conspicuously open. Then he moved forward. "Well met, *mademoiselle*. I thought to find you from home, dancing the evening away at some ball."

"I had not the heart for it tonight. My father may have mentioned to you that my brother is missing?"

"A disturbing business, I don't wonder that you are distressed. He called on me that morning, you know. If only I had been available."

"You didn't see him?"

"Lamentably, no. He said he would return, or so I was told, but he did not."

"Told?"

"By the hotel clerk who spoke to him."

"And did my brother give no indication of where he was going so that you might follow?"

"Only that he would be no great distance away."

"Yes," she murmured. Was this yet another sign

pointing at Rio? She hated to think that it might be so.

The count took a step toward her. "How I wish you would allow me to remove this burden from you. As your acknowledged betrothed, I would be your shield against such tribulations. Place your troubles upon my shoulders, and I shall certainly discover the whereabouts of your brother and return him to you."

"Certainly?" She met his eyes, her own cool. It might be the result of her earlier discussion with her father, but his florid promise had the sound of coercion to her ears.

"I would move heaven and earth to secure the ease of your mind. No task would be beyond me."

He could not be such a villain as to know her brother's whereabouts but keep it from her until he had her tied to him. It was far too suspicious of her to even think such a thing. "I am sensible of the compliment you pay me with such sentiments, *monsieur*," she said with care, "but I am of the same mind as before."

Moving closer, he thudded down to his knees before her and grasped her forearm, fumbling down it until he clutched her fingers in his damp hand. "Fair Celina, do not be so cold toward me, I beg you. I erred in my conduct when last we met. My feelings for you overcame my better judgment, leading me into behavior that must have been shocking to one so gently reared. I acknowledge the fault and crave your forgiveness."

"Count de Lérida, you must not. Please, get up." She tried to regain her hand, but he had it in both his, pressing it to his forehead.

"Do not be so cruel as to turn from me. Regret and fear that I had destroyed your regard have been my constant companions since last we met. Give me hope. Tell me that you absolve me of wrong and will consider our betrothal, even if not yet consent to it."

This was awkward in the extreme, a farce she had to end before it became something more distasteful. "You are forgiven, Monsieur le Comte, from simple charity. As for your proposal, I could not think of such a thing while my brother is missing—even if my sentiments had changed, which they have not. Now I must leave you. Here is my father arriving, and I'm sure you have important matters to discuss that are not my concern."

The count glanced around, then released her and heaved himself to his feet. "As you will, Mademoiselle Celina," he said in a rumbling voice too low to be heard by her father who had just entered the salon. "But this is a refusal you may well live to regret."

Celina had turned away to make her escape through the side door. She swung back toward the count. What she saw there chilled her to the heart. And she wondered, suddenly, if the value she had placed on her own free will, her own freedom, might not be too high.

Alone in her bedchamber, she sank down on a slipper chair while she tried to think. "*I must see you*," she had written to Rio de Silva. She had thought to discover the scope and details of his search efforts, also to see if there was anything he was holding back because it might upset her. Mostly, she had wanted to speak to someone who did not belittle her concern for Denys.

Yes, but was that all? Her heart beat faster at the mere idea of seeing him. As appalled as she was at the risks he took to be private with her, she was also flattered and enthralled by his willingness to undertake them and the ease with which it was accomplished. She was growing addicted to the thrill of having him suddenly appear when she least expected it, entranced by his male presence, his understanding, his touch, his smile.

It was ridiculous, a reckless display of indiscretion. She should know better, and did, but couldn't force herself to stop. Not now, while Denys's whereabouts were still unknown. Not yet.

Regardless, Rio could not be allowed to come here tonight while her father was at home and closeted with the count for an unknown length of time. It was far too risky.

Yet how to prevent it?

They should have established a signal, she thought with an almost hysterical urge to laugh, some banner or scarf that she could drape from her balcony as a means of indicating that all was clear. Though in reality, it was never truly safe.

She could think of only one way to stop him.

To have a purpose, a reason to act instead of waiting for things to happen, was such a relief that she sprang to her feet. Moving to the bellpull beside the fireplace, she rang for Suzette, then went to the armoire to take out her cloak of midnight-blue velvet trimmed with braiding and cords. She was still adjusting it over her gown when the door opened.

"Mam'zelle, what are you doing?"

"We are going out," she said in crisp tones. "Get

your wrap and meet me in the porte cochere. Make sure you aren't seen, particularly by Mortimer."

"Where…"

"There isn't time. You will learn everything later."

Suzette didn't move, but stood staring at her with suspicion dawning in her eyes. "Mam'zelle, you wouldn't!"

"Quickly," Celina said in firm tones. "We must go at once."

She was glad of her heavier outerwear once they were in the street. A cold wind was blowing from the north, whipping around corners and whining under the eaves of buildings. Its chill breath had driven most men home or into the warm conviviality of the gaming houses, coffeehouses and barrooms. The only ladies out were those on their way to or from some entertainment. Celina drew her hood closer over her head to conceal her face and tied the cords under her chin. Holding her skirts high, she set out with a fast and purposeful stride.

Olivier answered the bell. For an instant, it seemed he would not admit them, then he glanced up and down the pedestrian way and drew them quickly inside. His smile held a shadow of pain as it lingered on Suzette. Watching them made Celina's chest ache. She had no compunction whatever about leaving them together while she went alone up the stairs to the sitting room that lay just off the main fencing salon.

Rio was shrugging into his coat, perhaps because he'd heard their voices and footsteps on the stairs. His movements were a shade careful, or so it seemed, but she had no time to consider it. "I am sorry to descend on you again without warning," she said as she came forward.

He took her hand, carrying it to his lips. "I have no quarrel with it except as it may affect you."

"It was necessary to come at once while my father was occupied with a visitor."

Humor rose into his eyes, turning them silvery. "A convenient time, I agree."

"You may think it comical, but I cannot."

"I know," he said, handing her into a chair before the fire. "Forgive me, and tell me how I may be of service."

Though his words were nearly the same as those spoken to her by the count, they did not set her back up but made her ready to comply. It made no sense when both men seemed intent on forcing her to their will. Was the difference some weakness within herself? Or could it be merely that Rio de Silva's tone was layered with sympathy. Well, and the fact that he had broad shoulders and a face to make women swoon compared to the count who reminded her forcibly of a bullfrog?

"Is there still no word?" she asked.

"None. I'm sorry."

She let out her breath on a sigh. "So am I."

"You didn't come here to ask something that could easily be put in a note, I think. Tell me what concerns you."

She looked at her hands, which were clenched on the edges of her cloak. "There is another matter. We spoke of it briefly when last we met, but it lingers in my mind. It is so very…"

"Please," he said, cutting across her words. "Just tell me."

"A third person has suggested that you were the last to see Denys before he disappeared. This circumstance comes up again and again when there is no other sign."

He stared at her a long moment while his eyes turned storm dark. Then he rose and moved to stand with his back to the fire. "Who else has told you?"

"What difference does it make?"

"A great deal, if the only way they could know is that my movements are being watched."

"This time, I fear it was the…"

"Count de Lérida," he finished for her.

"How did you know?"

"It makes sense in a situation where little else does. Tell me, if I swear that I have not harmed your brother, will you believe me?"

That was, of course, the question. She searched her mind for the answer, wanting to be positive.

"Yes or no, Celina. It isn't complicated. Simply say what you feel."

She looked at him as he stood there, making no effort to explain or convince her by pleading his case. His expression was direct, his back straight, his hands clasped lightly behind his back. He did not move, gave no sign that he was being judged. The candlelight gleamed as it fell across his features from girandoles on either side of the fireplace, searching out the lines of character and valor imprinted there, touching the snowy whiteness of his shirt collar, the black of his casual cravat.

How could such a man be a liar?

"Yes," she said. "I will believe you."

His smile was an accolade. Drawing a deep breath,

he let it out again, and then rolled his shoulders as if they were stiff. When he spoke, his voice was deep and even. "I can assure that Denys was alive and well when last I spoke with him."

The magnitude of her relief was a measure of how much she had feared it might be otherwise. She looked away, toward the fire, unwilling to let him see. Then her shoulders twitched, and abruptly she was shaking all over.

He went to one knee at her side in a movement of athletic grace in marked contrast to that of the count less than an hour before. Taking her hands, he stripped away her calfskin gloves with practiced ease. Then he chafed them between his own for an instant before placing them against the warm, muscle-clad wall of his chest. He reached with a strong arm to encircle her waist, drawing her to the edge of her chair. As she slipped from it to her knees, he caught her close, clasping her against him with warm strength.

The silk of his waistcoat was smooth under her palms. She could feel the padding of muscle beneath it. His scent, compounded of starched linen, a hint of English bay rum from his hair and his own male essence, made her feel dizzy. Or perhaps it was the press of her breasts against him as she slid her hands higher, his touch as he smoothed over her back and down her spine, or the way he tilted his head to look down at her lips.

Her tension flowed away. Her trembling stilled. She lifted her lashes, meeting his eyes for endless seconds. They were dark gray and slumberous with desire, yet seemed to hold some tenuous pain layered with regret. Then his attention flickered to her lips once more. He dipped his head, hesitated, then took them.

She had been here before, in this room at night while firelight danced on the walls. He had kissed her then.

It was nothing like this.

His lips were gently caressing, an incitement to dreams of languid possession, of infinite sensual enlightenment and power controlled by invincible will. They molded hers, parted them for access even as she opened to him.

She tasted him, wanted more. He gave it to her, encouraging her exploration, inciting it with skilled sweeps of his tongue while the spread fingers of one hand spanned the slender concave of her waist, slid upward along her rib cage and measured the curve of her breast.

It was magic, an intoxication of the blood that banished fear and doubt. She moved against him, murmuring in her throat. His grasp tightened, grew more purposeful. She felt herself lowered to the carpet before the fire, felt his weight and heat, even through her skirts.

Then he stiffened. Suddenly she was free as he eased away from her and sat up, raking a hand through his hair. A sense of desertion moved over her, leaving her cold and somehow afraid.

"I'm sorry, abjectly sorry. But this…it's impossible."

The disjointed words were an indication of his disturbance of mind, she thought. Strangely, that relieved a portion of her own. "Why? What is it?"

"I'm a fool, still there is something I must make known to you. The problem is that I don't know where to begin."

"Monsieur Rio! Monsieur Rio, come at once!"

It was Olivier, plunging into the room, interrupting whatever he had been going to say. The manservant, usually so imperturbable, was breathless and his eyes huge in his face. With him came a whiff of something that smelled like smoke.

"What is it?" Rio demanded, already leaping to his feet and starting toward him.

"The St. Louis Merchant's Exchange and Hotel, *monsieur!* It's burning!"

15

Acrid smoke was thick in the air. They could see a great black plume of it mounting toward the sky well before they reached the front of the great exchange and hotel. The block-long building, foursquare and stalwart, had an orange-red glow around its dome, and curls of fire decorated its entablature like icing on a cake. People swarmed out the front doors and from beneath the columned portico. Others climbed out of windows on makeshift ropes of sheets or drapery cording. Men shouted and women searched for children. An older couple stood white-faced and staring, clutching the few belongings they had been able to gather. Some here and there were still dressed for the evening, but most wore capes and cloaks hastily thrown on over their nightclothes.

Church bells rang out the alarm. They had begun with the great voices of those in the twin towers of St. Louis Cathedral and were taken up by those from St. Anthony's, Christ Church and others farther away. Their dolorous triple notes, endlessly repeated, sounded a dirge for the ill-fated building, a musical counterpoint to the drumlike roar of the fire.

Spectators and volunteers summoned by the bells

were arriving from every direction. Men began to take off their coats and roll up their sleeves. In the house across the street, a woman was dragging her household furnishings onto her gallery and heaving them over the railing to the octagonal paving stones below, lest embers from the fire set her house ablaze. Something would be saved.

Fire-engine bells began as a distant tinkling sound, increasing to a nerve-shattering clangor as they came nearer. An engine rounded the corner, pulled by four horses that strained into their collars while the whites of their eyes shone. Firemen piled off and began to unroll lengths of canvas hose. Another engine came down the cross street, scattering the crowd as it pulled up near the first. Instead of making ready to fight the fire, however, its crew jumped down and attacked the firemen from the first engine on the scene. The battle was joined.

Celina wanted to scream at the men. She was well aware the engine crew that claimed to have been first to reach the fire received a hefty bonus, but the flames were gaining momentum, hissing and crackling with ominous force. The hotel could burn to its foundation before the two crews decided ownership.

"Nothing can stop this blaze, not against the wind," Rio said, eyeing the roofline where the tiles had begun to steam. "It's being driven toward the Passage. We'll be lucky if the houses facing the hotel don't catch. If they go…"

He didn't finish the thought, for there was no need. If the houses in the opposite block of rue Saint-Louis caught, then the entire Passage behind them might go up in flames. From there, the fire could spread for blocks in every direction.

Even as Celina measured the danger, glancing from the hotel to the surrounding houses, she was aware of Rio turning to Olivier and giving instructions in a voice too low to be heard above the din. Olivier nodded, briefly squeezed Suzette's hand, then turned and sprinted in the direction of the atelier they had just left. Seconds later, he was lost in the growing crowd.

Rio turned back to Celina and Suzette. "Try to stay out of harm's way," he said. "I would remain here to protect you, but…" He swept his hand toward the fire and the melee between the two fire-engine crews.

"I understand," Celina said, moving back a few steps as she spoke. "Please don't concern yourself about us."

Cinders were falling around them. One drifted down to rest on the pristine whiteness of Rio's shirt collar, a feathery black curl. Smoke stung Celina's eyes, so she had to squint against it in order to see.

"I'm sorry," he said, the words abrupt.

"Why? It's not your fault."

"Perhaps, but still."

He turned from her then and waded into the nearest fight between uniformed firemen. Moments later, two men lay sprawling and another nursed a bloody nose. The rest shook hands and reached for their hoses.

As at a signal, other men set to work to bring order to the scene while smoke swirled around them and cinders and ash rained down on their heads. They shouted at the crowd of hotel guests, bystanders and the ghoulishly curious, forcing them back in case the walls toppled, and also directed the efforts of the fire crews toward the worst of the flames.

The pitiful streams of water produced by the hand pumps were no match for the conflagration eating at the great building. It was going to be too little and too late to save the structure. One fire crew turned its attention to preserving the Girod house on the near corner and those buildings that had concerned Rio.

A man carrying a huge iron cooking pot staggered from a side door of the burning building and crossed the rue Royale to the relative safety of the covered banquette opposite. Behind him came a train of men burdened by more pots, stacks of plates, trays of glasses and cups. One rotund individual had an armful of bottles that sloshed as he walked. Another had a great ham, while a third carried a side of beef across his back.

"Alvarez," an elderly gentleman nearby said as he stared after the man leading the parade. "Give you ten to one the fire started in his restaurant."

"Done." His friend next to him held out his hand to seal the bet. "He'd not have gotten so much out if it had originated with his cookstove, you know. More likely the cause was a faulty gaslight or lamp, or maybe a cigar left burning in a washroom."

Any of those things or a half dozen more were feasible, Celina knew. Fire was a constant danger, and city ordinances aimed at prevention were passed regularly. The blaze from a building the size of the hotel could scatter sparks for blocks, more if the wind did not abate. The whole city could burn as it had twice in the past.

She should return home, she knew. Any chance of speaking further with Rio was unlikely. The whole town had to be awake by now, roused by the alarm bells and the smell of smoke. Her aunt and her father might soon discover that she was out. Nevertheless, she couldn't bring herself to leave.

Then Celina saw Oliver pushing his way back through the milling throng. He seemed to be searching for his master, turning his head sharply this way and that until he caught sight of him. Plunging to Rio's side, he caught his arm and dragged him close to shout something in his ear.

Rio drew back to stare at the manservant. His voice, pitched to carry above the din, came faintly to where Celina stood. "You unlocked the door?"

"The lock was smashed. And *monsieur,* the young gentleman inside…I could see. He doesn't move."

Rio turned to face back along the Passage while his lips formed what appeared to be a virulent imprecation. Moving at top speed, then, he wrenched out of his coat and thrust it into the stream of water splashing from the nearest hose end. When it was wet through, he balled it into his arms and spun in the direction of his atelier.

Olivier made a grab for him, but Rio sidestepped with a quick twist of his body, then broke into a run. The manservant started after him. Rio stopped, put a hand on his chest and pushed him back. The faint sound of an order spoken and rejected came to where Celina stood. Rio gestured toward her and Suzette, repeating the command.

Olivier ceased struggling. Still, he didn't move from where he stood until Rio had disappeared among the curiosity seekers streaming up pedestrian way.

"Where is he going?" she asked as the majordomo

approached with reluctant footsteps, still staring over his shoulder. "What's wrong?"

"The atelier is on fire," Olivier told her, his voice tight, almost defensive. "Monsieur Rio has gone to do what he may to save…that is, to see what may be done."

"But it's more than a block and a half away."

Olivier's features had an uncomfortable cast as he lifted his shoulders in a helpless shrug.

"You should go after him. He may need your help."

"I must stay with you, *mademoiselle.* My orders were clear."

"Then we will all go. There is nothing we can do here except get in the way." She picked up her skirts and started down the Passage.

"No, *mademoiselle.*" Olivier didn't move from where he stood.

"Why should I not?"

"I…Monsieur Rio would not like it."

"That can't be helped."

"*Mademoiselle*, wait." He put out a hand as if to detain her.

"Really, I don't understand you. We must hurry or the fire there may be past help, too."

She thought the majordomo protested again, but she didn't remain to hear him. Coughing a little from the ash in the air, she hastened back along the narrow way to where a separate pillar of smoke, smaller than the one above the hotel, climbed into the night sky to be wafted away by the wind.

The arcaded front of Rio's building was untouched as yet. The smoke was coming from the rear, indicating the area where the blaze had started. A crash sounded from that direction. She strained her eyes trying to penetrate the gray shadows behind the windows of the upper floor. Nothing moved there or gave the slightest indication that anyone was inside. Where had Rio gone? What was he doing?

Suzette and Olivier caught up with her, and they were joined by others attracted to this new excitement. Among them were several *maîtres d'armes*, Rio's friends and competitors, she thought. A few she recognized on sight, while others could be placed by their fine physiques and athletic vigor as they exhorted and commanded, helping the elderly and the young move back out of danger while organizing a bucket brigade to fight the fire. They seemed formidable as they worked in unity and with determination. Just the sight of them raised her spirits.

Concern for Rio was at the forefront of her mind, yet mixed with it was rising doubt. Something was wrong. Rio's words had been strange, his anger and concern excessive. Olivier's manner had also been peculiar. The majordomo had not wanted her here, and she could not think it was purely for safety's sake. What else it might be, she could not imagine, did not wish to imagine, but the feeling rose inside her like sugar-fed yeast.

Just then a gentleman approached from down the Passage, then paused as he caught sight of her. "Mademoiselle Celina, how is this? Surely you are not alone?"

Her stomach took on a hollow feel as she recognized Etienne Plauchet, her cousin Sonia's husband and the host for the soiree she had attended a few nights ago. "An accident, Cousin," she said after only a small hesitation. "And of course I have my maid."

The gentleman gave Suzette the barest of glances. "Your father, where is he tonight?"

She was saved from having to answer by the exclamations of those around her. Swinging around, she saw a tall form emerge from under the arcade of the atelier. His shirt was torn on one shoulder, and so smoke-blackened were his features that it was almost impossible to recognize him as Rio. In his arms was a limp figure whose head and shoulders were wrapped in wet cloth. Moving with loose-limbed grace, he shouldered past the bucket brigade and strode from under the arcade into the passageway. There, he knelt to place his burden on the paving stones.

Celina started forward. "You're safe. Thank heaven."

He seemed not to hear her in his concentration on the man he had carried from the burning building. Reaching out, he pulled away the wet covering that had protected him. Then he sat back on his haunches.

Celina came to an abrupt halt. She couldn't breathe, couldn't think or move for the appalled recognition that bloomed in her mind. It was Denys who lay on the paving stones, Denys who had been carried from the smoke-filled atelier behind him. Rio had known he was there, had raced back to rescue him at the first word of fire here. It followed that if Denys could not manage his own escape, then he had to have been held in some fashion, held under lock and key, the smashed lock reported by Olivier to his employer. Everyone who said Rio was the last person to see Denys had been correct.

At that moment Rio looked up to meet her eyes, his own smoke-gray with pain and what might have been remorse. She stared into them while a terrible sense of betrayal cut into her heart like a sword thrust. Then she moved forward again almost without being aware of it, sinking to her knees beside her brother in a billow of skirts.

Denys's face was white, his lips bloodless, his eyelids closed. An ugly bruise marred his forehead, livid purple surrounding split skin from which blood trickled. She reached with unsteady fingers to lay her hand along his cheek. His skin was warm, she discovered, and a pulse beat with a faint movement in his throat. Her relief was so great that she felt lightheaded for an instant.

"He needs a doctor," Rio said, his voice abrupt.

"Yes," she said then took a sharp breath. "Yes, at once. Then I have to get him home."

Suzette touched her shoulder. "Shall I go for the carriage, Mam'zelle?"

"Or I?" Oliver added.

"That will be unnecessary." Her cousin by marriage stepped up to loom above her as he spoke. "My barouche is a mere half block away, on the rue Royale. It will take but a moment to transport Denys to the Vallier town house. The doctor may attend him there."

"Lead the way," Rio said, his voice grim. Without waiting for more, he scooped up Denys again with a stifled grunt, then stepped aside. As he turned, Celina saw that blood stained his shirt at his shoulder and across his back. Oliver saw it at the same time for he stiffened. The majordomo's expression of con-

cern reinforced her instant guess that Rio had somehow reinjured his dueling wound.

Olivier reached out his hand to help her to her
feet. Her cousin elbowed the manservant aside and
took her arm in a firm grip. "Come," he said, dragging her upward. "The sooner we get you and Denys
out of this, the better." With a brusque gesture indicating that Rio was to follow, he started off.

The barouche could carry only four, particularly
as one of them was an injured man. When Denys
was deposited inside, Rio stood back. Celina thought
he meant to speak, but he was given no time. Etienne
Plauchet shut the door and called up to his driver,
and then they rolled away.

The brief journey to the town house seemed to
take an eternity. The streets were filled with people
and carriages as many made ready to escape the possible spread of the fires, and the horses were fractious
and hard to handle. They stopped and started so the
carriage rocked back and forth, making Denys moan
where he lay with his head in Celina's lap. Her relative was short-tempered, fretting with impatience
over every delay. She was soon out of charity with
him, since he hardly spoke to her and then in tones
of the most extreme disapproval. When they reached
home, he got down and went in search of her father.
Celina and Suzette were left alone to get Denys into
the house. It was just as well; they did not require the
gentleman's officious aid. Summoning a pair of menservants, Celina had them dismantle a window shutter and use it as a makeshift stretcher to transport her
brother up the stairs.

Through it all, Denys did not regain consciousness. He did not awaken as he was carried up the stairs to his room, nor did he stir when Tante Marie Rose threw herself across his chest, sobbing in fear of the worst. Washing away the smoke grime failed to wake him, as did the examination of the doctor and the bloodletting decreed by that worthy gentleman against the possibility of brain fever caused by the head wound. Hours after the doctor had drunk down a glass of sherry, taken his fee and departed, Denys still lay unconscious, his chest barely rising and falling with his breathing.

His condition did not alter during the remainder of the night. Celina watched at his bedside as the long hours turned into morning. Tante Marie Rose took her place then, allowing her to rest during the daylight hours. After an early dinner, Celina resumed her chair at Denys's bedside with her embroidery in hand.

It was some time later when Denys moved his head, turning it restlessly on his pillow. Celina sprang up, certain he was about to awake. He didn't, however, nor did he move again.

She stood for long moments, staring down at the still form of her brother on the bed. He looked so young and defenseless with his head swathed in white bandaging and more of the same at his injured wrist. She had thought for a time that he might be lost to them; that he still could be haunted her.

It was her fault that he had come to this, her doing that he lay there. To be forced to live without her brother's warm smile, his teasing and laughter would be more than she could bear. If he would only open his eyes and call her *stupide* once more, she would gladly retreat into the pose of a good sister and daughter, doing only what was expected of her for the remainder of her days.

Denys lay still, breathing with a rough wheeze caused by the smoke he had inhaled. Not even an eyelash flickered. Sighing, Celina turned away and took up her embroidery once more.

Their father came into the room perhaps an hour later. It was not for the first time. He had been in and out all day, and had even sat with his son for an hour while Tante Marie Rose ate her evening meal. Now he walked to the bedside, staring down at Denys while he tapped his leg with the sheet of foolscap that he held in his right hand.

"Any change?" he asked after a moment with a brief glance in Celina's direction.

She gave a weary shake of her head.

Her father sighed, then reached to feel Denys's forehead, brushing back the soft curl of hair that had fallen onto his forehead. "Where in the name of Jesus, Joseph and Mary could he have been all this time? What was he doing?"

The last thing Celina wanted was to set her father on course toward a confrontation with Rio that he might not survive. Rather than answering, she asked, "The fire, is there news?"

"The hotel was a total loss, but already they talk of rebuilding. Some thirty guests were injured, with the only death being that of an older gentleman who succumbed to a stroke. A few nearby houses had minor damage. They're calling it a miracle, though most credit the quick action of a couple of men on the scene."

"And the other?"

"The fire at Monsieur de Silva's fencing salon, you mean? The damage was mainly in the cellar area where it apparently began. The sword masters who have their ateliers on that street put out the flames before they could spread—protecting their own livelihoods of course."

Celina indicated her understanding. At the same time, she thought there was a deeper element behind the cooperation of these men. She had seen them working together, had sensed an odd brotherhood between them, a camaraderie of the blade or something very like it. But what did it matter? Rio had deceived her, that valiant master of the sword. He had taken her brother and shut him away while pretending to search high and low for him. Why should she find anything good to say about him or his kind?

Her father paused, as if at a loss. "You have everything you need here, everything Denys may need?"

"Yes, Papa."

"That's good." He hesitated, bringing up the paper he held, tapping it against the fingers of his other hand. "I very much dislike bringing this matter to your notice under such trying circumstances, but time grows short. I have here your marriage contract. You really must sign it, *chère*, and without further arguments."

She searched his face in the soft glow of the whale-oil lamp, noting the lines of weariness, yes, and age that marked it. "Why now?"

"The time for discussion is past. It has become a question of family honor." He walked to the secretary desk that stood near the French door, opened the inkstand, took up a pen to dip it and held it out to her. "Sign, Celina."

It was an omen. Had she not just been thinking that she should be glad to do what was expected of her? This might be as close as she could come. Nevertheless, the image of the count rose up before her and she could not quite make herself obey.

"Do not try my patience," her father warned. "I had a most unpleasant interview with Plauchet last evening after the doctor had gone. He tells me you were seen in the Passage with de Silva, this *maître d'armes* who bandied your name in public and pierced Denys's arm, that you went out on the street alone, perhaps to meet him. Is it so?"

"Yes, Papa." Her voice was hardly above a whisper.

"You went from this house with only a maid to preserve your good name and without informing either your aunt or myself. Anything might have happened to you, anything, and I would never have known."

"I thought…it seemed something had to be done to find Denys. And I did find him."

"Thank God for that," he said with fervor. "And thank God that you returned home safely. The fault is mine that you risked it, however, I do realize that. I have been away too much, have grown lax in my care of what is left of my family. I thought all was well, could not imagine it otherwise. I see now that I was wrong."

As much as she deplored his past behavior, she could not bear this contrition. To offer comfort was instinctive. "You did your best, Papa."

"It matters little. Things must be different henceforth. I vow to be a better father, but you must do your part. Such conduct as you have shown cannot be permitted. Only think how your dear mother would have felt, what she would have said."

"I know," Celina said. Indeed she did. Her mother had been the most conventional of women, never dreaming of anything that might call for censure, much less undertaking it.

"News of this escapade of yours will soon be whispered in every salon. Your reasons weigh little against the unseemliness. We must do what we can to salvage your good name. The only remedy is marriage, and as quickly as possible." He thrust the pen toward her again. "Sign the agreement, my dear Celina. Yes, and pray to *le bon Dieu* that your betrothed does not renege in disgust when he hears what is being said."

"But what of witnesses, a notary?" It was grasping at straws to bring up such vague legalities as she had heard about in passing, but the best that she could do.

"I have friends at the city court, so these may be attended to later." He proffered the pen again.

Now was the time to tell him that the count would be gaining an impure bride, Celina thought. She should fling it in her father's face, enraging him so that he would send her from the house in disgrace. It was the only way she could avoid the alliance, the only way she could ever be free.

She couldn't do it. She might have if he had been angry, if he had stormed and accused. It was impossible while he was so concerned and penitent. The habits of a lifetime were too ingrained, her reluctance to disappoint him too strong to be overcome. More than that, Denys needed her, needed the care she could give him. She could not desert her brother, nor could she risk being sent away before he recovered his senses and his health.

Tears began somewhere deep inside her, rising in burning pressure to the back of her nose. They filled her eyes, welling up so that the piece of foolscap her father held on the desk wavered in the lamplight, became almost indecipherable. She had tried so hard to avoid this, had twisted and turned like a hare caught in a trap. All for nothing and worse than nothing.

"Take the pen, Celina. Sign now."

The fighting, the hope of another life, of freedom and joy, love and happiness was at an end. All her dreams had brought only pain and injury to those she cared about. Nothing was left now except obedience.

"What of Suzette?" she asked with a slight lift of her chin.

"What of her?"

"She is to be free. You promised."

"Yes, yes, included in your dowry, to be disposed of as you will...or as your husband wills."

She hesitated, not liking the sound of that last, though she was fairly certain it was the best for which she could hope. Perhaps it would be enough.

Accepting the pen, she steadied her hand on the flat surface of the secretary and signed her name. Or she thought she did. She could not be sure for the tears turned her signature into a blurred line without meaning.

Her father took the foolscap, pressed the silver blotter to the signature line, and then waved it in the air to dry it. "You did the right thing. You'll see."

"Let us hope so."

"Yes. The count will be happy to have the news, I'm sure."

A species of panic seized her at the thought of that gentleman's possible reaction, his undoubted expectations. "But the wedding need not be Saturday as he requested? I mean, I cannot leave Denys so soon."

"Not Saturday perhaps, but the instant he recovers his faculties. It's imperative, given the talk." Her father turned, moving toward the door. At the opening, he looked back with a nod toward the bed. "Call me at once, please, if there is any change."

"Of course," she whispered. He had shown more concern in the past twenty-four hours than she had thought possible, both for Denys and for her. He did care for them, in spite of everything. It was some small comfort.

When her father had gone, she sat staring at nothing. She felt drained. She should begin to contemplate wedding plans, she knew, think of speaking to the priest, requesting use of the church, choosing a gown, penning invitations, arranging the nuptial feast and a thousand other details. Her mind refused to grapple with any of it. The idea of standing before the altar with the Count de Lérida was so foreign that she could not conceive of actually doing it. Yet she must accept that it would happen.

She must, but not now. Later, when she was not so tired, perhaps the idea of becoming a bride would be more real, less appalling. She closed her eyes, leaning her head against the back of her chair.

The faintest squeak of a hinge was her only warning. One moment she was alone with her brother in the dim room, and the next Rio de Silva stood at the French door that opened from the *garçonnière* bedchamber onto the gallery overlooking the courtyard. He appeared much as usual, with the exception of a little more bulk under his cloak at his injured left shoulder and the implacable look on his face. Removing his hat, he placed it under his arm with his cane as he came forward.

Celina sprang to her feet so the embroidery hoop in her lap fell to the floor. Stepping to the fireplace, she put her hand on the pull for the bell. "You must leave at once," she said firmly. "Otherwise, I will have to ring for Mortimer."

"I'll leave when I am assured that you and your brother are well."

"Yes, both of us. Now, please go. You have no right to be here."

"Go, just like that, without a fond kiss goodbye or even a smile? Oh, yes, and without a word of gratitude?"

"I should be grateful to you for saving my brother's life when it was you who endangered it?"

"Is that what you think?" He watched her, his face without expression.

Something about the way he stood or the hollows of pain and sleeplessness under his eyes made her uncomfortable. She even doubted for a brief instant the certainty of his guilt that she had reached with such painful exactitude. In sudden awkwardness, she asked, "Your shoulder is…that is to say, you suffered no permanent injury?"

"It's well enough." The words were clipped, almost angry.

"Then that's all right."

Quiet fell between them, one so profound that they could hear the soft rasp of Denys's breathing. The whale-oil lamp made a soft popping sound as it fluttered on its wick. They both looked at the fire inside the lamp globe, like a miniature of the conflagration the evening before. Their eyes met above the bed for an instant before they looked away again.

Rio thrust his fingers through his hair, smoothing down the shaping of his head to clasp the back of his neck. When he spoke, his voice had an exhausted sound to it. "I can explain if you will listen."

"Can you indeed? And I am to believe what you say?"

"Believe it or not, as you will."

"Whatever possessed you to take and hold him in such a way? Wasn't it enough that you had me in your power?"

"I meant to tell you last evening. I would have except for news of the fire."

"You lied to me! You said that he was safe and well when you last saw him."

"It was the truth. He was perfectly fine when I carried wine to him before dinner that evening."

"That's hardly the same thing." She would not allow that sign of civilized detainment to weigh with her.

"Oh, agreed," he answered without noticeable remorse.

She swung from him, pacing in her agitation. "All the time that you were demanding my surrender in exchange for finding him, you had him shut up. You could produce him at will, yet required that I dance to the tune you played. Did you never think that he must make known what you had done the instant he was free? Did you have no consideration for what might happen then?"

"Perhaps I thought the prize was worth the cost."

She refused to meet the hard glitter of his gaze. "Or perhaps you meant to kill him all along."

"You can't believe that."

"I don't know what to believe!" she cried, spinning back to face him. "Have you any idea how degrading this is to me? Can you even begin to realize how it makes me feel?"

"I think I have an inkling," he answered. "The question is what you intend to do about it."

"Nothing. Nothing at all! What can I do that will not endanger someone I care about? I am left with only disgust so strong that it sickens me and a wish that some day you may feel as I do now."

"You are assuming that my reasons for holding Denys are base. I wonder why that is?"

She stared at him an instant in disdain. "How can it be otherwise?"

"Suppose I meant to keep him safe until I could remove what I perceived as a greater danger?"

"And what form might this danger take?"

"Kidnapping, shanghaiing, even death."

"A far-fetched assessment."

"Not if you think about it. Who will stop at nothing to get his hands on your fortune? Who would have the most to lose if Denys learned of past dealings that cast him in a less than favorable light? Who would gain if his bride became sole heir to her father's fortune?"

Celina blinked as that last question struck her. It made a terrible kind of sense when she considered the challenge that Denys had intercepted and the fact that he had been present when Broyard accosted her. It was, she thought, the half-discerned pattern that had been eluding her. Or was it? "You mean the count. His faults are many, but I can't believe he would deliberately cause harm to my brother."

"Because he is noble by birth? Or is it simply easier to believe that I am the culprit?"

"You detained Denys at your salon. That cannot be denied."

"I told you why. Denys came to me with his doubts about the count. He had been to the count's hotel to speak to him about certain things he had discovered, but missed him so meant to call again. It seemed unlikely that he would be allowed to leave after that discussion."

"You think the count would have tried to kill him in his rooms? That's absurd."

"Not at all. The fire at my place had all the earmarks of arson. It was set deliberately because someone knew Denys was there. The count was aware that Denys meant to confront him, must have guessed that the matter concerned serious allegations. To dispose of him before he could spread whatever he had learned would be logical."

"And how was he to know where to find Denys when even I could not guess?"

"Couldn't you? I rather thought that was why you came to me that evening."

It was true enough. The count could have surmised his location just as easily since he had certainly known that Denys was last seen at the salon. Still, she could not allow herself to be persuaded so easily. "The hotel fire was very convenient then, wasn't it, allowing the appearance of an accident when your atelier also caught fire?"

"*Convenient* is the word."

"You mean…?"

"The lives and property of others matter little to one such as the count. He was staying at the hotel. A splash or two of lamp oil, and the thing is done. Fire has served him well before."

"Then a brief walk down the Passage to your cellar in the midst of the excitement?"

"If I had not sent Olivier to free Denys, just in case, the outcome might have been very different. Your brother was meant to die. He was stuck on the head first in order to assure it."

It was a stunning revelation. If Denys had been unconscious, then he would surely not have survived without Rio's intervention. "You mean he was not hurt during the rescue? I assumed…"

"No, I swear to you."

"I can't believe anyone could be so vile as to leave him to burn to death." She hugged her arms around her to counteract the shuddering chill she felt inside.

Rio lifted a brow. "You prefer to think that I detained him because I wanted you in my bed?"

"It's what you've wanted from the first."

"You have no idea what I want or what I…" He

stopped, took a deep breath. "I was angry when I asked you to pledge a night with me in exchange for finding your brother. I wanted to hear what you would say. But I would not have carried through with it unless it was your will."

Unless it was her will. And it might have been, heaven help her. "How can I believe that when you deliberately tricked me? The fact is that you dared lay hands on my brother. If you hadn't done so, then he would not be lying here now."

"Believe that if you must, but hear this. I did not harm Denys, nor would I ever do anything to hurt you. All I have done is tried to prevent any damage to you and your family because of me."

"Because of you? Why should that be?"

He shook his head. "Some things are best left unknown for your own protection."

"Yours, you mean," she suggested with a twist of her lips.

"No, *chère*. The dowry of a dead bride is as easily spent as that of a live one. Perhaps more easily."

A shudder moved over her. A dead bride. "You are trying to frighten me."

"I hope I've succeeded, for Denys's sake as well as yours. Whatever he learned is dangerous to you both. Consider well before you trust him to anyone in his present state, or before you trust yourself to any man."

"You being the exception, I suppose." The urge to tell him that she had signed the marriage agreement beat up into her brain, but she suppressed it. She had no wish to hear what he would say against it.

"For Denys, yes. For you, by no means." He took

her hand, carrying it to his lips. His voice, the whisper of his breath against her fingers was like a caress as he went on. "I am your greatest danger and most forlorn hope, Mademoiselle Celina. I am both your shield and the sword pointed at your heart. Trust me at your peril. But my danger is merely to your comfort, your pleasure and your lovely body. Others will take everything you hold dear, including your life."

She could not speak, could think of nothing to say. She only watched as he released her hand and backed away before turning with a swirl of his cloak. He moved to the window, where he swung around with one hand braced on the frame and a smile as silvery as steel in his eyes. "Oh, yes, and a reminder, should you need one. I did bring your brother to you, according to our bargain. I kept my word, and expect those who treat with me to do the same. I am owed a night in your arms."

"But you said…"

"There is no question of force, how can you think it? But neither do I release you from the obligation."

Heat suffused her, threading through her veins like poison. The problem was that it was impossible to say if it came from rage or desire. "If you think for one moment that I shall come meekly to your bed, then you are quite mad."

"Oh, not meekly," he said on a choked laugh. "Come in anger, come in hatred, come in a passion of resentment and the need to annihilate me with kisses, if nothing else. But come you shall, and soon. It is, after all, a matter of honor."

He was gone then, vanishing without a sound. She listened, expecting to hear the creak of a railing, the rumble of a drainpipe or a thud as he leaped to the ground. There was nothing. She might have dreamed he had been there except for the disturbance of her mind and her doubts about tomorrow. Yes, and all the days thereafter.

16

"You must stop, Monsieur Rio. You have blood on your shirt."

Rio grimaced as he took the damp towel Olivier handed him along with the warning, but bowed to the inevitable. It was his day to work with special clients at the salon. The exercise was strenuous, and he had been at it all morning. Disappointing those who came to his salon went against the grain, and he needed the money. Added to that was the fact that any failure to take the practice strip could give rise to claims that he was slipping. If that happened, the vultures would begin to circle again.

His shoulder hurt with a fierce, burning ache. The wound from the Broyard duel had torn open as he broke down the cellar door to get to Denys Vallier. This morning's efforts had not helped the healing process. A warm trickle down his side was a clear indication that he needed attention before someone other than his sharp-eyed friend and majordomo noticed.

All was well in the salon. The upstairs room was packed with men drawn by curiosity about his recent exploits, as well as the fire. Men stood in groups or lined the balcony outside the open windows, smoking the Desoelo regulars from Havana that he provided or drinking the burgundy and claret being circulated by a young free mulatto whom Olivier had befriended. A pair of men had faced off on the second of the two fencing strips that centered the room, their clothing pared down to open-necked shirts and pantaloons along with protective masks and torso padding. The clashing scrape and bell-like ringing of the contest was loud enough that voices had to be raised above the noise, though most of those watching preserved the traditional respectful quiet.

What talk there was centered around when the St. Louis Merchant's Exchange and Hotel would be rebuilt and who would get the job as architect, also whether tenants like the restaurant owner, Alvarez, and Candide Avinence the jeweler, would reopen, but also encompassed cotton prices, arriving ships and various affairs of honor or the boudoir. Rio's last lesson of the morning was done, and he had no other actually scheduled until midafternoon. It was as good a time as any to excuse himself for a few minutes.

In the bedchamber, he stripped off his shirt and washed away the sweat of his exertions, then surrendered to Olivier's ministrations. The manservant carefully peeled away the bandaging from his shoulder. The linen strips were stuck to the wound in places. Gritting his teeth, Rio endured the pain of having them removed. No point in whining over what could not be helped.

"A cheerful crowd today," Olivier observed as he worked. "Full of news."

"You heard something of interest?" Long experience told Rio that Olivier seldom spoke without purpose.

"A matter concerning Mademoiselle Vallier, one which may not have been mentioned in your hearing."

"Not bad news of her brother?"

"No, though they say he is better, that he moves and calls out in his sleep. The gossip is that *mademoiselle* was seen in Passage on the night of the fire. They say that she was keeping an assignation with you, and the two of you were seen with your heads together in a most intimate fashion."

Rio muttered a quiet curse. He had feared something like this. "I suppose they will force her to marry the count now."

"Or he will repudiate her."

"Unlikely. She is still the daughter of a wealthy planter." The groom might despise her, however, Rio thought, and make her life a purgatory after the wedding.

"There is little to be done," Olivier murmured.

"Short of killing the count, no."

"He won't fight you."

"Wise of him," Rio said.

"Of course the lady might make an escape."

Rio glanced over his shoulder at his majordomo. "You are suggesting I could help her?"

"Or steal her away. She could be grateful for it."

"She could also hate me."

"A temporary situation, one you should easily be able to overcome."

"Your confidence unmans me, Olivier." As he spoke, a third option occurred to Rio. He hesitated, turning over the ramifications in his mind, but there was little doubt that he could carry it through. "I believe there are houses of assignation here in the city where a lady might meet someone in reasonable comfort and security. You have heard of these places?"

"Indeed." Olivier's voice was cool.

"Of course you have. Why did I ask?" Olivier did not approve. Neither did he, if it came to that. Somehow, Rio had never availed himself of such a rendezvous. Visiting his amours in their homes meant that preventing discovery was his responsibility alone. Yet the changed circumstances made invading the Vallier house too dangerous. "You know where such a house might be located then, something respectable, quiet, secluded?"

"Inquiries could be made."

"Undertake them, and then make the arrangements. I think an afternoon would be best, since Mademoiselle Vallier might have more difficulty getting away at any other time."

"How is she to travel there? To walk might be dangerous and to order out the family carriage is clearly impossible."

"A hired hack waiting for the lady in a quiet street is customary in other places, I believe."

Olivier dipped his head. "I will see to that, as well."

Rio hesitated, half-inclined to countermand the whole idea, troubled by the insult to Celina of expecting her to come to him in so clandestine a manner and the added scandal if they were discovered. But he thought longer of holding her, of sweet kisses and exquisite joinings.

"Yes, do so," he said brusquely as he reached for a clean shirt. "Then inform Suzette so she may make the appointment known to her mistress."

Returning to the salon, Rio moved through the room, greeting clients, welcoming new patrons, stopping now and then to answer a question or give an opinion on some weighty matter such as the quality of the fancy dance performed by Madame Celeste at the current Bank's Arcade exhibition, or who owned the fastest horse scheduled for the first race at the Métairie course in two weeks' time. Since Olivier had brought it to his notice, however, he became acutely aware of remarks suddenly broken off as he neared, small silences as he passed and odd looks slanted in his direction. He carried on with purpose, smiling, bowing, offering liquid refreshment, but his temper rose to a slow boil.

It wasn't that he cared for himself; he had little good character to preserve beyond the tenants of personal honor. What enraged him was knowing that these gentlemen of good family and normally superior manners were sniggering and whispering behind their hands about Celina, especially when he was well aware that whatever she had done of an imprudent nature could be laid at his door. Above all, he was infuriated that his own actions had placed her in this position. It was the last thing he had meant to happen.

A short time later, as he soothed the nerves of a young gentleman who had just lost his first practice match so was theoretically dead, someone approached from behind him. A prickling at the back of his neck made him whip around.

"Forgive me," Nicolas Pasquale said. "I didn't mean to approach on your blind side."

"Not at all." Rio sketched a polite bow.

Pasquale returned the salute with casual grace. "A nice place you have here. Impressive clientele."

Rio thanked him before he went on. "This isn't one of your days to be open, I perceive?"

"Alas, no. You, Croquère and Dauphin are too much competition, not to mention Llulla. I am available on alternate days."

"Caid, as well, O'Neill, that is. You have met?"

"It happens that we have. I like him."

What was he to make of that? Rio wondered. Was it a simple statement of fact, or a backhanded way of saying that Pasquale didn't number present company among the favored? One thing he was sure of: he didn't care for the tone of the Italian's voice. "A likeable fellow, Caid."

"He speaks highly of you as well, especially your skill with the blade. Of course your prowess is touted everywhere by those with less reason to appreciate it." Pasquale smiled with a lazy movement of his lips. "So much praise invites curiosity. It would be a pleasure to cross swords with you if you will grant the honor."

Rio wasn't up to a match with another master at the moment, even if the Italian's motives weren't suspect. It wouldn't be the first time a pedagogue of the sword had attempted to steal away clients by showing up a rival in his own atelier. "I regret that I can't accommodate you just now," he answered. "Another time perhaps."

"By all means." Pasquale tipped his head with another smile. "I do understand your reluctance. I would feel the same if I expected to entertain a lovely visitor this evening."

Rio stared at him for a frowning instant. "I beg your pardon?"

"Everyone talks of the latest conquest of the Don Juan of New Orleans, the famous Silver Shadow. Mademoiselle Vallier, is it not? A fair prize indeed."

Rio was reminded, abruptly, of Caid's assertion that the count had sought a master to take him on. That Pasquale dared bring Celina into it was no great surprise. She was his weak spot, after all.

Rio had been so certain he could protect her from scandal. His anger at Pasquale for forcing him to face that fact that he could not was strong enough, but his wrath at his own failed judgment was blighting.

Mounting temper gave a dangerous edge to his voice as he spoke. "You will retract that, if you please."

"And if I don't?" Pasquale inquired, his voice soft.

Heads were turning in their direction. Conversation faltered then died away. That odd sense of avid dread that always accompanied such a confrontation seeped into the air.

"You malign the lady, and that I can't allow."

"Then you deny the rumors?"

He stared the other man down, or attempted it. "I deny that she is at fault in any way, and object to her name being used so carelessly."

"You might have thought of that before pursuing her."

The Italian dared censure his conduct. It was insupportable precisely because it was earned. "It seems you are determined to have a match, *monsieur*."

"For the sake of the lady's good name? That is surely the province of her future husband."

The idea was no surprise; still Rio felt as if a hand had reached into his chest and squeezed his heart. "The betrothal is official? She marries the count?"

"He is in transports, naturally, now that the marriage contract has been duly signed."

"But will he defend the honor of his bride?"

"Possibly, though there is no assurance of it."

The words were almost cordial, yet deadly in their implication that in the eyes of her groom, the bride might have no honor to defend. Rio spoke instantly. "A lady can never have too many champions. My seconds will attend yours."

"I expected no less. May I say I salute your principles, however misguided? And that I look forward with pleasure to this test of steel."

Nicholas Pasquale turned and walked away, his back straight, shoulders·level, stride long and easy. Rio watched him go in confusion. The man had neither the sound nor the look of a hired assassin, yet what else could he be?

To challenge the Italian had been a mistake; Rio had been sure of it before the words left his mouth. His opponent was in superb condition, well rested, free of the tension of recent episodes on the dueling field. He had none of those advantages. Still, there was nothing else he could have done. Nothing at all.

By the following morning, Rio had two fixed appointments. The assignation with Celina had been arranged for that afternoon and the duel for the morning of the following day. The last had been at Caid's insistence as chief second. Rio needed the time to recover, he said, and it was well within the parameters of the Code Duello to allow a man as much as a week to set his affairs in order. The span of days was also codified as a cooling-off period in case more rational thought allowed for an apology. There would be none in this case.

No word had come from Celina either accepting or declining their rendezvous. Rio liked to think she would have the consideration not to leave him waiting in vain, but it was not guaranteed. She had not felt kindly toward him when last they met, and he had given her little reason to change her mind. He had also known women who delighted in disappointing men as proof of their control over them.

Celina only wanted to control her own life, or had until the night of the fire. That must be at an end now if she was to be wed. He wondered if this was his fault as with so much else, if she had agreed solely out of anger over his interference where her brother was concerned. She could hardly be blamed, but that didn't mean he would accept any failure to appear on her part.

The house of assignation was in the Faubourg Marigny on the rue d'Amour, a coincidence that annoyed Rio as much as it amused Olivier. It was modest enough, a raised cottage with four commodious rooms and two cabinets, as the small rooms on either side of the back gallery were known. It included a salon, dining room and two bedchambers, with an outbuilding that served as a kitchen and servant quarters. The cabinets connected to the bedchambers and were fitted out as dressing and bathing rooms. The last usage was particularly important, since removing all sign of an amorous encounter was of primary importance.

The furnishings were not cheap, but neither were they the best. Fireplace mantels of carved wood painted to imitate white marble sheltered leaping flames. Brocatelle in soft rose covered the settee in the parlor and the dressing table stool. The walls were hung with cream silk in a moiré pattern. The bed coverlet was cream matelassé, and the pillows that were strewn over the cotton mattress were of satin and silk in every shade of the rainbow. Everything else was velvet the color of claret with a lining or edging of lace. It was so blatantly a setting for seduction that it made Rio's back teeth ache. What Celina would think of it, he couldn't begin to imagine. That was, of course, if she deigned to put in an appearance.

He moved from the parlor to the bedchamber and back again, checking the wine set in a silver bucket of cracked ice brought downriver from Massachusetts, the serving trays of savories and pastries, the candles that burned against the dimness created by tightly closed draperies. Time was fading into the past with every heavy beat of his heart, and so were his hopes.

The sound of a carriage rolling to a stop outside brought his head up. He could hear Olivier greeting Suzette and taking her in charge, then calling up to the hack's driver to bid him return in three hours. Taking a stance with his back to the parlor fireplace and his focus on the door, Rio waited.

She came into the room in a whispering rush of skirts and cool air. Her cape belled out around her as she turned to close the door behind her. Then she swung back to face him.

Her eyes were bright, her cheeks flushed with either cold or excitement, and her breathing was so quick that even the heavy merino of her braid-edged cape could not disguise it. She was everything fresh and lovely that he had ever imagined, and he knew with sudden conviction that she was slipping away from him because he was unworthy to have her.

"I didn't think you'd come," he said, his voice a little hoarse.

She unbuttoned her gloves of lavender kid and peeled them off, tucking them into a pocket in her cape. Reaching up to remove her bonnet, she said, "I very nearly did not."

"What changed your mind?" Forcing himself to move, he came forward and took her bonnet and wrap, placing them on a rack near the door. The gown she wore was of gold silk, with a simple heart-shaped neckline and smooth skirt ornamented with only a row of scalloped cording at the hem that echoed the neckline. The standing collar and bishop's sleeves were edged in lace so fine that it gave her a fragile air; the score or more of tiny buttons that closed it up the back made the ends of his fingers tingle and his pantaloons feel too tight.

"Honor and obligation, I suppose," she answered without quite meeting his eyes. "Does it matter?" She glanced around her. "This is very…cozy."

"Would you care for wine?"

A smile curled one corner of her soft lips. "For

courage or to stimulate passion? Either way, I accept."

He had moved to the table set with wineglasses and picked up the bottle. Now he paused. "If you would rather leave…"

"Playing the coward? I think not." She moved away from him to a table crowded with bibelots, nothing very fine but an amusing collection if you cared for Far Eastern erotica in carved ivory. She reached for a small figure, focused on it a bare second, then quickly put it down again.

He suppressed a smile as he filled the wineglasses and picked them up, carrying hers to where she had taken his place before the marble mantel. "Better than playing the martyr."

"Better for whom?"

"For me, of course." He transferred the glass to her hand and noted with some satisfaction that she jerked a little as he touched her cool fingers. She was as on edge as he was.

"I shouldn't think it would matter to you what I feel."

"Your mistake. A courtesan in training should have at least some small enthusiasm for the business at hand."

"Oh, please," she said, finally meeting his eyes an instant. "That was a foolish notion, like a young boy running away to sea or to join a sideshow."

So much for his main reason for this assignation, which was to allow her the chance to carry through with that salacious threat—and even take advantage of it. Regret touched him for an instant, but was easily overcome by his relief.

He sipped his wine, suddenly enjoying her valiant efforts at self-possession. "You no longer think of Paris?"

"No. No longer."

It appeared that she was not going to tell him that she had signed the marriage contract. He wondered why, since he had half expected her to use it as an excuse to avoid her part of their bargain. "Too bad," he said, his voice deep and suggestive. "I was looking forward to the role of instructor."

She almost spilled her wine as she took a quick swallow. He watched the movement of her white throat as she drank, and thought of pressing his lips to its softness. He would, soon. For now, it seemed best to present a safer topic. "How is your brother?"

"He talks in his sleep. The doctor says he is very near to consciousness, that it is only a matter of time and rest. I fear he is merely trying to ease our minds."

"I'm sure he isn't. Denys is young and strong. He'll recover."

"I pray it's so. I can't speak for what my father may do if he dies."

"I understand that," he said simply. "But for now…"

"For now, the need to prevent scandal takes precedence over all else."

"Many would feel the same," Rio murmured.

"Yes." She drank the rest of her wine and set the glass on the mantelpiece. "What of you?"

He tilted his head in polite inquiry.

"Please don't pretend with me." The words were remote, a reminder that she need not necessarily believe the reason he had given for holding her brother.

"If you are inquiring again after my shoulder, it will do." At least, it had not bled since the day before.

"Unless someone challenges you."

"Even then." Did she know? Was that the root of her questions and her appearance here, concern over his meeting with Pasquale? He had no intention of asking. Pity was not something he required.

What he needed was to touch her, to hold her close, to feel her warm skin against his in the benediction of a naked caress. And yet he didn't want to force her or even to have her think that physical contact was all he wanted. It wasn't, in all truth. The problem was that what he most desired lay forever beyond his grasp.

"Shall we leave this fencing for the dueling field then?" she suggested. "We both know why we are here. To pretend otherwise is too false to be borne."

He searched her face, noting the shadows painted there by sleeplessness and worry, the moist corners of her mouth that had a tendency to tremble. Perhaps he did need answers. Taking a deep breath, he let it out in a rush. "Why are you really here, *chèrie*?"

"To discharge the debt, of course, as I told you. Yes, and perhaps for a memory."

Her honesty was nearly as painful as the defeated look in the golden-brown depths of her eyes or her bravery in doing what she considered right instead of merely what was selfish. Against the scream of his own blood, he said, "Suppose I said that the debt was canceled?"

"Please, don't," she whispered.

"Don't?" He wasn't sure he'd heard correctly.

"I need… I would prefer to keep my word."

A sardonic note that he could not prevent invaded his voice. "Out of fairness?"

"Yes, but also because…oh, because everything is stupid and I must still accept my fate. Because you are not a part of the living death that my life will become, and I would like to step outside it for a short time in a manner only you may allow."

"Even though you despise me? Or is it because of it?"

"You are different. With you, I can be myself without pretense or artifice. With you, I can forget for a little while, set aside who and what I am—what we are—and simply…feel. She reached to touch his lapel, smoothing it with a fingertip while a rim of tears shimmered at her lower lashes. "Will you help me to do that?"

He reached to place his wineglass on a side table, then stepped closer. "It will be my pleasure," he whispered as he placed a hand at her silk-clad waistline, encircling it to pull her against him, "and my very great honor."

Her mouth tasted of wine, the salt of swallowed tears and something so sweetly seductive that he almost groaned as he accepted it. The feel of her warm curves under the smoothing caress of his palm was sheer incitement. The knowledge that he could have her raced through his head with dizzying power. The blood coalescing in the lower part of his body vanquished reason, leaving him dependent on instinct while he clung desperately to some vestige of principle.

Never had he felt such a compelling response,

such desire melded to infinite tenderness. He wished, suddenly, that he was as new to love as the woman in his arms so they could discover the joys of passion together. At the same time, he was profoundly glad that he had the experience to make certain that her escape into his arms was worth the risk.

She was his, he could have her. Yet there might be consequences, and often were when passion compelled men and women in their desires. If so, they would not be his to remedy or even to know. He drew back a little, opened his lips to speak.

"Don't, don't," she whispered. "I have sought and found enough objections for us both and learned that they made no difference. I refuse to have regrets, now or later."

How could she know what was in his mind? Was he so transparent in his concern, or was she a sorceress with the ability to steal his thoughts, his breath, his very heart? He neither knew nor cared, but under the beguiling spell of her permission, let slip his grasp on doubt and sanity and surrendered to her unknowing allure.

He kissed her with fervor and a shade of desperation, molding her to him past forgetting. She became gracefully boneless, leaning into his support, denying nothing to his hands that cupped and held, teased and tempted.

Exultation surged inside him, turning his blood to molten desire. She met it, fueled it as she slid her hands up to clasp them behind his neck, delicately scoring his nape as she trailed her nails through the thick curls that grew there.

He shuddered at the edge of control, took a deep

breath then stepped back from the precipice. She deserved more and so did he.

Bending, he placed an arm behind her knees and lifted her against his chest. His shoulder protested, but he barely felt it, easily ignored it. Striding into the adjoining room, he glanced around. The fire had burned low, and there was no time to replenish it. A chaise with a padded sloping back and enough length for comfortable lounging sat next to the mantel, however. He carried her to it, depositing her on the silken surface. Kneeling beside her, he kissed her deeply again, then moved to where her slippered feet rested on the silk.

In a few practiced moves, he loosened her slippers and dropped them to one side. He slid his hands along her ankles, following with his mouth up her sweetly turned calves to her knees and above where her garters were fastened. He untied these, first one then the other, while soothing with kisses the marks they had left behind, then stripped away the silk hose they held and let them fall. Her insteps required saluting, as did her knees. From there he trailed a damp path back along the slender lengths of her legs to where the opening between the soft, lace-edged linen legs of her pantaloons gave access to the center of her body.

She writhed in breathless protest as he centered his attention there. He smiled but was ruthless in his gentle exploration, his delicate handling, as if she were a sweet and succulent fruit that could be bruised by less care. And she was very like it as he inhaled her fragrance, tasted her like some exotic delicacy that might drive him to the edge of madness with her intoxicating essence.

She cried out, convulsing in his arms, then lay flushed and panting in such lovely, wanton upheaval that he felt his heart sunder in his chest as if cleaved by a sword.

He gathered her to him then, undoing the dozens of buttons down her back, freeing her of her silken gown and all that was beneath. She urged his coat from his shoulders, and he let her ease it from him, half amused, half destroyed by the care she took not to hurt him. She stripped away his shirt, trailing her fingertips over his chest and the flat surface of his belly before manipulating the fastening of his pantaloons.

She would have served him as he had her, but her touch on his hot, strutted flesh was almost enough to unravel his defenses. He took her face in his hands and captured her mouth, letting her have his tongue, probing deep in an intimation of what was to come.

Then he shucked off his pantaloons, boots and half stockings and joined her on the chaise. He covered her, taking her hands in his, meshing their fingers while he eased over her, letting her feel his weight, memorizing the satinlike curves of her body against him, her heat, and the mind-bending glory of her open, welcoming thighs. The shudder that gripped him, the goose bumps that beaded his skin like a virulent rash were warnings that he knew well to heed.

He entered her, his way eased by his own moisture, and hers, and her moan of completion nearly took off the top of his skull. He began to move, capturing her mouth again as he set a rhythm that was easy and slow and invited imitation.

She joined him, gasping a little with the effort, with the feeling, with what he hoped was the pleasure. And abruptly they were flying, caught in the elemental surge of blood and brain, heart and imagination. It took them higher, faster, until he clung to restraint and tenderness and care by only a hairbreadth of control.

Then it went from him, and all that was left was the urge to seize and to claim with hard power, demanding that she allow him the right. He opened his eyes, staring down into hers, his own burning with effort and a terrible need that had no end. She stared back at him, her expression wild and yearning, touched with desperation that thrust him headlong into the most violent paroxysms of release he had ever known. He buried himself in her velvet heat, straining to go deeper, deep enough to reach her heart. And knowing all the while that he must fail.

Afterward he lay beside her, covering her against the coolness, taking the pins one by one from her tangled hair and easing the strands into smoothness, watching the firelight play over her face like the caress of a lover, watching her sleep. In that moment, he would have killed any who tried to wake her. In that moment, he was reborn. In that moment, he swore to all the saints he knew or had ever heard extolled that he would not give her up to anyone else, least of all to Damian Francisco Adriano de Vega y Ruiz, Conde de Lérida.

He would not lose her, not now, not ever, not even if he had to forfeit his every hope and dream to keep her. No, even if he had to forfeit his life.

17

How did you say goodbye to a man, to rapture and to a dream, all in the same moment? Celina thought she must surely have botched the task. She had been too prim, too contained because to be otherwise meant shattering into a thousand pieces.

Or had she?

Waking naked on the silk chaise, naked against Rio's chest with her legs twined with his, she had pressed herself to him. She had wanted more of the bliss only he could supply, more of the oblivion. He had given it to her without stinting. Moreover, he had drawn her above him so she straddled him, then drew her hair down around them like an enclosing curtain. Within that screen, he had allowed her to take what she wished, as she wanted.

She wished for so much.

When the tumult passed, she traced his body with her fingertips, memorizing it by touch, as well as scent and taste and sight. She reveled in its smooth and rough textures, its sculpted perfection and its power, never quite comparing it to the overstuffed decrepitude of the count, but near it, very near.

She discovered just how far his injury extended,

and how deep. She had known, of course, from Suzette, who had it from Olivier. Finding out for herself was different. A distant terror had invaded her
mind as she thought of the duel that was to come,
and she almost wished Olivier had kept that particular news to himself.

Rio could not die. He was too vital, too strong
within himself. Such a man should be invincible, beyond the pains and disasters of mere mortals. Regardless, he had been hurt, his armored defenses
damaged. He wasn't immortal.

She feared for him.

She had felt cherished during their afternoon of
love. He had offered food but she could not eat. She
had wanted only him, only his whispered words, his
touch, the white-hot slide of his body against her, the
power of him captured inside her, the unwinding of
her being that only he could bring.

He had loved her a third time. She used that word
in her mind as she clung to him, but she did not say
it aloud. She didn't say it as he helped her dress then
called Suzette to attend to her hair. She didn't say it
as she kissed him goodbye, nor even as he handed
her into the hack and gave the order to the driver.
What was the point of it? Their affair, if it could be
called that, was over. What had been between them
had no bearing on her duty or her future. Her love
would not protect him.

Inside the hack, she glanced at Suzette. Her maid
was staring out the small window at nothing while
tears made wet tracks on her face. Celina wondered
briefly how Suzette and Olivier had occupied themselves during these past hours, and if they had also

said goodbye. This parting was theirs as well, after all. There would be no more messages, no more meetings that required a go-between, no other assignations.

Rio had spoken of there being no limit this time, to their bargain, had set that stipulation on the night in the garden. She knew better. Once married to the count, she would sail for Spain or some other place, and all would be at an end. She would keep her wedding vows as she honored all her commitments. She would, in spite of everything.

As her own anguish rose up inside her, flooding her eyes with stinging salt tears, she reached to take the hand of her maid. Sitting that way, they rode back toward the town house.

As evening stained the sky and reflected lavender-blue under the wings of the pigeons that flew above the rooftops, Denys awoke. Celina was standing at the window with the curtain pulled aside, watching the fading light. She heard the stir of bedcovers, then a croaking whisper.

"Lina?"

Tears hovered so close these days. She blinked back their rise before turning toward the bed. "Finally," she said in husky raillery. "I thought you would sleep your life away."

He held out his hand and she moved to take it, smiling down at him through a haze of unshed tears. He was almost as pale as the bandage that circled his head. His soft brown curls tumbling over it gave him a rakish look completely at variance with the softness in his eyes. He was her younger

brother, but he was growing up, and much too
quickly.

"*Stupide*," he said. "Of course I wouldn't." He
paused, frowning. "I have the most terrible headache. Why is that? What happened?"

"I was hoping you could tell me."

"I don't remember. At least… I was at de Silva's
place in the wine cellar. I remember smelling smoke,
hearing a commotion about the Exchange being on
fire. I could do nothing about it, so lay down on the
cot provided for me. Then nothing."

"Nothing?"

"Pain, but I don't know why unless someone hit
me as I slept. I really remember more about talking
to Rio, then having his man, Olivier, come up to me
on the street and insist that I return. He took me to
the cellar and first thing I knew I was locked inside."

"On Rio's orders, I'm sure. Why would he do such
a thing? It's beyond belief."

Denys gave her a wry smile. "I was in his way, if
you please. Though if he objected that much to me
speaking with the count, he'd only to say so."

"What on earth are you talking about?" She put a
hand to her throat as she stared down at him.

"I went to Rio's to discuss with him something I'd
heard. He didn't seem particularly surprised, which
led me to think he already knew. I suppose he was
merely playing a deep game." He put a hand to his
neck, mimicking her movement. "Might I have a
drink? I'm as dry as a cockfighting pit."

Celina reached to pour water for him from the
crystal carafe on the bedside table. She should prevent him talking so much, she knew. He needed to

conserve his strength. She also needed to hear what he had to say.

Holding the water glass to his mouth while she supported his shoulders, she asked, "What kind of game?"

"I'm not sure," he said hoarsely when he had swallowed. "Politics, maybe, or maybe not…did you know the count has ties to Mexico? That he is against American expansionism—or no, that's not right. He cares not at all for American or Mexican aims, I think, as long as he receives Mexican gold to supply his habits."

"Gold? But he is a man of wealth."

"So he would have us believe. The word in the gambling hells is that he can't pay, that the rich hidalgo pose is a sham."

"So in exchange for money, he has become a spy?" The idea did not shock her as much as it perhaps should have.

Denys drank again, then indicated that he was done. "Not exactly. He was supposed to suborn those who fawn over him, convincing them to turn their backs on our neighbors across the Sabine."

"Is there really anyone who would listen to him?" She set the glass back on the bedside table.

"Some few, maybe, those easily led."

"And you think this…this treachery is why Rio, that is, Monsieur de Silva, holds him in such dislike?"

Denys almost shook his head then stopped with a grimace of pain. "I don't know. But the feeling is mutual…or else the count has something to fear from Rio. He tried to have him killed on the street the other night and has been quietly circulating an offer of thousands to the man who will kill him on the dueling field."

"Dearest heaven," she whispered. This was the man she had agreed to marry, one who refused to face his adversary but fought back with guile and trickery.

What could cause someone like the sword master to hound such a man? she wondered. For it was suddenly clear to her that he had been doing just that all along. This was the reason Rio had spoken publicly of her in a way that caused Denys to challenge him in the beginning. Was it also the reason he had agreed to what she asked with all the consequences that it brought? Had he, in fact, come to her in the night for no reason other than that she was the chosen bride of the count, someone he could use to further his scheme against him? It all made a terrible kind of sense, finally, though she could hardly bear to think of it.

Why else would such a man as Rio, who could have any woman he chose, look at a simple, inexperienced female? And she had begged him to take her, which was the most humiliating thing of all.

"Rio made me an apology for detaining me, you know," Denys said. "Quite a handsome one, in fact."

As if that absolved him. "But he gave no explanation?"

"He said it was for my own good," he replied with a small grimace of distaste. "And to prevent me from running into danger."

"Instead, he is the one at risk."

"How is that?"

She told him, and in detail. Denys's amazement was transparent. He had no memory whatever of the fire at the atelier or being carried out of it, could hardly believe that the duels stemming from his own meeting with Rio were still playing themselves out as indicated by the meeting with Pasquale.

"Are you sure that's what this is?" she asked. "Another would-be usurper?"

"What else could it be? But wait. What of his shoulder?"

"Painful, I fear, at least somewhat."

"And still he accepted this challenge? It's suicide!"

"Why do you say that?" Her voice was as sharp as the fear that pierced her.

"Pasquale is said to be formidable with a blade. He fights in the Position Sinister."

"What on earth do you mean?"

"With the sword in his left hand. It gives him an advantage, since it requires that his opponent defend in an abnormal position, to work twice as hard. Of course it also means that he must present his left side, closest to his heart, to the sword of the man he faces."

"A pleasant thought," she said, wincing.

"You did ask."

So she had, though she might wish it otherwise. "There must be some way to stop the meeting."

"You tried that once," her brother said, a warning in his voice.

"Yes." She turned away from him. "Oh, I can't stand this. How I wish..."

"So do I. Do you think I might get up tomorrow? It would be no great thing to ride out in the carriage to watch."

"You can't," she cried, swinging around again. The doctor says you must remain still or you could still have a brain fever."

Disgust crossed his face before he released a sigh. "I suppose I must, though I would give anything to see this match, or at least hear of it."

She stared at him a long moment. "Perhaps I could go."

"You can't. It isn't done. Besides, the coachman won't take out the carriage without an order from Papa."

"There are other means of transportation."

"A hack? What do you know of such things?"

"Never mind. I've kept you talking too long. You must rest."

He looked distinctly unhappy. "How can I while knowing you may do something outrageous?"

"It's just an idea that may come to nothing," she said soothingly.

"Lina?"

"Please don't fuss, Din-Din. I'll have to listen to that soon enough from my husband."

He took the bait, as she hoped he might. "Husband? You don't mean you have signed that infernal contract."

"I have grown resigned," she answered. "Is that not a good thing?"

With the discussion that followed, Denys seemed to forget her intention to be present at the duel. But Celina did not forget.

Creeping down the outside stairs at dawn was a severe trial. She moved with great stealth while making as much haste as possible. It wasn't the possibility of waking her brother, her aunt or her father, so much as the possibility that Cook or Mortimer might be up early and about their duties. The last thing she needed was to be bundled back into the house like a naughty child.

No one stirred in the servants' quarters, however; no alarm was raised. She and Suzette passed through the porte cochere without incident. They saw only a stray dog and a pair of Choctaw squaws laden with baskets to be sold at the market. The hired hack waited at the cross street as arranged. They stepped into it and were off.

The rattling journey to the Allard Oaks seemed to take forever. The shell road was shrouded in fog that deadened sound. Trees and houses appeared ghostly through the mist. Dampness seeped into the hack, bringing out its smells of sweat and tobacco and an unsavory intimation that someone inebriated to the point of sickness had been a recent passenger. It was not truly cold, yet Celina felt a deep internal chill that nothing could reach.

The Oaks loomed ahead of them, and the hack driver pulled up in the field well back from the pair of trees known as The Twin Sisters where the duelists would meet. They were early. One other carriage stood not far away with the occupants still inside. It wasn't Rio and his party, so it had to be the other principal in the duel, Celina thought. She drew back well behind the leather curtains that had been let down against the coolness. The less attention she attracted, the better.

Glancing across at Suzette on the opposite seat, she saw that the maid was huddled into a blanket, staring at her feet. "You're very quiet this morning," she said. "Are you all right?"

Suzette only shook her head.

"Come, out with it. What is the matter?"

"Everything. Nothing. I just…nothing."

"Is it Olivier?"

Suzette pressed her lips together an instant, then she burst out, "It's everything, don't you see? I hate the idea of knives and swords—just the thought makes me feel sick, as if I can feel them thrusting into my body. This dueling is madness, madness."

"Yes. I understand exactly what you mean."

"More than that, what will happen to Olivier if Monsieur de Silva is killed? Where will he find work? Who else will appreciate his skills and his honesty? It's extremely important to him to have a place, a livelihood. Oh, I know it's a terrible thing to think of now, but how can I not? Yes, and if Monsieur de Silva is victorious, what then? You will marry this count and go to Spain. What will become of me then, since I belong not to you but to your papa?"

"Oh, Suzette." Celina had not told her of the bargain with her father for fear something might happen to prevent it. Though she did not doubt her papa's word, she was wary of the count's interference. It would not be for Suzette's betterment if the count should claim the maid as his property. A husband might control the use of a woman's dowry, including slaves and property, but any gift or her inheritance were her own to do with as she willed. Celina still hoped to persuade her father to sign the manumission papers before the wedding. Suzette could be considered a gift and freed at will. Such caution seemed cruel, however, in the face of Suzette's distress.

"There is no need to worry. My father has promised that you will be mine when I wed the count. What you do then is your choice."

Suzette sat quite still. "Mam'zelle, you didn't, you wouldn't. Not for me."

She shook her head with the ghost of a smile. "Not entirely, but it seemed someone should benefit."

"This is too… I can't think what to say."

"Then say nothing. It isn't required, I promise you, for it hasn't yet come to pass."

"But the prospect, just think of it! Olivier won't believe it when I tell him."

Celina put out her hand in a quick staying gesture. Not only might it still be prevented, but she wasn't at all sure she wanted Olivier to know since he was sure to tell his master. Rio had accused her before of sacrificing herself, and this could look like more of the same. "It might be best to wait."

"Oh, but Olivier must know. It's his happiness, as well."

Suzette meant that to be together would mean happiness that was shared. Yes, that was undoubtedly true when both loved. "If you like, then," Celina said, and turned her head to stare out the window again.

The maid slid from the seat, going to her knees beside Celina and catching her hand. "I thank you, Mam'zelle, from the bottom of my heart. You are so good. Surely this joy I feel will be yours someday. I will pray that it's so."

"Please," Celina said against the tightness in her throat. "Please, do."

The clip-clop of hooves and grating of carriage wheels on the shell road announced the arrival of others. Before the vehicle could draw to a halt, more appeared behind it. They were joined by still others until the hack was surrounded by a motley collection of broughams, barouches and sporting carriages, with also another hack or two. Men began to get down and stroll toward the dueling ground. A few shouted back and forth, exchanging bets. An up-ended flask gave off a silver flash in the rising sun. The scents of whisky, warm horses, trampled winter grass and cigars drifted in the air.

"There is Monsieur de Silva," Suzette said. She nodded toward where four men were descending from a black barouche with yellow trim around the doors and on the wheels.

Rio's party moved into the oak's shade, and his opponent, with his seconds and doctor, emerged to join them. Two men from each group met in the space between the oaks where they consulted together for a few minutes. A coin was tossed for position, then instructions were called out. Rio stepped to one end of the designated area, facing the carriage, while Pasquale took the opposing end with his back to Celina and Suzette. Immediately, they began to remove their coats and waistcoats. Both men stripped off their cravats and opened the collars of their shirts for easier breathing.

"They seem well matched," Suzette said in colorless tones.

Celina had been thinking much the same thing. The two men were very similar in size and body frame, both tall with broad shoulders, lean waistlines, and the impressively muscled lower limbs of men who spent strenuous hours every week working on the fencing strips. They were both dark and gifted with the innate grace of natural athletes. The difference between them was that Pasquale was fit and whole, while Rio moved his upper body with obvious stiffness.

The preliminaries took a few minutes more. In the midst of them, Olivier detached himself from Rio's party and walked toward the carriage in which they had arrived carrying Rio's discarded clothing. When he had put the things inside, he turned back toward where the dueling strip was being marked off with powdered chalk. Suzette looked toward Celina in strained inquiry, and she nodded her permission. The maid jumped down from the hack and ran to intercept Olivier behind the protective cover of carriage wheels. They spoke for a few moments with their heads together.

To watch them felt like an intrusion. Celina looked away, leaning her head against the window frame. Through the slit between it and the curtain, she could see the spectators appraising the two duelists as if they were prized horses, discussing their fighting styles and stamina and placing more wagers. They seemed to have no qualms about watching two men enter a contest in which one might die. Celina closed her eyes, feeling a little ill.

The crowd was growing larger. It seemed the attraction of watching two *maîtres d'armes* cross swords was great. Then she heard the commotion of a new arrival. She lifted her lashes in time to see a familiar figure alight from a splendid carriage. He pushed his way to the front line with arrogant assurance, brushing aside protests as if he didn't hear them. Dressed in a flamboyant combination of green coat, yellow waistcoat and plaid pantaloons, he appeared obscenely bright for such a solemn occasion. He pulled out his purse and placed what had to have been a sizable wager, if the eyes of the man who received it were any gauge. That done, he turned back to the field. He bowed as he caught the eyes of Pasquale, but did not look to Rio at all.

It was Count de Lérida, come to see the spectacle. From his satisfied air, he apparently expected it to be much to his liking.

"Mademoiselle Vallier? Forgive the intrusion, but I should like to add my gratitude to Suzette's." It was Olivier, standing at the carriage door. He was handing Suzette back inside as he spoke.

"You are very welcome," she said quietly. "That is, you most certainly will be if manumission is accomplished. As I tried to tell Suzette, it isn't guaranteed."

"You cared enough to make the attempt. That is enough." He put a hand to his breastbone. "I would say more, all that is in my heart, but there are no words and also no time."

Behind him, Rio and Pasquale were approaching each other across the greensward. "Yes, you must go. But one small moment, if you please? What do you know of this Pasquale?"

Olivier's lips set in a thin line. "A man to be respected on the field. I have not seen him fight, but they say he is deadly."

Denys had been right then. The knowledge did nothing to calm her fears. "He is really that good?"

"Indeed. But Monsieur Rio is the best of them all."

"His injury, what if it is too much?"

"Who can say? Monsieur Pasquale is also reputed to be a fair man. We must hope so." He paused, a worried line between his eyes. "I hesitate to suggest it, Mademoiselle Vallier, but…"

"Yes, Olivier?"

"Are you certain that you would not like to leave? Now, before it begins?"

She caught the inside of her lip between her teeth as she considered it, but still shook her head. "How can I, before knowing the end?"

"Monsieur Rio would not like you to see, I think, not if this Pasquale is the victor."

It wasn't a mere victory to which Olivier referred. The fear of more drastic consequences had been with her from the moment she left the town house, and grew more blighting with every second that passed. Yet to turn away now seemed a betrayal, like abandoning him to face the prospect of death alone. She would stay, though the very thought of what might come was like a dagger in her chest.

She moistened her lips, met his eyes with their liquid darkness, and their concern. "Perhaps, in that case, this so formidable swordsman will be satisfied with a show of blood?"

"Indeed, so we must hope."

"Yes," she whispered. "Take care of him, Olivier."

"As ever, Mam'zelle."

He had deliberately given her the title of informal affection reserved for family. She was touched. "Thank you," she said, and held out her hand to him.

He bowed over it with a polished gesture, then turned and walked away.

It was only as she watched him go that Celina realized that Rio was staring in their direction. He must have seen Suzette, perhaps had guessed that her mistress was also present and watching from inside the carriage. Would it be a benefit to him or a hindrance? She could not begin to guess. Nor could she imagine what he might think or do about it.

It was the one thing, out of all she had considered before deciding to come, that had not occurred to her.

Then the waiting was abruptly at an end. One of the seconds, sword in hand, walked to where the two men stood. He held it aloft between them and they crossed their blades over it. The cry of *"En garde!"* came loud and clear across the clearing.

The second stepped back, whipping his sword down to release those of the duelists. The two men brought up their rapiers in salute, then swept them down again.

The match had begun.

18

Rio spared the crowd a brief glance as he waited for the signal to begin. It was sizable; word of the meeting had doubtless spread quickly. He might almost suspect the count of giving out the details, a breach of etiquette, certainly, but not of the formal dueling code. The purpose would be to gather an audience for what he expected to be the humiliation of a foe by his paid champion.

His task, Rio thought with grim resolution, was to see that the count was disappointed.

It would not be easy, of that he had little doubt. The Italians had invented swordplay. Their fencing schools turned out masters who were something more than proficient in the art. Pasquale's reputation came as much from these facts as from the braggadocio that surrounded him. Which wasn't to say that the man touted his own skill. Such a thing wasn't necessary; those who had seen him fight took care of that chore for him.

A duel was primarily a battle of intelligence, however, or so the old fencing teacher to whom Rio had apprenticed himself always said. He wondered if Pasquale was aware of it.

Rio's gaze flashed beyond the crowd to the vehicles that were pulled up under the trees or else lined the road. Olivier stood with Suzette at the open door of a hack near the edge of the grassy field. His business there was plain even before Rio glimpsed a pale face and shining gold-brown hair in the vehicle's dim interior.

Celina was here. It was incredible. That she would risk such exposure astounded him. Women did not belong at these events. Their presence was a threat to concentration. Concern for their safety and sensibilities could become fatal distractions.

There was nothing to be done about it at this point except see to it that her attendance did not interfere so much with his skill that she must bear witness to his death. He turned his attention back to the match.

He and Pasquale touched blades with a ringing clang then allowed them to be supported by Caid, who again acted as his chief second with Gilbert as his fellow. In that brief moment, Rio did not look at his opponent but at Pasquale's sword. The tip glittered like a star above his head while light ran down the blade to the hilt like a flash of blue lightning. It was a finely crafted weapon, and the hand that held it was steady, with a relaxed grip that yet hinted at latent power. Its touch against his sword tip was neither threatening nor timid but confident as they stood at the ready, anticipating the first move in this ancient and dangerous *pas de deux*.

"Begin!"

As Caid stepped back from the thirty-yard strip that had been measured off, Pasquale initiated a fast, hard attack. The move, Rio knew, was designed to complete the main objective of a duel, which was to wound the adversary as quickly as possible while sustaining no similar injury. Rio parried easily and whirled into a riposte. Then they settled into a series of forays, seeking any weakness, any mistake in form or training that might be exploited. The moves also served to plumb the heart and mind of an adversary, discovering what he was made of, the kind of person he was inside. In the space of that first minute, Rio knew more about the man in front of him than he might have learned in weeks of conversation. He knew him with instinctive, brotherly intimacy, and he was puzzled.

Pasquale had no obvious weakness, made no mistakes. He was disciplined, agile and intelligent, a fast yet careful fighter. His skill was well honed, his strength above average, his will relentless. He had none of the flashy moves dictated by ego or arrogance, did not attempt to overwhelm with fancy technique. Matching swords with competence and impressively varied maneuvers, he seemed to be feeling out his partner with the same intent concentration that Rio brought to the task. His mechanics were perfection, but added to them was a touch of inspiration, the intuitive genius that made him truly formidable.

That Pasquale was left-handed was a distinct disadvantage. From that point of attack, Rio's own right arm provided little protection for his chest and his parries had to be wider and more forceful to shield this target area. In addition, the blade of his opponent circled counterclockwise, the opposite of the norm, so forced adjustment in his own moves. He was not

unused to the changes; he had fought left-handed opponents before, had, on occasion, assumed the style
himself. Still, their combined effect demanded extra
effort, extra vigilance.

Time and place receded, leaving nothing except
the man who faced him. The two of them existed in
an odd half world where the only reality was the rapiers in their hands and the need to use them. The
melodious chiming of the blades provided the
rhythm to which they advanced and retreated across
the grass strip. Rio fought with the discipline of thousands of hours of practice and the lightning reflexes
and instincts instilled by the exercise while his mind
worked at speed and in instinctive unity with his
hand and arm.

Beyond intellect, the deciding major factor in any
match between swordsmen of equal skill was courage.
A part of the equation was which of them had the most
to fear from the other, but just as important was what
he did about it. Rio saw no fear in Pasquale. Was there
any within himself? He could discern none, yet caution hovered at the back of his mind. Its main cause,
he thought, was doubt about the Italian's intentions,
but he also had an awareness that the man he faced
was perhaps the greatest threat he had encountered
since coming to New Orleans. The only other he had
found that came close was Caid, and the engagements
between the two of them had been with blunted
swords and for sport, never with intent to draw blood.

The Italian, for all his lack of malevolence, was
not merely sparring for the exercise. His purpose
might be his own, but it was a serious one. Pasquale
meant to win.

The rising sun poked hot sunbeams through the branches overhead. They fell to the ground in patterns that dazzled the eyes and touched Rio's back like firebrands. Sweat glazed both him and his opponent. He could feel it seeping around his bandaging, stinging as it reached his raw wound. His every lunge pulled at the injury, breaking its newly made scabs. The pain was an irritant and a handicap in the way it affected his timing.

He wasn't on his best form, could not quite reach that perfect blend of mind and body where the battle became effortless and victory certain. He knew it, and thought Pasquale might guess it as well, for if he could read his adversary, then the reverse was also true. There was nothing to be done, however, except to try his utmost. To persevere when the odds were against winning was perhaps the truest test of courage.

A *phrase d'armes*, or round, of a duel lasted until there was an injury. This one seemed endless as neither of them could find or manufacture an opening. Feinting, parrying, eternally testing, they moved back and forth over the grass while their chests began to heave and their breathing rasped in their throats.

Pasquale's patience gave way first. He lunged into a virulent attack that Rio parried with a scraping of blades that sent blue and orange sparks showering into the grass. He retreated deliberately then, meeting the silvery, flickering tongue of the blade before him in quarte, in sixte, drawing on deep reserves of power he scarcely knew he possessed. Sensing the chalk line behind him that to step over meant a charge of cowardice, he swirled with speed and precise timing into an abrupt stop-thrust that made Pasquale's eyes narrow.

Immediately Rio seized the offensive, counterattacking in his turn, driving the other man back before executing a lunge with such power and precision that Pasquale was forced to resort to a twisting backward leap to avoid being stabbed. Rio's blade sliced through the Italian's shirt, raking across the skin under his left arm.

First touch to him.

Rio disengaged at once, even before the opposing seconds shouted out the order to halt. That call was almost drowned by the cheers of the crowd. He should have been pleased by their partisanship, but it left him unmoved. His adversary did not deserve that anyone should be glad at a show of his blood.

Stepping back, Rio waited for an assessment of the damage he had done. It proved to be a small slice that barely parted the skin. Pasquale allowed it to be swabbed with alcohol but refused a surgical dressing or sticking plaster that might impede movement. Resuming his shirt, he moved once more to the strip and signaled that he was ready.

The opposing chief second stepped forward, bowing to Rio as the challenger as he put the formal question. "Sir, shall we stop?"

No one expected it. The wound was trifling, the fight barely begun. Still, Rio hesitated. The anger that might have propelled him to kill would not come, nor would the contempt he had expected to feel for the count's chosen champion. The edge these might have given him was missing. This bout seemed more like an exhibition of prowess between masters rather than a fight to the death. It was obscene that one of them might die for so little cause. Yet his curiosity was strong. Could he best the other man? Was he capable of it?

"We continue," he said.

The salute was performed once more. Caid stepped to the center and called out, *"En garde!"*

Rio brought up his sword.

Pasquale did not. Rather he stepped back and let the tip trail in the grass. With a frown between his dark eyes, he nodded at Rio's shoulder. "You are injured, friend, and the touch was not mine."

Rio glanced at the sleeve of his cambric shirt. It was turning red in a long streak down his left arm. The back of his shirt at the shoulder felt suddenly cool also, as if the bleeding from his opened wound had soaked through the bandaging.

A buzz of comment ran through the watchers. Rio thought he heard the count's voice raised in outrage, and why not? Such an honorable stance by Pasquale could hardly be satisfactory to him.

"It's nothing," Rio said. "Disregard it, if you please."

His adversary observed him through dark, narrowed eyes. "Impossible. I refuse to have it said that I took advantage of a wounded man."

"If we continue now that you are injured, the same charge could be made."

"A different matter altogether since mine is little more than a salon touch and sustained in the fight. Any injury in the heat of a meeting is hardly felt while an old one…" Pasquale lifted an expressive shoulder. "I am done. I make you an apology in form for my remarks that brought us to this ground, but I will not lift my weapon against you again."

The point of honor was a fine one. As much as it irritated Rio to be the recipient of it, he still appreciated the distinction and also the high standard of his opponent which caused it. This was the code of champions who competed on the fencing strips and dueling fields, that all deeds and actions should portray the best of a man, with generosity and grace under provocation as watchwords. It was proof, if more were needed, that the man who faced him was no more a hired assassin than he was himself.

"Why?" Rio asked in tones so soft that they could be audible only to the two of them. "Why did you force this challenge?"

"You refused me a bout, among other reasons."

"That these reasons involve me and my dealings with someone else is the rumor. What I fail to understand is why you might choose to strike such a bargain with the devil."

The seconds, watching from their posts, frowned as they conferred among themselves. For a duelist to declare himself unwilling to go on was not uncommon, but to be held accountable for it had little precedent. Those gathered to watch were more vocal as they talked excitedly among themselves, craning to see while speculating and arguing about the cause for the halt in activity.

"It could be," Pasquale answered in quiet suggestion, "that I disliked the idea of standing back with my hands in my pockets while a less principled *maître* entered the contest for mere money."

"So you would save me?"

Amusement for that idea shone briefly in the dark coffee-brown of Pasquale's eyes. "Or at least make certain it was a fair fight." —

"A noble aim, but it appears less than adequate."

"Perhaps because it is." Pasquale's smile held disarming honesty. "I object to those who would bring a lady into their quarrels. And I would add that your enemy is also mine."

He could only mean the count. "So you fight the man's battles for him?" Rio inquired with irony. "An unusual vengeance."

"Rather, I prevent the untimely removal of one who may become an ally. Vengeance is like swordplay, my friend. To achieve victory is no less satisfying for being deliberate and based on strategy. Do you not agree?"

"Within reason." Rio met the other man's gaze, his own searching.

"Then?"

"Then I accept your apology and suggest that we continue this discussion at another location."

"I don't believe so."

To refuse such an overture under these circumstances was perilously close to insult. Rio hovered between suspicion and annoyance as he inquired, "You have a reason, I suppose?"

"You may be sure of it." Pasquale's dark gaze was gently mocking. Swinging away, he moved off the strip where he held up his arms, facing the crowd with his sword still in hand. *"Messieurs!"* he called out. "Attend to me!"

The assemblage turned expectant faces toward the tall Italian. Quiet descended, save for the distant call of a crow. Someone coughed, hawked, then was silent. On the gathering's far edge, the count's face had an uneasy cast to it.

"I am Nicholas Pasquale, known as La Roche, lately come to this fair place directly from the island of Cuba, and before that by way of Spain, France and my own Italy. My travels were not for pleasure but on a vengeance trail. I am Italian! Born of a patrician mother and an Englishman who bedded her out of wedlock, I am a bastard. But know you that I had a younger brother born of legal union, a fine youth and gentle poet who loved words and the ladies in equal measure. He died, my brother, died by his own hand after bringing dishonor to his family name. He was led into this disgrace by a man pretending to nobility but of ignoble spirit. He used my brother to gain access to the highest circles of Rome where he bled many of their wealth then fled like a coward, leaving my brother to face their anger. This selfsame trick he used in Paris and Havana, one he had perfected in Barcelona from whence he came. Then he took ship for New Orleans, this monster. I followed after him as I have hunted on his trail across Europe and the Caribbean. For I am Italian, as I have told you, and the sanctity of family and revenge against those who harm me and mine is everything to me."

"Who is this gentleman?" a man called out. "Let us know his name."

"He is a man of parts, one who gives himself high title though his actions are base. I saw him here, recognized him from descriptions given to me. I made his acquaintance, gained his confidence, and what do you suppose?"

This Pasquale had audacity, Rio thought, and something more that might be called magnetism. He commanded attention through sheer personality and internal strength. The crowd was with him, waiting to hear what he would impart to them.

"I was asked to kill for him."

A hush descended. Even Rio, who had half expected the announcement, felt the shock of it.

"Unbelievable, is it not?" Pasquale inquired with a swift gesture. "The mind recoils. Still, it is true. I was asked to manufacture a challenge for a fine swordsman and annihilate him on the field of honor. This, because the noble Spaniard was too much the coward to risk the task himself."

An elderly man stepped forward from the ranks of the gathering. His voice stern, he asked, "The duel today is the result?"

Pasquale bowed. "As you say. I am also a swordsman, though never a *maître d'armes* until I arrived here. But of course I wished to try my skill against this master. It is a vanity, I know, but what would you? Then there is the matter of responsibility. If I did not accept, could I not be blamed if another swordsman accepted this task and de Silva died? So yes, I agreed. But I did not know, this I swear, that he had already been grievously injured. Count Damian Francisco Adriano de Vega y Ruiz did know. He knew because he came to me and offered a fortune if I would strike immediately. He swore that I could not fail. Just now, I saw why. This, *messieurs,* is the quality of the man who stands now among you."

Pasquale had publicly branded the count a coward. All eyes turned toward that gentleman to see how he would take it.

"Preposterous," the count blustered, sweat shining on his cheeks in the morning light. "This Pasquale admits to being a nobody, a bastard who seeks to make his fortune with a sword. I do not associate with such riffraff."

It was a trap, Rio thought, and the count had walked into it with his eyes blinded by arrogance. That surmise was proved an instant later.

"Your pardon, sir," Pasquale said, his voice soft. "I thought I heard you name me a bastard."

"So I did! And why not, when you said…"

"What I may say is a different matter from what I will hear from another without redress. My seconds will call on yours."

Pasquale turned to Rio. "Will you do me the honor, *monsieur*?"

"With pleasure," Rio said. The irony of the reversal of roles did not escape him, but that was the way of the Duello.

"No!" The count glared around him like a cornered wharf rat.

"No?"

"I am not obliged to fight one who is not my peer."

"You are saying again that I am inferior?" Pasquale leveled his sword at the count as he took a step forward.

"In rank, yes, also blood and breeding. Do you deny it?"

"I deny nothing," Pasquale said, moving forward with a swordsman's grace and deadly purpose. "But I will tell you that the title of bastard was honestly gained, unlike some who are known to have stolen their honors. Nay, to have wrested them from their rightful owners by blood and fire. Did you really think no one would ever know? You laughed at my brother before he died, telling him he was as weak as your own elder brother and your nephew whom you had destroyed. You told him many things, all of which he committed to the letter he wrote before ending his life. The names were there and the deeds. How do we judge a man who inherits his title over the bodies of his relatives but is yet a bastard in conduct?"

He knew. Pasquale knew of Rio's own past and stolen patrimony. Rio was dazed by the realization. Then, as he saw the count staring at him with black hatred in his eyes, he understood that the nobleman also recognized him for who he was, who he had once been. How he had made the discovery was a mystery, still it explained many things. It wasn't the threat to his marriage plans alone that had led the count to attempt murder.

"Nonsense," the count shouted, Celina's scratches on his face standing out in livid streaks, like cracks in the skin of a boiled plum.

"Prove it," Rio said, his voice harsh as he moved to stand at Pasquale's side. "Prove on the dueling field that you are not the ultimate coward, one who dares not wield the weapon himself but hires others for the task."

Pasquale gave him a single, flashing glance of approval before adding, "Just so. Do it now, if you dare."

The count did not. That failure of nerve was in his

rigid stance, his staring eyes, his hesitation to defend his honor. Of all these, the last was by far the most damning. A man could be a scoundrel of the first order and still be accepted in New Orleans. But to be proved a coward was to be forever disgraced.

It began as a slight shifting, a few men turning away, speaking under their breaths to their neighbors. Others drew apart in a slow realignment with friends and acquaintances. One man spat on the ground. Within seconds, the count stood alone.

He was being shunned. It signaled his finish in the city. He was done, and he knew it.

Abruptly, the count gripped his cane in a stranglehold, tugged his hat brim down over his eyes and spun in the direction of the carriages. He marched away with his shoulders hunched and his mouth set in a tight line.

It was too easy. Instinct brought a frown to Rio's face as he stared at the retreating back of the man who had been his nemesis for a large portion of his life. "I think…" he began.

"As do I, my friend."

He and Pasquale exchanged a quick glance, then turned as one and sprinted after the departing figure.

The count looked over his shoulder, perhaps alerted by the sound of their footfalls. Flinging down his cane, he broke into a run. His heavy legs churned, his arms pumped. Faster than he had any right, given his bulk, he covered the distance to the carriages in thudding strides. He seemed to be making for his own gaudy, heavy barouche—until he swerved abruptly toward the hired hack that stood closest to the road.

Rio redoubled his effort.

"What is he doing?" Pasquale demanded as he kept pace beside him.

"Mademoiselle Vallier is in the hack."

"If he harms her..."

Rio gave him a bleak look, all too aware of the grim note in the Italian's voice. "Or compromises her?"

Swift communication passed between them. It was enough. The lady's name was already besmirched, and there were those who would consider any sort of marital alliance a fair remedy. In addition, they both knew that the count had no aversion to killing when the odds were on his side. He might well take Celina's life from rage and frustration, or to prevent anyone else from having her.

They redoubled their effort. Natural athletes in superb condition and half his age, they would have him in a few more strides.

Abruptly the count halted, drove plump fingers into the pocket of his waistcoat and turned with a pocket pistol in his hand. His hand and arm shook. His face was fiery red, his breathing harsh and wheezing. His voice held the growl of a cornered animal as he called out, "Stop! Stop now, or one of you will die."

Rio and Pasquale skidded to a halt. For long seconds, the three of them stood in frozen tableau while men shouted and called behind them. Caid and Olivier pounded up, to be joined seconds later by Gilbert.

The count spared hardly a glance for the others. Stepping back until he was near the hack door, he reached behind him and jerked it open. He mounted the hanging bar step and lifted his voice to call up to the driver with an offer of ten silver dollars if he arrived in the city ahead of any other vehicle.

The driver, staring with his mouth agape until that moment, kicked off the brake and reached for his whip. The crack of that black snake above the horse between the shafts was like a pistol shot. The hack lurched into movement.

The count dove inside. Rio caught a glimpse of Celina's pale face, saw her lunge away from the count as if to escape out the opposite side. Then the door slammed shut.

The wheels of the light hack spun over the spring grass and out onto the roadway. The vehicle clattered away in a billow of white, blowing dust.

19

The hack careened down the road, the wheels dropping into ruts and potholes and bouncing out again. Celina, jerked to the floor by the count as they lurched into motion, struggled back onto the forward-facing seat beside Suzette. Across from them, her betrothed pocketed the small pistol he carried before leaning to snatch the window shade from its holder and toss it aside. He thrust out his head, staring back toward the dueling ground.

Celina glanced at Suzette who clung to the strap for balance in the swaying vehicle. Her maid was pale but composed as she stared at the count. Celina could feel dislike amounting almost to hatred pour along her veins. The sight of the pistol pointed at Rio moments before had made her throat close in terror. Now the casual way it had been put away, as if she and Suzette posed no threat at all, was so enraging that her voice shook when she spoke.

"What are you doing? Stop the carriage at once and get down!"

"Be silent," he snapped.

"Do not order me, if you please. We are not married, nor are we likely to be after what I just heard. This is my carriage…"

"It's a hired hack, and few back there know you are in it with the exception of de Silva and his new-found friend. But that will change if I decide to throw you out onto the road."

"Monsieur de Silva will follow us."

"For what good it may do him. Cease yapping so I can think."

The urge to reach for the door handle again and snatch it open was almost overpowering. Celina repressed it with an effort. She could not leave Suzette behind, for one thing, but it was also a move with scant chance of success. More than that, giving the count an excuse to lay hands on her again did not seem wise. She had to cling to her temper while searching for a more feasible way of parting company with him.

"Where are we going?"

"A place where we may be private," he answered without taking his eyes from their back trail. "One where you may be taught obedience, among other things."

"An alarm will be raised, a search party sent to find me."

He turned on her then, his pale eyes glacial. "But not soon enough, I think. Afterward, it will make no difference."

The tone of his voice would have told her his intention, even if common sense had not. Panic brushed her only to be swiftly banished by disgust. He might force her, compromise her, but she would make it as difficult for him as possible.

Beside her, Suzette reached to touch her hand. It was a reminder that she was not alone, that the count must deal with both of them. Celina appreciated the gesture more than she could express, but put little faith in its message. When the time came for the count to make good on his threat, it was doubtful she would be permitted the protection of a chaperone.

The hack had a head start, but she was certain they were being pursued. She could not see, so judged mainly from the harried look on her abductor's face and the way he shouted up at the driver for more speed. Then as they rounded a curve she glimpsed a dust cloud trailing them. It was fast moving, but too far back to be of great comfort.

A short time later, they reached the outskirts of the city. The count called up instructions. They swung smartly into a side street that was little more than a rutted lane, and then turned again only a few blocks farther along. A tense silence prevailed for some distance. All commotion faded away. As they turned yet again, the count sat back on the leather seat with a smirk of satisfaction on his round face.

"We have lost them, I believe. They thought they had me, those two, but they will have to get up early in the day to catch this old fox."

"I have no doubt," Celina said, her voice tight in her throat as she fought to conceal her dismay. "It appears you have had some experience at running and hiding."

"Mam'zelle," Suzette said in soft warning.

"You had best heed your maid, *mademoiselle*. My patience with your insults is at an end, and I will be repaid for them all."

She gave him a single, clear look. "Lay hands on me and you will regret it."

His short laugh held more anticipation than humor.

Celina wanted to annihilate him. The need was so strong that her hands shook with it. Now was not the time, however, not while he was watchful and they were shut up in a moving vehicle. Turning her face away, she stared out the window.

The neighborhood they were passing through was at the outer edges of the Faubourg Tremé, she knew, though she seldom had occasion to travel through it. Nothing appeared at all familiar. Shanties lined the street's edge, and the people who sat on the stoops of doorways appeared to be poorly dressed laborers or their wives and children. In the side yard of one house, a woman stood over a great iron pot that was blackened by the fire that heated it. A washerwoman, apparently, she stirred the boiling clothes with a stick while keeping an eye on a pair of toddlers.

The hack turned yet again. This new street was quieter and more orderly. The white painted houses with their heavy shutters were neatly kept but still small, mere cottages. The lots were narrow and construction in the shotgun style, so-called because a shotgun blast fired through the front door could travel through the rooms lined up one behind the other and exit out the rear door. Celina had never ventured into this secluded thoroughfare in her life, but she knew it instantly.

The rue des Rampart, it was the street of the Vieux Carré that once had marked the rear wall when New Orleans had been a fortified city. A mere four blocks

from rue Royale, it was worlds away in status and respectability. It was the street where lay the houses in
which gentlemen kept their quadroon mistresses.

The hack pulled to a halt before one of the more
modest dwellings. The count stepped out, calling up
to the driver on the box to wait. Then he turned and
held out his hand to help Celina alight from the hack.

"This is infamous," she said without leaving her
seat. "You can't mean me to get down here." It was
not that she objected to the neighborhood or even
being presented to the count's mistress, if that was
his intention. Rather, she feared he meant her to take
the quadroon's place.

"Enact me no tantrums for I have no time for them.
You will get out. Now." The order was peremptory.
Hard on it, he took out his pocket pistol once more
and pointed it at Suzette. His attention was not on the
maid, however; he paid no more attention to her than
if she had been a piece of furniture. She was a nonen-
tity to his mind, Celina saw. He scarcely seemed to
register her presence except as a means of forcing her
own obedience.

Celina gathered her skirts and left the hack,
though she refused to touch the count's hand. Back
straight and head high, she crossed the short distance to the front door with Suzette following and the
count herding them. He moved ahead to push open
the door, and they stepped inside.

A young woman stood in the archway that
marked the opening from the front sitting room to
what was apparently the bedchamber. Her face had
the softly rounded outline of a girl still in her teens,
though her shape under a thin wrapper of lace-edged

silk was lush. Chestnut hair drifted around her shoulders in a dense cloud, and her skin was the creamy tint of old parchment. Her gaze flickered from Celina to Suzette, then to the man behind them. Color rose to her cheekbones, and she pulled her wrapper closer around her with an embarrassed gesture.

"Monsieur le Comte, I was not expecting you," she began.

"Get dressed, and be quick about it," he commanded. "I have an errand for you."

"But I must see to our guests." Her expression was as concerned as that of any lady caught in the same situation.

"Go," he said, the word a snarl of anger as he gave her a shove toward the bedchamber behind her.

Was this debasing treatment of his *placée* habitual or for her benefit? Celina wondered. She was sorry for it either way, but particularly if she was the cause. "Surely, there is no reason for her to be dispossessed?"

"You prefer an audience, or perhaps three in a bed?"

"Nothing so vulgar was in my mind!"

"Too bad."

The count removed his hat and tossed it onto a chair, then reached for Celina's arm. He half led, half dragged her to a small settee and pushed her down onto it. Turning then to the secretary desk that sat in a corner, he took a sheet of paper and a steel-nibbed pen from a drawer and began to write. For long seconds, the only sound in the room was the steady scratching of the pen on the heavy paper.

Celina used that moment of inattention for a quick inventory of the sitting room. It was a pleasant enough space, with a settee covered in brocatelle, an Aubusson carpet in the subdued colors of such floor coverings, and a wooden mantel over the fireplace that was topped by a painting of a ruined Roman villa in the current Romantic style. A frame holding Brussels's work sat near a fireside chair with a brass lamp nearby. The air smelled pleasantly of coal smoke, beeswax used to polish the furniture and a faint whiff of morning coffee. Altogether, it was a tasteful if not particularly opulent retreat, but it held no poker, no letter opener, fruit knife or anything else lethal enough to be useful as a weapon.

The count took a silver blotter and rocked it back and forth over his penmanship. As he folded the letter, Celina asked, "What are you doing?"

"Arranging our future, if you must know." Rising, he took a candle from the holder built into the secretary desk and lit it at the coal fire, then dripped wax on the flap to seal it.

"What can you mean?"

He made no reply, for the *placée* returned then, holding her bonnet by its strings and still adjusting her bodice. Handing over the sealed message and a handful of banknotes from his purse, he said, "Take this to the captain of the barque *Paul Emile* now loading for Tampico. I have requested a cabin with places for two for departure on the evening tide. If you don't let him overcharge you, there will be enough to pay off the hack."

The young quadroon's eyes widened. "We are going to Mexico?"

"I am going. You will remain here."

"Oh, but Monsieur le Comte…"

"This house is yours, thanks to your harpy of a mother. Let that be enough for you. Now go, and do not return when you are done."

The young woman gave him a long look, then turned and left the house. She seemed glad enough to get away now, and who could blame her?

"You intend that I should go to Mexico with you, I suppose," Celina said. "I tell you to your face that it's impossible."

"Not at all," he said, moving to the window and looking out, perhaps to see that the quadroon followed his orders. "We shall be married at sea, and then send from Tampico to inform your father and let him know where to ship the settlement for your dowry. The proceeds derived from the sale of the property included can be collected later."

"You must be mad if you think my father will do such a thing."

He gave her a brief look over his shoulder. "He will, and with gratitude after the time we shall spend here together."

She glanced away, biting the inside of her lip a little as she tried to think. The count might well be right. How could she say? Something must be done. What that might be, she could not think, but it seemed left to her.

She noticed a cup and saucer left on a small table before the fire. Rising to her feet, she removed the bonnet and cloak she wore and set them aside. "My maid and I left the house before we had coffee this morning," she said with stiff decorum. "Perhaps a cup of café au lait and slice of buttered bread could be found for us?"

"The kitchen is in the back. Your woman can look after all three of us while she's about it."

"A visit to the necessary would be appreciated. As I said, we left home early."

"You may avail yourself as long as you remain in my sight."

Celina had hoped for a moment of privacy with Suzette, but it was clearly not forthcoming. "Perhaps the matter isn't quite so urgent, after all."

"I had thought that might be the case," he said snidely.

She could have slapped him. As it was, she used the flare of anger to turn away as a thought occurred. Her father was at home with Denys. He could be here in a matter of minutes. He might not forbid the marriage, but his presence would thwart any physical assault by the count.

Facing Suzette with her back to the count, she mouthed the words, "Papa. Bring Papa." Then she said aloud, "You heard, I think?"

Suzette had always been sharp-witted. "Yes, Mam'zelle, café au lait for you and the gentleman. I shall no doubt have to brew a fresh pot, so may take some little time at it."

She whisked from the room without waiting for further permission. After a moment, the back door closed behind her as she made her way out to the detached kitchen. Or at least Celina hoped that was where the count would think she was going.

She could not afford for him to consider the matter too closely. As a distraction, she hurried into speech with the first thought to come into her head. "So you are leaving the city. I can see why it might be necessary."

"Can you indeed."

His caustic words were not meant as a question, but she pretended otherwise. "I heard Monsieur Pasquale's challenge and your refusal, you know. You won't be received after today. Ladies will turn away from you on the street. Men will avoid you in the coffeehouses and drinking establishments. It will be quite uncomfortable."

He made a sharp gesture. "As if the censure of such provincials matters to me."

"Perhaps the elite of Tampico will be cosmopolitan enough to overlook such conduct. I'm sure I hope so, for otherwise it will be no better there. You may have run out of countries in which to play the noble count."

"Play?"

She had gone a little too far. "That is, if what the Italian sword master said is true."

"A master of liars, that Pasquale."

"But if everyone believes him…"

"If so, you must share my disgrace."

"Indeed?" she said with a challenging tilt to her chin. "Perhaps I would prefer being disgraced here, instead? Society is a dull business, and bearing endless children while my husband amuses himself around a foreign town is no recommendation for marriage. Here, I can always live with Denys or become a nun."

"You would not care to be at the beck and call of God, much less a brother."

"You know very little of me if you think so."

"I know you are strong-willed. That is one of your many attractions for me. I can't abide a woman who weeps and droops without fire or fight."

"And yet you think to tame me. Isn't that a contradiction?"

"I relish the challenge. Believe me."

"To assert your control gives you pleasure." She hardly knew what she said in her need to keep him talking.

"Precisely." He ran his tongue over his fleshy lips as he watched her.

"Then I am more certain than ever that we should be badly paired. I am determined to be mistress of my own fate."

"You may be my mistress, if you choose, before you are my wife."

"Intolerable. I wonder that you can speak of such a thing."

"You would prefer to be kept by a lowly sword master like de Silva?"

The only man she could even begin to consider in that capacity was Rio de Silva. The truth of that was so clear that she was stunned by it.

Taking her silence for uncertainty, he said, "But of course I can allow you no such choice. You must come with me."

"Why? You care nothing for me."

"Don't be naive. In addition to the pleasure of bending you to my will and your usefulness as a brood mare, there is the money. The many thousands of dollars in your dowry are both incentive and necessity."

"You can't really believe my father will release it into your hands after he discovers…discovers that you have abducted me, coerced me?"

"He is a reasonable man. He will understand that I had no choice."

Anger moved over Celina in a wave. "Do you actually think he cares so little for me or what becomes of my life? He is my father!"

"And you are an ungrateful daughter who disregards his wishes and flaunts his authority. Why should he not wish to be rid of you at all costs?"

"To the point of marrying me to a trickster and gambler who pays others to fight for him? Never!" Though she denied it, the fear that the count might be right was a cold ache inside her.

"Your welfare is the last thing on his mind now that your brother is injured. A man values his sons."

"You dare speak of Denys? My father may wish to discuss his health with you before he comes to marriage settlements. He will be fascinated to hear about my brother's visit to your hotel and what came afterward."

"The poor boy has not told him all? Or is he too ill to speak of it?"

"You would know if you had called, as most betrothed men would have under the circumstances."

"I have been rather busy. Besides, the situation has been a little strained." He gave her a pious smile. "I did not care to intrude during what must be a delicate time."

"The sentiment might do you credit, if I believed it."

"You doubt me? I am wounded."

"And if you were sensitive at all, you would not press your suit just now."

"To relieve your father of the weight of responsibility for you must be my aim. As for his questions, I'm sure I can satisfy them. Have no fear, my dear. We shall be married, and then this unfortunate day will be forgotten."

"By you, perhaps, but not by me." His sublime confidence in his ability to gull her father into accepting whatever lies were handed him made her feel sick with rage. The urge to prick that overweening conceit pounded in her head, urging her toward the final and most desperate defense.

"By you, as well," he said with a dismissive gesture. "I shall see to it. That is, of course, if the novelty of being a *condesa* doesn't occupy your mind to the exclusion of all else."

That cynical estimation of her character was the final goad. "Odd that you would be so determined to bestow such honors on one you consider a mere provincial. I'd have thought you would look to the highest ladies of Europe, or at least to the daughter of a Spanish grandee. Certainly, I would expect you to reject a tainted bride."

"Tainted?"

He appeared stunned. It would have been gratifying if not for the hard set of his mouth. "Impure," she said with exactitude. "A recent change, but one of importance, you must agree?"

"Why was I not informed?"

"My father is not aware, of course."

He appeared to swell like the frog to which she had compared him in her mind. "And how was this impurity achieved? Who was the bastard who had you?"

"Does it matter?" she asked with an attempt at nonchalance. "The result is the same."

"It was de Silva, wasn't it? He came after you, had you, even impregnated you in order to sully my prospective bride. He did it from the malice of vengeance and nothing more. And you, empty-headed little chit that you are, spread your legs for him out of spite and preening vanity at catching the eye of a handsome sword master. I could kill you."

There was no bombast in the accusation, but only cold, cruel hatred. She had thwarted him and that he could not forgive. The words he used were meant to flay her for it. And they did, oh, they did.

She had known Rio had come to her for some reason that had little to do with love or desire, but had not suspected it was anything so calculated as revenge. Surely the gentleness of his touch, the magic of the love he had made to her, could not have derived from something so ugly? Yet even as the thought came to her, she knew better.

"You didn't realize, did you? How droll. Could it be that you cared for him, thought he desired you for yourself, even cared a little for you in return? What a foolish notion. De Silva is a man possessed. He has risen from death itself to hound me, following me across continents and oceans for one reason only, and that is to seek his vengeance. Nothing else matters to him, nothing can be allowed to stand in his way. He will use anything, particularly any woman who will serve his purpose. And when he is done, he will leave you behind and never look back, never think of you again."

Every word was like a blow. She flinched inwardly with them, but refused to allow him to see. Her breath felt tight in her chest. Her eyes burned and her throat hurt with the need to weep. She would not do it. Staring straight into his eyes, she said, "If revenge is all that matters, why has he not killed you? Nothing could be easier. He is a sword master, after all."

"Death is not enough. He prefers to destroy me by ruining me financially and holding me up to public ridicule."

"I would say you have abetted him."

"Oh, granted. He knows well how to play on a man's weakness, or a woman's. But you know that, don't you?"

"It wasn't like that!"

"What was it like, then? Did he declare himself? Did he make promises? No, I thought not. Still, he may have felt something, who can say? And if he did, how better to show him the futility of using you for his ends than by doing that which he tried so hard to prevent? Marry me, and his intentions will no longer matter."

"I cannot."

"You would save yourself for him? That offends me. I think I must have you as a tarnished bride rather than permit it."

"There was never a question of promises," she said, her voice strained.

He pursed his lips. "No, it isn't done. He would not make them knowing how unacceptable a mere sword master would be to your father. Still, you yearn for the forbidden."

Did she? Was it in her mind that she might live

with Rio as lover or wife, sharing his rooms and the uncertainty of his calling, bearing his children? It was impossible, still the image had enough bright, golden promise about it to tell her that she had dreamed. What harm was there in dreaming?

"How foolish of you," the count said on a coarse laugh as he moved toward her. "And what of him, I wonder? Will knowing that I possess you be another way to destroy him? It seems possible, and so let us have done with talk and get on with the reason we are here."

She was to be punished for trying to escape him, she saw, and also for preferring Rio. The rest was merely an excuse. Retreating before his strutting advance, she said, "He really will kill you."

"Unlikely. I refuse to submit to honorable murder, and he is too noble to act otherwise. It's a handicap, but one I don't share."

"He will pursue you wherever you go, regardless of how you try to hide."

"For your sake? Are you sure?"

"He has reason enough without that," she said with contempt. "Then there is Pasquale. The Italian will follow you as well, I think. Never in this life will you be able to run fast enough or far enough to escape them both."

He cursed as he reached for her. She whirled away from him, but his fingers caught in the fullness of her skirt. She snatched free, tearing stitches at the waist as she backed away from him. "Why?" she demanded in a breathless attempt to delay his purpose. "Why do you hate Rio so?"

"I don't hate him, or I didn't until now. His father,

yes, but not the son. Riordan was merely a threat that must be removed."

"Riordan?"

"His English mother's surname name, you know. Or is that another thing he failed to tell you?"

"I only knew Rio, but you…"

"Oh, yes. I was there for his christening. He was named after me, his dear uncle who was also his godfather, but his English witch of a mother never cared for me, so called him always by her own choice."

"His uncle!"

"Oh, I shall deny it to the rest of the world, but you deserve to know how you have been used, and why. It's a family matter of the most vicious kind."

"His father was the brother who died, leaving you the title," she said as the outline of things she had been told began to come together in her mind. "But no, that can't be right. His son would have inherited."

"Lamentably, he was not available."

"You saw to that, didn't you? You killed his family, and afterward…"

"Young Riordan was supposed to die, but the greedy bastards hired for the task sold him instead to an Arab sea captain bound for Algiers."

"From which fate he escaped to become your enemy."

"He says so, but can he prove it? It was all so long ago. My nephew was barely eighteen at the time, a strong young bull but hardly likely to have escaped the clutches of the dey of Algiers."

"You killed his family. You burned them alive."

"No, no. They were quite dead first."

He made it sound a virtue. Her voice hardly more than a whisper, she said, "His sisters, too?"

"Such a waste, almost as much as it will be to destroy you," he said, his voice hard but inescapably reasonable. "I had not realized you were quite so close to him, you see, though I should have. He has told you far too much."

He lunged, clutching her arm. Stunned by the things he had said, she was slow to react. He hauled her against his bulk, encircling her waist with a hard arm. Hefting her against his side, he dragged her, kicking and struggling, into the small bedchamber.

The bed took up most of the room. He threw her on it and would have fallen across her if she had not bounced up, heaving herself over, rolling away. Cursing, he grabbed her skirts, using the widths of cloth to haul her toward him again. She fought him with her teeth set so hard that her jaws creaked. Her nails raked his wrists, reached for his eyes, making him jerk his head away. Still, he pulled her back down on the mattress, managed to throw himself across her chest. She felt something hard press against her rib cage as she heaved and squirmed, bracing an elbow under her in the attempt to push him off her. It was his pocket pistol, she thought. If only she could reach it.

Abruptly he stiffened, let out a sound between a squawk and a grunt.

"Piggish behavior, even for you, dear uncle," came the hard taunt from above them. "I suggest you release the lady—unless you'd like your gullet slit like a shoat for the roasting."

Rio.

His words were quiet and even, their cadence unmistakable. He was here, looming over them with one knee on the bed and his sword in his hand. The tip of the steel blade gouged the roll of the count's chin so a single drop of blood clung to it. Rio watched it, the look on his face implacable.

The count's grasp went slack. Celina slid from under him, pushing away in revulsion and trembling rage until she was out of reach. He let her go, turning over with care as she moved away, struggling to a sitting position with one hand pressed to his stomach and his bulging eyes fastened on the blue length of the sword at his throat.

"Rio," she began as she saw him massage his abdomen as if he felt sick. "He has—"

"Just so," the count said, and lifted his hand with his pocket pistol cradled in it, pointing the black and deadly bore in Celina's direction. "Now let us see who dies like a pig. Or should that be like a sow?"

20

"Don't!" Rio exclaimed. Then he said again more softly, "Don't. I am the one you want. To threaten the lady is needless."

"Plead for her, by all means. It will make killing your whore all the more amusing. Remove your sword now, or I will decorate her lovely throat with my shot. From this distance, I can hardly miss."

Celina saw the swift flicker of cogent thought in Rio's eyes. To withdraw the blade would be to abandon his advantage, leaving them both to the count's dubious mercy. She also saw the instant when his attention flicked down to the count's hand, apparently judging the chance of a quick slash to disarm him.

His mouth tightened and his eyes turned as hard as silver. "I could spit before you manage to squeeze the trigger."

"Do so, if you are willing to take the risk."

The count was sweating, the droplets running down his scratched face along with the pomade that he used on his hair. Still, he spoke with the hauteur of one who had grown used to feeling both superior and invincible. He did not think Rio would kill him. Though he himself had murdered others and stood ready to do so again, he refused to accept that he could die.

Rio glanced at her, his eyes dark and infinitely measuring. Then his lashes came down to veil his expression. With an abrupt movement, he drew back the sword. It flashed in the morning sunlight coming through the window as he lowered it to his side.

"Very wise," the count said with a twist of his lips as he left the bed and straightened his coat with a jerk. "Now this is much better, though I'm not sure how you found us so quickly."

"A matter of deduction," Rio said. "You could not take a reluctant woman to the St. Charles Hotel where you have removed since the fire, and arranging another venue on short notice would be difficult. This place has the advantage of being close by and already dedicated to your pleasure. It was obvious."

He stood relaxed, to all appearances, with his sword tip resting on the floor. Celina thought it was a sham. His reflexes were coiled tight, ready for the least wavering in the count's guard.

"So you made a sneaking entry," the count said with a harsh laugh. "And after all your prattle of honor."

Rio inclined his head. "You must forgive me. It's become a habit. And the back door was open."

"That maid of yours went out the back way. What's keeping her?" Count de Lérida scowled in suspicion as he looked at Celina.

"It is a strange kitchen," she offered, the words jerky, "or maybe she ran away. Anyone would be frightened."

"Or you sent her away." His grasp on the pistol firmed. "Where did she go?"

"I am here, *monsieur*," Suzette said from the doorway.

"As am I," Celina's father said as the maid stepped aside. Stalking into the room, he whipped off his hat and stood tapping it against his right leg. Nor was he alone. On his arm, her face so white it appeared she was about to swoon, was Tante Marie Rose come to carry out her duty as chaperone.

Rio gave a short laugh. Celina, standing still under the muzzle of the count's gun, saw nothing amusing in the situation, particularly as the count began to swear forcefully and with variation.

"What is the meaning of this, Monsieur le Comte?" her father demanded. "I am told that you made off with my daughter."

The count moistened his lips. "It was a necessity, *monsieur*. I regret to tell you that your daughter has engaged in immoral conduct with this…this *maître d'armes*. I thought to retrieve her good name by compelling an immediate marriage to myself."

"Don't listen to him, Papa!" Celina cried. "He meant to take me away to Mexico for the sake of my dowry."

"The intention was to compromise Celina first," Rio added. "For the most exalted of reasons, of course."

"Better by far than your aim," the count said on a snarl. "You despoiled her in order to make her ineligible as my *condesa*."

"Not at all," Celina declared roundly. "It was at my request."

"Silence!" her father thundered.

"Oh, my poor *chère*," Tante Marie Rose cried, starting forward with tears in her eyes. Heedless of the pistol trained on Celina, she trotted around the end of the bed and enfolded her in a vetiver-scented embrace.

Celina thought disjointedly that her nerves were more overwrought than she knew, for she was glad to be held. At the same time, she did her best to shield her careless aunt from the line of fire.

"It seems an excellent thing that Celina sent for me," her father said grimly. "Monsieur le Comte, you have a pistol trained on my daughter. Remove it at once."

"This man had his sword to my throat just minutes ago and stands ready to return it there."

"My view is somewhat personal, but it appears to me that your proper target would be the man who threatens you."

"She is with him," the count declared with a violent gesture of the pistol in Celina's direction. "She is his whore."

"For this supposed crime against you as her betrothed you feel she deserves to die? Do you think that I should not care? She is my daughter, one of my own, my family. Should she fall at your hand, her death is mine."

A hard knot formed in Celina's throat as she listened. Her father did care for her welfare. "Thank you, Papa," she said with difficulty. "But the count can conceive of no love for those of his blood. He paid to have his older brother and all his family killed. Rio is his nephew, yet he tried to have him killed with the others, attempted it again when that failed, and yet again today on the field of honor by paying a man to force a meeting while he was injured. He would remove him without a qualm at this moment except for the inconvenience of an audience."

"Lies, all lies," the count shouted as he turned to wave the pistol at Rio. "This man, this de Silva, is not my nephew. He is an impostor!"

Tante Marie Rose, still holding Celina, stiffened to attention. "You are mistaken, *monsieur*."

"I have heard him make no such claim," Celina's father interrupted, his voice stern. "Even should he do so, it's not a killing offense. Put down your weapon before it goes off by accident."

"He will murder me."

"Before witnesses? I hardly think so. Monsieur de Silva?"

Rio lifted a shoulder. "I have restrained the impulse these many weeks since coming to New Orleans. I suppose I can do so a little longer."

"You see?" the count demanded. "He admits that it is his aim."

Celina's father gave Rio a stern look. "You came here for this purpose? To be avenged?"

"It has been a long quest, *monsieur*. It is what kept me alive when I learned that my entire family had died. It sustained me while I was beaten and starved as a slave aboard a ship bound for Algiers, then during my short stay at the palace of the dey, before the French captured the place and put me on a ship for Paris."

"More lies!"

"The men paid to kill me had scant reason to think I might escape from slavery so none at all to speak untruths. They told me that my uncle had promised them a fortune in gold to kill my family as they lay sleeping, and were also given an entrance key to make it easier. My uncle was enraged that I had escaped, a detail he learned when they described those who had died at their hand, and so he had them set on me as I returned home with the dawn. It was intended that I should be buried in some secluded place so everyone would believe I had died in the fire. But these men had been shortchanged for their work, so decided to sell me for the remainder of what they should have been paid. Therefore, I knew the architect of my misery and I hated him. The need to be avenged guided me as I apprenticed myself to the *maître* of a famous Parisian *salle d'armes*. It directed my hand while I practiced with foil and épée, allowing me to see every opponent as my uncle. I harnessed my rage, honing it into a weapon fit to cut down one man and one only."

"A fantastic tale," the count said with heavy sarcasm, "or would be if there was a word of truth in it."

"Oh, but I know…" Tante Marie Rose tried again.

Monsieur Vallier lifted a hand. "Permit him to finish, if you please."

Rio inclined his head. "The rest is quickly told. When I was ready to meet my uncle, a man of worldly experience and endless guile, I sought him out in Spain. There I learned that he had gambled away the vast sums he had inherited when I was given up for dead, would have lost the estate that produced them except that it was entailed. He fled the country ahead of his creditors and enemies, hoping to repair his fortunes elsewhere. I followed him to Rome and on to Havana, but always it was the same. He had outlasted his welcome, been discovered as a Captain Sharp who leads men into gambling and other vices in order to fleece them. His trail led to New Orleans, and so I arrived here."

"As did I, and on much the same quest."

Nicholas Pasquale spoke those words, letting them fall into the thoughtful silence as Rio finished speaking. Close behind them, he strolled into the bedchamber as if he belonged there. Following him was Caid, with Olivier at his side. The last two hung back, ranging themselves along the wall like a guard of honor while Pasquale joined Rio, coming to a halt at his right hand where he surveyed the gathering with a steady regard. "Imagine my chagrin," he ended, "when on finally running the infamous count to earth, I discovered he was the rankest of cowards, one who paid other men to fight his battles so he need not bloody his hands. It seems to have become a habit with him."

Tante Marie Rose exclaimed under her breath, though whether in admiration or in horror was impossible to tell.

"Yes," Celina said. "Just as he allowed Denys to protect my good name after Rio—that is, Monsieur de Silva—used it as a ruse to draw him to the dueling field."

"A ruse as base as the man I was after," Rio said in low tones.

Celina would have replied, but the count cut across her words.

"Such calumny! Must I stand here and listen to this drivel while de Silva gathers his friends to overwhelm me?"

"Oh, it was not Rio who brought us here," Pasquale said with a brief glance at Caid and Olivier behind him. "It was you, *monsieur,* with your note to the captain of the *Paul Emile.* The young woman who carried it feared your intent toward Mademoiselle Vallier. Knowing of the interest of my friend de Silva, she came with it to his atelier. She met us at the door as we returned from the dueling field. De Silva had left there abruptly and alone, so was not there to receive this message. Something required to be done as it seemed the thing might be a trap. We came to be of service in springing it."

"Yes, and ready to swear anything for one of your own kind. I should have known…"

"After hiring me to face an injured man on the dueling field? So you should. If you had understood anything about those who live by the sword, you would know that the most rigorous honor is the bedrock of it, since it's the only way that two men can face each other on the fencing strip without a maiming for every match. For the man who uses his sword for money, there is no word of adequate foulness. I accepted your commission for two reasons. One of these I gave on the dueling ground, to prevent harm to a fellow swordsman that could come if another, less scrupulous *maître d'armes,* like Broyard, was tempted by your offer. The other was because of Mademoiselle Vallier's brother."

"Denys?" Celina asked before anyone else could speak. "What have you to do with him?"

Pasquale looked at Celina. "I sought him out some days ago because of the count's connection to your family. Your brother is most engaging. He reminds me of my own brother, Giovanni, who died a suicide.

We talked for some time at a barroom, and during the course of the conversation, I told him many things about the count, things I had learned from Giovanni. When he left me, it was to seek out the count or, failing that, go to Rio for his counsel."

The count sputtered invective while spittle flecked his lips. "How they hang together, these accursed hellhounds of sword masters. Sons of whores with the devil's own talent for twisting the truth. Liars and impostors, all of them!"

It was then that Tante Marie Rose spoke up in quavering yet stringent tones. "That is quite untrue, *monsieur*, as I've been trying to tell you all. My dear friend Madame Calvé nearly swooned on seeing Monsieur de Silva at the musical evening not three nights ago. She said it was like seeing the ghost of the gallant cavalier who courted her in Barcelona when she was a girl. He is the very spit and image of Don Antonio Jose de Vega, once Count de Lérida, though a little taller and with lighter eyes. It gave her such a turn, for she had once thought to become his *condesa*. In memory of the past, she gave me this love token in hope that it would be returned to one who has more right to it. And she asks only that Monsieur de Silva should visit her so she may look on him more closely, and perhaps speak with him of the man who was his grandfather."

The item she held out was a miniature in an oval frame of heavily chased silver. It depicted in bright and clear oils the face and shoulders of a *hidalgo* dressed in the style of more than fifty years before. Proud, imperious, handsome in an austere fashion, he was the image of Rio de Silva.

The count gave a cry of rage and reached for the

miniature with his free hand. Celina was before him, snatching it from her aunt's grasp and holding it close against her heart. He cursed and brought up the pistol, glaring at her above the barrel.

She saw the bore, as big and black as a cannon's mouth, saw his finger on the trigger, knew when it began to tighten.

Then light flashed, a silver streak in the morning sun through the jalousie blinds. A noise like raging thunder shook the world. Something struck her and she was flung backward, turning, thudding against the wall as she went down.

Pain burst inside her head. Faintly she could hear her aunt screaming, shouts, voices babbling, a clamor of sound without meaning. Her eyes were dazed, focusing only on a glow of white. Hard bands encircled her, held her immobile. They should have troubled her, but did not. She felt secure, protected, safe. She closed her eyes.

Safe.

"Tell me where you're hit, *querida*," Rio said, his breath warm against her temple. "Please, tell me."

The bands were Rio's arms. The white only his shirtfront. It was his shoulder that had struck her, she thought, knocking her from the line of fire.

"I have the miniature," she murmured.

"Damn the miniature. If he has hurt you, I swear by all the saints that I will…"

"No, I'm not hurt. Except…I think I hit my head."

"I'm sorry, but I could not help it. It was necessary to act quickly."

"I know," she said, resting her forehead on his shoulder. "I know."

A man appeared beside them, knelt with a rustle of clothing. Caid, she thought, even before he spoke. "The count is dead, and the sight isn't a pretty one. We need to get *mademoiselle* out of the room."

She tilted her head back to look up at Caid. "Dead? But how…?"

"Pasquale. A matter of snatching Rio's sword. He was closest and Rio had a more important duty. Shall we go?"

Duty. That had an unpleasant sound to it, though now did not seem the time to question it. She was expected to move. She didn't want that, wasn't sure she was able, but the effort had to be made.

It wasn't so difficult, after all. Rio rose and took her hands to pull her up, supporting her for an instant until her world righted itself. Then while the other swordsmen provided a shield with their wide shoulders against sight of the blood-soaked body, he escorted her from the bedchamber to the small salon where Tante Marie Rose, inhaling from her smelling salts bottle as if it were the elixir of life, waited for her with Suzette. Her father took charge of them, bundling them from the house and into the carriage outside. Moments later, they were driving away, leaving the chaos and death behind.

Celina leaned her head against the hard leather seat and closed her eyes. She could feel her head throbbing with pain, feel her pulse racing with life, feel her heart beating warmly in her chest. She was alive and it was over. Finally.

She still held the miniature, even now. The edges of the silver frame pressed into her palm. It hurt, but she did not release it.

* * *

"*Mademoiselle*, a visitor has arrived."

Mortimer's voice was portentous. It was also significant that he closed the door behind him before speaking. Celina looked up from her embroidery, aware that she was suddenly warm in spite of the cool day. "For me?"

"*Mais non*, for your papa. He is with him in the study now. I am to bring wine."

Frowning a little in perplexity, she asked, "His name?"

"A most peculiar thing, Mam'zelle. He called himself—"

The door opened again at that moment, and Suzette whirled into the salon. "Monsieur Rio is here, Mam'zelle. Come, you must tidy yourself at once." She glanced at the butler. "*Tiens*, why are you here? Bring the wine immediately. Go, go."

"Yes. Thank you, Mortimer," Celina said as she set her tambour frame aside and rose to her feet. When the elderly man had shuffled away, she went on, "No one has sent for me?"

"Not yet, but of course they will."

"Then I will wait until it happens." She sat back down and picked up her needle.

"What is this, Mam'zelle? You must know why he has come!"

"No, I don't, and won't until someone tells me. It's been two days without a word. Why should I assume this is anything more than a courtesy call?"

"Oh, Mam'zelle!"

To be ruined, Celina had discovered, was an odd thing, almost like being an invalid. Everyone as-

sumed she had no interest in going out. She was spoken to in the hushed tones used toward the bereaved
by her aunt, her father and even Denys, who was almost recovered. Not that anyone seriously thought
she mourned the count, but all recognized the meaning behind the end of her betrothal coupled with the
loss of her good name. The true tragedy, and what
roused their sympathy, was that she would most
likely never marry.

Celina didn't mind being in disgrace. The relief of
knowing that she need never see the count again
seemed worth any cost. She felt no different inside.
Certainly, she wasn't ill or in danger of going into a
decline. Her feelings were hardly engaged at all, or
so it seemed. She had moved through these past two
days in deliberate numbness, carefully holding at
bay the wretchedness she could sense hovering at the
edges of her mind.

The source of that distant disquiet, she knew, was
the lack of word from Rio. She had expected him to
send a note, appear in her room, or perhaps pay a social call. He had done none of these things, either on
the evening of that day on the rue des Rampart or
since.

He did not owe her that consideration. She had no
right to expect it. Still, they had shared something
more than a mere social flirtation. She had thought
she mattered to him. It was disturbing to discover
that he could not be bothered to tell her what he
meant to do now that he had achieved what he
wanted in New Orleans, whether he meant to leave
since it was done, or when he would go.

Now he was here. Suzette, ever the optimist, took

a romantic view of the call, but Celina could not. That Rio had asked to see her father indicated his purpose was perhaps a polite apology for involving the Vallier family in his intrigues or even a formal farewell. If that was it, then she might not see him, or else the meeting between them would be so brief and public that it hardly mattered. She would endure it as she was then, in her simple day gown of teal-green French merino without ornament of any kind and her hair drawn back away from her ears in a smooth chignon. If she appeared drab, almost in demi-mourning, what did it matter?

"If you are sure…" Suzette said with resignation.

"I am."

"Then I will leave you, if I may. Olivier is downstairs and I…"

"Yes, certainly. Go, by all means," Celina said with a brief movement of her hand.

The maid did not wait to be told again. Celina, listening to her footsteps on the stairs, smiled ruefully to herself as she turned once more to her embroidery.

She did not have to stay in the salon. She could appear in the study as if on some errand, or else simply barge in on the conversation taking place there. Her need to know what was taking place was great, and she didn't believe her father would send her away given the extreme consideration shown for her feelings of late. What held her in her chair was dread of what she might hear. It was possible that she really did not want to know what was being said.

The summons came a short time later. She smoothed a hand over her hair, shook out her skirts, then left the salon and moved out onto the gallery, preceding Mortimer to the study. He opened the door for her and she stepped inside.

"Come, *chère*," her father said, holding out his arm in an invitation to join them where he and Rio stood at the window. "You know this gentleman, but under another name. May I present, most formally, Don Damian Francisco Adriano de Vega y Riordan, the rightful Count de Lérida."

"He is my namesake…"

The count had spoken those words, but she had not realized he meant them quite so literally. The only difference was the addition of Rio's mother's surname in the Spanish manner, one which he had taken, at least in part, as his nom de guerre. And of course the count; the usurper was dead now, along with Rio's father, which meant that Rio had reclaimed his rightful title. Still, it felt like a farce as she held out her hand.

"Monsieur le Comte," she said, the syllables difficult on her tongue.

"Mademoiselle Vallier," Rio returned, his voice grave but the look in his eyes bright as he took her cool fingers in his warm grasp, bowing over them. His appearance was rigorously correct, from his beautifully tied cravat and broadcloth coat to the black ribbon trim that ran down his pantaloons and under the instep of his soft calf boots.

"You will be pleased to know that this is an official visit, Celina," her father went on. "The count has said everything that is proper concerning your past acquaintance, and has most graciously indicated that it is his intention to honor the marriage agreement drawn up in his family name. He is not the bride-groom intended, but feels it to be his duty to take his uncle's place. The honor of his family has been greatly tarnished, and the first step in erasing the many stains shall be this substitution."

"The honor of his family." She repeated the words without inflection.

"It is small enough recompense for all you suf-fered at the hands of my relative," Rio said quietly. "And mine. I once pledged, if you remember, to guard your good name. I failed in that regard, but this may mend it."

Somewhere deep inside her, she could feel her blessed numbness disintegrating. Pushing it aside was the pain she had expected, but also something more, a slow, burning anger. It seeped into her voice as she answered, "I require no recompense or mend-ing."

"Now, *chère*," her father began.

"I have been released from a betrothal that was odious to me. Anything beyond this was of my own will and in clear acceptance of the consequences. I will not marry because of a contract signed under du-ress, and I certainly will not be married as a duty."

"Don't be foolish," her father said, his voice rising. "This is a boon you had no right to expect. You dare not throw it away!"

"Monsieur," Rio began, laying a hand on his arm.

"I do not want a husband as a boon," Celina said in scorn. "As for what I deserve, it is something more than to be handed over to a man who says he will take me merely for the sake of his family name."

"Celina, I forbid—"

"Monsieur Vallier!" The whip of a sword slash was in Rio's voice as he cut across her father's words. "Say no more in my defense, if you please. I will plead my own case, if I may speak to Celina alone."

Her father looked from him to Celina and then back again. "It's most irregular."

"The entire contract is irregular, and you have allowed this once already with its designated groom."

"With results I am unlikely to forget."

"I pledge that they will not be repeated."

Her father hesitated, and then gave a nod. "Very well. Five minutes only, by the clock."

Rio thanked him. Her father departed, leaving the door open. Celina, with her hands clasped in front of her, moved away a few steps to put distance between her and the new count. Then she turned like a doe facing a swamp panther. A constriction in her throat made it hard to speak, still she forced words past it.

"Why are you doing this? There is no need whatever for it."

"There is every need," he said, moving after her with his inimitable grace. "But first, are you well? How is your head? Your skin is fair at the best of times, but so pale just now that this bruise seems a sacrilege." He reached with gentle fingers to touch the sore place on her temple where she had struck the wall as he flung her out of the line of fire.

"Don't." She moved away again, almost undone by that tender gesture.

"I regret that it was necessary to hurt you, and apologize for it most sincerely."

"I am perfectly well."

"Well, I'm not," he said with strain fretting the

edges of his voice. "My shoulder hurts like hell, I have inherited a multitude of debts and time-consuming duns from my uncle along with his title, and in trying to make amends for the pain and trouble that I've caused you and your family, I seem to have enraged you. Why is my suit so unacceptable?"

If he could not see that after what she had said, then there was no way to make it clear. She only shook her head.

"Is it because I have been a *maître d'armes*? It's an honorable profession, but I will be one no longer. I must return to Spain to reclaim my name and my heritage and salvage what I may from the estate. It will take time and much work before the land can be put back in shape to produce an income. But once it's done, I shall be as idle a gentleman as you could wish."

"Your profession has nothing to do with it. It never did."

He studied her a long moment, his gaze silvery with consideration. "You fear I will not be a conformable husband, perhaps. I swear that no one could be more respectable than I intend to be. You never need worry that I might embarrass you, and the only challenge I will accept from this day forward is that which cannot with honor be avoided."

"I had not thought otherwise."

"You see me as the Don Juan I've been called, ever seeking new conquests? That is not my true guise. You would be the only woman in my heart or my bed forevermore. This I also swear."

The only woman in his heart. The sound of it in his deep voice brought the ache of tears to her throat. "Please don't. I...it can't matter."

"It's because you don't care to leave New Orleans, then. I would prefer to have you with me in Catalonia, but would not insist. I can attend to the necessary business and then return here, with perhaps a yearly visit to see that all remains in order."

"You would do that?" she asked, her eyes widening with her surprise.

"If it means your happiness. What must I say to convince you, my Celina? I need you near me as the guardian of my honor. I nearly lost that, you know, in my obsession with revenge. It was you on that first night who made me see the danger, when you charged me with the baseness of my motives. It was having them pointed out so clearly that alerted me to what I had almost become, a man not unlike the one I pursued, ready to sacrifice everything to achieve my ends."

"You knew it before," Celina said with a small shake of her head. "If you had not, then you would have accepted the bargain I offered on the spot, and…"

"And none of the rest would have happened? Perhaps not in its particulars, but something very like it. I wanted you, meant to have you, from the moment you stepped into my room that night. I would have forfeited anything to have you."

"Yes," she said, remembering the moment when he had lowered his sword rather than allow her to be shot, and later, when he had chosen to save her rather than strike out with his blade. "Yes, even your revenge."

"It no longer had meaning compared to the risk of losing you. You are everything bright and good that is missing from my days. You taught me the need to protect those near to me, showed me what it means to belong, finally, not to some great society but to the inner circle of family. With you, I may gain in respect and honor and the joy of the passing days. Without you, I am only an apprentice of the sword, master of nothing."

"How can you say that? You saved Denys and me."

"I owed a rescue to your brother because I put him in danger in the first place by shutting him up in my cellar. I protected you because it was the only way to save myself."

"You give me too much credit. You are the Count de Lérida. When you return to Spain, you may take your place at court and among those of your station. Nothing will be closed to you, not the homes of those with marriageable daughters, and not the hearts of these eligible brides. Whatever you want can be yours."

"And if I want nothing and no bride other than you?"

"You will, when the time comes." She believed that to be true, or at least feared it.

"Never."

"You cannot know, not until you are comfortable with your new title and honors."

"Damn the title. Marry me, Celina. Come away with me."

What did she want, now, at this moment? Were the things he had said enough? Could they be when nights grew long and she was far, far away from those she loved in a country where she was a stranger? "I cannot."

"You could, but you won't."

"As you say." The effort it took to speak those words left her weak, barely able to conceal the trembling in her hands.

He swung away, taking two long strides before stopping with his back to her. "I could force you. Your father would abet me for your own good."

"You wouldn't!"

He turned to stare at her with a black scowl between his brows. Then he closed his eyes, exhaling on a sighing breath. "No. I couldn't do that to you. I am not my uncle."

In the silence that stretched between them, she could hear the quiet rustle of his clothing as he turned once more and walked to her father's desk. The sheet of foolscap that lay there crackled as he picked it up in one hand. Reaching toward the silver holder of phosphorous matches that sat beside the cigar humidor, he lit one and held a corner to the paper.

The foolscap caught with a curling plume of gray smoke. The paper turned brown, twisting as orange and blue flame ate into it. The fire leaped upward, eating at clauses and conditions, seals and signatures.

The marriage contract was burning.

It was burning, destroying all her nebulous hopes and dreams, the promise of her future and her children. It was burning, turning to ash the family she might have had, the long nights of passion she might have known, the love she could have shared. It was burning, and the ache of it seared her heart.

It was burning, tainting with its smoke the single red rose that was attached to it with sealing wax and curling ribbons.

"Stop!"

Rio dropped the contract, put a booted foot on the flames and ground them out. When he was sure that no ember remained, he picked up the charred piece that was left and held it out to her.

"It's yours," he said. "Do with it as you will."

"I will marry you."

"Accepted, and gladly," he said at once. "But why? What is so different?"

"I changed my mind. I thought…"

"What? Tell me."

Grasping desperately for any reason other than the real one, she said, "Suzette. My father has sworn to give her to me on my wedding day and I promised to grant her freedom so she can marry Olivier. I can't disappoint her."

"An excellent reason, but not one that calls for such panic." His voice was grave but his eyes silvery with dawning amusement as he took a step toward her. "Try again."

"I wish to be a *condesa*!"

"So you shall be," he said, reaching for her, taking her into his arms. "And what else?"

"I've never traveled more than fifty miles from New Orleans, and have a great desire to go across the ocean on a steamship." This was muffled against his shirtfront as she was gathered close.

"And?"

"Court," she whispered. "To wear a coronet and curtsy to the queen should be…"

"Deadly dull," he supplied, "but we'll do it if you like. And if you will just say that you love me."

"I do," she said, with tears crowding her throat. "I

have, since the night you first came to my room. And I will, when we have our children and grandchildren around us and are too bent and gray to do more than hold hands."

"That," he said with such conviction that he had to be believed, "will be never."

"Never?"

"Never, my adored one, not as long as there is breath in my body," he said, and prevented any possible argument with the heated demand of his lips.

Celina allowed herself to melt against him, breathing in his scent, reveling in the strength of his arms around her. As she lifted her hands to the back of his neck, the contract fluttered from her fingers.

It fell to the floor and lay there, intact, smoking gently. But she kept the rose, holding it tightly in her hand.

Author Note

Challenge to Honour is the first book in a series that was a long time in the making. The idea came to me over a decade ago, when I first ran across mention of the *maîtres d'armes*, sword masters of old New Orleans. What a fascinating concept: a group of men of fearsome athletic power and reputation who were idolised by society in much the same way as the sports heroes of today. Followed in the streets by small boys, they were copied in their manners and styles of dress by young gentlemen and their company was sought by older men, yet they were never introduced to young ladies from good families. Exchange Alley, known to the French Creoles as the *Passage de la bourse*, housed over fifty of these fencing masters. Oh, the possibilities! Other stories intervened, but the idea would not go away. It's my great pleasure to introduce, at last, these dynamic Masters at Arms.

The next book in the series, *Dawn Encounter*, features the story of Caid, Rio's Irish friend. A tale of secrets and lies, revenge and redemption, it's set against the intriguing backdrop of 1840s New Orleans, a port city second only to New York in ship traffic and wealth, and arguably number one in exotic charm and sophistication. Lisette, the heroine, is a spirited Creole belle who, when Caid kills her husband in a duel, demands the sword master's protection as her right. Lisette must then defy society and even Caid himself in order to claim the love and family she craves. Still, who can blame her for being seduced by the powerful allure of one of these ultra-romantic Masters at Arms? I've fallen in love with them myself – and it's my hope that you will allow yourself to be enticed into their special world, as well.

Warmest regards

Jennifer Blake

MILLS & BOON®

The *Regency*

LORDS & LADIES
COLLECTION

*Two glittering Regency
love affairs in every book*

*Available at most branches of WH Smith, Tesco, ASDA, Martins, Borders,
Eason, Sainsbury's and all good paperback bookshops.*

REG/L&L/LIST